Playing Hannah

Playing Hannah

a novel

by Eric Beauregard

LAUGHING GULL
PUBLISHING

CHARLESTON, SC
USA

ISBN: 978-0-692-50529-8
    0692505296

Library of Congress Control Number: 2016902690

Contributing Editor: Tammy Morissette
Original Cover Art: Libby Manahan
Visit author: playinghannah@hotmail.com

Note: Excerpt from "All the Lovely Ladies" is used with Gordon Lightfoot's permission.

for Kate Spinoso

Inside

Playing Hannah

Act One

The beginnings of things, of a world especially, is necessarily vague, tangled, chaotic, and exceedingly disturbing. How few of us ever emerge from such beginnings! How many souls perish in its tumult! — **Kate Chopin**

It's all theater. — **Mary Carney**

-1-

The alarm clock slammed into the morning, like the fist of Iron Mike Tyson in a Las Vegas scuffle. It nearly bit off Hannah's ear. She countered with a horizontal roundhouse, but missed the timepiece and whacked an Anne Tyler novel on the bedstand instead. No dinner at the homesick restaurant this morning.

"Shut up already," Hannah moaned. It was too early to curse.

A second attempt at the clock proved worse when she came down with pugilistic vengeance atop the remnants of a multigrain bagel with chive cream cheese, toasted, prepped and forgotten in the night. Now Hannah was railing. "Son of a bitch!" Now she was waking up.

With all the grace she could muster, she tapped out, ceding the match, grateful only to be awake; for Hannah had been dreaming, and she didn't much care for most of her dreams; and Dr. Jung's interpretations only seemed to make them worse. She had better luck with alarm clocks than with Swiss psychotherapists.

She'd been suffering a grueling round on *Jeopardy,* with the relentless host grilling her in mathematics and the sciences. Hannah couldn't question any of the answers correctly, her own fault for having wasted life in pursuits of the arts and histories. Still, without the knowledge to back it up, her game show thumb kept pressing at the signaling button held fast in her sweaty hand.

Atop being taunted by Alex Trebeck, like that wasn't bad enough, Hannah was wedged between a pair of disagreeable co-contestants. On her left was the same raggedy doll from her other dreams. It was a full-size doll, but slightly animated, not unlike one of Hannah's favorite actresses, post-*'Virginia Woolf*, and seeming present for no other reason than to remind Hannah that she wasn't the only raggedy girl in the show. The doll never rang in. She did not speak.

On Hannah's right was a pint-size version of the commander-in-chief, a spot-on facsimile of the president, though about forty years younger, four feet shorter and dressed like a cowboy. Hannah reckoned they called him Billy Jeff. The program's staff had the little guy propped on a plastic stepstool assisting him to camera level, and once that camera was leveled he was the star of the show, much to Hannah's dismay, as he spent the entire half-hour correctly questioning all of her failed responses, and each with a roll of his shifty politician-like eyes, determined to let the studio audience know, as well as those viewing from home, that Hannah's platform was weak, that she couldn't be trusted, and she was just plain stupid. Then, once comfortable in his position and having grown full of his smart little self, the cowboy took to reaching over and grabbing handfuls of Hannah's ass, behind the lecterns and away from audience view.

Making dream matters still worse, as disgusting as Hannah found the budding world leader, his touch was starting to turn her on. She began thinking he was sort of cute in the southwestern motif. It was a *ridin' the range* and *ropin' dogies* ensemble, made all the more west winning with twin, imitation pearl-handled, cap blasting six-shooters and a shiny tin star pinned to his puffed out chest. The vest struggled to mimic leather—*close enough*, Hannah thought—and all around dripped with fringes and a tassel here and there. Metal tips capped the toes of his boots, and though the spurs were plastic, Hannah could overlook those as well, and even give a wink at the horse tethered to the arcade in the mall, ready to giddy-up-and-go with the persuasive deposit of four bits.

Thinking, *ah, what the hell*, and absolutely nothing else, Hannah quick-like made a grab for the cowpoke's ass, just the one time, for any fun there might be in it. Not as discreet as her opponent, though, Hannah's move was seen by everyone. The buckaroo let go a scream, tapped the microphone for a sound check and asked for an adult, leading the way to Hannah being chastised on national television for the lascivious conduct.

"But I'm a minor too," she retorted.

"You should be ashamed of yourself," returned the angry Canadian host, his moustaches poised like a pair of militant caterpillars threatening to leap over the lectern in defense of the smirking cowboy. And Hannah was ashamed of herself, something to which she had never been a stranger. The host then mumbled something else she couldn't quite catch.

"This isn't fair," she whimpered, her arms gone akimbo. Hannah sounded whiney and she knew it, only adding to her shame, as she was certain her parents were watching the program at home, not having bothered attending the taping in person, but rather anticipating a later trip to Culvert City when their daughter would compete in the upcoming tournament of champions.

At last the game was over. "Thank God," Hannah sighed, exhausted and near tears. The final round was a wash. She was several thousands in the hole, the doll had broken even, and the cowboy was left to ride alone into the sunset, the prize money stowed in trail-weary saddlebags tossed over the haunches of his polyurethaned horse.

Hannah shook off the dream and let go her unpleasant playmates.

As lately she'd been making some attempts at prayer, particularly during those times when she chanced to think of doing so, Hannah reasoned this might be a good day to make an offer of herself. In the past she had reached for celestial powers mostly when she was jammed up, during those times when her ass was afire; and though currently all was well, all in all, she wondered if maybe she shouldn't bank a prayer or two, just in case something came up. Something was always coming up.

She lay awhile wondering if she should be on her knees at the bedside, if those celestial powers would smile more favorably on the attempt at humility; but if the powers were all that powerful, they would know she was already as humble as she could possibly be; besides, those celestial powers probably had enough going on that they couldn't care less what sort of prayer position Hannah Mae Fields adopted, and especially when she wasn't planning to ask for anything this morning, but rather wanted to give up some thanks for what she already had. Still, it bothered her as selfish that she only went to her knees in times of struggle, so she begrudgingly slid to the floor, but she went with a tinge of spite, along with the declaration that the celestial powers would have to take her as she was, and that was wearing a little bit of cream cheese and nothing else. Hannah did, however, mind her posture; slouched with her elbows on the bed left her bare ass rounding out, and she thought this might push the spiritual envelope too far.

She began with staple thanks for mom, dad, birds, trees, books and the like. She tossed in a small measure of gratitude for an alarm clock sparing her what might have been another game show dream, the one where she spins a great big wheel to still more harassment from that other host and his southern accomplice. Lastly, Hannah asked for strength to get through the day; another first day at another new school.

Two weeks prior, Hannah had moved to Vermont at her parents' behest. They were always behesting her somewhere, and Hannah's youth maintained that she remain the reluctant behestee. Until recently these moves had been up and down the California coast, temporary set ups between Eureka and Encinitas; but this latest behest came as somewhat extreme. Connie and Art had roused her from sleep, declaring in excited unison, "We're going to Vermont!" The daughter was nowhere near as excited. Startled, groggy, and never much for geography, Hannah rubbed the sleep from her eyes and asked, "What state's that in?" She then checked her watch, prepared to protest being awakened at such an hour, and with such fatuous plans; but Hannah found she hadn't much weight for the argument, as it came on about two o'clock that afternoon.

Hannah was starting to live comfortably in Monterey when news of this latest relocation came. Coming so suddenly and unexpectedly as it did, she wondered if the family was going on the lam, but such was how Art and Connie Fields operated. It was how they worked before Hannah came into the picture, and little changed once she was born. They were movers and shakers, moving and shaking along in a quest for financial security through the manipulation of struggling real estate markets, and although children had been discouraged from joining in this quest, a long weekend in Reno proved the safe sex they'd been practicing wasn't nearly as safe as they had supposed. Far from safe, Arthur Fields returned from Nevada with a low back strain, while Constance ended the weekend with the beginnings of a child, along with some bothersome chafing. The couple then convinced one another that something beautiful might come of such an amazing weekend, and so they decided to have a go at parenting. The same trip to Reno prompted a decision to stay away from roulette and stick with blackjack.

Art and Connie eagerly negotiated the stacks of child rearing manuals as they sipped lattes at Barnes & Noble. They quickly mastered the arts of disposable diapers, tough love and college prep. By the time Hannah made her entrance in the summer of '78, they were giddy and ready, encouraging the baby girl's every move, as they read in one of the books this was what they were supposed to do. But business, pleasure, parenting and moving and shaking often proved too many balls in the air for these purveyors of real estate. Between the two of them they could account for only one of the hands juggling those balls, while they remained desperately dependent upon outside help for another. Quality childcare was difficult enough to find, and no sooner would they locate an objective provider when one or the other, in the midst of their juggling, would forget to pick up the child. It was not long before the business of rearing textbook progeny gave way to a simpler system of winging it.

Flowering as an attractive young woman, forming at the hips and at the will and starting to turn some heads, Hannah was at an age to begin dating when the family gathered for a discussion regarding sex. The daughter maintained eye contact and a sympathetic smile when the conversation showed itself more difficult for the parents than for her. Hannah let them go on a few minutes before politely asking to speak.

"No one," she told them, then repeated herself for punctuation, for their peace of mind, and for any dramatic effect it might carry; "no one except the doctor and me puts anything inside, ever, and then it's only once a year—for the doctor, not me." Her father decided they needn't discuss the issue further.

And when Hannah began skulking about, the family gathered once more, this time for a discussion regarding the dangers of drugs. Again Hannah listened dutifully. Again she asked permission to speak. "I do not use drugs, nor do I ever intend to." She went on to tell them of the cracks she believed drugs created in one's psyche, in the spirit; she threw in the word *soul*. "And it's through such cracks where all the bad shit—I mean, the bad *stuff*—gets in, shit like the lies and fears that would make it impossible for us three to have meaningful discussions like this." Finding the metaphor packing wallop enough to end the conversation, Hannah then moved in for the kill. "And I love you guys way too much to ever let that happen." She asked, "May I be excused?" kissing both on her way past.

Connie and Art sat still and stifled, tears tracking three of their four cheeks. What Hannah had neglected to tell them (as her sins of omission tended to outnumber those of commission) was that she was afraid of drugs and of how they might mix with the alcohol, because what Hannah really liked to do was drink; *cocktailing*, she called it, having heard the expression in a film and liking the sound of it. She didn't allow the social lubricant to make her unmanageably slippery, never sloppy, word slurring or falling down silly, but rather she enjoyed the effects brought about by 'a few.' A few helped her to forget her fears. A few helped to quiet the guilt of disliking herself, as well as the disliking herself for the guilt. Hannah liked the way a few made her feel, and she especially liked the way a few allowed her to not have to feel.

Finally, when Hannah's parents believed their daughter was growing too distant and aloof, the family gathered for a discussion regarding friendships. Hannah had no stock explanations this time. She might have lashed out at them for dragging her about and making it difficult for her to develop meaningful relationships, but instead she calmly assured them she simply wasn't "all that good at making friends," and that it was no one's fault but her own, but she would continue trying and even trying a little harder. She didn't tell them those labors would be for their benefit and not hers, as she'd rather no one got very close. Hannah then asked to be excused, so she could go upstairs to enjoy the effects brought about by a few.

The family had decided on Christmas break for the move east. While a few months to prepare for matriculation would have been nice, Hannah had to make do with about three weeks, and those same three weeks ran out at the same time the cream cheese ran from her fingers into the drain of the shower.

Not unlike others her age, as well as some of those older and most everyone younger, Hannah wanted freedom. She loved and respected her mother and father without question, but it was in much the same way that she loved the armed forces; they were strong, forever hovering and sadly necessary, but she sure wished she could get along without them. They were busy doing what she called their *real estate thing*, while Hannah had a different sort of plan. She liked to imagine a life of initiating change and helping those less fortunate (a daunting task, as, compared to Hannah's well taken care of self, nearly everyone else on the planet was less fortunate). She liked to picture herself in a jungle somewhere (it didn't matter the jungle), wearing bloused khaki pants and a beret, working with the Peace Corps (or some other corps), and helping the poor souls of developing nations by swapping cultures, beads, herbs and recipes. She imagined herself teaching those jungle souls the beauty of the English language and how to read her favorite books.

But today Hannah was once again the new kid at another new school, a position causing her such self-consciousness she might as well arrive at class naked. *A real big deal*, she thought of herself, wanting to help those jungle souls when she hadn't the backbone or patience to help herself. Defeated and deflated, she returned her altruism to a hope chest spilling over with selfishness, wondering if her desire to help others wasn't only more of that same selfishness, still more self-gratification. Hannah was also well acquainted with self-gratification, evidence of which ran into the drain with the cream cheese. She was pampered, by herself and others, and the fact that she so enjoyed the pampering disgusted her. Shamed in the spray of hot water, she pondered the likelihood that there would be no such hot showers in the jungle of her imagination. Hannah would have to work around this, but for her life she could not begin to imagine how.

The new kid toweled off and wiggled into some undies. Reaching for a bra, she eyed her tiny boobs in the mirror and said aloud, "Why bother?" Still, Hannah needed something to go with the tiny knickers—anything—so she went to the window for fashion cues. The night before was bitter cold, as many January nights in Vermont are wont to offer. It would take her some time to get used to the cold. But at least it was dry. Hannah liked it dry. Birkenstock dry. She could already see enough of the coming day through the shades to know that it was Birkenstock bright; but, once the shade was up, she gasped, dazzled as such to confuse her rods and cones. A thick, heavy blanket of fresh Vermont snow covered everything Hannah's confused eyes could see. The blanket was a shade less than two feet, but her shock and confusion pumped it to ten; her amazement then brought it to twenty, putting the snow just above the second-story window at which she stood wide-eyed. There were two shapeless white mounds in the driveway where the cars had been the night before.

Returned to speaking with celestial powers, Hannah said, "You can't be serious."

They were.

"Wow." She looked on, still dazzled, but thinking the fluffy blanket kind of pretty. "No Birkenstocks today. More like mittens and mukluks."

Hannah Mae Fields, dazzled and fearful, gathered herself to begin the second half of her sophomore year; the new kid at another new school.

-2-

Between the White Mountains of New Hampshire and Green Mountains of Vermont rests the quiet Preston valley. That the elevations are labeled differently by their respective states means little, as only the whims of the nature mother determine the complexion of the range. Part of the larger Connecticut River Valley, the land was whittled through the millennia, then smashed by the heavy hand of a valley carving glacier some 15,000 years thawed. An arm of the Appalachians, the rolling Preston hills are great-grandparents to the pubescent Rockies, the Himalayas and Alps; they are but mere children by geological comparison, biding their time before wearing away and washing to the sea. It's not a land that time forgot, this valley within a valley, but a place rather ignored and gotten back to periodically, perhaps even reluctantly.

Once the glacier dust settled, woman came with a rugged northern spirit and her man in tow, braving the deep snows and rocky fields with ambitious plans of taming the unfriendly landscape. The mighty oaks, maples and pines were felled, availing the valley for farming and affording wood for shelters to get the rugged people covered. *We've got it covered*, was the collective cry once out of the caves and under their own roofs. They are a hearty folk.

Then the age of machine industry lured the progressively less rugged people from farming and lumbering and into the factories of the newly built cities. Waterwheels started spinning, harnessing the river and spinning the people into a future of capital. They are an enterprising folk.

Off the beaten path, the valley is now home to sleepy hamlets, mom and pop stores, and weathered covered bridges; rustic bridges constructed in centuries past with the vision that, for future generations, they would be touted in North American travel guides as a means to generate tourism revenue. The locals liked to say that their ancestors, those who built the covered bridges, way back when before they were weathered, weren't nearly as excited at the prospect of having their waterways spanned as are the many tourists who seasonally flock to the northcountry to photograph the bridges. This makes the locals smile. They are a good-natured folk.

The city of Preston, just over ten thousand souls and little more than a pistol shot in length or breadth, boasts specialty shops, artist co-ops, fraternal organizations and a bustling downtown, recently made all the more bustling with the construction of a strip mall. And surrounding the city proper, running her streets, forever looming, are thousands upon thousands of the trees annually tapped and sapped and reduced into genuine Vermont maple syrup—a sweet and sticky treat even more popular with the tourists than the weathered covered bridges.

Centered in this rural, Thornton Wilder-like collage of Americana is the ivied façade of the Preston Valley Union High School. Preston High sat in the test pilot's seat of a school consolidation movement in the '60s, and has had its collective hand on the ejection lever since. For many of the valley students this merging of classrooms was their first exposure to others who were not their neighbors and kinfolk. Most valley transplants—less than affectionately referred to by the locals as *flatlanders*—were yuppie couples without children in tow, so very few non-valley teens ever darkened the halls of Preston High. Once in a while, though, a strange student braved sneaking into the tight and familiar group. For the youth of the valley, *strange* constituted any young person who did not ride in on the bus from "betwixt that there yon clumpa trees." They are an educated folk.

Rarer still at the high school was the introduction of any new instructors. Those charged with classrooms at Preston High were, what they liked to call themselves, *real Vermonters*: musty, dusty, and more than a little set in their ways, held fast in the self-constructed confinements of a green v. white mountain paradigm. Much the same as the students, anything new thrown into the teachers' mix brought with it the prospect for change which few had ambition to accept. *Yup, the applecart's shaky enough without kickin' at the wheels.* They're a close-knit folk.

Hannah's ennui and loneliness in her new surroundings grew until she finally winnowed and weeded, trudging the snow and looking for a friend. Many Preston boys showed keen interest in becoming Hannah's friends, most of them concurring that the new student was *hot*. They said she looked like a certain pop star, as the Lotharios and Romeos of Preston invariably used pop stars for their locker room comparisons. Hannah wanted none of that. She was on the lookout for a girlfriend, a certain special friend, someone who might understand a girl who often felt misunderstood. But, because Hannah was hot and looked somewhat like a pop star, and because her fears and insecurities were often mistaken for a snobbish, west coast affectation, the girls of Preston tended to ignore her; or they tried to ignore her, except to speak of her with hushed voices in ways which made them feel a little bit better about themselves. Some of them may have agreed that the new girl looked a little like a pop star, but it sure as hell couldn't be the same pop star the boys were comparing her to.

Much the same as back in Monterey, Hannah took refuge in her books and cocktailing, awaiting her chance to travel to the jungle of her imagination, to a place where she'd be understood and perhaps even appreciated. She sometimes said aloud to no one, "Why bother?" and finally gave up on the search for a special friend. At just the time Hannah gave up, that special friend found her.

Katie was a Preston native, though never quite at home in the sleepy valley. Her father boasted that he was *Preston born and Preston bred, and when he died he'd be Preston dead.* It made his daughter wish to hasten the second line of the couplet.

Katie never fit in, in large part because she didn't really want to. She wasn't a small town girl, and found her surroundings boring—*passé*, Katie would say—and so she spent most of her spare time trying to make the whole of her young existence more interesting, more exciting and even a little more dangerous. Her approaches at spicing things up were most times deemed inappropriate by those around her, against which Katie took pains to show that appropriateness was relative and must be weighed against results only later realized.

She was a strikingly handsome young woman of black Irish descent; more in truth, Katie referred to herself as *black Irish*, though she had but a vague definition of the reference. She liked to romanticize her heritage a la carte, finally subscribing to a myth involving the Spanish Armada wrecking on the shores of the motherland. In Katie's myth there were boatloads of washed up sailors, all sad, beaten and lonely, while the local girls rushed to the beach to greet them, most of them rather kindled and horny. Katie couldn't quite back up her myth, but as it sounded adventurous, dangerous and a little dirty, she liked to consider herself of the ilk. She sometimes even used it as a defense for her ribald behavior. "Que voulez-vous?" she'd feign tied hands; "but it's my nature." She had the face to launch all the ships of her armada, but behind there also lurked the inclination to send every one of them to Davy Jones' locker.

Katie had long, shining dark hair, with still darker brown eyes, and she was uncommonly muscular without having ever stepped foot into a gym. She chanced to bloom early, and bloomed generously, and all the while enjoyed a proud and ostentatious display of what she considered a rather precious array of attributes. And Katie possessed, what she herself came to call, after extensive self-exploration, *a concupiscent promiscuity*. Her mouth watered with the admission. It sounded so cool. It sounded so hot.

Abhorring the small town secrets of Preston, Katie worked hard to provide for the local gossip, then she watched and listened as the lyrical slander rippled through the little city like silk on a wind, until her simple walking down the street brought with it a whispered "*psst, psst, psst*"—so much *psst*, it sounded like nails were tossed under rush hour traffic. Those whispers were often accompanied by tragic commentary from the older and more forgiving residents: "It's too bad, really. She's such a pretty girl, and a smart girl, too." Katie's peers, on the other hand, by nature more honest and less forgiving than their elders, had whispers of their own, as well as adjusted commentary: "*Psst, psst, psst*—slut."

Katie thought of her life as a knot of Gordian complexity severable only by a sword of Rabelaisian sexuality, so right out of the gate she adopted a sex goddess frame of mind; Katie moved like she meant it, she often treated herself roughly, and she treated others like they'd been stolen. She could have played *the girl next door*, but only if one lived near a munitions factory within the red light district.

Her grandfathers were partners in a small grocery market they opened upon returning from the Korean peninsula in '53. Each old soldier had one child, and it was early decided that these children, Michael Pauley and Catherine Ross, would one day unite and take charge of the prosperous business. Eventually the elders left the store, and left the earth, and left the young family at the helm of the County Store.

The older of Catherine and Michael's two girls, Madeline, showed more of an interest in caring and curing than in canned goods, so she left Preston for the nursing program at the University of Vermont, bringing with her few fond memories of coming of age in the Pauley household. The younger daughter, Katie, fifteen years old and stuck, to her own dismay as well as that of many others, worked for her parents at the County Store, now grown into a specialty foods market catering to the up and coming in the valley—the *flatlanders*. Venturing that Katie *worked* leans towards dramatization, but still payroll kicked a weekly check for her thirty hours whether or not she was actually in the building. Katie was at the store only when she had to be, unlike her father who opened and closed every day (except Sunday), and proudly boasted the fact with a sandwich-board sign with bright red, four-inch block letters on the sidewalk at the front entrance: THE OWNER IS IN THE BUILDING. "That's what sets us apart from the chain stores," was Michael Pauley's favorite and oft-quoted retail expression, something in which he took a measure of comfort as a tangled montage of X-chromosomes worked to strangle him at home.

Cathy Pauley, Katie's mother, spent a good deal of time at the market as well, but for altogether different reasons. There was one passion, and only one, that the mother shared with her younger daughter, and that was in games of seduction with the County Store's employees. Thanks to the Pauley women, Catherine the elder and

Katherine the younger, Preston had silk enough to fly the winds of the approaching millennium.

The town's annals were peppered with lascivious tales involving the pair. They eventually became, by all outward shows, bent upon showing one another up, with each wearing well, and even with pride, their hard-earned cloak of licentiousness; that is, until it all came to a geometric head atop an obtuse triangle claiming the career of the County Store butcher.

Miss Pauley had been grounded by Mrs. Pauley, as was often the case; however, Katie took it upon herself to leave the house just the same, as was just as often the case. She went to the meatcutter's apartment and quietly admitted herself with the key he kept covertly hidden under the *welcome* mat; but Katie found herself much less than welcomed, when she discovered her secret lover in bed and making the beast with two backs, with one of those backs belonging to her father's naked wife. The double-backed beast prompted Katie to let go a scream which tore through the streets of Preston. Old Mrs. Clogston had heard it on Riverside Avenue, reasoning it had to do with the Pauleys. It usually did.

Katie's mythological, black Irish instinct convinced her she had to pull a knife from the block on the kitchen counter; the black Irish settled on the curved-blade, six-inch boner. Blind with rage, Katie lunged for the beast, but caught her foot in the rug—it was an imitation bearskin rug; she tripped on the imitation paw—and went airborne the last few feet. The boner brushed her mother's ass, severing the flower from the stem of her rose tattoo, then went on to carve into the meatcutter's hip. While neither of the wounds was any more than superficial, Katie was plenty successful in murdering the bed itself, dumping nearly three hundred gallons of water onto the neighbors below.

The butcher was bandaged and banished, and this time Katie's mother was sent packing as well. Casually picking at her teeth with the proverbial last straw, with plans to meet up with the meat man in another time, another place, Catherine Pauley quietly left the little city, and left her ex-husband and ex-daughter to mind the store. Katie was no sooner rid of her mother's competition when another young lovely strolled into town.

-3-

Hannah spent the first of her time in Preston *feeling out* the new arrangement. Without straining to listen, she heard the silk on the wind blow past with rumors of the local black Irish girl. Hannah loved everything she heard, whether it was true or not. The silk whispered that this same girl was the valley's black sheep, piquing Hannah's interest even further. She wondered if they might become friends, and found chance in Mr. Balzac's American literature class to test the viability of such a friendship.

Theodore Balzac was of the aforementioned crusty Preston academia, with an approach to the instruction of literature running along the lines of *if it ain't broke, don't fix it,* and none could convince Teddy that it was, in fact, *broke*. His teaching style had gone out with the Nixon administration, and many thought it unfortunate that the tenured Teddy hadn't gone with it.

The teacher assigned beat up copies of Steinbeck's *The Long Valley* at the beginning of the session. Katie's copy, wrapped in a cloth of coincidence embroidered with threads of irony, was the same volume her mother had been assigned in Mr. Balzac's class some twenty years earlier; 'Cathy + Michael = TLA' was inscribed on the title page. Written with a felt tip, the inscription was destined to last longer than the actual relationship.

Only a couple of days into the term, Mr. Balzac selected from the volume and bid the students read 'The Red Pony.' While Hannah loved the short story—she pretty much loved stories in general, and especially the stories of John Steinbeck—she held no such feeling for the instructor. This same lack of feeling begged that she project on the difficulty of spending the next forty weeks with the man. Soon her projection was verified and vivified when the teacher called her to the carpet. Having been the new kid in other schools, Hannah believed herself an easy mark for teachers like Teddy Balzac. While it never failed to singe her self-consciousness, this time her anger was fired as well. She decided then and there that she wouldn't have any more spotlights shone upon her; henceforth she alone would choose when and where she performed; from here on out she alone would light the lights.

The teacher looked over his glasses at Hannah, half the room's length away. "What are your comments on the passage I assigned, Ms. Fields?"

Eyes in the classroom turned, as eyes in high school classrooms invariably do. Disconcerted and alone, Hannah's claws protracted. She looked down at the worn book on the desk. She looked back to the man in the front. "I didn't read it, Mr. Balzac. I perused most of this musty volume over the weekend, but I couldn't bring myself to read that pony thing again. I like to think I'm beyond horsey stories."

The teacher abruptly recoiled from this whack by Hannah's insolence stick. Worn out pride and ideological immunity then prompted Balzac to whack back. "Well, young lady, if you *perused* the volume, as you claim, please enlighten the class on those works you did find interesting."

Hannah picked up the book and scanned the front matter. Though still under the spotlight, she now felt more comfortable in the performance. "Here's one got my attention," she announced, more for her fellow students than the teacher; 'St. Katy, the Virgin.' That's something I didn't expect to come across around here."

"Explain yourself, Ms. Fields," requested the instructor.

Hannah perked up. "Since coming to Preston, I never expected to hear the words *Katy* and *virgin* used together—not even in the same conversation."

The room was pin dropping silent. Hannah turned to face Saint Katie sitting at the desk behind. She struggled for a look of innocence, but couldn't quite pull it off. Katie traded a toothy smile. "Good one, new girl. Real fucking clever."

"Watch your mouth, Miss Pauley," said the teacher.

Katie couldn't remove her eyes from the new girl. They looked at one another for a moment longer than their smiles lasted; and in that moment, Hannah, nimble like a cat burglar, quickly heisted the jewel of friendship and ran with it. She even had a little time to spare. And it was in that same moment, Hannah and Katie would later agree, when each became the greatest friend the other would ever know.

With Saint Katie's attention, and that of the rest of the class, Hannah returned to the instructor and continued sagaciously, "If we have to read Steinbeck, why not *In Dubious Battle*? or *'Winter of Our Discontent'*? Furthermore, it's unprofessional, even downright rude, to use a student's first week at her new school as an opportunity to flaunt some sort of imaginary power. You should be ashamed of yourself for picking on me, putting me on the spot like that." She considered conjuring some crocodile tears, but decided the occasion did not warrant them. "That said, you can have your stinky, little book back." She lifted the volume between her thumb and forefinger, holding it away like something from the back of the fridge. "We've a fresher copy at home, thank you very much." This last put her off; Hannah disliked the use of *thank you very much* at the end of a statement, disliked the affect behind it, but it had slipped out and could not be brought back. She wasn't going to let the faux pas impede her performance.

Tension filled the classroom, like cigar smoke in a pool hall, like the tear gas at Attica, until the teacher finally mumbled, "You're getting off on the wrong foot, Ms. Fields—the wrong foot, I assure you."

She returned with her insolence stick once more, "With just the two feet, I only had a fifty-fifty chance. Now you can watch those same two feet carry my ass outta here." She gathered her belongings and made for the door, slinging her backpack over her shoulder in stride, placing the mildewed volume of Steinbeck stories on the teacher's desk.

"I hope you're aware you need this class to graduate."

"Then I won't graduate, Mr. Balzac. Simple enough. Trust me, it'll fuck up your numbers more than mine. I'll simply seek my education elsewhere, thank you very much." *Damn! And used 'simple' twice?* Hannah was chastising herself, making mental notes on closing performances, when she noticed Katie was also gathering up her gear. In preparation for her exit, though, Katie's foot got caught in the leg of her desk, sending her tumbling onto Jennifer Novak.

She quickly recovered. "Sorry, Jen."

"Not a problem, Kate," Jennifer returned, contentedly caught in the spectacle.

"I'm outta here too," Katie announced, as though she felt she had to.

Hannah and Katie left the room together, and few would argue they looked good doing so. If Katie was black Irish, then Hannah was white as light, as bright as Katie was dark, with blonde hair on her shoulders, creamy white skin and crystalline eyes. Alike in many ways, the pair was different in more, so that they complemented and completed one another. Each brought the other closer to perfection, while at the same time helping one another to remain at a comfortable distance from perfection, something they would likely have found boring. Neither could see any boring perfection from where now together they stood, but if one was to get on the shoulders of the other, craning her neck, she might discern the direction they would follow toward perfection, if they wanted it, which they didn't. There was harmony and balance together that could not be contained apart. And Katie, much like her new friend, was also exhausting avenues of approach in finding something to justify a seeming paltry existence. She now believed in her black Irish heart of hearts that that something was found. *Serendipity?* Katie wondered; but just as quickly she decided that any word ending in *dipity* was too foo-foo sounding to accurately describe what she believed was coming about—say nothing of *serendipity* sounding like a hair gel laced with nerve agent. What Katie was thinking was … maybe *fate.*

April in the Preston Valley found the welcomed spring struggling to melt a record snowfall. The Connecticut River moved swiftly, its freshets tumbling and carrying the smaller stones lying in its path, and boldly eating away at the rocks it could not yet move. Water came from the mountains to form little streams in the streets, carving small canyons through the built up sand and salt; a timeless erosion to wash another winter of discontent from the city and into the river, down to the sound and out to sea. The inexorable season had left the land aching, scarred and worn out, but glassy, sun-filled puddles dotting the fields reflected the semblance of rejuvenation.

The valley people busied themselves in their newfound freedom from the elements. An iced lethargy became energy. The wearied were invigorated. Returned birds sang merrily, as awakened squirrels, lean from sabbatical, scampered across the saturated landscape in search of another season's storage. The air was alive with excitement and anticipation for the annual renaissance, blessing the old with reprieve and the young with determination, all swimming in the intense and optimistic beauty of an emerging season.

The pursuits of students and faculty at Preston High were heightened by the comforting weather and preparation for finals. They planned for their summer vacations, and planned for the futures of those graduates who would soon pass beyond the valley boundaries to still richer, greener lands of hope and prospect. The casual observer, looking over the picturesque community in all its Rockwellian splendor, might comment on the tranquility and peace of mind seemingly blanketing the valley; but the casual observer does not see and hear the goings on beneath the superficiality; the outsider is not privy to the whispered secrets of uncertainty.

Hannah and Katie shared a bench in Memorial Park on the soft side of summer. Both were enrolled for the summer session to make up the course in American literature. They laughed at the episode, believing deep down it was worth it, until it occurred to Hannah that the summer instructor might be Theodore Balzac.

"I never thought of that," Katie returned. She was eating corn chips from a bag, wiping her mouth with a napkin after each one. "No, old timers don't teach in the summer. At least I hope not."

Hannah was working on an orange, collecting the peel in her lap and wishing her own skin was as thick. She nearly gasped when she spoke. "I can't stand this place a minute longer, Kate. Barely six months in Preston and already I'm so sick of it I could scream." There was a fire of frustration in her eyes, passions, dreams festering and boiling, looking for even the smallest crack through which to escape. "Let's just go. Let's just get on the bus and go. We'll stay at Aunt Patty's till we're situated—get jobs or something."

Katie loved and shared all of Hannah's passions. "You know I'm with you, like ninety-eight percent—rich and famous or running from the law, it really doesn't matter to me; but whatever we do, we have to do it right, and we have to do it with some class. Still, irregardless of what we do—"

"Could you *please* not say that?" Hannah interjected.

"Say what?"

"*Irregardless*—it's not even a word."

Katie looked at her in silence, almost dumbfounded. She did not know whether to kiss her or slap her, so she did neither, but rather went on, "*Whatever* we do, we're only getting one chance to do it, and I'm not using my one chance to hop some fucking Greyhound to Boston. While we're at it, we can wrap some toothpaste and tampons in a bandana and tie it on a stick—goofy fucker. We have to tough it out for now. There's no way around it. I promise we'll go after graduation, but we have to graduate. I'm not going anywhere without the diploma. As that makes the most sense, that's what we're going to do."

"Okay, that's what we'll do."

"A bus to Aunt Patty's? Where do you even get such shit?"

"I was kidding about the bus part." Hannah smiled and lowered her eyes.

Katie patted her friend's leg with enough confidence for them both. "We'll get through it, sweetheart, don't you worry. We can get through anything."

Hannah went on peeling. "I never would have made it this far without you. You're an alright person." She took a break from the orange to look Katie up and down. "And you're the hottest friend I've ever had—you know, in a redneck, whore-like sort of way." She went back to her produce.

Katie studied her briefly. "If someone threw a hand grenade at us right now, I'd jump on it to protect you."

Hannah didn't bother looking up. "You know that isn't true."

After a time, Katie had to admit, "No, I suppose you're right. What I mean to say is, I love you and I'll do anything to keep you safe, make you happy."

"Me too," said Hannah, stepping up her relationship with the fruit. No less than a half-dozen big, fat tears splashed in her lap.

The tears made Katie smile through the beginnings of her own. "Knock it off," she said, leaning in to kiss her.

Hannah wiped her cheeks on her sleeve and *sniff*ed. "Sorry. Must be my period."

It was not Hannah's period, but rather an exclamation point punctuating the excitement Katie had brought into her life. In her gratitude, she asked, "You want to go across the river and see that fortune teller?"

Katie quickly decided against it. "She's actually a palmist, but to be honest, I'd rather not know. I don't want to spoil the surprise. One thing's for sure, though, we're gonna have us lots of fun. I can foresee that much of our future, and you can rub my crystal balls if ever you need to know more."

"Thank you."

Hawthorne might also have had a fun time with the pair. *Behold, verily, there is the woman of the scarlet letter. And, in truth moreover, there is the likeness of the scarlet letter running along by her side!*

Katie could have been the Hester Prynne of the Preston Valley, while loving any infamy coming from such a comparison. She'd proudly wear a big, red *A* embroidered on her reputation, convincing herself, and one day everyone else, that it represented *Awesome*. Hannah, Pearl-like and happily guilty by association, but planning to keep some tidbits to herself, would have her own *A* stand for *Ambiguity*.

Come, therefore, and let us fling mud at them!

-5-

It often comes to pass when a great deal can happen in a relatively short period; short like the two years' time since the California winds blew Hannah Fields to Vermont. When a host of personalities exist in close quarters—close like the small city of Preston—characters get caught up, weaving in and out of each other's lives and creating the collective fabric often generously referred to as human*kind*. Courses change and conditions alter, as people lead one another onto contrary paths, toward different destinies. The lives oftentimes come away enriched, enlightened and all-around better for the experience; but just as often those same lives, in the flicker of an instant, can be destroyed.

"John, Mrs. Green is here to see you."

"Thanks, Beth. Show her in."

John Stanson had been sitting at his desk trying to imagine how bad his day was going to get. The sudden appearance of Mable Green brought him uncomfortably closer to the dismal picture he'd been painting. He muttered, "Let the games begin," as he went to the door. John knew his attitude was unprofessional, but any boost of professionalism now would be akin to closing the gate after the horses were out. And the horses were already out—way out. They were bucking and bouncing off one another in distant fields, and the more John wished to corral them, the more elusive they became, and further off in the fields. Some of those fields were troubling to John, but troubling him most at present was Hannah Fields.

"Good morning, Mrs. Green," he said. "How's everything in the wonderful world of mathematical studies?" He saw the old woman to the chair before taking his own. It was only the beginning of what would be a long and arduous day. Such days once were rarities, but of late they had become commonplace. "Students are treating you well I hope?"

The old woman still looked disapprovingly over her glasses at him, she still had eight inches of ass hanging over either side of the chair, and John still had great admiration and respect for her. Though never his favorite teacher, Mrs. Green was instrumental in seeing that John kept clean and present during high school, and made it safely to graduation. Like a monkey with molasses hands, she held fast to his back all four years, possessively guarding against any other primates wanting to set up shop. John remembered the smiling pride swimming in the old woman's eyes at his graduation, with the tearful nodding of her head and the handkerchief in her gloved hand.

Mabel Green always favored John with a bit of reverse discrimination, he being one of only two black students at the school, in Preston—in Vermont, the whitest state in the union. Mrs. Green had wondered if John was at high risk for winding up on the Preston scrapheap, wondered if contemporary society as a whole might ensure him a spot on the heap. She wasn't going to have any of that on her watch; and her watch didn't end when John finished high school, for nearly fifteen years later she was on the floor once again when he took his PhD in Boston, and still with the handkerchief in her hand, with the same smiling pride dripping from her eyes.

"The world of mathematics, Dr. Stanson, is not as wonderful as one might hope—"

John could never get used to her addressing him so formally. When he sat in her classroom he was *Johnny*, or *Mr. Stanson*, or *young man*, all dependent on where he presently stood in the woman's graces, on how much his current actions were mirroring her vision of the model student, the student she was adamant in seeing young and black John Stanson become.

"—and it seems a world I'm scarcely part of these days. The distance between myself and these students grows all the time. After forty years, I'm completely out of touch. I honestly believe the time has come for me to move on."

John often heard Mrs. Green's complaints, damn-near daily, but now she was visibly upset. *Move on?* John was sure he'd retire before she did. He tried to dance around the elephant in the room, but wasn't able to pull it off, his attempts at Gene Kelly offering only left feet. "I understand they can be trying at times, but they're pretty good kids for the most part, not much different than we were—a bit braver and more outspoken perhaps. It's tough out there these days, especially in a town like Preston."

At thirty-five, John was staring down the barrel of his third decade in Preston. Until recently the experience had been as smooth and rewarding as he could have hoped for. He'd been looking forward to seeing the school and the city into the new millennium.

He began at PVUHS as a student, then spent some time there as a young educator before moving on to higher education. When the cost of that higher education proved higher than John's resources, he looked to the G.I. bill for financial assistance, offering in trade a four-year tour with a marine expeditionary force. Subsequently, as part of a reenlistment agreement, he applied to Officer Candidates School, graduated with honors, and began another tour, this time with force reconnaissance. He was a first lieutenant, tapping at the door of captaincy.

One year after his reenlistment, John's body was splayed with bullets from Iraqi assault rifles. Once healed, he returned to the valley to head up the guidance office at Preston High. In all his travels, through all the trials, John wasn't sure if he'd ever found what he was looking for, but he did come away from the Carolinas with something that had not been part of the quest; a wife, the lovely and talented Lauren Thatcher of Chapel Hill.

John went into the guidance office believing that the kids of Preston needed some guidance. He'd graffiti'd some buildings back in the day, smoked a little dope and raised some hell, and years later he still considered himself among the more troublesome youth. But compared to kids in the classes today, he had played a game of Albert Schweitzer, while they were libertine devotees of the Marquis de Sade.

Mrs. Green asked, "Is there any word on when Mr. Dollar will be returning?"

John had hoped the conversation wouldn't turn to the subject of Lincoln Dollar, but there was no way around it now. "I haven't talked to him for a couple of weeks," he replied. "He said he'd be away for a bit, that's all. You know about as much as I do." John did know more, but he was keeping it to himself. He knew Lincoln was back in New York. The phone message he'd left had said, unconvincingly, that he *needed some time to work things out*.

Mrs. Green was near tears. "The students are whispering of something happening during the class trip to New York, something having to do with Hannah Fields and Mr. Dollar. And now she's not been in school these same three weeks since we've seen him. Hannah's parents said she's staying with relatives, nothing more—just as secretive as the students. It makes no sense for her to suddenly pack up and leave, not when everything was going so well."

John didn't enjoy the thought, but if Lincoln Dollar and Hannah Fields were away somewhere together, at least there would be potential for an explanation; contrary, he saw no good coming of the two of them missing separately. The past three weeks had been a waiting game which John was not up to playing. Stuck in the middle of something, he didn't know what, he knew it would prove to be riddled with complications. In fact, he had told his wife that very morning as he left the house, "Wait and see. This is going to turn into a huge shit sandwich without any bread."

When Lauren suggested he may as well hold the mayo too, John kissed her goodbye, but his heart wasn't really in it.

-6-

Lincoln Dollar had arrived in the blooming Preston Valley at an awkward time to begin his new occupation, but as a blessing to the other teachers in the department. The staff was drawing straws to see who would stand over the summer session when Lincoln dropped his duffle bag on the floor in the teachers' lounge. He didn't know it going in, but the summer classes would soon be his.

While the bulk of the staff and studentry geared up for their favorite part of the year, certain slackers dragged about the weight of engaging in another six weeks of concentrated study to make up for their unwillingness during the regular term. Hannah Fields and Katie Pauley, not surprisingly, were among the slackers. They and their fellow students, while not pleased with sacrificing vacation for education, at least found some mischievous comfort in knowing they would be breaking in a fresh, new teacher. The odds were already in their favor, as the slackers were thirteen strong and the educational force but one, plus the slackers had a home team advantage. So the student-warriors prepared for battle; singly, and in small units, they mapped and planned their campaign strategies like so many impish mercenaries. Upon arrival at the front, the troops engaged their enemy in the customary theater of operations.

One coming on the scene would have had trouble discerning the instructor from the students. With their attempts at appearing older than their years, coupled with his just as silly attempts at trying to pass himself off as younger, one might be left wondering who was actually in charge. The teacher wore a frayed denim jacket, worn at the sleeves and collar. He was stationed casually in the chair, one hand in the pocket of his jacket, the other flipping through the pages of textbooks on the desk, sometimes reflecting mild pleasure at what he found between the covers, but more often grimacing with shows of distaste at some hackneyed story or passage.

The long hand crept on the hour as the desks filled. Lincoln couldn't help but notice how the seats filled oppositely those at a rock & roll concert, and more akin to pew seeking for Sunday mass; the seats near the back seemed the desired destinations. Soon the room was a dozen people including the instructor, though the class manifest advertised thirteen slackers. Lincoln reasoned that the eleven of thirteen present would rather have been anywhere else; twelve of fourteen when including himself.

He turned to face the blackboard, writing his name, L-I-N-C-O-L-N-D-O-L-L-A-R, and immediately felt foolish for having done so, then was close to erasing and starting over when there came a startling kicking at the door. No others showed the initiative, so Lincoln went to open it. Hannah and Katie pushed past him and into the room, their hands full of trays and bags of coffee cups and bagels.

Hannah went to the instructor's desk, sliding its contents aside with her forearm. She put down her parcels and looked at the chalky scrawl on the board, putting out her hand. "Ah, so you're the new teacher. My name is Hannah Fields, and this is my friend," she indicated with a cock of her head in Katie's direction, "Katherine Pauley. There's dairy and sugar in the bag if you need it. Bagels are whole wheat with veggie cheese, courtesy of the County Store. We should have enough for everyone."

Lincoln took the cup handed him and put it off to the side of the desk. He declined the sugar and cream, but accepted the wax paper-wrapped roll. He sat back at the desk as the girls went about the class, breaking the fast. Once all were served, Katie performed some tidying up, during which Lincoln couldn't help but notice that the service and meal took the better part of twenty-five minutes, twenty-five of the allotted ninety. He spent the twenty-five sipping his coffee and scanning the texts. A few of the students had brought the assigned book, a couple were even thumbing it, but most sat in idle conversation, in pairs and in small groups, enjoying, Lincoln surmised, the same disregard for education that had introduced them to the summer session to begin with. Cyndi's back was to the teacher, she and Jennifer holding hands, acting all in love, whispering, laughing under their breaths.

The class was past out of hand when Lincoln, for lack of a gavel, let the heavy text fall from some height to the desk. The room grew silent with all eyes to the teacher, except for Cyndi's eyes, which remained intent on Jennifer's gaze. He asked, "Is anyone here at all interested in the study of literature?"

There may have been a couple of shrugs. Perhaps a few thought the question rhetorical. Having garnered such a feeble response, Lincoln rose and put the bagel in his jacket pocket. He inserted two of the textbooks into the crook of his arm. Picking up the coffee, he made for the door, addressing the class along the way, "Read the first one hundred pages of the Poe work in the text, the novella, and we'll have our first examination tomorrow morning, accounting for twenty percent of your final grade. Enjoy the rest of the day."

Cyndi sat closest the door. As the new teacher was so loaded down with his books and beverage, she graciously moved to open it.

"It was nice to meet you, Cyndi. I'll see you tomorrow." He started out, but turned back and leaned in close to her ear. "We're not really having an exam in the morning," he whispered, "but don't tell anyone else, except maybe Jennifer."

"Okay, Mr. Dollar," she whispered back.

Once he was gone, the class had to know what he had said.

"He said we're lucky we don't have to read that whole no-vella," Cyndi announced.

The students returned, begrudgingly—some closer to prepared, though most still were not—to the classroom on Tuesday morning to find a note of instruction taped to the door: MEET BEHIND BUILDING BENEATH WILLOWS. COME ONE, COME ALL AND COME PREPARED. YOURS IN SERVICE, LINCOLN DOLLAR.

The fire exit at the end of the hall was propped open with a folding chair. Cyndi and Jennifer each took a chair from the rack and began the short walk across the parking lot to the school lawn beneath the weeping willow trees. The rest of the students soon followed, and there found the new teacher, Lincoln Dollar, sitting cross-legged under the trees with the morning sun on his back. He wore the same denim coat as the day before, with pants of the same worn material. He still kept his hand in the pocket of the coat. Covering shortly cropped dark hair was a cap advertising a product he'd never purchased. His shoes were almost as old as the students. Lincoln Dollar sat with the textbook in his lap, opened to the final pages of *The Narrative of Arthur Gordon Pym'*. He might have been twenty-five, or fifty-two, it was difficult to tell, for his were years maybe remaining dormant before jumping up all at once.

The slacker-students entered the mock classroom and formed a semi-circle. Those with chairs unfolded them. Some sat on the grass. "I count eleven present, and once again a pair of stragglers picking up the rear."

He addressed the group with the voice of a disenchanted actor rehearsing a poorly written monologue, as part of a stage drama in which he would rather not perform. Lincoln Dollar could only vaguely remember having auditioned for the role. "We got off to an awkward beginning," he said, "but that's okay. Beginnings are often awkward. Some might even say they're tangled and chaotic. So, let's get to know one another—sort of untangle the chaos—before we begin again."

He paused as Katie and Hannah joined the group. "Regardless of what anyone has planned," he went on, "our class plan is to spend part of the summer pursuing American lit. We'll read several works and discuss plots, themes, characters, style and such, and see how they all relate to the host of letters we've come to call American literature. As we have only six weeks to cover four hundred years' worth of material, everyone has to be here every day, and on time." This last comment seemed specifically directed toward the tardy two.

"There are three rules regarding this class and any other class I might have the opportunity to instruct. Anyone uncomfortable with the rules should leave right now—no hard feelings, I promise, and no questions asked. Participation is number one. I've committed myself to being here and I'll require the same from you. Number two—and I can't be too adamant about this—we won't tolerate anyone coming late. If you are running late, don't bother running. We can't have the class being disrupted once we've started. Rule three, read the assigned works, read them all, so the entire group can add to our dialogue. Kinda easy-peasy, right? Three rules: be here, be on time and do the work—no exceptions, no excuses, no loopholes, no bullshit. Come, come on time and come prepared. Any questions?"

There were no questions, yet, but there was a good deal of stirring with boredom and seemingly defiant indifference, prompting Lincoln to add a disclaimer, even smugly: "I'm not here to make friends; I already have some friends." However, he thought briefly, then had to disclaim the disclaimer: "They're not really *friends*, per se—more like enemies who finally gave up."

Katie let go a laugh.

Hannah whispered, "A passion for Poe and a shitty attitude. Not unlike old man ball-sack."

"But considerably hotter," was Katie's hushed return. "Much hotter, and kind of funny."

Lincoln continued, "I'm sure no one's all that excited about being here, and I can appreciate that. I'd rather be out enjoying the summer as well, but this is my cross to bear for starting a new job, while it's your atonement for not doing your job sufficiently during the regular term. Let's all work together and get through it. We might even have some fun."

Again the indifferent eyes were rolling.

"I spoke with a few of you yesterday. Ms. Partlow, it's good to see you again. Ms. Novak, Mr. Hazzard, welcome to the class. And you're Katherine Pauley. We were sort of introduced yesterday. I'm Lincoln Dollar."

"Please, professor, my friends call me Katie. It's indeed a pleasure to meet you, again."

Hannah slapped at Katie's thigh. "Please excuse my associate, but she doesn't get out much, and so finds it *indeed a pleasure* to meet just about anyone. *Professor*? She thinks you came in here off the set of *Gilligan's Island*." Katie nodded in agreement with whatever Hannah had said. She stuck out her chest a bit, but it was an act more second-natured than of any conscious exhibition.

"And you're Hannah Fields," said the teacher. "Thank you for the breakfast yesterday."

"You're welcome."

"Is that *Hannah* as a palindrome?"

"Yeah, my parents are clever that way. I've a sister Eve with a racecar, and a baby brother, Otto, in a kayak."

"Delightful," the teacher returned, though unimpressed. "I understand you had a problem in Mr. Balzac's class last term—you and your … *associate*."

"You understand rightly, but don't believe everything you hear in that teachers' lounge. My departure from old ball-sack's class was on account of an eye problem I was having."

"How so?"

"I couldn't *see*—as in, couldn't see spending another minute in that class. I blew outta there so fast my ass was smoking." Exceeding flamboyant, she went on, "You see, Mr. Dollar, that guy's wannabe testicularity was simply too much. He tried backing me into a corner, and I wouldn't have it. I couldn't have it, him trying to bust my balls because I was new in town. Granted, I'm young, but I've been around enough to know I got some rights—like the right to be treated gently, and with kindness and fairness and respect. I'm here because I want to be, not because anyone's forcing me. That said, I already sense we won't run into the same problems with you, so I'd like to welcome you to Preston Valley Union High School."

"Thanks for having me."

Hannah caught herself doing something with her hair, realizing she was doing it for the new teacher and no one else. She cursed herself for it, then cursed herself more for having taken the time to notice and to curse herself. She leaned back on an elbow and stretched out on the grass. She let her hair be. "It's all about choice, but enough about that. You don't really look like a high school teacher. Got any credentials?"

"The people in the main office seemed to find them in order."

"Where's the main office? Bangor? What about the Vermont office?" It was Hannah's day, and the new teacher was making it all the more fun. "When were you born?"

"Born December the 20th," he answered, "1968."

"The year of revolt," she said, with some surprise, "and a Sagittarius at that. Interesting." The date already held a spot in her head, but she couldn't quite place it.

"It was the year of revolt. I'm a product of the revolution."

"Kate's a Sagittarius, too, and now that we're on the subject of birthdays—" Hannah had made sure the subject would turn to birthdays "—today just happens to be mine." She was happy she was able to share the information with the class. "A not-so-sweet sixteen."

Lincoln was musing on the relativity of sweetness when it occurred to him there were a dozen others in the group.

"Excuse me?" said Hannah.

"Excuse me?" Lincoln returned.

"Nothing. I thought you said something. Anyway, if it's any consolation, Mr. Dollar, the years seem to have treated you kindly."

"Please, call me Lincoln."

"Nope. I'd rather not begin on such informalities, *Mr.* Dollar."

Hannah was smiling in a manner seldom seen by others when there was suddenly a splash in her think pan. *December 20th, '68?*

Lincoln went around the group with introductions, his first class since receiving certification. The students found him tolerable enough, in a teacher sort of way, his steely blue eyes, squinting in the out of doors, offering the young men what they suspected might be a seasoned individual, perhaps a force to be reckoned with, but by another, more brazen volunteer. Occasionally the guys at Preston High tried to strong-arm their teachers, especially any new arrivals, but there was a silent, collective agreement that there would be no such strong-arming here. The young women were impressed by the simple, rugged look of the new instructor, and by the same eyes, but for altogether different reasons. The group was warming up nicely to Lincoln Dollar, and soon the battle lines began to fade.

He dropped the initial speech and moved into something unrehearsed. "I'll be honest with you, you're my first students. I've never, ever in my life taught a literature class. I got the certificate, having been found certifiable, but I never thought I would actually have cause to use it, let alone in Preston, Vermont, so I would really appreciate it if you guys worked with me. As I said, we're here to read and discuss literature, but it doesn't have to be all rigid and formal. I don't believe these artists had such rigid formality in mind when they wrote this stuff. And I'm not coming in here with a bunch of windy lectures and an ego full of answers. I've got questions of my own, and I'll look for your help in answering them. We'll study what the bosses say we have to study, and we'll look at what we, as a group, think is important. I hope there's a difference between the two. By the end of the summer we'll put some things together, and perhaps have a better understanding of present and future writings in this country. Perhaps you and I will be a part of those writings. If everyone comes to class every day and on time, I guarantee everyone will be juniors in September—even you, Ms. Fields."

Hannah didn't feel the comment warranted any reply, but at the same time she rather enjoyed the simple way of being singled out.

"If anyone's not cool with this, I might have another section of this same class in the fall. You'd be welcomed to try it again, and again and again, until you accept the fact that you've got to swallow this material if you want a diploma. Personally, I think this is important stuff, and not only because it's American, but because it's part of something bigger, something far more important. If you can't dig the material, that's okay—you won't hurt my feelings—but you will try my patience with any shows of disrespect towards this class. We have to be here, so don't fight it. I've been there, trust me, you won't win." He tried for an expression of vital importance, managing well enough to hide his amusement.

Hannah saw the teacher's amusement, and she saw something else, and she wanted to believe it was only she who saw it. She met his eyes briefly. There was an instantaneous, synaptic flash of familiarity, leaving her believing she had met Lincoln Dollar somewhere before.

"I'll now launch into my first ever block of instruction," he said. "Wish me luck."

"Good luck," said Cyndi.

Lincoln Dollar had a passion for literature, American and otherwise, though the passion wasn't so much for the works of Poe; but his new bosses were the ones to determine what was and was not contemporarily pertinent, and they had suggested the Baltimorean make an early showing in the term. It was far too soon for Lincoln to upset the established curriculum. There would be plenty of time for that later on. "Let's talk about this gothic literary movement."

Attached to a hand raised in quasi-classroom formality was Hannah Fields. "I have a two-part question, Mr. Dollar."

"Please, proceed with part one, Ms. Fields."

"Why would you even assign such an irrelevant passage of literature? It's mundane, windy, dated and trite, and I'd have to read it more closely, but I believe it also lacks in continuity, which isn't surprising, being written by a junkie. Worse still, you forced us to choke down well over half of it in one sitting, a chore for a Poe scholar who actually gives a shit about the material, say nothing of a bunch of hostage high schoolers who should be on summer break."

"I'll grant you windy and dated," the teacher rebuffed, "but not irrelevant." Addressing the group, he went on, "Regarding windy, we can assume Mr. Poe was paid by the word. As for dated, it was the 1830s, but still, when viewed within Marxists' or a new historicist context, even the work of a junkie can help us to piece together the period. Poe is relevant, in that he speaks to, and represents, a rather important transition in the literature of the United States. And Poe was assigned because my bosses said to assign it, and for the new guy on the block that's a pretty strong persuader. Lastly, this tediously long piece was chosen as punishment for your flippant display of using yesterday's class time for a social hour. It was my way of lashing out because somewhere inside my feelings were probably hurt." Just as quickly, though, the new teacher recovered from the supposed injury, returning with a proposition. "I'll try and keep my feelings in check, if you'll do what you can to make my new job a little easier. We'll then assume the class is well versed in gothic literature and disregard this morning's exam, then move along to something not so dated and windy." Now Lincoln was winded. It had been a while since he managed so many words in a single morning.

Hannah was entirely engaged, spending half her time thinking him brilliant, and the other half thinking him somewhat goofy. She liked both halves. Thus engaged, Hannah christened him, hands-down, the best looking teacher she had ever had. At first she thought he was kind of cute, but upon closer inspection she found the adjective wouldn't serve. It was then the blood came into her face, and Hannah directly knew whence it came. *Oh shit!* thought she. More blood followed on the heels of her embarrassment, and still more by way of a humbling shame.

"Please proceed with the second part of your question, Ms. Fields."

Hannah was so deeply engaged that it took some time for her to resurface. "The second part, yes. Why do you keep your hand like you do? In your pocket all the time. Is it some kind of Napoleon thing? Like some Napoleonic Code?" (There, now the teacher knew she was a little bit versed in old French law. Hannah thought herself clever, and she wanted the teacher to agree.)

Katie gave her a poke, leaving Hannah unsure whether it was meant to urge her on or to shut her up; she assumed the first, continuing, "I was talking to a friend last night about it, about how you keep your hand tucked in your pocket like that. It's kind of affected. No offense."

"You seriously sit around after hours discussing the people who work at your school?" the teacher asked. "This is only a suggestion, you know, with all your birthrights and what-not, but if you put that time into your studies, I bet you'd pass your classes the first time round. Now, let me ask, why do you constantly scowl like you do?" He mocked her mock-seriousness, enough so that a couple of students laughed. "Is it some misplaced pseudo-intelligentsia? A brooding artists' mien? Your impressionable mug is apt to retain the disposition as it ages, which would be a shame, unless you plan on moving to Taos. No offense."

Anyone else would have been told "fuck you," but, darn it if Hannah didn't rather enjoy the teacher's gentle rebuke; and besides, she deserved it. She was being a smartass, and the teacher had merely called her on the behavior. Hannah was cool with that much, however crushed in other regards. Definitely crushed, she was sure. "This is my deep in thought look," she said, slowly relaxing the facial tension—movements barely perceptible, though painfully obvious—"as in deeply thinking and wondering why you always keep your hand in your pocket."

Katie nudged her once again, this time in protest.

"So let the outward shows be least themselves; the world is deceived by ornament."

"What's that supposed to mean?" asked Hannah.

"It means you can't judge a book by its cover," said the teacher. "Written by a guy named Shakespeare."

Lincoln rose and walked the outside perimeter of the group, moving through an opening to where Hannah was among the inner tier. He placed the end of his arm on the back of her neck, up under her hair.

She shuddered against the sensation.

"Sorry about the chill. It never warms up till around lunchtime."

All but Hannah saw the plastic shell and steel hook where Lincoln Dollar's forearm should have been. With his pocket filled again, the teacher returned to the front of the group, sitting on the grass and believing that now would come the round of questions for his stock-ready answers. Subtle tension mixed with mild curiosity began simmering beneath the weeping trees.

Once Hannah was recovered from the chilly shock of the metal, she looked to Lincoln Dollar with hard, questioning eyes. She imagined him as a sort of gatekeeper she'd been seeking of late, imagined he might be holding a certain, valuable key. She vowed she was going to get that key from him, even if she had to steal it, even if she had to kill for it. That youthful treachery, however, soon gave way to curiosity, to general inquisitiveness. "Let's have a look at that thing."

Lincoln pulled the contraption from his pocket and landed it on his knee in mock display. He turned it from side to side, affording different views, as a vendor might do while trying to hawk the apparatus. Hannah moved forward to obtain a closer view.

In demonstration, he opened the steel slightly, to the mild interest of the class, and to some interest not so mild. "Sweet!" "How'd you do that?" "Fuckin' cool!"

Lincoln briefly explained the shoulder harness, the simple shrugging movement to open and close.

Hannah's Taos scowl had returned. She looked deeply into his eyes for some sign that she could trust him, and though she could not find any, at the same time she discerned no sign of why she should not, so she placed her index finger between the steel grips and quickly took it back out. She inspected the prosthesis, his face, his other hand and again the hook. Once again her finger went in, but this time the steel jaws closed fast on the playful digit. Hannah giggled, trying to pull it free, and when after a moment he released her, she would have been lying if she said she was glad he did. She gave the instructor a wink and returned to her spot on the grass next to Katie. In route Hannah did something strange with her arms—slightly, even passive-aggressively waving them in a comic attempt to keep her shirt off her braless torso, for she wasn't certain if her time in the clamp ... then, to further deflect the group's attention, she broke the drawn out, awkward silence: "It's like a big, built-in roach clip. If I had one, I wouldn't hide it."

Laughter spilled from the schoolyard. Passersby on the street wondered what could possibly be so entertaining about the summer session at Preston High.

"When I was in college, maybe," Lincoln returned. "Now it's primarily a back scratcher."

Katie leaned in toward her friend. "Yummy. He can scratch my back anytime."

Hannah turned on her with something near violence in her eyes. Through pursed lips, she asked—all full of cynicism and rhetoricism and pissed-officism—"Is it your intention, Katherine, to screw the whole of mankind one at a time?"

Katie needed to ponder the question, but it would have to be later, as presently she was taken aback. She had guessed that her remark would be met by some mild amusement. Hannah was always amused before. *An anomalous event*, thought Katie, but only briefly before realizing why her friend could not find her entertaining at the moment.

A student asked, "What happened to your arm, Mr. Dollar?"

"Tiger shark off Key West, and call me Lincoln, please."

"You must've been freaked, Lincoln Please."

"For a long time I was. It bothered me to no end until I finally decided it was only fitting, and maybe even destiny. You see, I've been eating seafood all my life, so it stands to reason some seafood might want a little taste of me."

More laughter rang in the outdoor classroom. Jen laughed so hard she peed. As the group remained preoccupied with boisterous guffaws, Katie took some time to test her hypothesis, once again getting close to her friend's ear. "I wouldn't mind a little taste myself."

Hannah wouldn't acknowledge Katie's comment, nor was she particularly amused by the teacher's fishing tale, but she smiled with the group just the same, stretching herself on the school lawn. It was then that Katie knew for sure, and of course she was happy with having her test proven and conclusive. In her happiness for Hannah, Katie decided the new teacher would be forever off limits. Lincoln Dollar was sacred ground upon which Katie would dare not tread.

-7-

The Preston Valley Union High School Board held its quarterly meeting on a sunny afternoon in the summer of 1994, right about the same time Lincoln Dollar was meeting with his first group of students.

A minor topic at that board meeting was the reformation of a long-forgotten drama club. Some thought it might be a good outlet for those students without interests in hockey, football and chess. Some even imagined their own kids in productions of *Oliver,* maybe *Evita,* but not *Hair*. It had been years since the club disbanded, and some nay-sayers—so long on the board that their asses were shaped by the conference room chairs, and vice-versa—questioned whether it was worth the time, the effort and the money to bring it back.

One board member suggested, "What the hell, why not give it a shot?"

Another questioned, "But what's it going to cost?"

A third countered, "It can't be all that much for a couple of shows a year. A bake sale or two should cover it."

One nay-sayer asked, "Who's going to run it? That was a problem last time."

A board member reminded, "The new guy in the English department had a theater major."

Another cautioned, "He doesn't strike me as the Preston drama type."

An impatient member urged, "Let's see how he works out and talk to him after the break."

"Alrighty then. All in favor?"

In rushed efforts to get home to *Law & Order* reruns, the board was unanimous, providing everything needed—a spot of cash and a few assumptions—to wake a sleeping high school drama club in the Preston valley.

Lincoln considered the proposition, mulling it over for a couple of hours, but waiting two weeks to return his version of an answer: "Why not?"

He settled into a small apartment close to the city center. He made himself comfortable, but not too comfortable, as it was a far cry from anything he'd known before. He walked gingerly at first, reconnoitering the new area of operations. Having made the commitment, he resigned himself to the fact that he was now *locked in*, at least metaphorically. He'd been locked up before, but never really locked in.

The building was quiet, with the students not scheduled to return for another two weeks. Lincoln smiled as he turned the handle on the door to John Stanson's office. The smoked glass read 'Guidance Office.' *Guidance?* Lincoln thought; *more like the blind leading the blind.*

"Good afternoon, Elizabeth. Boss around?"

She usually didn't care for people using her given name. It reminded her of being scolded. But the new one-armed teacher seemed to infuse the name with a certain sense of poetry. It sounded almost Elizabethan. Beth liked it, and she liked Lincoln, and she took pains to show him just as often as she could.

Beth Bronson was head of the committee welcoming Lincoln Dollar to Preston High. It was a position—actually several positions—she enjoyed that summer. He was someone to share a movie with, or a dinner out of town, and someone with whom she could share her bed once the Preston sun was down. He was kind and manly, not too openhearted and always discreet, which worked well for Beth, as she wasn't interested in getting into his head or his heart, finding his pants to be most sufficient. The committee head was enjoying her time with the new teacher, and the new teacher was taking kindly to the committee head.

Holding him in her gaze, Beth picked up the phone. "John, there's a Mr. Lincoln Dollar here to see you." She hung it up. "Go on in, Linc. I'm going to lunch. Tell him I'll be back in a few margaritas."

He watched her walk out of the office, a delicious, young secretary's cheeks dancing in her skirt. Beth turned on leaving to ensure her performance wasn't without an audience. It wasn't. Lincoln was so far into the skirt that he didn't notice her smile when the door closed.

He entered John's office, finding his colleague with his feet on the desk. "Beth said to tell you she's out to lunch."

"That's for sure," John agreed, adding, "I just got the news. I'm glad you decided to stay on."

He then quickly went for a more professional manner, lest any walk down memory lane should take them farther than he wanted to go. John returned his feet to the floor. His hands went to work straightening paperwork on the desk, paperwork already neatly placed. The men had shared an arguably vivid past, in a time and a world far from that they presently shared, though which still left John wondering if it was but a thin line dividing the two.

"Something else on your mind?" Lincoln asked, however quickly deciding his tone too defensive for the occasion and company. He looked into John's eyes, looking to be sure the friend who once was still was. "Come, come, you've been walking on eggshells since I rolled into town. Lose the kid gloves, Cap'n, and I'll do my best to be a good boy. Let's just take this thing as it comes, maybe even have some fun— you know, like the old days."

This facetiousness was lost on John. "I don't want it like the old days. Are you sure you're ready for this?" The interrogation wasn't without justification. "This is Preston, man. It isn't Europe, it isn't South America, and it ain't the Middle-fuckin'-East."

Lincoln hit back. "I appreciate you getting me in here, John, and I'll go out of my way not to tarnish your standing in the community. Jesus, all these years, and I'm still asking forgiveness for the day we met, when it was me who wore the black eye for a week."

Both men reflected on the day, sharing a short laugh at the recollection.

"Anything else?" Lincoln asked.

"Yes there is. Lauren said you're to come over this weekend for steaks on the grill, and, as she doesn't handle rejection well, it'll be easier on me if you show up."

"Anything else?" Lincoln asked once more.

John had to admit, "Yes, I really am happy you finally came. And I'm glad you're staying."

Once Lincoln was gone from the room, John slowly shook his head with the confusion one experiences when entangled in something with potential for going all the way, but who's still unsure of the direction.

"I've noticed," said Lauren Stanson, approaching the guys on the deck with fresh cocktails, "when I'm not around you boys whisper of bygone days, but then the conversation invariably shifts when I show up. Why is that?"

"It's a financial thing is all," answered John. "If the secrets of my colorful past were revealed, I stand to lose fifty percent of all I have, and I'm broke enough as it is."

"Colorful past?" Lauren laughed. "The only thing coloring your past is your NAACP membership."

Young, fresh and full of life, Lauren was a dancer, as one might easily gather when eying from her neck to the floor. Her legs were long and lean. She was full, hard and strong, always smiling and genuinely grateful. She kept a studio downtown, catering to jazz, ballet, chorus-line and funk, but in her heart she was a saucy tango, through and through. She taught these same styles at the school, a member of the only wife-husband team at Preston High.

John had Lauren to thank for the comfort and stability in his life. She was, at least in his adoring eyes, the most beautiful woman ever to take breath. Naturally, he often reminded her of as much, at which she would lower her eyes, smile and turn from him, leaving him all the more smitten. At times he wished they were able to have children, if only to bless the world with others of her likeness, but more often he was selfishly thankful for not having to share her with anyone else.

John felt good on the deck in that August afternoon, and it wasn't only the gin. He liked where he was, he had accepted where he'd been, and most of all he looked forward to where he was going. The future looked so bright that he was happy he was wearing sunglasses, hiding eyes now Tanqueray glassy, while his voice rang warm, sure and sincere. "You two." He was waving a finger of his free hand between them. "I'm a lucky son of a bitch."

Lincoln and Lauren laughed.

"Don't goddamn giggle, goddammit. I'm trying to be serious here. Seriously, I say to myself, John, you're a lucky son of a bitch. Lord knows, I've had to bust my ass, but it was worth it—everything was worth it, and today's the pay off, right here. Right now I am one hundred percent." He canted, continuing, "Now, I'm going to take credit for about twenty percent of everything that's come my way, and I'm giving the other eighty to you, to both of you"—again he waved his finger—"whom without I would not be here today in this little lounger chair, and having these little cocktails. Thank you both very much, thank you. That is all." John lowered his head with inebriated flamboyancy.

Lauren, despite the feigned comedy, was called to look seriously upon their years together; the ups and downs, the trials, the separation. She wouldn't change it if she could, nor could she change it if she would; so difficult now to remember a time they weren't together, and even more difficult trying to imagine them apart. She soon decided, though, that her husband was quite long enough in the spotlight for one afternoon, then turning the focus on his friend. "How do you find living in Preston? Not quite what you're accustomed to, I'm sure."

Lauren was happy he had opted to stay on for the year. In the few months since his coming to town, Lincoln had grown quite popular, not only at the school, but at large within the community. He was new to the profession, but Lauren believed he brought with him a life experience more valuable than any learned in a classroom. Her husband had forewarned her that the new teacher was likely to push a few buttons, leaving Lauren to wonder if the staff, the studentry, and the city of Preston might all benefit from a little button-pushing. She also thought Lincoln's presence in Preston was somehow beneficial to her husband; and best of all she believed Lincoln's coming to town was good for Lincoln.

The one-armed teacher said, "I'd like to stick around awhile, so long as no one minds having me."

"Minds having you?" John chided his friend's modesty. "They want you, my friend. You're the talk of the town, you are—toast of Preston, the big cheese—but there's always a catch, right?" Realizing his wife had not yet heard, John sought to update her. "Preston High has a new theater section, and guess who gets the honors."

She was exceeding pleased. "That's great! Finally bringing some culture to Preston. And you studied theater—it's perfect!"

John let go a captious laugh.

"What's funny about that?"

"Far from perfect, honey girl. This town loves the one thing in the world I know this man cannot stand—musicals." He poked some fun his colleague's way. "So, what's on the fall program, Mr. Director? *Annie*? *Sound of Music*?" He gave them his best, "The hills are aliiiive…"

Lincoln clipped the hook of his arm onto the frame of his sunglasses and removed them from his face. "I've got just two words for you and the school board.

"And what are those, Mr. Director?"

"No—fucking—musicals."

With a toast, John reiterated, to verify for the group as well as for the neighbors on either side, "No fucking musicals!"

Their three tumblers *clinked*.

-8-

Word spread quickly through the valley confirming that Lincoln Dollar was staying on for the coming year. Most were pleased at the prospect, including the parents of Katherine Pauley and Hannah Fields. The young women began the previous summer to show greater interest in their studies, when any interest at all would have been a welcomed improvement. The parents credited this newfound interest to Lincoln Dollar, agreeing that his approach to the classes breathed new life into a sleepy curriculum. It wasn't as noticeable to Hannah's parents, as they were new to the area, but Michael Pauley, a lifelong Prestonian, assured them that Lincoln represented a needed break from worn out tradition. They took comfort in believing their daughters were coming around, and not a moment too soon.

Many families shared this same comfort, with discussions around the city's dinner tables regarding the one-armed teacher: "In Lincoln's class we're reading this," and "Mr. Dollar's having auditions for that." In the queue at the County Store, or filling up at Miller's Garage, residents began introducing themselves as the parents of such-and-such.

Lincoln put names to faces and relaxed into the community. He knew for sure he was making some progress when he told the students to read the story of Melville's scrivener, and over half the class said they "would prefer not to;" the rest then did not have to.

The students, however, did read *The Crucible*, and those same students decided to use the Miller play as the flagship production for their new theater group. Classes were held instructing in the auditioning process. Notices were posted. The director let the students do most of the work, as it seemed they got along well enough without him; besides, he had already done quite enough, having gone against all he knew of fairness by pre-casting two students for the show.

Katie and Hannah had lately grown accustomed to finding some pretext affording them the opportunity to stay in the classroom after their peers were gone. On one such afternoon, Lincoln asked, "Have you ladies ever been on a stage?"

Hannah went with the obvious. "Like a horse-drawn carriage?"

"Not bad," he replied. "Your material, while low brow, still speaks to the naïveté of pained adolescence, but I was referring to a theatrical stage."

"Are you suggesting we try out for the play?" asked Katie, not so quick to disguise her interest.

"I'm *suggesting,* if you audition, I'll get you in, just between us. You'd be doing me a favor, and I guarantee it'll be a good time."

Katie stepped up. "You can count me in. I really like that play, but I think we might have read *into* it a little too much. I think it's meant to entertain, but we turned it into some kind of history lesson. One minute we're on the witches of Salem, and the next we're talking about commies in Hollywood, like we care about that shit." She went to work enlisting the other. "What do you say, sport?"

Hannah had furrowed her brow and tightened her lips, like she was struggling with some weighty, monumental, life-altering decision. Looking down at the floor, she began slowly shaking her head. "I don't know if I'm into it. Have to give it some thought, see if I got the time. I kinda got some other projects going right now."

Put off by her cavalier attitude, her take-it-or-leave-it flippancy, her attention to projects which may or may not exist, Lincoln wanted to tell Hannah not to worry about it, they would find someone else, even someone perhaps better suited for the part. He wanted to tell her all this and more, but he couldn't. Lincoln wanted her in the role. He hadn't considered any others, but he could never let Hannah know as much. "You give it some thought, and give me an answer on Monday morning, one way or the other. It'd be nice if you could postpone your other projects, just long enough to help us out with this. And there might even be some extra credit, if you work like you mean it."

Katie reminded him, "We're already in the high-90s."

"So you are, and so what. I'm not going to beg you, and it's already bad enough I'm pre-casting, so I'll throw this on top of it: It's both of you, or neither; work it out yourselves. I know you're all about choice. Do it, or don't do it; your choice. Now kindly go away."

Hannah wanted to know, "What are your plans for the weekend, Mr. Dollar?"

"Hang out at home and grade a pile of papers. Why do you ask?"

"No particular reason. See you Monday."

Katie added, "Have a nice weekend with your papers, Lincoln," as she followed Hannah out of the room.

Once outdoors, Katie took Hannah's arm and spun her round. "What do mean, *give it some thought*?"

Hannah was looking over her shoulder at her own reflection in the door. "Do these pants make my ass look big?"

"Big? It's like a postage stamp—without the scalloped edges, thank God, and hopefully not as sticky." She slapped it. "You *have* to do this with me, you know. Plus, we've been looking for something to turn things around here, and we might even owe this little bit to Lincoln. Please, please do it with me."

Hannah smiled. "It so turns me on when you grovel, knowing I've got that kind of power over you. It's really quite delicious." She took advantage of that power, staring Katie back and down. "For starters, I don't *owe* Lincoln Dollar shit. Owe him for what? Making me read plays and write papers? Screw that. He's my teacher and there it stops. As for the play, of course we're doing it, you crazy bitch." She added, if only to show she was capable of some self-sacrifice, "Besides, he said it has to be both of us, and this is obviously very important to you."

Hannah looked to the sky and let go a sigh. "We're going to be actresses, Katie-Kate. Imagine that. Maybe get famous, huh? *People* magazine's worst dressed, name in lights, limousines, lifestyles of the bitchin' shameless. Look, I'm getting goosebumps!" Sure enough, and she presented the flesh of her arm as proof. "This is the start of something, girl. I can feel it."

Arm in arm they sauntered away, their feet barely touching the ground as they basked in ambitious dreams. Passersby on Main Street honked to greet the pair. Katie returned coy waves with happy hands. Hannah flipped hearty birds.

Lincoln watched, from the second-story window, the two young women walking away along the sidewalk. He knew he had two of the principals for the show. *Katie'll be a showpiece*, the director mused, and mused rightly, as he moved the stainless steel slowly back and forth along his chin; *Hannah, she was born for it*. He thought back to the second day he knew her, to the day she playfully put her finger in the vise. He knew it then, of a morning under the weeping willow trees, Hannah was a performer. She had hopes and fears, desires and passions; the ingredients for artistry, the makings of an actor.

Almost out of view, he was still watching after them when Hannah quickly stole half a glance over her shoulder. She could not see him for the distance and glare, but somehow she knew he was there. She wanted him to know she knew. Hannah suddenly felt bold, sure and confident, the likes of which she had never known until just a few moments before. She had played at these qualities in the past, but now she no longer needed to pretend. She wanted Lincoln to know that she was through with pretending, so she bid farewell to the sideshow attraction, to the bearded square peg and the monkey-face freak. As they left her, Hannah desperately wanted to cry, but having no plausible excuse for doing so, as crying would call for questions, she was finally able to let them ride away on a sigh. "Wow," she whispered.

"Wow, what?" asked Katie.

"Nothing, I guess. I don't know, just—wow. Wow!"

Katie agreed. "Yeah, fucking wow."

"I'm a little nervous," Hannah confessed, slowly descending from the frightfully head-lightening heights.

You've been nervous," Katie reminded her, "and getting nervous-er, and it's got nothing to do with this play." She took Hannah's hand. "Just keep it in check, will you? I can't have you setting yourself up."

They walked on a bit in silence.

"We're lucky to have each other, aren't we?" said Hannah.

"Yes we are." Katie squeezed her hand, swinging it high and back. "We're totally lucky to have each other. Don't you ever forget that."

-9-

There lies potential for reward in dabbing oils on canvas, in molding lifeless lumps of clay, in chipping away at stone and scratching words on paper. With struggles often disheartening, and efforts often painful, and provided the muses and important gods are kind, occasionally something of beauty will emerge. For the disheartened struggler who was Lincoln Dollar, stone, paper, canvas and lump all found him in the guise of Hannah Fields.

The director and actor were able to learn from one another their crafts. With intelligence, projection, determination and beauty, she was stage worthy, stage ready, a director's dream. *A natural?* Lincoln wondered. He once questioned whether they existed, but he would not question any longer. Hannah was a natural. Having made the conscious decision to go into the theater, she went like a starving fish into murky waters. Given time and space to swim around, the fish continually fed itself—and the fish found plenty to eat. A subtlety of direction allowed her plenty of time and room in which to work, to swim, to feed. Against egotistical want, the director stayed as best he could near the wings, as the greatest results came from the simple encouragement of Hannah's performance, and with allowing the rest of the cast to fall in.

Lincoln watched from the darkened theater, amazed by her acting abilities. She not only longed for that stage, but absolutely had to be on it—life or death. *That's the real Hannah,* Lincoln mused, caught up in the irony of seeing the *real* Hannah when watching her play someone else.

She took the part of Elizabeth Proctor, the vengeful wife in the popular drama. Katie slid sleekly into the role of Abigail, the seductress, a part barely taxing her blossoming method-acting capabilities.

Students, faculty and parents busied themselves building and painting sets, sewing costumes, adjusting lights and sound and rehearsing lines. The show was so much a collective effort that not only the cast and crew, but most of the audience, suffered with opening night apprehension. The first show's attendance read like the local census, with nearly the entire valley experiencing varying degrees of stagefright.

None, however, were more stagefrightened than Hannah Fields.

The auditorium was bright and busy, the patrons taking their seats, when the search for Hannah began. Finally found, she was huddled in a corner of the darkened set. Her fellow actors ran about backstage, unable to conceal their excitement, while Hannah sat in hiding, cowered in fear. Her lunch had already backed up and gone, having lost an argument with her apprehensions about going on stage. She was dressed in 17th-century garb and paralyzed on the floor, her face chalky white. Beads of sweat poked from her every pore; like goose-stepping soldiers, they merged to march down her forehead and temples. Her lower lip quivered. Tears of fear washed her wide, lost eyes.

Some moments before she had looked out past the curtain, peeking through a part in the draperies. What she saw frightened her. There was no way she was going to stand in front of those people. No way. Even the ushers intimidated her. Oblivious to the lines she had worked tirelessly to memorize, Hannah wouldn't have been able to identify with any certainty the play in which she was supposed to perform, but in which she was now not going to perform. She shook uncontrollably.

Lincoln moved quickly about the group, giving hurried instructions and advice, and one- and two-word reminders. He had purposely avoided seeking Hannah, not needing her and reasoning himself unneeded. He'd just considered looking when Katie found him. "This isn't good. You better come quick." She led the director to the frightened actor.

Lincoln knelt in front of Hannah. She was like a stranger; a frightened and angry stranger. "What are you doing?" he asked, as he needed to know her intentions. Many tickets had been sold, with no understudy to stand for her.

"Leave me alone!" she snapped through clenched teeth. "Get away from me. If it wasn't for you—" She sniffed, spitefully wiping away tears. "Just go. Get out! Go!"

Lincoln stood, preparing to depart.

"Don't you dare leave me!"

Once certain his smile was gone he turned back and again went down. He knew it would be the last time that he ever saw Hannah as he knew her, so he wished to bid her a lasting farewell. More so, he wished her to get ready to go on stage, not for her sake alone, but for the production. Avoiding further fanfare to commemorate the departure, he said, "Break a leg." It came out almost like a question.

"I'd rather break your neck. I can't go. I won't do it. I've never been so scared in my life."

"You *can* do this—and you're going to. Stop this … this sniveling, get out there and do your job. You'd like to think this is all about you, but it's not. None of any of this is about you, Hannah, and the sooner you realize that, the better off everyone's going to be. You've got hundreds of people counting on you tonight—hundreds: Katie, your family, your friends, the playwright. If you're willing to turn your back on everyone, now's the time to do it. You know where all the doors are."

"That's what you think? You're calling me *selfish*?"

He pointed to the fire exit, if only to let her know it was still an option. He grabbed for her hand and a walk for the door. "Come. I've got some experience with this nonsense. I can help."

She pulled her hand back. "Seriously, Lincoln—fuck you."

"That exit's the soft way," he said, "the easy way out, but once the door closes, it closes forever. You're finished." All amusement was gone from the situation. Hannah's fear was contagious. "You'll be second-guessing yourself the rest of your life; I promise you, as a friend. Even if by some miracle you managed to make it back, you'd come back to infinitely less than you have right now. But if you go through that curtain, and I promise this too, every door you ever come to will swing wide open for you. Now is the time to choose, and you really need to hurry. Please, we have to do something. It's a sold-out house. Get your head out of yourself, if only for just a few hours, and give these people some quality entertainment. At least give them their six dollars' worth."

She hid her face in her hands, whispering to herself and breathing deeply. She asked, "Do you have a tissue?"

Lincoln gave her a crumpled paper towel from his pocket. Working around her makeup, she calmly and carefully blotted her face free of sweat, tears and snot before handing the towel back. At last she stood.

Lincoln stood with her.

Nervously smiling, with eyes sparkling, questioning, probing, she took his steel in one hand and his flesh in the other, squeezing both. "Tell me something good," she said, nearly begging. "Anything to help me out there, help me through this nightmare. Please, say something."

He groped at words all coming as paltry and trite. "When you're playing Emily Proctor, you're still just being yourself—only bigger; continue being yourself, and no one can ever accuse you of doing it wrong. Just be big, Hannah, bigger than you've ever been."

She looked so deeply into him she wasn't sure if she'd be able to get back out. It was as though Hannah was seeing Lincoln Dollar for the very first time—seeing something for the very first time. Soon the color came back to her face, even more so than was her usual.

"You're a talented actor," he added. "You're really good at this, and it's important for you to know that, and to believe it—to believe *in* it. Give it everything you got. Even if you end up drowning, it's always better to do it in ten feet of water, as opposed to ten inches." He lastly reiterated, "Be big. Okay?"

She nodded. "Be big, be myself, drown—got it."

"You're cool with this?" he asked, though he was now certain she was.

Hannah feigned bravado. "Cool? I'm gonna go out there and make you proud. I'm gonna be so cool, you'll never, ever want to let me go."

She instantly shrank and shuddered and looked away. "Now we better call wardrobe, 'cause I think my Freudian slip is showing. What I meant to say is, I'll try my best not to let you … you people down."

Lincoln let all her comments slide, unable to venture any response. He did admit, "You could never let me down," and then desperately wanted to hug her—this student, this friend, this actor—to take her even briefly into his arms, but instead he told her, "Have a great show," and left to take his seat in the crowded auditorium.

The set was macabre, dark, thick and heavy with gloom, washed in blood red light. It was a powder keg and Katie was the spark. She hit the stage, and the doo hit the voo. Everything came to life. She moved about, fast, large and loud, begging others to either keep up or take cover. The cast was enrapt, as was the audience, as she fed them morsels of emotion, tidbits of intensity. She was sensual and seductive and twenty shades of sexy, bringing the show from PG-13 over to NC-17. Few were surprised; contrary, it was but a fine line between the Abigail of Salem and the Katie of Preston—a razor's edge upon which the actor shook, shagged, shamed and shimmied.

The show was comfortably into the initial act when the character of Elizabeth Proctor made her entrance. Deathly afraid, intensely curious, Hannah saw only those with whom she interacted, and periodically those in the peripheries of the make-believe world. An angry wife seeking retribution, she took the stage and Salem and Preston and wrapped them into a storm, a tempest, a whirlwind of passion and thought-provoking motive, laced with crafty innuendo. Hannah was transformed and transported, wishing to transform others, to take the whole of the world into her sweaty hands, to squeeze it and mix the juices in with her own.

The eyes in the house were fixed on Hannah and Katie, back and forth, like spectators at Forest Hills. There was whispering, "My son helped build the set," and "Isn't that your daughter playing Susanna?" but no one could deny that Hannah and Katie were the stars. Michael Pauley sat on the seat's edge, elbows on knees, his chin resting in his hands, his interrupted breathing on the neck of the patron in front. Connie Fields, a gently older reflection of the thespian daughter, beamed from the fifth row, as Hannah's father struggled to show indifference, but beamed as well, remembering how he once smiled at a little girl's threats of making the world a prettier place, while at the same time watching his little girl doing that very same thing. Part of him wondered if he had some sort of hand in it.

Lincoln forewent a director's custom of consulting with cast and crew during the intermission; instead he kept his place in the auditorium to impatiently accept the greetings and compliments of the townsfolk. With curiosity and eager anticipation, he watched as the house lights grew dim and the stage lights returned. He caught himself nibbling his lower lip during the second act, quickly putting an end to it, only to start biting again with still greater fervor. He watched as the magical, mystical gate to the freedom of expression was unlocked, and Hannah stood mesmerized under the lights holding the precious key.

At last it was over. Lincoln was happy to have it done. Rumbling, thundering applause filled the room when the actors returned to the stage. The building shook with enthusiasm when Katie came back under the lights. Finally, Hannah entered, sleepwalking through a cloudy struggle of humility with grace, with tears of joy and of self-recognition streaming on her face. When at last she could open her eyes, the entire house was out of their seats.

Her first reaction was to seek out Lincoln. She recognized his silhouette in the light of the lobby at the back of the house, but in one deft movement he was in his coat and out the door. She'd never seen him move so quickly.

The snows of New England had playfully fallen while the show was on, with flakes so large and fluffy white as to cast discernible shadows on fore-fallen flakes in the glow of the streetlights. It rested in a thick, soft layer, blanketing the small city of Preston and the rest of the entire world.

Lincoln quickly brushed half the windshield with his sleeve. He heard the applause and whistling as he got into the car. The hair on the back of his neck was snapped to attention, as by some follicle drill sergeant, as he sped away from the parking lot, with the tires spinning and sliding on the cold, slippery streets.

The telephone reminded him of how easily-shattered is the illusion of solitude. He contemplated not answering. Mellowed, withdrawn into a couple of drinks, long and neat, Lincoln was most content to speak with no one.

"Are you alone?" Hannah asked.

"I'm visiting with my friend, Jack."

"Oh, I'm sorry. I'll only need a minute."

"That was a joke."

"Really? Good comedy. Clever, while low brow, and speaks to your goofiness. Where did you take off to in such a hurry?" Hannah was stretched on her bed with her partner and an assortment of berry-tasting wine coolers. "Kate went to get you for the final call, but you were already flying out of the parking lot. Didn't you like the show?"

"You were up on everyone's lines," he said with a director's reprimand. He noticed that she sounded different; and reasoned, henceforth, she would always be different.

"They were slowing things down."

"And you're still too rough with John Proctor," he added.

"He's lucky that's all he got," said Hannah, "that philandering … son of a—you-know-what." She was angry with the character who was her husband in the play, enmeshed in a sort of fictional domestic dispute, a problem maybe calling for fictional couples' therapy. "The way he treats that poor woman, someone should take that play and smack him on the ass with it. The man needs to grow up."

"Where's Katie?" he asked.

"Right here." Hannah tossed the phone across the bed.

"What'd you think of the show?" Katie asked.

The director attempted more reprimand. "There's too much sexual innuendo with Proctor."

"Sorry about that, but I was so turned on. Being on stage … I can't even describe it. It was just like you said. I tried giving to the audience, the same as they were giving it to me, like you told me, and the more I gave, the more they wanted, just like you said."

However excited, Katie was receiving impatient glances from her partner. "I got to let you go. The starlet's getting jealous."

Hannah swapped the phone for a threatening glare, snatching it, mouthing *bite me*, at which Katie snapped her teeth.

"I'll ask again, did you enjoy the show?"

"Of course I did. I loved it. You were amazing, so raw and powerful and beautiful and, well, striking."

"Hmmm," said she, sort of. She cupped her hand over the receiver and whispered excitedly, "He said I was beautiful!"

"No shit," Katie replied, having told Hannah the very same on many occasions, but having never garnered anything near such a response.

Hannah's tone grew serious. "If you were so pleased with the show, then something's troubling me."

"What is it?"

"I'm wondering why you weren't clapping at the end with everyone else."

Lincoln could hear Katie laughing in the background. He laughed in spite of himself. "*You* should stick with the tragedies, and *I* don't do no applausing."

"Did I make you proud tonight?" She was already sure of his answer, but desperately wanted to hear it from him. She tried to imagine his mouth saying the words.

"Arthur Miller could not have been prouder writing that play than I was watching you perform it. You were brilliant. Everyone was. I'm sure glad we took the chance. Aren't you?"

Katie watched on as Hannah grew rosy, awash in the teacher's compliments. "I am," Hannah answered, "thanks to you." She repeated "thanks to you," but the echo got lost on its way to her mouth. She swallowed hard. "I'm looking forward to seeing you at the cast party tomorrow night. We got champagne—a whole freakin' case!" She knew just then that she sounded juvenile, but just then she wanted to, having suddenly felt the need to reclaim her position as a high school student. "It's gonna be fun."

Lincoln paused, just then feeling the need to reclaim the position of a high school teacher. "I'm sure there's something in the rulebook I never read about drinking champagne with students," adding, and almost thankful for the excuse, "besides, I'm hopping an airplane in the morning, going south for the break. I have appointments need tending to."

There was a lengthy pause, an awkward silence, so long that Lincoln wondered if she was still on the line. "That seems kind of sudden," she finally said. "I mean, you never said anything about taking off. You'll, well, you're going to miss the rest of the shows." She was genuinely taken aback. Lincoln down in Louisiana was never a part of her holiday plans.

"As far as the show's concerned, my job's finished. As stage managers, Jen and Cyndi are in charge. They're the bosses. Besides, if the cast is one-tenth as good as you were tonight, there's nothing to worry about. We'll crunch the numbers when I get back, find a way to launder the cash before the school gets hold of it. Maybe dinner for the crew, maybe a show, whatever you all decide. Give your family my best. I'll see you in a couple of weeks. Again, you were wonderful tonight. I'm happy for you. I feel fortunate having been around to see it happen. And the best part is, I knew you'd be great, and I love it when I'm right. It's such a good feeling."

Hannah wasn't ready to let him go. "I've got a good feeling, too." She hesitated, looking for words. "I kind of felt something tonight, like something may have come over me. Once I was under those lights, it was like I wasn't me anymore. I wasn't the dumb old, stumbling, awkward Hannah. It's like I was somehow out of myself, like I was actually looking at myself—me watching me, if that makes any sense. And things looked pretty good for a change."

Prepared to beg, he was aching to know. "How's it feel?"

Her words were far away and dreamy. "I feel like I'm at the top of the world, and not at the center, like I was before. It feels like I'm finally playing my part, and nothing can ever take my part away. Nothing has that power." However, while Hannah said as much, in reality she had little idea of how the performance had left her. She finally admitted, barely whispering, "Make sure I'm grounded, Lincoln. I'm apt to get all Icarus-like and fly off. I'd hate to melt these things after all the shit I went through to get them."

"You'll be fine. Stay on top and away from the center, right?"

"Right … I hope. We'll see you back here in January? You're sure about that?"

"Absolutely sure. Tell Katie I'll see her soon."

"Hold on," Hannah stalled, looking to bridge the oppressive span to the second week of January. "Thanks, for everything. I really … well, never mind. I'm just … just kind of happy you came here, to Preston High, I mean. I'm happy you came."

"So am I. I'll see you soon."

Lincoln slowly, gently, returned the receiver to the cradle. He tossed back, not so gently, the remnants of the whiskey, speaking into the empty glass, "I guess I'm happy I came here, too."

He briefly entertained the inanest of thoughts, but just as quickly shook it off. He smiled at it—*whiskey thought?*—then scolded it, dismissed it and let it fall away. He was left with only the slightest tinge of guilt for having allowed the thought a single moment—or moments.

Act Two

-1-

It was two years after Lincoln Dollar arrived in the Preston Valley when Hannah's parents made their way to John Stanson's office for a second visit. The first regarded their daughter's lack of performance in Theodore Balzac's literature class; this second meeting was to address a situation not so easily swept under the small town rug.

Otherwise, by Preston standards, they had been a couple of pretty good years.

Lincoln had done his best to keep the promise of *no musicals*, and to barely minor public outcry. When pressed regarding the absence of a musical program, he merely maintained how such productions were beyond the range of his "limited artistic capabilities," leaving the townsfolk almost believing he was doing them a favor. He did find it increasingly difficult to evade the school's orchestral director near casting time.

The new theater group began to amass a small pile of cash. Ticket sales were consistent. Everyone went to all the shows, and most more than once or twice. The box office could gauge within twenty or so how many seats would be sold for any given performance, variations dependent on how many Prestonians had visitors from out of town, or on how many of the valley's residents would be away. Also keeping costs down was all the labor being free, with some of it even indentured. The director's red pen easily coaxed students to work either on the stage or behind the scenes, if not during one term, then certainly the next. Other methods coaxed employment from staff and residents. Nor were there any rental fees for the spaces the players played; of the high school auditorium, the senior center, the minimum-security lock-up on the outskirts of the city and the park downtown—the green—none of the venues charged. Apart from some nominal advertising fees, the group had virtually no overhead. When a length of board was needed to build a set, it was most often *borrowed* from the high school's wood shop, often in the deep dark, dead of night; until Katie and Lincoln were apprehended by third shift security, by a guard seeming adamant in introducing them to a little concept he liked to call *Justice*.

Katie let go some of the buttons of her blouse with hopes of diverting the guard's attention.

The rent-a-cop gently laid into the thieves, while moving the cheese doodles from the desktop to a drawer. "I've been on to you," said he, thinking himself a vigilant, johnny-on-the-spot sort of guard. With his fat belly and even fatter ego satisfied, albeit anticlimactically, the thrill of the chase was over. He knew they were stealing the wood for the theater, so he thought, *What the heck, no big deal*, with plans to release the burglars. Meanwhile Katie had both her breasts near fully exposed, unable to grasp why the guard focused his attentions more on the director than on her—on hers. In her jealousy, she cussed and cursed and accused him of a couple of things. Then the guard called for the police.

Petty larceny was bad enough without indecency charges added, so Katie tucked herself in. The police called in the principal. Processing the paperwork, the principal released the nighttime thieves with a stern warning: "No more stealing wood, and I mean it this time." On his way past, he added, for only Katie to hear, "For Heaven's sake, Katherine, would it hurt you to wear a brassiere like the rest of the girls?"

The troupe was stealing lumber for construction of a fire escape for the set of *The Glass Menagerie*. Brian Robison, self-proclaimed theater critic for the upper Connecticut River Valley, wrote of Hannah's portrayal of Laura Wingfield as 'memorably fragile and moving.' He suggested his readership 'keep an eye on this up and coming local talent.' Regarding the review, Hannah remarked, "Local, my ass. I am *so* not from around here. Theater critics are feeble-minded philistines and douche bags—sycophants with poopie pants."

Lincoln's second summer in the valley brought two Shakespeare productions to the open air of Memorial Park in the heart of downtown Preston. As the only summer theater in the region, all the shows were well received. Half the valley attended with a genuine appreciation for the medium, while the other half attended to create the impression for their neighbors of some appreciation for the medium. The broad, level lawn was a fine setting to lay blankets and sip wine under summer stars, with the large memorial monument, Rock of Ages granite, serving well for a stage once the Gettysburg Address was covered and flats erected, ramparts affixed and curtains hung.

Katie's portrayal of Hero stirred much ado on the city green. Her Juliet, said Robison, was 'heartbreakingly tragic.' Shakespeare for Katie was second-nature. She moved well through the shades of past eras where she could engage in intrigues with the potential for high tragedy.

Hannah, meanwhile, did all she could to see that Katie remained comfortable in her new world. Her present position was to support Katie, while also serving as stage manager, fill-in prop master, and, in her words, *all-around costume and makeup bitch*. Hannah loved working behind the scenes, from where she could watch Katie, from where she could bask in Katie's success. Watching her perform, Hannah grew lost in the love and respect she felt for the pains the other took in bringing the dramas to life. Katie brought it from the page to the stage; she made everything make sense.

Only a year before, Hannah had been aimless, alone and afraid until Katie tripped into her life. Lincoln Dollar soon followed, and with them came the wind and the rudder, the motivation and direction. Hannah's little world was opened up, blasted wide apart, and the resulting explosion enabled her to escape her adolescent vacuum. With this escape came change. Hannah no longer flipped off passersby. She grew more conscious of her bearing. She tried to concern herself more with her inside than outside. And she let go of many imaginary problems, focusing instead on those couple or few that were real. Through it all, Hannah hoped that being in love wouldn't become one of those real problems, because she was, by now, very much in love. Hannah was blown-in-the-glass, dyed-in-the-wool and totally knee-deep—times two. She could have fun with one of those at present, but the other would have to wait.

Unfortunately, among those couple or few real problems was Hannah's impatience. She soon discovered, though, that keeping busy helped her to not mind so much the waiting; so she stepped up her work in the theater, only to find that the more she was in and around the theater, the more entangled in the love she grew. This eventually became her biggest real problem, so much so that she told Lincoln one day, "I think I've got a problem, and I don't quite know what to do about it."

Without waiting for elaboration, the teacher-director knee-jerkly identified. "If ever I don't know what to do about something, I simply don't do anything, hoping it clarifies itself later on. Eventually most things work themselves out, or with time I mostly forget they ever existed. So, what's the problem?"

"Nothing, really. Forget I mentioned it." Not knowing what to do, she opted to do nothing.

Meanwhile, the townsfolk complimented her on the stage performances: "My, but you perform so well in those plays," prompting Hannah's reply, "Well, thanks, but never mind me; Katherine Pauley is the greatest Shakespearean actor since Olivier." And those same townsfolk complimented Katie on her performances, prompting her invariable reply, "Thank you for coming. Thank you so very much."

Hannah allowed Katie the run of the house. She gave her the summer green, hitching her cart to Katie's star, biding the time until September when she could get back inside the auditorium.

She asked Lincoln one summer evening under the stars on the green, "What are we planning for the fall production?" He was minutes before going on stage to recite the prologue beginning the tragedy of Juliet and Romeo.

"Never mind the fall. Let's get through this production first." He waited for a lighting cue to make his entrance.

Hannah wouldn't let up. "You've got something planned. What's in it for me? I've been working my ass off. I need to get back up front."

Despite Lincoln's stage experience, he was presently reminded of the nervous tension one might experience when facing an entrance. He was mouthing the lines he would soon deliver, pausing to tell Hannah, "Leave me alone."

She grabbed hold of his arm. "I wish I could, and I'll start trying a little harder once you tell me what I'm getting in the fall."

He turned on her. "You're a pain in the ass, you know that?"

Hannah accepted the comment as a compliment. She knew she could get on a person's nerves if she had a mind to. She had a way of wedging herself under the skin, not unlike a sliver and with much the same irritability.

They were just over a year into their mentor-protégé relationship, and already Lincoln had lost all control of any reins he thought he may have once held. Hannah was in charge of Preston's theater department, with Katie coming in as second-in-command. Lincoln by now had been reduced to the lowly rank of private observer. In fact, they had given him tonight's monologue mostly so he wouldn't start feeling left out. Another teacher might have been threatened by the role shifting, but Lincoln allowed it to speak to his proficiency. In fact, he came to enjoy witnessing the changes in the actors. Regarding her personal life, Katie still flew by the seat of her (often exceedingly tight) pants, but once she was on stage she was in complete control; Katie's version, anyway, of complete control. For Hannah, the drama club was a vehicle; her vehicle had four-wheel-drive and lots of clearance, and she had plans to drive it hard and fast for another year before trading up to something with a sleeker styling, cleaner lines and a great deal more power.

Lincoln hadn't choice but to relent to Hannah's backstage harassment. "You're doing *Born Yesterday* in the fall," he finally said. "It's a fun piece, the cast is small and it's light—we've got to do something light. You can pick what you want for the spring, within reason, that is. Quid pro quo, remember? Now, kindly release me and let me enter your stage."

"You always seem to say just what I want to hear." She spoke to the side of his face, while he grew more and more impatient for his entrance. "You know, if you were a few years younger and I was a few years older—"

"Yeah," he turned on her, "I wouldn't have had to suffer this past year with you. Please let me go."

Hannah released his arm. "Who's holding you? Break a leg, sport." She mumbled something about the hypersensitivity of actors, as she returned the headset to her ears and brought the microphone near her mouth: "Kirk to bridge. Kirk to bridge. Warp speed, Mr. Sulu."

In the booth, Jennifer Novak brought up the 750-watt Lekolights and the 500-watt Fresnels. Jen knew that Hannah was in a pretty good mood, having heard her entire conversation with Lincoln, as Hannah had forgotten to turn off the mic. Jen liked that Hannah was in a good mood. She liked how Hannah was liking him, because Jen really liked them both. She was smiling as she moved the controls forward.

Lincoln crossed through the curtain and moved to center stage. He kept his left arm tucked behind his back in a display of theatrical Italian affectation. With only fourteen lines, it was the shortest role he was ever called on to play. It would soon prove the simplest he would play for a long time to come …

The which, if you with patient ears attend,
  What here shall miss our toil shall strive to mend …

Again the leaves went from green to myriad autumn colors. Withered under the pressure of change, they let go their hold. The snows came.

Hannah seized the opportunity to recreate the role of Billie Dawn. The piece was light, helping to cushion the coming oppression of another Vermont winter. Lincoln gave in to pressure from the music department and staged a haphazard production to get a melodic Marley and Scrooge on stage for the silly season, all the while eagerly looking forward to the break. For the first time since he had arrived in Preston, he wanted to get away. He needed to get away.

-2-

"Go on ahead," Hannah said to Katie. "I'll call you later."

The girls were passing by the high school on the way home from holiday shopping. Hannah wanted to pitch her plan before Lincoln left for the winter break; before, in her opinion, he ran off on another silly adventure. Hannah had little knowledge of where he went or what he did, and with whom he did what she had so little knowledge of. She only knew that she did not enjoy his being away. Not at all.

"Don't let him tell you no," Katie warned her when they separated. "Don't let him talk you out of it."

Hannah turned up the walkway, trudging the knee-high snow. She made her way through the darkened, abandoned building—empty, apart from a couple of custodians and the drama teacher—coming at last to Lincoln's makeshift office. His work area was a cleared out, partly renovated storage space adjacent to the teacher's lounge.

He had a red pen in hand, reading and grading papers, correcting them and being corrected by them, when Hannah walked in. She left her shopping bags by the door. Removing her hat and mittens, dripping with melting snow, she put them under a chair next to the desk. The *desk* was actually eight milk crates—four stacks of two—topped with the door he'd removed from his new *office*. Hannah felt comfortably at home in the storage closet, and she liked how Lincoln was a low-maintenance kind of guy—not that it was any of her business.

She dropped herself in the chair, fumbling through her pockets for a cigarette. Her hair was mussed. Her cheeks were bright and flush from the cold and the sudden warmth.

"Smoking in here is grounds for losing my job," the teacher protested.

"There's other jobs," she assured him, lighting up. "I'm not sure we wouldn't all be better off."

Lincoln took the offered cigarette, relieving it of its filter. He accepted her light and found a cap from a pop bottle to use for an ashtray. "Have you seen the write-up for the Christmas show?" He found a copy beneath the layers of paperwork and slid it across the desk.

Hannah had the same article already affixed in her scrapbook. She didn't need to see it again. "I'm glad I wasn't in the show."

"Robison says that's one of the problems." He mimicked the critic's pen: *"As we've seen before, there is a painfully obvious void when Ms. Fields is not among the ensemble.* I thought it was a pretty nice compliment."

"More like a compli*sult*. He talks about how good it is, *but —*" Hannah didn't like the critic's criticism; her own was quite enough, thank you very much.

"He's still raving about your Billie Dawn," said Lincoln, "you painfully obvious void, you."

"That philistine disgusts me," said Hannah, curling her lip, "the way he sits back and talks shit about the theater instead of actually getting on stage and doing something about it. The real *painfully obvious void* is in that fucker's ambition."

"You never minded his reviews before."

"He never dissed our shows before, but enough about him. How was your birthday—the big two-seven?"

"No noticeable change. Thanks again for the book. That was nice."

"You're welcome. You know, you were born on the very same day that John Steinbeck died."

"That's right. And you're the very first person I've ever met to make the connection, not that there is any connection."

"There is to me," she said. "I grew up by his place out in Cal, and was a big fan of the guy till I met you. Now I have trouble reading his stuff without thinking of you—of the connection, rather. It kind of spoiled it for me."

"Sorry."

"Well, it's not your fault. What are you doing for the holidays?"

"Riding the train to Louisiana."

"Visiting? Family? Friends?"

"Visiting some friends. Going to do a little fishing, maybe some writing, see some shows, raise some hell. No snow down there."

"Who ya going with?" Hannah tried letting the question ring casual, in keeping with the conversation. It may have sounded so to him, but it certainly didn't to her. She nearly lost eye contact.

"I'll be traveling alone. Why? Would you like to come?"

She came close to jumping on his facetious invitation with a hearty, "Yes, yes—please! Let's go on a trip together!" but instead she quietly asked, "You got no family anywhere? No brothers and sisters? No kids? Nothing like that?"

Lincoln shortly shook his head. "All my family's in Preston. And all my exes live in Texas."

Hannah wanted to say, "Not for long," but put it to rest with, "Enough small talk."

She took a long last pull from the cigarette and snuffed it in the pop bottle cap. She spent some time rubbing her teeth on her lower lip to get at a piece of chapped skin. "You haven't forgotten the deal we made over the summer, right? Remember that night? We were under the stars when you took me in your arms—well, arm—and whispered those sweet, fantastic promises —"

Lincoln jumped in. "Yeah, I remember the evening somewhat differently, but I can see where you're going, and the suspense has been killing me. Just remember, the cast has to be small—our talent pool has all but dried up—and it has to be clean, nothing too racy."

This was Hannah's last performance in Preston. The triune was soon to disband. She wanted to give the teacher a little theatrical something by which to remember her. She wasn't going to let him forget. Ever. Hannah began thinking, *If only he wasn't my teacher, or if this town wasn't so goddamn small, or—*

Lincoln brought her around. "What's it going to be?"

She suddenly considered getting up from the chair and running, running, thinking of how everything would be so much easier. Wanting something so badly reminded her of how she was seldom disappointed when she wanted nothing, when she kept her expectations at a minimum. Instead of running, however, Hannah blurted the words—so quickly she was unsure if she'd said them correctly—"I need to play Miss Julie." There, she took in and let go a deep breath, she'd said it.

Lincoln rested an elbow on the desk, using the hand to support his head. "You want to end it with some Strindberg?" he asked, rhetorically as it was, for he could clearly see this was what she wanted, this was what Hannah *needed*. He had never seen her glow so adamantly.

"The cast is small, and we had a deal."

It then occurred to Hannah that she hadn't prepared any defense, hadn't planned for meeting with possible opposition. Having neglected to do so put her off her guard, and hearing herself nearly whine *we had a deal* was simply too much. She would not grovel. She wasn't going to pout. She would have what she wanted. Besides, they *did* have a deal.

Lincoln imagined her in the role of Miss Julie. He could hear her reciting the lines of the naturalistic drama to a cloudy male lead. "That's one of my favorite plays."

Hannah well knew it was among Lincoln's favorite plays.

"I staged it with a friend in college—used the money we made to finance my post-graduation foray into the American west." Lincoln's thoughts drifted to Lake Mead, Hot Springs and Vegas; to the Hoover Dam, the Bellagio, Cirque du Soleil and roulette wheels. He was nearing an intersection perhaps returning him to some of Sin City's lesser-advertised attractions when the visions of Hannah playing Miss Julie steered him back to a somewhat professional course.

"You're perfect for the part," he said, "and the part is perfect for you, but—"

Don't you do it, thought Hannah. *Don't you even dare.*

"—but we've got no one to play Jean. There's no one around here to keep up with you. Without someone to rise to your performance, you'd have to dummy-down. You'd come away from it resentful, feeling cheated—"

She interrupted. "I know someone who'll rise for me.

"Not from this neck of the woods," he flatly returned, though with a curiosity aroused.

Hannah searched him, as bravely as she could under the circumstances.

At exactly the same time Lincoln realized who she had in mind for her male lead, he realized also the futility of the coming debate. He looked to the papers on the desk for support, but they were all taking her side. Backed into a corner, he began shaking his head and laughing—noticing, uncomfortably, how she was positioned between himself and the exit.

During their acquaintance, Lincoln had had cause on many occasions to enjoy laughing with Hannah; he was soon to find that laughing *at* her wasn't nearly as fun. Not for either of them.

"Forget it," he finally said. "I haven't been on stage in years. I let you talk me into that prologue last summer, but that's as far as I'm going. It's not going to happen. Find someone else, or pick another play." Then, thinking, believing, hoping his side of the debate was rested, he went on to laugh a bit more at the proposal.

The makeshift office became infinitely smaller still.

Hannah found his first round of laughter—cagey, nervous, giggly—somewhat offensive. Quickly processed, the offence brought some anger. But this second round of his *tee-hee-hee* was more than she could bear. A mist came to her eyes, trying to grow heavy, but Hannah fought it off. She would not, could not, let those tears have their way. She rose quickly and moved for the door.

"Wait," he called.

She stopped, giving him a momentary view of her back, gathering herself up as best she could, although her best wasn't very good. She turned and forcefully walked the three long steps to where he sat. Her flushed cheeks were now stained with tears, but Hannah no longer cared if he saw her cry. She no longer cared about Miss Julie, August Strindberg, any plays or any playwrights. She didn't care about Christmas and she didn't much care for Lincoln Dollar, deciding to let him know as much. "Don't you ever laugh at me, you one-arm, paper-pushing coward. You're as bad as the fucking critics, sitting on your ass pretending—*acting*!—like you're teaching others how to act. You do nothing for the theater." Hannah was consumed with the anger, the contempt and sadness, but still she went on. "I can't believe the one person on this planet who's capable of hurting me would actually take advantage of it. I truly don't believe it! You're a real piece of work!"

Though wearied, she gathered herself up just enough to let him know how things would be from here on out. "You go to Louisiana with your friends, and have a merry-fucking-Christmas. You can stay there for all I care. You and I, Lincoln Dollar, can no longer be of service to one another." At the door she turned back once more. "You're inept and spiritless, you know that?!"

She was gone into the corridor.

Lincoln stood, confounded. He might have heard her say, "I thought you were my friend," as she stormed away, but he wasn't sure, though it hurt just the same. Her footfalls suggested she was angry with the hallway as well. Echoes called out confirming that the stairwell was duly punished for its part. She took still more of it out on a door. Her steps became quieter, but still they were angry steps. There was another defenseless door—*slam!*—and Hannah was gone, gone, gone.

Now, Lincoln Dollar, the same as most part-time, one-armed theater teachers, occasionally did things not making a whole lot of sense. After some thought, he decided that laughing away the opportunity to play one of the greatest roles in modern drama, and opposite one of the most exciting performers he'd ever known, made no sense whatsoever. It was plain stupid, yet still he had done it. *What's the problem this time?* he wondered. *Really? Same old excuse?*

He slammed the hook into the pressboard door-desk. It punched through two student essays before sticking into the faux wood. He chastised himself. *Actors don't have hooks? Or is it something else?*

The entire door lifted as he worked to free himself. *And don't you dare blame it on Miss Julie. She didn't start it.*

Lincoln put on his coat. He picked up Hannah's bags, and her mittens and hat from the puddle on the floor, turned out the lights and made his way down the corridor, out into the dusk.

It was but a short walk from the school to the Fields' home on Maple Street, and though there was some light when he began, he arrived in near blackness. A large wreath hung on the front door with a heavy brass knocker nestled inside. Lincoln let it fall three times.

Connie answered, little surprised to see her daughter's teacher standing on the stoop.

"Hi," he said, handing over Hannah's things. "She left these at the school."

Connie put the parcels behind the door, stepping aside to let him enter. "What's she all bent out of shape about now?" she asked. "The S.S. Outtamyway just sailed through, slamming every door in her wake. I swear, that kid goes from thirty to thirteen in the blink of a frustrated mother's eye."

Connie had been wrapping gifts. She set about clearing the holiday away from the sofa and coffee table. "Let's fix you a drink," she said, taking his coat to hang over the banister.

"Whatever you're having—big and straight."

Connie poured a single-malt into two highball glasses. She put a couple of cubes in hers and joined him in the den. "Tell me all about it. What's the crisis du jour?"

"Seems I pissed her off," said Lincoln. "She went as far as to suggest that I extend my vacation indefinitely. I've never really seen that side of her. Then she went in for name calling." He took a large bite of the scotch and smacked his lips, reckoning with no small satisfaction how the whiskey had gone into the barrel at about the same time he went into high school.

"That's the thirteen year-old Hannah," said Connie. "She'll curse you gone, but if you left she'd be the first to go looking. What kind of names did she call you?"

"Started with *one-armed paper pusher*—I kind of liked that one; then I was a *real piece of work*—an *inept and spiritless* piece of work, at that. It went downhill from there."

Connie laughed. "That's what she says to the kid at the market when he doesn't rotate the milk. I certainly wouldn't take it to heart. But you obviously upset her. What happened?"

Lincoln was beginning an explanation when the Vermont winter blew Katie in. She was hurriedly closing the door against the cold when she saw Lincoln standing in the den. Looking at him with scorn, she asked, "What the fuck were you thinking? Man, you sure are a piece of work." Katie didn't wait for any response, but rather shook her head in disgust as she made for the stairs.

Lincoln turned to Connie. "We've established I'm a piece of work, and I didn't make any friends today."

She agreed. "I should say not. But on the bright side, fewer friends means less people to shop for at the holidays. Think of the money you'll save." Their cocktails met with an agreeable glass on glass *clink*.

"Let me guess," said Connie. "Hannah asked you to do the Strindberg, and you blew her off. Please, tell me I'm wrong."

Lincoln's eying the floor said she was not wrong.

She led him to the sofa. "It's time we had a little chat." They sat. "What's stopping you from doing the play? I hope you're not above sharing a stage with my daughter. Are you worried she's not up to it? Or, are you afraid she'll upstage you?"

"It's nothing like that. I'm not sure what it is. I'm looking for reasons not to do it, but can't come up with anything valid."

"Are you afraid of my little girl?"

"Perhaps a little."

"Hannah and I are pretty close," she said. "Sometimes a little too close. And she tells me just about everything—sometimes a little too much. I used to think it was strange how she rarely spoke of you. She might drop your name in some passing story, but she couldn't quite seem to put herself and you into the same context. I thought it was strange until I realized why."

Lincoln sometimes wondered if this conversation, like a viper, might one day strike. Now he'd been snaked. The fangs were deep inside his neck, though the venom was not as painful as imagined.

"It's best to put difficult things simply," she said. "Hannah's in love, simply enough."

When he offered nothing, she added, "What to do about it is the question."

Lincoln left the conversation in his head to rejoin her. "I hope I haven't done anything to make her think—"

But Connie spared him, giving him a chance to re-hit the scotch. "We're naïve if we think we can put ideas into Hannah's head, and even bigger fools thinking we can get an idea out once it's there. Just be careful with her, that's all. She's a lot tougher than she was, but there's still some vulnerability, especially when it comes to you. She can melt away the troubles of others, but she still has a hard time dealing with her own."

Connie thought briefly of how different her daughter had become. "I thank God every day for Katie coming into our lives. She's been such a gift, Lincoln, so good for Hannah, Hannah good for her. They'll be going off to school soon. Who knows? Maybe it's a crush and it'll blow over. Maybe it won't. We'll have to wait and see."

"But why do that play?" Lincoln asked, more wondering aloud. "She knows it's too much for—" Then it hit him, like a sledgehammer in a slaughterhouse. "Which is, of course, exactly why she wants to do it. She's something else, that one. *She's* the piece of work."

Mom embraced this for the compliment it was. "She wants to do it because it's special to you. This play's not about her, Lincoln. It's for you."

He finished off his drink and went for his coat. Connie followed to the door. "Before I forget," he brought an envelope from his pocket, "I thought they'd enjoy a weekend in Manhattan for the break. They've certainly earned it." Lincoln smiled to himself at the thought of Hannah and Katie in Manhattan's theater district because they'd earned it.

"Art wants to talk about NYU," she said. "Think they can get in?"

"They can probably go wherever they want. We're taking some classes to the city in April. They can check it out then."

Connie put an arm around his waist and pulled him close. "We appreciate what you do. You're a good teacher and a good man, a good friend. This might sound cliché, but it's really a pity there aren't more like you."

He thought to say something self-deprecating, like "There are those who would argue;" and he thought to wax humble with something, like "It has very little to do with me;" instead, Lincoln said nothing, but looked long about the room trying to gather in the holiday cheer. Sparkling tinsel dripped on the tree with gifts spilling from beneath. The soft, warm candlelight, the track lights and decorative lights all melted into one gentle glow. Much of what the holidays represented was lost on Lincoln Dollar, but he wasn't so much thinking of that just now.

"What will you do for vacation?" Connie asked.

"I've got people on the Gulf of Mexico. Leaving in the morning."

"You know, you're welcome to spend the holidays with us."

"I appreciate it, Connie, I really do, but it's messy enough already." He hugged her, thanked her and wished her happy holidays, lastly adding, "Would it be better if I didn't come back?"

Connie pulled away quickly, firmly and sternly, nearly angry. "That would be the worst thing for her, and it wouldn't do you any good either. You've got too good a thing going here to let this drive you away. If you're to continue teaching—a strapping buck like you—

you'd better get accustomed to the attentions of your students. Don't let the first one scare you off."

Lincoln took his leave and his regrets, still wondering if his ticket should be changed to one-way. He closed the door and was returned to the cold and dark Vermont winter, the air crisp, hollow and empty. He stood on the walkway, unsure of which direction to go, but before he could decide the door opened behind him and Hannah slipped out.

She was mellowed by a large cocktail while waiting for Katie, and another smaller one once Katie arrived. Her place on the upper step put her a couple inches taller than the teacher, a position she enjoyed a bit before coming down.

"You caught me off guard," he said, not searching long for forgiveness. "I wasn't laughing at you."

"I know. I'm sorry I called you those names. *One-arm paper pusher?*" She was shaking her head. "That was mean and cheap and I apologize for it. You just get me so worked up sometimes. You're the one who told me to *be big*; this is big—as big as I can be, here and now."

Had Hannah suggested he walk on water or build a time machine, his question would have been the same: "What about the arm?"

"I was able to write it into the script. Had to doctor it up a bit, but it kinda makes Jean's relationship with Julie's father even stronger— more history, more at stake, more conflict equals more drama. I used the Sprigg translation."

Hannah's speech was rapid, smooth and clear, her pitch rehearsed, lest she meet with any more opposition. But she knew, by the very conversation, that he was doing the play. Lincoln would be her Jean. And why shouldn't he? She had played plenty for him. It was time he did some playing for her. She had asked little of him in their two years together. She would ask for even less in the future. Her wants would be minimal, but she would have what she wanted, quid pro quo.

"You added a few lines?" In stalling, Lincoln began looking for unneeded verification. "To Strindberg? When I met you you'd never been on a stage, and now you're *doctoring up* one of history's greatest playwrights?"

"I know. Pretty cool, huh?"

Lincoln was wary, past denying that he played some hand in what had transpired. Only time would tell if he could take some credit or have to shoulder the blame.

"I might be a natural," she said, "if there is such a thing—doesn't really matter, I suppose." She stood close to him, her eyes intent, arms tight behind her. Her cheeks were red from the recent cry, her short-lived lapse in confidence, whence Katie had rescued her—Katie and the vodka.

"This is for you. Open it later." She stuffed a small box into the pocket of his coat. "And this is for you, too." Her other hand produced a copy of the Elizabeth Sprigg translation of *Miss Julie*. "I marked the changes in the text. If we're off book by February first, we can start right in with some blocking and staging." Hannah tried to present herself as serious and professional, but couldn't quite pull it off. "All I need you to do is direct this thing and throw me a few lines—a fucking monkey can do that. I'll take care of everything else." She looked into him, trying to read his thoughts. They were cloudy, but still she got the gist of them. "It'll be incredible, I promise."

Resigned, Lincoln stood holding the script in the jaw of his arm. "And Kristen?"

"Well, Kate's playing Kristen—who else?" This was a detail obviously long since settled.

"Of course," he conceded.

"And we'll need a small chorus," she said. "A couple of guitars and flutes, maybe a mandolin—shouldn't be a problem."

"Of course," he re-conceded.

Hannah thought she detected some residual apprehension. "Buck up, buddy. I guarantee it'll be fun." At last believing the deal to be sealed, she moved in close and wrapped her arms around him. Holding tightly, she whispered close to his ear, "Just remember, you're doing this for me."

There was a rustling in the glow of the window as Connie let the draperies fall. Her daughter was getting away from her, and nearly gone. She loved to watch the girl grow, but it wasn't without concern. Connie trusted Lincoln Dollar explicitly, but could she trust him enough to put his trust in Hannah? She smiled as the curtain fell. It was long past out of her hands, so she went back to wrapping gifts.

Hannah pulled back, but continued holding him, looking in his eyes. He was warmth against the frosty night air. "This means a lot to me and you're the only person who can make it happen." And, though she desperately fought the urge, she moved in quickly and kissed his unsuspecting and receptive mouth.

Had there been time to move away, Lincoln might not have taken advantage of it. He managed to say, "You shouldn't have done that," but only because they were the words he thought he was expected to say, and because *thanks* would have sounded too awkward.

"You're right. Let's call it rehearsal."

"Rehearsals are for acting on stage."

"Oh, pooh. All the world's a stage, and tonight I'm cast in the role of one who's quite taken with the character you're playing."

She kissed him once again, staying longer on his mouth this time. She then rested her forehead against his chest. Hannah momentarily shuddered with a memory of the earlier tiff. "About this afternoon," she said to his ribcage, "I won't ever let that happen again, I promise. It's just … I've never wanted anything as much as I want to do this play with you. I … I should just shut up."

But Hannah couldn't shut up—not yet, anyway. She considered her next request a little longer before putting herself the rest of the way out. "There's one more thing," she said, hesitating, stumbling, recovering with no going back; "will you please stop seeing Mr. Stanson's secretary? Could you not see Beth anymore? I don't know why I'm asking. I just am. Could you stop? Please?"

Some words came into Lincoln's mind, but could not make it to his mouth, to his lips still warm from her touch.

"Will you do that?" she asked again. "For me? And so I don't have to ask again? Just till I'm gone. Please?"

Cyndi Partlow and Jennifer Novak, chilled for lack of a heater in the rusty Mustang, were cutting a path through the snow on Maple Street with a Christmas tree tied precariously to the patched cloth roof. As they passed the Fields' home, Cyndi said excitedly, "I knew it! Check it out, Jen. Hannah and Lincoln making out on the stoop."

"I don't blame him. She's pretty hot."

"Never mind them," said Cyndi. "Keep your eyes on the fucking road."

Lincoln never said that he would stop seeing Beth, but he didn't really have to. He did manage to say, "Have a happy holiday, Hannah." The 'h's left his mouth dry. He turned from her and walked down the path. When he met the city street, he looked back to an empty stoop, considering his holiday plans might be one-way after all, wondering if there would be any returning from this trip.

Hannah had watched him halfway down the walk before going back inside. She continued to watch through the window as he moved down the street, watching until he was around the corner and out of sight.

She knew every word of the revised script, knew the work cover to cover. Hannah first read the play the year before, having heard Lincoln mention the title in passing, knowing that one day she would play the role of Miss Julie. After the evening in Memorial Park, when Katie played at Juliet and Lincoln played at promises, she took up the text, memorizing the lines. A natural's instinct asked that she put bodies on her mind's stage, and though Hannah did not plan for it—or did she?— one of those bodies was Lincoln Dollar. She never imagined giving the lines to anyone else. If it couldn't be him, then it simply couldn't be. But it had to be.

She spent eight weeks researching and writing the dozen lines she added to the play, wanting to believe they were among the best in the script—Katie even said this was so—but she could no longer allow herself to think along such lines. This was no longer a high school drama.

She had reentered the house with fresh tears in her eyes, falling all the harder as she watched him walk away. Hannah did not enjoy looking at his back. She let the curtain fall and went to her mother, who conveniently waited for her in mother-like fashion on the sofa. Hannah curled up to her, seeking warmth and love and protection, and fighting a long-past habit of wiping her eyes and nose on a mother's blouse.

Connie draped an arm over the girl. "He still won't do it?"

"He's going to, but I'm not sure if I can."

"Be careful, Hannah. You're seventeen, he's your teacher, and that's the way it's got to stay for now. Don't freak him out. When guys get scared they run—happens every time. Let it stay the way it is for now. I believe he loves you, but he's fighting it, and it must be terribly difficult for him. If it's meant to be, it will. Just remember, though, it's not always best to take the first one who comes along. You might want to shop around a bit."

Hannah's default mode was currently argumentative. "I *do not* want to *shop around*, mother."

"Of course you don't, sweetheart. Of course you don't." Connie leaned in to kiss the top of her head. "I'm so proud of the woman you've become."

Hannah couldn't see her mother's face, but she imagined there were tears. "You're not crying, too?"

"No, I'm okay," Connie replied, wiping her eyes, and she really was. "Go up and get Katie. Let's go shopping, have some fun."

Lincoln walked the length of three cars before finding a pair of empty seats. Removing the bag from his shoulder, he wedged it in overhead. He had a book, a little white box, a disheveled pack of Camels and a lighter; nearly everything needed until the layover at Pennsylvania Station. He took a silver flask from a pocket of his travel bag, placing it on the seat; the balance of what was needed until the layover at Penn. A young boy and his mother sat facing, so Lincoln kept stowed the end of his arm inside the pocket of his vest, lest it grab too much of the kid's attention too soon into the journey.

He took the seat closest the window, facing the mother and child. Unscrewing the cap from the flask, he put it to his mouth for a short sip. It tasted pungently of sour mash and charcoal. As a neighborly gesture, he offered the flask to the woman across the way. She politely shook her head. Lincoln then offered it to her traveling companion. Eight or nine years old, the boy looked up at his mother, only to receive the *no whiskey for you* shake-of-the-head a lot of guys get from the ladies in their lives.

Lincoln took another long salutary pull before replacing the cap, putting the flask on the empty seat and trading it for the book: *Six Plays of Strindberg*, translation by Elizabeth Sprigg. The translator's name recalled Elizabeth Bronson, recalled the not-so-covert relationship, beginning the week Lincoln came to town, and lasting until the theater troupe wrapped the summer shows on the green. The relationship had been moved to a back burner, as Beth had other lovers and Lincoln had a theater department begging more and more of his time. As there had been no entanglement, there was no separation, nor was there any break up. They had simply and quietly stopped being lovers—an open ended ending that now appeared closed. Lincoln was unsure exactly why, but he was sure that the relationship with Beth Bronson was over, finalized as soon as Hannah requested it should be.

The locomotive slowly, laboriously began a departure from the station.

He thumbed the book to the work planned, arriving first at the author's forward, next at the dramatis personae. Three characters were listed at the top of the page: Julie, Jean and Kristen; Hannah, Lincoln and Katie. Beneath this cast of characters was written, in Hannah's distinguishably tight, no-frills script,

Forbidden fruit a flavor has,
That lawful orchards mock;
How luscious lies the pea within
The pod that duty locks.

The undefined Dickenson daunted Dollar. *Was she teasing?* Lincoln wondered. *Mocking?* Did she play at some schoolgirl's game of cat-and-mouse? He answered *no* to all his own questions. He had to. Resting back his head, closing his eyes, Lincoln could picture her answering the same *no*.

He returned the book to the seat, picking up the small box she had stuffed into his pocket, untying the hemp string and removing the cover. Inside was a chained white gold cross, with an onyx stone at the intersection of the upright and transverse beams. Hannah sometimes spoke of this intersection where the stone was set. She called it *home*.

Always quick to point out that she was by no means a religious person, Hannah did fancy herself as having adopted a certain spirituality, and more so as of late. She'd been on the hunt for some sort of god, and stumbled upon a special place, a place she imagined was somewhere between her head and her heart, a place where all her ideals could come together and converge: Justice, Beauty, Love and Freedom—every couple of weeks she would add an ideal. Eventually she came to call this special place *God.* The vertical beam of the cross represented her relationship with the special place, with her God; and

Hannah likened the horizontal beam to her relationship with others—humankind, and the not-so-human kind. At the intersection of the post and transom was the place she called *home*.

The woman across smiled. "It's beautiful."

"It's from a beautiful person." Now, while Lincoln had always thought Hannah beautiful—even uncommonly so—giving the thought voice somehow made it truer than ever. Turning the cross, he found an inscription on the back; however, squinting, he tried in vain to read the tiny script. "Can you make this out?" he asked, handing it to the woman.

Beginning a half-meter from her face, she brought it closer until it nearly touched the tip of her nose. Looking back to him, she shrugged. "The beautiful person wants you to work for it."

"That's not surprising."

"Here, mommy." The young boy, having curiously watched the interaction, unsheathed a bulky Swiss Army knife, producing a magnifying glass from its superfluous array of implements.

Mom put the plastic lens between her eye and the cross. "Says *Welcome Home*—as sweet as it is small." Handing it back, she asked, "Have you been away?"

"I suppose I have." Pulling the end of his arm from the vest pocket, Lincoln asked, "Would you give me a hand putting it on?"

The woman stood and, having achieved the Amtrak equivalent of sea legs, leaned in and brought the ends of the chain together. "From your girlfriend?"

"A friend," Lincoln replied, admiring her perfume.

Once the clasp was set she stepped back, using his shoulder for balance at an awkward rail. "It's beautiful," she reaffirmed, sliding back into her seat. "Your beautiful friend obviously thinks you're a special guy."

"She's actually my student."

"Then the beautiful student thinks you're a pretty special teacher."

The woman continued looking at the cross hanging from the neck of the man on the train. The boy's gaze was fixed on the hook at the end of the train guy's arm, his young thoughts swimming about in all the romantic possibilities associated with such a sight. He wore an unmistakable *should I ask, or will mom get mad* expression, the same as most boys wear when seeing guys with hooks for hands, and especially on the train.

"What's on your mind?" Lincoln asked.

"Are you a pirate?" the boy inquired.

Lincoln adopted an appearance of sorrow to accompany his reply. "Nope—just a teacher.

The boy's disappointment was immediate, obvious, but soon he sensed the train guy must be feeling pretty low, what with leading such a lackluster existence; figuring the train guy must have been a pirate at one time, waving a scimitar, parrot on the shoulder, buckling swashes and all sorts of what-not; and the boy assumed some nautical accident took the guy's hand, then something really bad came along and forced a total career change. From the heights of piracy to the depths of teaching was one glorious extreme to another not-so-glorious. So, naturally, the young boy felt for the man. Who wouldn't?

The train guy looked out the window at wintery-white New England flipping past.

Two more miles of track had gone beneath when the boy stretched his short leg as far as it could reach, gently kicking at the train guy's foot. "It's okay, mister. Teachers are kinda cool too—I guess, sometimes."

The train slowly rolled through the valley.

Lincoln once again opened the book of plays. Reading the script, his mind unconsciously ran through a production of *Miss Julie*. Called upon to put faces to the names of characters, for the first time in a long time one of those faces was his own.

-3-

Over the hump of a tumultuous decade was primetime for revolution. Women were demanding a defined identity, and African Americans were protesting centuries of abuse; Natives would have an accurate historical accounting, and an entire postmodern society was disheartened with still another war. The people were pissed, and the more the government wanted to quell the tension—the *pissed*ness—the more the cities smelled of tear gas, gunpowder and fear; the more the streets and jungles ran with blood.

Nathan Dollar decided to enlist, rather than wait for the imminent notice. His irrational side believed that if he went to them before they came to him, he might secure a safer assignment. But there weren't any safe assignments. He knew there weren't any safe assignments.

By the skin of clenched teeth, he was able to return to Brooklyn the following year. A snake wrapped around a dagger was tattooed to his forearm, and there was contempt in his fellow travelers at LaGuardia not present before he was tattooed. They called him *murderer, baby killer* and *pawn*, and though he had heard that some of the guys were spit at, no one spit at Nathan Dollar. They simply turned away from the soldier in the dress-green uniform, the Green Beret wearing spit-shined jump boots.

The airport was draped with the holiday cheer of reds and greens, colors conjuring fast images of a bloody jungle for the soldier still tasting napalm as he hoisted his duffle bag from the luggage carousel.

Charlotte Curry, CeeCee, had often written Nathan with her vows, until at last the holidays brought the man upon her doorstep. He quietly melted into the small apartment, into blue jeans and heavy sweaters, trading his combat boots for unseasonable loafers. Half a world away from booby traps and snipers, he had only to brave the snow and slush of another Brooklyn winter.

Through Christmas and New Year's, they watched the tensions grow to outsize the black and white screen. When the NVA moved into the embassy, Nathan knew he was soon to return to the jungle. When CeeCee suggested they get married before he left, he happily agreed. It was the two and the pastor and as good as it could be. And still the tensions grew.

Nathan made furious, desperate love with his new bride as Lieutenant Calley's riflemen moved into My Lai 4. He was nestled in her breasts when the soldiers used candy to lure the village children into a ditch. Nathan returned to his uniform, returned to the 7th-Group.

CeeCee Dollar took to crying more than was her right. Lonely in the tiny apartment, she cried as the Reverend King lay lonely on a Memphis balcony. Her stomach was starting to grow when Bobby fell in LA.

The Great Society was far from great when baby Lincoln was one hundred hours removed from CeeCee. He stared at his mother from the bassinette on the floor, while outside the snow fell quietly on Brooklyn streets. Daddy wasn't coming home for Christmas, but still the baby giggled as best as he knew how. Mom trimmed the lonely tree, unable to share in the child's amusement. The tinsel reflected her fear, boredom and apprehension.

Nathan Dollar spent the holidays of 1968 on the border of Laos, where a six year-old approached him for instructions pertaining to the use of hand grenades. The lesson didn't get far, lastly resulting in the Department of Defense sharing news of the brief lesson with the widow Dollar on Christmas Eve.

The grief clung to her like guilt, like a shame, but still CeeCee carried on, if only trying to keep busy. She burned her bras in freedom fires and rallied for a democratic society. She protested the war that killed her baby's father. CeeCee was finally detecting an inkling of equanimity when Crosby, Stills and Nash took the stage in upstate New York. Dancing at the three-day music and arts festival, exploring her own marijuana-induced nakedness, she chanced to notice the small lump in her widowed breast and returned to her husband six months later.

The State of New York took the little boy into protective services. The first foster family prompted him to imagine in his little boy's mind that there had to have been another family before; eventually, as he grew, his imaginings of the first family faded to something more like a feeling. With each new family the gulf widened, until all the original memories were vanished, the filial imaginings, the feelings.

The boy had his father's eyes and his mother's drive. He took refuge in the concrete jungle, the mousetrap of Manhattan, learning warily and wisely to walk the delicate line between the flavor of the bait and the violence of the snare.

-4-

Connie and Arthur Fields didn't wait for Beth Bronson to ring up her boss; rather they walked past her desk and directly into John's office, where he was wiping his palms on his trousers, reluctantly heading to meet them at the door.

"Connie, it's good to see you. Mr. Fields, I'm John Stanson. Good to finally meet you." This last wasn't true; John would have been content not having to meet the man, especially under the present circumstances.

Once seated, Hannah's mother didn't waste time in coming to her point, her voice hurried and anxious. "We don't know what the hell is going on. Hannah's at my sister's in Boston. Says she's not coming home. And now Lincoln's disappeared?"

When neither of the gentlemen ventured commentary, Connie went on, "If they ran off together, I could understand that—hell, I'd be happy for them. But something bad has happened, John. I know it."

Art Fields broke his silence. "I'll be all over this fucking place if that guy did anything to hurt my little girl. I swear to God—"

John jumped in, hoping as a shield to cushion the blow of incoming threats. He had kevlar intentions, however a muslin zeal. "Let's not let some small town gossip blow this out of proportion. I've known Lincoln Dollar a long time. There must be—"

Connie joined in Lincoln's defense, albeit with trepidation. "For Christ's sake, Art, after all he's done, do you honestly believe he would do anything to hurt her? He couldn't." Of John she asked, "Could he?"

John couldn't risk fueling the fire. "I haven't talked to him for a while. How can I get hold of Hannah? What's she said about all this?"

Connie stared in her lap, slowly shaking her head. "That's just it. She's not saying anything, other than she doesn't want to see us. Patty said she's into the drinking, even more so than usual, won't go outside. The poor kid. She's always been prone to capriciousness, and we've always tried to accommodate, but it's never been anything like this."

John wrote his private number and slid it across the desk. "When you talk to her, give her this. Tell her to call." He put himself up as collateral. "Trust me. I'll work this out."

"You'd better work it out," said Art, grabbing for the slip of paper. Signaling the end of the meeting, he stood, offering a final threat as he made for the door. "Or I'm gonna work it out for you."

No sooner were Hannah's parents gone before Katie was in John's office. Getting her there was easy enough, but getting her to speak would take a bit more doing. John knew she'd be hard to reach, only to have it confirmed when she opened with, "You can keep your thirty pieces of silver. I'm not saying shit without talking to them first." She was wrapped in silence, an armor of fearful restraint, and John didn't want to press too closely, lest she shut herself away even further.

Trying to convince her he was not the enemy, John appealed first to Katie's reason, then to her emotions. "I can't get into details, but I'd do anything I could for Lincoln Dollar, regardless of the circumstances. Whatever's happened, Katie, I need to fix it, and I can't do it without you."

He gave her time while stealing some himself, as the possibilities rode about his mind like bumper cars. *What have you done this time, Lincoln?* he wondered. *What happened with her? You promised you'd play it cool, but this ain't fucking cool.*

He asked Katie, "What happened in New York?"

She was ready to accept his help, any help. Katie needed it. Her eyes were red with sorrow and anger. No stranger to loss, still this current abandonment was far beyond anything for which her fragile sensibilities were prepared.

She told him what she could, that she and Hannah had shared a room in the city, that it was their last night there, that all the students had tickets to *Phantom'* or *Cats*, "but Hannah got ticks for a show off-Broadway; *Journey at Night*, something like that. She said she was doing a paper on O'Neill, going to the play to do some research, and taking Lincoln with her. But that's bullshit, Mr. Stanson. She wasn't working on any paper. I hate it when she lies to me, like she doesn't fucking trust me."

Katie went on to tell of a brief argument between the two, and of how Katie left the room in anger, and of how she looked through the peephole in the early morning to see Lincoln in the hallway, with

Hannah pressed against the wall. "He looked crazy. I've never seen him like that."

Met with a ghost from the past, John had seen the same Lincoln Dollar. He'd hoped never to see it again.

Katie spoke of the blood on Hannah's mouth, the bruised cheek, the torn blouse. She told of the vodka Hannah nursed in the bathroom before getting into bed. "I held her, but she only cried harder. When I woke up she was gone. Patty must have come to get her. That she would go anywhere with Patty rather than stay with me and Lincoln doesn't make any sense. We rode back with the other chaperone and I haven't seen them since. I can't believe he would do anything to hurt her, but if he did—"

"What are the students saying?" asked John quickly.

"Everyone's talking shit, as usual. I don't know what to think anymore. I don't know what to do. I'm lost without her—and him."

John saw the fruitlessness in getting any further with Katie, and right at the same time Katie was through with him. "Fuck this. I need to do something. If you talk to that whack-job, tell him to call me, please. Tell him he better call me." She slammed the office door, taking catlike pains to ignore Beth Bronson on her way past.

John's day was rich enough already with these visits from Hannah's parents and Hannah's partner, but there was something in the present ringing of the phone speaking of still more richness to come. The ring sounded the same as it did every other day, but somehow it felt different.

"It's me," said the shaken voice. "What's she saying about all this?"

John nearly yelled into the phone, "About what, Lincoln? Nobody's talked to Hannah since you were in New York. What the hell happened down there? Let me help. I owe you that much."

John immediately recoiled from the last of his plea, having agreed years before not to bring it up again. He had promised.

Lincoln bit back. "You don't *owe* me anything. Let it go already." He tried to calm himself, only partly succeeding. "I didn't know where I was—or who I was. I'm still not sure. Feels like my head's turned inside-out." He was taking large breaths, quick and deep. "Where's Hannah?"

John sensed the man was slipping away, losing touch. "What are you into down there? Tell me what's going on."

"The less you know the better. Just tell me how to get hold of her."

"Man, I don't know how. No one does! Everyone's on my ass to get you here and straighten this out. The way her father's talking, the cops'll be here soon enough. It's a bad day in Black Rock, and I ain't got a fuckin' clue. Regardless of what you say, I do owe you. What did you do to that girl? Did you … did you hurt her?" John was already regretting the implication of his words before they passed his lips. The call abruptly ended.

Rich and getting richer, the day was full of worries before the call, afterwards filled with weighty concern. The person on the phone recalled too much the man John had served with during the 100-Hour War. He was reminded of the all-too-gung-ho psychosis he had seen in Lincoln's eyes in the Persian Gulf, imagining those same eyes again down in the city, caught up in the concrete maze of the big mealy apple.

Captain Stanson had been in the vanguard, platoon leader as the group advanced on Baghdad. It was not a position which John enjoyed, but did only because it had to be done. He gave every bit of the marine in him to the assault. John gave it all to every assault, believing that each bit of distance covered was less the distance separating him from home, from Lauren. Foot by foot, he pushed to narrow the span, his thoughts of being near her again helping to drive the mission, thoughts enough to produce a sandy smile. Then the first of the mortars flew in.

Like the angry hand of a vengeful god, the explosion lifted John from the vehicle and threw him to the sand. Dazed, confused and alone, when the smoke finally cleared he checked on the Humvee, resting overturned atop the driver, all four wheels turning in the air. The windshield had severed the young man's head, releasing rivulets of marine blood to roll and mingle on the dusty desert floor.

Deafened by the blast, with his face in the sand, John's desert world engulfed him in dream-like peacefulness. He'd been hoping it would be the last assault and decided it definitely would be, as his shoulder had been shattered in the crash.

The captain thought it wisest to remain where he was and wait, but such being the wise course, John opted for the opposite, the same rationale that had carried him through many past missions. He waited several moments gathering the strength to move. Maybe it was several hours. He couldn't be sure. He wasn't sure of anything but the pain, having grown louder and louder, transmitting in rushing waves from his wrist into his chest.

Pulling the morphine injector from his cargo pocket, John tore the package with his teeth and stabbed the needle through his fatigue trousers. It was only a moment—*ahhh*—before he no longer cared about the shoulder. Treating himself to a second injection, John didn't care about anything. Engaging all that was left of his faculties, he was again semi-vertical, but had no sooner achieved the feat when a bullet splashed into the broken shoulder. John danced about like the ragged marionette of an epileptic puppeteer, spinning, falling near to his original resting place. The desert was quiet.

The break in the shoulder was difficult enough to contend with, but the bullet's belligerent behavior made matters all the more muddled. Still, John felt disposed to help himself, venturing to get upright again. Using his rifle as a fully loaded crutch, he dug into the sand, willing his legs should hold, and after great effort was erect once more, and once more feeling like a marine. He spit the sand and blood from his mouth, shook his head clear and laughed aloud; it was an angry, cynical laugh, full of contempt, full of fear. The young captain looked south toward Kuwait, whence they had come; just as unsteadily he looked to the north, onward to Baghdad. He was a moment in deciding on a direction to go—bewildered, unsteady, resentful—when a quick succession of five more rounds struck, two in each of his legs and one in the hip. John was down again and he wasn't getting up; so he was at last resigned, but only after another feeble, near comic attempt.

John's life ebbed on the sands of the Syrian, though his dying wasn't as bad as he thought it would be. The morphine swam in his veins, diplomatically addressing the physical realities of his situation. Again he spit in the sand, wiping a bloody mouth on his sleeve. John thought of his mother, of her coming sadness; he thought of how his father would have found the mission half-assed, incomplete and unsuccessful. He began to cry.

Lastly his thoughts were of Lauren. He had been on the edge of a proposal when the force was deployed, finally deciding to wait until his return, as to be close by in case he had to do some begging for her hand.

He imagined her back in North Carolina, in the studio working on some new routine, all luscious legs, laughter and love. He ached to see her once more. He would have given all that he had, but John had nothing left to give, nothing but his lonely tears, blood and sweat, all coming together and swallowed into his camouflage sleeve. "Good bye," he whispered.

As those lonely syllables left the captain's sandy mouth, the young sergeant appeared out of the smoke, out of the flying sand and solitude. *He never said a word,* John recalled, sitting alone at his desk at Preston High now five years later; *he just winked at me and smiled. It was the first time I ever saw the man smile.*

John recalled his subordinate taking him over his shoulder and carrying him to cover. His next memory was of a Turkish hospital. Three days had passed. He was covered in gauze and racked with pain. Hardware was installed while he slept.

When he finally opened his crusty eyes, in the next bed was the same sergeant who had carried him over the dunes. "Rise and shine, Captain. Looks like we're going home—what's left of us, anyway. What's left?" he repeated, holding up his left arm, its end an angry, bandaged, blood-soaked stump. Republican Guard soldiers with AK-47 assault rifles had removed the sergeant's arm between the wrist and elbow.

The two men were somewhat acquainted before that day in the desert, but had never quite hit it off. As a hard scrapping, hardworking, hard headed NCO, Lincoln Dollar never cared much for most officers; John simply didn't care much for Lincoln Dollar. He worked with him and he tolerated him, but he did not like him. During their stay in the hospital, however, the two became friends. Five years later John Stanson sat in his office hoping that friendship was still alive.

As they watched one another's wounds heal, whiling away the time, John painted for Lincoln a picture of a life teaching high school back in Vermont. Lincoln shared of his growing up in New York's theater district. They were many days in the Turkish hospital with many stories swapped. Other fallen marines around the wards were sharing another story. It was the tale of a young marine sergeant coming upon a man lying in the sand. The sergeant returned the man to cover, gave him narcotics to ease his suffering, and left him in search of other comrades. Bullets in the story splashed around the sergeant, seeming to hit before he arrived at one place and just after he'd left another, his own dumb luck forcing him to smile.

He found another wounded man, and another still, until three broken marines lay side by side between the sandy dunes of natural cover, natural safety. The sergeant dressed their wounds, eased their pain and called for the corpsmen. It was all he could do. Lastly, he prepared for another trip into the maze of dunes, into that valley of destruction, but this time was restrained, as, seeming unnoticed by him, he had lost an arm the last time out. The sergeant was, at long last, *hors de combat*. Actions far above and beyond all calls was the opinion of many in the Syrian that day. Others called the scene disturbing. Some thought the sergeant 'touched.'

Lincoln never spoke of that day in the desert. He didn't mind talking of other times in-service, even of the weeks in the Turkish hospital before returning to the States, but he never spoke of that day, like he'd rather wall it away, somehow leave it on the sands of Iraq. John wondered how the man could stow that day away with the prosthesis where his hand would be if not for that day. The end of John's wonderings, always and forever, were punctuated by question marks in the shape of greyish steel hooks.

Lincoln finished his degree at about the time John wrapped up his PhD. The two men had stayed in touch, and when Lincoln expressed a desire to break free of the concrete jungle, John lured him to Vermont with brochure-like offers of a slot at Preston High.

"You sure you want me up there?" the former marine had asked. "I'm likely to adopt some unorthodox teaching practices. I'd hate to get you into any trouble."

"I'd expect nothing less," John answered. "It would be an honor to get into another mess of trouble with you. Just come on up, whenever you're ready to start living the green mountain dream."

John Stanson stretched back in his chair, fixing his eyes on the ceiling, doing his best to ignore the pair of #2 Ticonderogas that a playful student thought would serve better in the tiles than at work on any assignment.

It's two years now since you blew into town, he recollected. *You said you wouldn't make any trouble, but it seems you've gone and done that very thing, my friend. I only hope it's nothing we can't fix.*

-5-

Concessions reached and deals made, Hannah was finally coaxed back to Vermont. Taciturn when she left, she was clam-tight once returned. She wasn't saying anything. And much the same as when she first came to town, she adopted an air warning others to not bother asking. The bricks were stacked, the mortar well set, and none would breach the wall; none but Katie. She never left Hannah's side, allowing others near on a case by case basis only.

Hannah had missed five weeks of classes, but few questioned the absence for fear of sparking fuel for an explosion to expose even deeper secrets. She was allowed to quietly ease back in, her silence proposing a *don't ask, don't tell—leave me alone and I'll keep my mouth shut* arrangement found universally acceptable. Once her averages were adjusted she would graduate with honors, though none were surprised when she didn't return the *RSVP* for the ceremony.

Lincoln Dollar sat alone in a small Manhattan apartment, wretched, until he couldn't stand being with himself any longer. His imagined thoughts of how Hannah was faring was eating away at him, bite by bite, eating away at the little not already mangled and chewed. The idea of leaving John holding the bag was more than he could bear. His world grew smaller and smaller until it could no longer contain the extent of his pain. He was choking, smothered in the dusty, stinking debris of his self, near his bottom, when he finally decided that, if he was to go, he was going on his own terms. He had started it, and so he would finish it.

As the jury in the courtroom of public opinion slept soundly in their beds, he slipped back in through Preston's back door. The glow of the coffee maker offered light enough to find a tumbler in the cupboard. Lincoln filled it to the top. Nearing midnight, he called John, opening the door for him minutes later. Lincoln refilled his glass and poured another for his friend.

John could see he was a little drunk, but there was also something unfamiliar about the man. Something was different. John believed it was fear. He had never seen Lincoln Dollar exude fear, and concluded that he did not wear it well. The one-armed teacher was staring with vague emptiness at the floor, his eight and twenty years flipping past like the pages in an obscure book, some of them dog-eared and worn, and others barely read. Having passed on attempts at any chronological assessment, at last he opened the book to John. His voice was rusty, parched from lack of use, the words coming from far away, sounding as yet discovered.

"I never had anyone, no marriages, no kids, no family to speak of. My parents had me and died, right off, back to back, almost like they had it planned. And then the foster homes said I didn't place well, whatever the fuck that means. But I did have Broadway, taking the train to the island every chance I got, since I was still small enough to slip past the ticket booths and under turnstiles. The stagehands used to let me in through the alley. And when I grew up I had the Corps. The theater and the Corps were the only things I've ever been connected to. I'd still be in if it wasn't for the hook, but there's not much work for a rifleman who can't hold a rifle.

"It seemed I was always looking for something, something to take the place of all the bullshit, the nothingness, the feelings of never placing well. Then you started in about teaching, had to put that idea in my head. I never claimed to have a lot to teach, but I do know the theater and I know a little something about books. I thought I could pass some of it along to some students. Now all this."

John could see the defeat. He shared of that defeat. He wanted to regret having ever invited Lincoln Dollar back into his life, but he couldn't. He wouldn't. Lincoln had given him the life, he could take it back, and he was seeming come to collect when John saw the beginnings of a change. He watched as that familiar conviction came down atop the man's despair.

"I'd do it again," said Lincoln, as though having finally convinced himself. "I wouldn't change a fucking thing."

"Change what?"

The dazed marine started back, punch-drunk, as though realizing for the first time he wasn't alone in the room. "We went out together, to dinner, to the Irish Rep; but, please, none of your lectures or judgments,

John—not now. I suppose I knew before, but it was then I stopped denying. I didn't plan for it to happen, but the things she said—every ounce of the crap I was carrying all those years was lifted. Everything.

"At the show she was going on about the production, the weaknesses of the actors, the set, a real pro. Finally, we stood for the curtain, and when she moved in to kiss me I didn't turn away. I was done turning away. It was just the two of us, like I wanted it. I barely remember leaving the theater. I didn't know what to do, or where we'd go. I wanted to take her away forever."

While John appreciated Lincoln's candor, broken by sips of whiskey, he didn't care for the direction the narrative was taking. He stilled himself believing that no laws had been broken—not yet. By state and federal statutes, Hannah was free to kiss whomever she chose. The city of Preston, however, had its own laws on the books, and the school had some laws, and all of these laws were written long before the likes of Lincoln Dollar and Hannah Fields came to town.

"We started walking, got a little off course when three doped up toughs pushed us into an alley … they had to have a gun, a shitty little, snub-nose 38." Lincoln's anger flared at the recollection. "Two hundred bucks in any pawnshop." The anger tried squeezing through his gritted teeth. "Those stupid, doped up—" He was nearly moaning.

"What happened?" John asked.

"He's got the piece jammed in my face, going through my pockets, while the other two had her on the pavement. They were in her blouse, pulling at her pants, and I'm standing there with this prick feeling me up, fucking helpless, and here's Hannah crying for help, my help. It felt … I felt like she was blaming me. I couldn't stand it. I just couldn't stand it. I'd rather eat the bullet.

"I smashed the guy with the hook. I could feel his skull cracking, right through my arm, up into my own. He was dead as soon as I hit him. It all happened so fast. This other fuck was fumbling with his pants when he splashed against the brick. The one on top of her, John …while he was on top of her … he rolled away … leaving his blood on … on Hannah.

"I tried to fix her up, but she started running. Somehow we got back at the hotel. She was crying the whole way about how I always made a mess of everything, about how I couldn't leave things alone." The memory of Hannah's words returned to pound him with the force of every bullet from every shitty little, snub-nose 38.

John listened in disbelief, working to envision the New York alley, three men lying in sticky, carmine pools, the terrified Hannah, her eyes were wide with fear.

Lincoln continued, his words drifting, disappearing into a whisper, "The next thing I remember is calling you. I took a friend's place on the island, locked myself in, self-medicated. What a mess. I don't care about the job, or the law. I don't care about all that. It's losing her. It's too much."

Lincoln brushed his face, wiping his hand on his jeans. Without looking up, he let go a short, sarcastic laugh. "You know, she's really got an eye for beauty; then, in typical form, being my fucked up self, I had to take her to the ugliest side of any life. And she blames me for it. I know she does, and probably always will. As much as I love irony, this is more than I care for."

John had taken to pacing the room. He poured them each four more fingers of the whiskey. "You got any intentions of going to the authorities with this?" he asked. "What do I say when they come to me? What can we do to make this go away?"

Lincoln was down, depressed, discouraged and drunk. Talking into the booze, he answered, "I don't know, but I can't stay around here. I'll go back to the city, maybe back down south. I can't hide in Preston. I've got to get out. I need to make these last two years go away, go away with the others."

"I'll do whatever I can," said John, though he hadn't any idea what it would be. He did know, however, that Lincoln was leaving. John was sure of it; he was as good as gone.

"I should've never come here. I should've left it alone. I should've … I should've stayed away from her." He drank long and painfully from the glass. "I need to be alone."

With reluctance, John acquiesced, feebly reiterating as he left, "I'll do whatever I can."

-6-

Lincoln took the rushed *indefinite leave of absence* offered by the school board. There were other options, though very little choice. The awkward stares and whispers were bruising, the ostracism none too subtle. His very presence in the town was inviting still more disruption, with some of his neighbors pledging too much support, and many others just the opposite. He was at the heart of an old fashioned, small town, *yer either with me or agin me* dispute. It was awkward; that is, Lincoln would have described it as awkward, were there anyone left to receive the description. He remained deep within himself while planning his departure.

The suggested indefinite leave was best; a chance to slip around and distance himself from the crisis which had followed him to Preston. He could quickly dress the wound with a geographical bandage, run from the trouble, but still it would eventually catch up. It always caught up. Lincoln Dollar was the common denominator in all such affairs, because no matter where he went, there he was.

The trouble began the year before when he returned from the Mississippi delta to share the stage with Hannah. The show had gone beyond racy, as Hannah had imagined and hoped that it would. It only snowballed from there, with many of the townsfolk wondering how much further the new teacher would attempt to stretch the city limits. They questioned themselves, and subsequently answered, *Where's he get off? In this town? And with a student?* By the time Lincoln began understanding the inner workings of the Preston machine, most of the damage was already done. A misty and ambiguous night in New York was but a dollop of distasteful icing on an already fallen cake.

The powers that be found the performances of *Miss Julie* inappropriate, at best, and though it was the student who perpetuated the theatrical scandal, the teacher would end up taking the rap. The pillars of Preston believed that certain business should be kept behind closed doors, where it has always been—in silence, as it's always been—and not on a stage for public view. This would never do. Hannah's staged performances incited strong public opinion, as being so blatant and brutally honest that—like the powers and pillars said—they were inappropriate. And this would never do.

Lincoln accepted the verdict, at the same time meeting increasing difficulty in keeping his opinions to himself. His thoughts and impending actions were growing base. Rather than watch it go from bad to worse, he wanted to quash the whole nonsense by taking off somewhere, anywhere, and immersing himself in something quickly, fully and completely. He thought to hole up and have a go at the great American novel, though he hadn't the presence of mind lately to compose a simple letter. He thought about another teaching assignment, but just as quickly dismissed that idea. Instinct begged that he simply start running, hard, fast and far, but where to this time? And why? He surely wasn't running from any grey matter on the pavement of New York City, having by now finished with questioning that night. He'd never un-ring the bell. Besides, it hadn't been much different than Lebanon or Panama, Berlin or the Syrian, and he'd already convinced himself that he would have done the same for anyone else lying on that same pavement, though conceded it might not have been to such extent. Concluding that it could have played out much worse, Lincoln let it go, let it go with all the rest.

He tried blaming Miss Julie one last time, but no way was she taking the rap. Instead, Julie hinted at a remedial course: *The Preston show's a wrap, but don't let it drive you from the theater. Whatever happens, you'll always have the theater*.

Lincoln was ready to start driving when he received a call from New York. He let go a relieved sigh when it wasn't the call he'd been half-expecting. Some friends were staging a production of *Death of a Salesman* and asked if he would come down to replace their Biff, who was "not quite working out," according to the stage manager. "We're barely in and already this guy's a nightmare."

Lincoln had played the salesman's son as a young actor, back when he had both his hands. The play and the lines were still somewhere inside his head, needing only to be rediscovered. He agreed to arrive soon. A couple more appointments with the V.A. hospital would have him up and ready. Now Lincoln's hope was bolstered. The opportunity to play someone else looked especially appealing in light of the past several months he'd spent playing himself. The character of Lincoln Dollar was oftentimes a difficult role to play—at least it was for him anyway.

He packed the moving boxes carefully, labeling each and sorting them out for storage. With each load he was reminded of how proficient he was at moving, and moving quickly. He was also reminded of how painful a skill it had been to acquire. Each trip to storage introduced Prestonians in the streets. Many averted their eyes. Many waved.

Jen Novak and Cyndi Partlow stopped by to fare Lincoln well, inquiring after his return. He left the question unanswered, and left them with his hopes of seeing them again. There were hugs all around. Cyndi was misty, squeezing her former teacher tighter than she might have. "I'm just happy you're okay, and don't you dare ever let her get away."

Jennifer added, "This place sucks anyway. We're leaving right behind you."

Lincoln had not spoken with Hannah since they were in New York those four months before. He hadn't anywhere near the words to express what he was feeling. He did send her a card by post, but apart from his name in signing off, the text included only that which came with the card. He last saw her from a distance as she walked in the graduation ceremony. The stage was set on the field when she took her diploma. Lincoln remained off the thirty yard-line. It was safer from a distance. Everything was safer from a distance. Taking pains to avoid her, still he thought of little else. Cradling a packing box, he opened the door for another reluctant trip across town. Hannah stood in the hall.

She had been there for some time feeling painfully out of place, debating whether or not to ring the bell, and finally deciding she had to. She had never been to Lincoln's home before, having declined his roundabout invitations, and having fought her many urges and circumstances to invite herself.

They were two former friends trying to make sense of a meeting. So much needed saying, but both could only stand and stare. Neither spoke. There were abandoned attempts at smiling, restrained wants to cry out, to reach out. And soon the threshold narrowed, having grown softer, gentler, until it melted away and was gone forever. All told, once complete, it took just over nine seconds.

Seldom at any loss for words, unless for dramatic effect, Hannah was first to speak. "I figured you'd be taking off. I had to see you once more."

"I've wanted to see you, too, but there's still too much going on around here."

She gathered from his eyes that he'd been wanting to see her. Hannah needed such information, gathering a bit more of it before moving to embrace him. She took hold of him roughly, tightly, but Lincoln broke from her and turned back into the room.

Hannah followed and took the nearest chair. She eased her head back with eyes closed, letting go a sigh, exhausted, conflicted and full of questions. Some of them she wanted left unanswered and others she didn't. "What can you tell me about this?" She pulled a folded acceptance letter from Tulane University from her pocket and threw it blindly in his direction. It bounced off the coffee table and went to the floor.

"An option," Lincoln replied. "You can't have too many options, but you should stay in school." He quickly recoiled, however, from presuming to tell her what she *should* do, and so amended: "You're great actors, you're talented, and it'd be good if you stayed with it—for the theater, you know. Go team."

Hannah and Katie were nearing the middle of their senior year when Lincoln sent their headshots and résumés to Tulane. He didn't have to see the letter to know that they'd be accepted. "Good people down there, quality instruction. It's a great school with an excellent theater program, and it's the nicest city in North America."

Lincoln was two years at Tulane finishing his undergrad. He held a dizzy fondness for New Orleans. Among his favorite places, he could easily imagine his two favorite people banging it up downtown in the Big Easy. He could picture Hannah and Katie dancing through the

French Quarter, moving fast and faster, mixed up in laughter and jazz. And there was Lincoln's home-away-from-home cabin on the Mississippi, downriver from the city, where he spent his idle time. He allowed himself to believe that the bayou cabin played but a tertiary role in his sending the girls' bios south—had even told John and Lauren as much when discussing his intentions with them—playing off the cabin's proximity to the university as more coincidence than anything else. They didn't buy it either.

"Why are you still bothering with all this?" asked Hannah. "Are you still trying to make everything right and pretty? You think you can say some more of those magic words, like that *be big* fuck-all bullshit, and everything's gonna be okay with the world? Like that's going to change what's happened? I get accused of having my head in the clouds, but you—you're in another solar system completely."

Lincoln didn't have the energy or answers for more angry questions. Given the choice, he'd continue packing. "You're my friends, for fuck's sake," he snapped. "I don't have many left. I've seen what you're capable of. Do what you want with it. Keep it to yourself, give it away, it doesn't concern me."

"Doesn't concern you?" she questioned to herself, though still the words came out.

Hannah thought back to the day, those two years before, when she waltzed into Lincoln's classroom with her arms full of coffee cups and bagels. She thought of the night he first coaxed her to the stage, the night he looked into her eyes as no one had ever looked into her eyes before. They were the same eyes she saw the night she forced herself away from the cold and into his arms, the night she gave up all hope of ever pushing him away. Hannah went back to a misty night when he stood over her, when she was nearly naked on the cold, wet pavement, one arm covering her breasts and the other shielding between her legs. Tears tried to visit now that she was finally alone with him once more, but she would not answer their call. There would be plenty of time for tears later on.

"Got anything to drink?" Without waiting for his answer, Hannah went to the cupboards. Settling on a glass from the sink, she rinsed it and poured a pacifying dose of Tennessee whiskey. She tossed it back, grimacing, her eyes gone wet. "Lord," she said, swallowing hard, "how can you drink this shit?" She shook it off and poured another. The burning ceased. The effect was quick, effectively rendering all bets null and void. Inhibitions waned as she looked to him with eyes half-mast, her head tilted to one side, as Hannah was prone when unsure of what to say. She worked much better with a script.

Lincoln was leaving. A quick look around said his departure was imminent. All that remained in the place was the furniture with which it came. He had one foot out of Preston while the other hinted at side-stepping out of her life. Part of her wanted to help him along, to nudge him, to give him a little push, but a bigger part wanted to bring him near. The bigger part won out.

"That night in New York," she began, "we need to put it to rest before you leave. You've done a lot for me and I appreciate it. My life was a puzzle before you showed up to help me put it together. The theater was the biggest piece. You showed me where to put it and how to put it, and how to work it so it works. And I'm grateful for that. I'll always be grateful. I knew that night in Manhattan, one way or another, I was going to be with you. I was never going to leave you, if only you'd let me have my way.

"I tried being careful, all the time hoping it was just some stupid crush. I tried forcing myself to believe it was." She laughed. "If anyone knew the thoughts I had … I couldn't talk about it, not even to Kate, afraid I'd jinx it. How pathetic is that? Silly schoolgirl romanticism. You probably think it's pathetic, too, but I don't care anymore. I don't care what anyone thinks. I was ashamed of myself, but not anymore.

"I was just getting ready to put it all out there when everything turned to shit. The puzzle you and I put together—*together*—was blown apart again, scattered. I couldn't even think of you without getting sick. But then I started putting the puzzle back together again, by myself this time. I think I've done it, and I think I'm a better person for having done it, but there's a piece missing. I suppose that's why I'm here. I'm pretty sure I'm in love with you.

"I was wondering if it was real, and now I'm sure it is—ninety-nine percent sure anyway; that other one percent is always going to pester me about my actual sexuality. All that's left is for us to get together.

And we will be together, somehow, somewhere, sometime. I'm so sure of it, I'm just going to keep on loving you, and I'm going to wait. Do what you have to do. Go where you have to go. I'll wait."

Hannah had a whiskey buzz. "But keep this in mind." She moved her hand up and down to advertise herself. "I know I'm not perfect—far from perfect, for sure—but I'm growing up good. There'll come a time when I'm a pretty prized package." She was half a cocktail from having difficulty saying *pretty prized package.* "Keep in mind, for what it's worth, this belongs to you if you want it. Personally, I think you'd be a fool to put me out. You need someone to love you, someone like me. It's win-win. Think about it. I'll do anything for you."

Against her better judgment, Hannah poured herself another, shorter drink. "So, now you're leaving—well, ta-fucking-ta. Who am I to stand in the way of an exit? I just want you to know what you're leaving. More importantly, I want you to know what's waiting for you when you come back, when you come home to me." Her voice fell to a winded whisper, speaking into his chest. "The first time I saw you, I knew I shouldn't, so I hid from it and tried to hide it from everyone else, but I don't have to hide anymore."

Lincoln suddenly got it into his head to test the theory of flight. "Let's not make this any more complicated than it already is."

Hannah didn't want the debate. "What's complicated about it? Besides everything? Maybe it used to be a problem, but not anymore."

Experiencing difficulties with takeoff, still Lincoln tried once more, kind of. "We can't," he said, a last-ditch effort to get airborne, but he was grounded, taxiing in small, frantic circles on the tarmac. Clipped, wingless, he wasn't flying anywhere.

His gentlemanly protestations may have been meant as sweet and appropriate, but Hannah found them annoying and time consuming, convinced that she didn't have a lot of time. "Perhaps we shouldn't," she told him, this side of agreement, "but I need to. Don't … well, you can't turn me away. I'd feel like an idiot."

Finally enwrapped in the man's voluntary hold, Hannah's instinct begged one last time that she run; now she concluded that instinct meant for her to run *towards* him, and she did. Hannah hit him with such force, and she got so deep within, from that afternoon until forever she was never again without. She whispered, "I've never—" stammering, hesitating, tangled up and embarrassed in her confession "— you know. I've been waiting, until I was sure. Now I'm sure." She looked well into his eyes and smiled. She was nervous, yes, but felt safe and a little happy.

They were only ten paces from the bed, yet she grew impatient with the journey. One thousand questions were raised, tossed about along the way, and all one thousand were quieted by his warm breath on her neck. But she was falling, falling into a misty dark, when her eyes opened with a start. Hannah shuddered. The memory always brought chills to make her shudder. Soon she was able to let her eyes close again. "Be gentle. I'm a little afraid. I'm actually a lot afraid."

Discouraged, Lincoln's hand came away from her breast to a cagey stop further south. Hannah brought the hand back up, up under her shirt and over a quickening heart. "Gentle, but not *too* gentle, okay?" she clarified. "I'm a little sensitive right now, but by no means fragile."

Her nipple hardened under his attentions. Hannah hardened her apprehensions as well, speaking through her nervousness. "Shakespeare said that all the world's a stage, and all I gotta do is play my part. I used to joke of being cast as someone loving you, but now it turns out it's not a joke. It's funny as hell, but it's not a joke. So let's get on with the show."

She went to the sliding glass doors overlooking the narrow deck to the quiet street below. "I'll work the lights," she said, reaching into the folds for the drawstrings to the shades. They made a dusty descent. "The box office is now closed." Hannah added, quietly and for no one but herself, "We offer discounts for seniors and students, and there's always plenty of free parking."

The curtains, also long undisturbed, came undone stiffly, letting go a chunky dust cloud coming to life in the feeble rays still trying to shine through. Along the way to him she pulled her shirt over her head; by the time she reached him she was using it to wipe her eyes.

Hannah quickly had him out of his shirt, eager to finally—at long last—try her hand at removing the rig; but she soon realized how little experience she had in removing prosthetic limbs, and just when she was really wanting to make a good impression. Not letting on though, she told him, "Just give me a sec. I think I got it … there."

Since the prosthesis was fitted by the technician, no one but Lincoln had taken it off. None had any call to. None had expressed the initiative. And this sat well with Lincoln Dollar, yes sir, with his fierce independence and all that what-not. It had never come up, and that was fine by him, yes sir. Hannah then pulled the unit from his arm. No one had ever done that. And she stowed the dangling straps before dropping it on the growing pile of clothes behind her. No one had ever stowed the dangling straps.

"There," she said again, having completed her task, more to herself than him, adding, "Not bad, if I do say so myself." Hannah was even a bit proud for having figured it out, as she stepped out of her pants and ambitiously went to work on his. In all her labors, in all the dusk, through all her tears, Hannah never once noticed the mist in her lover's eyes, and that was fine by him, yes sir.

They laid together, old friends, new lovers, traveling to the day's end. Hannah wept though much of the journey, and smiled through even more. She spoke little, save some colorful cursing and tactless references to the Messiah. On four occasions she burst into laughter. Twice she broke into song. Show tunes. With matted hair and sweaty eyes, she looked to him sadly, though intently. "Damn, I feel cheap right now."

"Why would you say that?" he asked, stroking her hair, kissing her forehead and eyes.

"Cheap, like inexpensive. I'm under a Dollar. Get it? Under a buck!" She began to cry once more. The movement began anew. Again she called to the son of God. She pulled at his hair. She pulled out his hair. So sweaty and warm and feeling so good against her, Hannah felt inclined to thank him, after which she bit him—twice—and then let the rest of the afternoon pass in whispers. She didn't know if he heard. She didn't care. Everything else was redundant.

Hannah woke first, slowly peeling herself away and rolling to one elbow, from where she could watch him sleep. With each passing second she came to love him a little bit more until, at the very moment when she knew for sure she would never be able to leave him, she did just that. Hannah couldn't wait any longer. She had to pee.

Her feet hit Lincoln's floor in the usual fashion, but those feet no longer felt like her own; nor were her legs the same legs she had gone to bed with. Her torso was also different, as were both her heart and her head. Hannah was changed. Everything was changed. She had purposely gone to Lincoln with expectations of change—she'd wanted change—but she hadn't any idea it would be to such an extent. She wondered if it was obtrusive, blatant. *Will mom notice? Will Kate?*

She sat on the toilet looking at her new *self* in the mirror. Hannah was not so changed that she couldn't still find the humility to laugh at herself, cutting a ridiculous reflection sitting naked on a strange toilet with her elbows on her knees, and glowing. Hannah noticed she was glowing, but she often glowed.

Washing her hands and face, she looked again in the mirror for signs of lost chastity. She found a few: a blushed complexion and kindly lovers' bites dotting her shoulders, her neck and breasts, and there was abrasion around her mouth from hours of kissing, and as much time biting at her own lips.

Hannah momentarily pondered the mirror's offering, wondering if she might be pretty. Upon close inspection she was pleased, and that was enough for now. She wasn't any knockout—which was okay—but on a good day she could pass for pretty. Besides, Lincoln thought she was pretty—she could tell by the way he looked at her—and that was more than enough for now. He'd certainly made her feel pretty. His robe was hanging on the door. She felt it for its softness. She smelled it for his scent.

Hannah reached inside the curtain to turn on the water. She stepped in, letting the warmth rinse her old body away. She ran soap over her arms and stomach, down her legs and between. Gently washing the intimate flesh, her mind wandered, taking her to the dark, wet alleys of a cold, hard city. Hannah wanted the wanderings to stop. She wanted the questions to stop. *What if? What would have become of us? What if it was taken—stolen!—that which I needed to give only to him?* The scene recreated in her mind, the same as it often did, bringing sobs to rise in her throat, and tears to flow as hard and fast as the water playing against her skin.

She was walking on the street with Lincoln, when suddenly he was gone. Strange men, like scavengers, were quickly upon her. Tangled in her clothes, she could do nothing to fight them away. Hannah wanted to fight, but couldn't. There was the rough stubble of a strange man's chin scratching against her face. It was the same stubble of the same strange man who had stuffed a weathered bandana into her mouth. It tasted salty with a strange scavenger's sweat. Hannah gave up and gave in as everything went to black. Still Lincoln was gone.

Of a sudden, an explosion pierced the concrete blackness—and another. The whisker-stubbled stranger relented, leaving Hannah taken aback with the sudden change of heart. Then Lincoln returned, speaking with someone, speaking at someone, and stubble-chin now lay on the pavement beside her. A portion of his head was missing in the front, its contents slipping to the asphalt, reflecting the moonlight. Stubble-chin now looked up at her much the same as he had looked down on her. It was an empty face, a stupid face—an angry face, made angrier still for the draining hole.

Another explosion.

The pavement was hard, cold and wet.

Hannah was brought back around when she dropped the soap. Bending to retrieve it, she *thump*ed her head on the handrail. "Son of a bitch!" she cried, feeling for lumps and signs of blood. She found neither, but it didn't stop her from rubbing the spot and cursing forth.

Her commotion produced a tapping at the door. "Everything okay?"

She looked again at her fingers for signs of blood. "I thumped my head."

"How'd you thump your head?"

"On this stupid bar. Why do you even have this stupid bar?"

"For older tenants, I suppose."

"Then older tenants suck."

"You know you don't mean that. Are you okay?"

"No, I'm not. I'm fucking pissed. And you're right; old tenants don't suck."

"Should I call for an ambulance?"

"No."

"You want me to go away?"

"No."

"Can I help?"

"Maybe."

He waited a moment before asking, "Did you like the sex?"

Hannah had to think. "I don't see what all the fuss is about, but it was okay."

"Are you mad at me?" he asked.

"A little. You wanna come in and sit with me?"

"Can I turn the fan on?" he asked.

"I kind of like it steamy."

"I could tell. Is it okay if I smoke?"

"Only if you turn the fan on."

Lincoln sat on the toilet, lighting a cigarette. "I've never had anyone in my shower before."

Hannah pulled back the curtain enough to show her face. "I've never been in a guy's shower before."

"What's it like?"

"I suppose I could get used to it." She pulled the curtain back all the way. "What was *this* like?" Other than her parents, a small handful of healthcare providers, Katie and the girls in gym class, no one had ever seen Hannah naked. She felt all the more naked awaiting his response. "Well?"

"Well what?"

"Don't you like me?"

"I do. Very much."

"I thought so. Tits not too small?"

"They're small, alright, but they're nice—both of them, really nice. You're all nice."

"C'mon. Guys only say that to get into a girl's …" She closed the curtain and leaned back in the spray, long past satisfied and content. "I want to put this to bed for good, forever. I'm not going to pretend it didn't happen, but what's done is done. It wasn't our fault. It just happened. I wish it didn't, but it did, and I want to forget that it did. If I feel the need to talk about it, I'll get a shrink or something. Until then, I want to let it go. What's done can't be undone."

"Are we still talking about the sex?" asked Lincoln.

"No, we're not still talking about the sex. I'm referring to something else."

"Okay then, I hear ya. What's done is done."

But it wasn't really done, for Hannah went on, "You own me now—you know that, right? It's written somewhere, some hippy-dippy, Zen Buddha thing. You saved my life, so now you own me. I'm indebted to you forever and ever. What do you think of that?"

"I'm not sure what to think of it."

Seeing that Lincoln now supposedly *owned* her, he thought to take the liberty of parting the curtain just enough for another quick peek. Her wet back was to him. She had one foot on the ledge of the tub, carefully drawing his razor near the top of her thigh. Looking vulnerable, she had gone past beautiful.

Hannah knew she was being watched and quickly finished. She turned to him, taking his head in her hands and kissing him deeply, making no efforts at keeping him dry. "And just as you own me, one day I'm going to own you." She stepped back under the water with the air of one quite sure of herself.

Lincoln watched her wringing her hair, having lost most of what she said. Maybe something about ownership? He could not respond, as his heart was pounding so.

Hannah turned off the water. "Much better," she said, stepping onto the mat. "Now, let's go back to bed and see if we can get me … yeah, let's just head on back."

Later that evening Hannah was laying comfortably, listening to the purr of his uninterrupted sleep and knowing that something powerful and special had now fully entered her life. She drew a line through that life. On one side was the old, and on the other the *here and now*. The old side seemingly insisted on returning, but could scarcely present itself as more than mere black and white line drawings, stick figures scratched onto a mixed up child's sketching pad. The *here and now* was colorful and vivid. The old was charcoal; the *here and now* was filled in by an assortment of 'Sharpies,' the hard lines drawn with a Hershey bar.

Hannah was gone from the dreary plains and alit smack-dab in the land of merry-*oh!* And not only was the *here and now* vibrant, there was a certain tingle in the air as well, and everything smelled really good.

Lincoln was fast asleep, his brow puckered and lips pursed. She watched him, wondering about his nocturnal thoughts. "What is it you dream, my sweet?" Hannah imagined him soon sailing off. In another galaxy she would steal away upon his star-bound ship, but at present she was content enough to watch from the wake. She had a vessel of her own in need of piloting. The ships' courses would have to intersect at some other time—hopefully. "Bye-bye, spaceman—for now."

Confident and satisfied, Hannah crawled from the sheets. She gathered up her clothes and left the room. She poured another short spot of the whiskey, at which she sipped while scribbling some lines at the kitchen counter.

The city of Preston was different. The sidewalk was different beneath her new feet. It was a little past midnight, and as sweet and kind an evening as any Vermont summer is willing to offer. The warmth of the night hugged her like an old friend. Enwrapped in the warmth of such a friendship, Hannah was halfway home before realizing she had nothing on her feet. She thought to use the forgotten sandals as an excuse to change direction, but she knew, once returned, she'd never be able to leave there again. So she decided against it and laughed aloud at herself, smiling the rest of the barefoot steps along the way.

Lincoln returned from his dreams. He might have thought them only the most pleasant of dreams, had there not been Hannah's scent on the pillow and a leaf of stationary atop the scent, and her sandals on the floor beside the bed.

The note bade him farewell with the sweetness of reluctance. As an afterthought, she'd written, 'I'll see you soon,' and closed with some sloppy kisses symbolized by sloppy 'X's. The after-afterthought said, 'You don't really own me. I was kidding about that part—ha-ha—but I wasn't kidding when I said I'll own you. That much is true.'

At the end of the after-afterthought, Hannah added, 'It was even better than I imagined—a lot better. Thanks.' She underscored *lot* before running out of paper.

-7-

With business in Preston wrapped, Lincoln set off with a carload of imperatives and plans to be in Brooklyn by noon. In fairness, he couldn't allow the events of the past few months to rain on the watercolor that had been painted. He was not casting any blame, but he wasn't taking it this time either.

Myriad memories danced about as he drove the exit streets. They were mostly good memories, and this was the most difficult of all to comprehend. None of the old stuff was coming up. He'd had a good run and was leaving Preston with infinitely more than he had brought with him. Accepting all the world as a stage, Lincoln wound up thanking the City of Preston for the brief scene change. It was, after all, the setting in which he acted in his first love story. And if the world truly was a stage, he had to commend the lighting department for the present scene, as well, for the warmth of the rising, perpetual spotlight shone with promise. He had one stop before his exit stage-south.

Lincoln pulled up to the curb in front of the Fields' home with intentions of leaving his parcel on the stoop and stealthily continuing on. He might have done just that, had Art Fields not opened the door, frumpy in his robe and slippers.

"Good morning," Lincoln stammered, like a kid caught elbow-deep in the cookie jar before the dinner bell.

"How do you want your coffee?"

Resigned that he was staying, Lincoln answered, "Black."

Art returned with two mugs and sat on the stoop. "You don't have to leave. We can work something out."

Lincoln also sat. "I don't think that's possible. Not right now."

"Hannah says you've got some theater gig lined up in Manhattan."

He nodded.

"It looks like she and Katie are going to Tulane in the spring, but they want to take some time off before they go, do some traveling."

At the beginning of the conversation Lincoln had been uncomfortable; now it was Art's turn. "Connie and I ... all you've done for her and Katie ... hell, all you've done in this town. We were worried about her, but I think she'll be okay. This whole business is gonna blow over. I know it is. These past couple of days, it's like she's in the clouds again."

Lincoln could imagine Hannah among the clouds—presently inappropriate, as in his clouds she was naked, the soft, puffy white accentuating her curves, while softening the rougher edges. She beckoned to him from the clouds to join her: *Come to me, my love. Come with me. Can you hear those mandolins and flutes?*

Like a snappy, sassy wind, Hannah's father dispersed the clouds. "I was always so wrapped up in the business, I couldn't see what was going on at home. One day I turned around and my little girl was all grown up, just like that. It's difficult for a father—at least it is for this father. Connie told me to slow things down or I'd miss it. I only hope it's not too late." It was a difficult dish for Art to swallow, but the coffee was helping to wash it down. "The worst part of it, I've even been jealous of you these past couple of years, like she was latching onto you because I wasn't doing my job, you know, the way I was supposed to." He paused. "Man, this is awkward."

Lincoln agreed.

Art rearranged his thoughts. "The thing of it is, if you're ever in the position, just be good to her. Hannah and her mother are all I got. And if you ever need anything, promise you'll come to us first." Now that the worst was over, he let go a short laugh. "Christ, you really stirred things up around here. If nothing else, it's sure been entertaining, and I know I'm not the only one who thinks as much."

It was a compliment coming in a roundabout way, but it arrived to find the former teacher somewhat moved. "Before this gets any more awkward, I'll end it by saying that Hannah's the person she is because of you and Connie. You have a real nice family, Art." He rose in preparation to leave. "Give this to her, please, for me" Lincoln handed off a small, hinged case with a black velvet covering and sterling hardware, accompanied by an envelope. "It's been looking for a home."

Art was putting them in the pocket of his robe when he noticed Hannah's footwear on the stoop. He caught himself before broaching the subject.

Lincoln offered his hand. "Thanks for everything, Mr. Fields. I hope to see you and Connie again soon."

Art received him with genuine affection. "Best of luck to you, Mr. Dollar. Call us, please. Keep us posted."

Lincoln turned and walked the brick pathway. He waved once more, then got into his car and drove down Maple Street, leaving Hannah's father sipping coffee on the stoop.

Art watched his daughter's lover fade into the morning, grateful that the man had come into his family's life. When the car turned on Oak Street and was gone, his hand, spurred by curiosity and some inherent fatherly nosiness, reached into the pocket. He paused in search of some justification for his snooping, found none, but still he opened the case just the same. There, resting atop a plush violet velvet lining, was the Purple Heart. Art eyed the decoration with the admiration he believed was its due. The gold trim captured and reflected the morning sun. He closed the case and looked again in the direction of Lincoln's departure. "Isn't that something."

He bent to retrieve Hannah's sandals from the stoop. Smiling, he went into the kitchen, poured another cup and sat at the table. While his wife and daughter slept, Art once more opened the case, marveling at the beauty and symbolism of the award. He was not long in making its connection with the missing arm, although a little longer in wondering how it should come into his daughter's hands. Seeming of its own accord, his admiration for Lincoln Dollar increased, so that again he said aloud to no one, "Isn't that something."

He closed the box and went quietly up the stairs to where Hannah slept. He placed the envelope and the case beside her head. She stirred slightly, and he thought he saw the hint of a smile on her lips, causing his chest to heave and his breath to catch. He ached to lean in and kiss her, to smooth her messy hair; but, rather than disturb his daughter's dreams, he left her to cradle in Morpheus's strong and gentle arms.

Had he enough curiosity and fatherly nosiness to open the letter as well, Art would have known that that particular Purple Heart meant little without someone to share of it. He would have learned more than he needed to know of what Lincoln felt was 'an incredibly special evening.' Had Art enough curiosity to open the letter, he would have known they would all share of one another's company again. Though, without opening the letter, still somehow he knew.

Act Three

-1-

The clouds of a promising Indian summer hung idly, like cotton balls swept from a dusty attic, until finally bullied they gave way to an overcast cuing the coming storm. The air grew cold; the rain was incessant. What had hinted at a pleasant September now threatened to fade into a dark and dismal November, without a care whether the valley got any autumn whatsoever.

Hannah and Katie loaded the bumblebee with clothes, books, stacks of music and a cooler. Accepting meteorological warnings, they were heading for warmer climes. Point A was the Preston Valley and point B was somewhere near New Orleans; otherwise they did not know where they were going, nor did they really care. Their only objective was to arrive, wherever *there* presented itself, with passion and some semblance of style. Above all else, wherever *there* turned out to be, they would arrive there together. With three months to play before reporting for classes at Tulane, the girls headed south.

The bee was Hannah's graduation gift. In the dealer's lot, while Art considered the safety records of Volvos, the convenience of mini vans and the versatility of SUVs, Hannah had wandered off and sealed the deal on a 1972 Super Beetle, bright yellow with a new black top. The car looked like a bumblebee, and although Hannah was deathly afraid of bees, she had to have the Beetle. Before the papers were signed she had christened the car *B,* and had decided that B would need fog lights, a bigger sound system, a new set of wheels and something to cover her modest front. More than anything she was excited for B to meet Kate.

Katie fell in love, just as Hannah reasoned she would. Giving B the once-over and declaring her among the coolest cars on the road, Katie wondered aloud why the Volkswagen Motor Company would stop making such an awesome model as the Beetle. Hannah replied that she didn't know, but reckoned "Yoko Ono probably had something to do with it." Upon discovering the motor in the rear of the vehicle, Katie was totally sold. "Instead of pulling me around, she'll be pushing me.

I'll have two whacky chicks pushing me around. Makes me feel kind of special." Katie, Hannah and B. And then there were three.

They sped along the highway on a quest to nowhere. Both were eighteen, and each straddling different lines between bitingly cute and somewhat beautiful. B, the oldest of the three, was also kind of pretty in her own right. There was barely an entire outfit between the three. B was the only one wearing a bra.

Running with the top down, their contrasting hair flew in the slipstream. The casual observer, at sixty miles per, might have viewed the pair as a Thelma & Louise for the new millennium, or something in the vein of Elizabeth Cady Stanton and Lucretia Mott. There was even a hint of Ma Barker and Bonnie Parker as B's stereo petulantly screamed about rocks and rolls. Hannah was at the wheel. Katie, a little high on wine and feeling playful, whiled away the miles by lifting her shirt and jiggling her breasts for the long-haul truckers, each flashing eliciting moaning, hungry wails from their thunderous horns. The girls waved boisterously, leaving the slow bulky rigs in their wake.

Hannah turned down the radio. She went along a ways in silence, occasionally looking to her friend. Now three years together, they were inseparable. They were a team, sharing interests and opinions, chasing the same dreams. If one was ill, the other suffered. When one was happy, the other was elated. If one was hurt, the other felt the pain. Hannah was nearly incapacitated, unable to stand the silence any longer. "I love you more than anything. You know that?"

Katie was touched, but only mildly, not really thinking much of it. "Yeah, I know." Her bare feet were pressed against the glove box. She was dividing her attentions between admiring the polish on her toes and staring blankly at the expanse of highway ahead; then, between those attentions another thought began coming through the haze of the sun and the murkiness of the wine. "But why would you say so just now? You're setting me up for something, so let's have it."

"You know me well," remarked Hannah.

"I know you better than anyone in this great big, fucked up world, and I know you're stringing me along, so out with it." Katie reached through the seats for the wine bottle in the back, pouring the white zinfandel over what was left of the ice in her travel mug. She offered her partner a taste.

Hannah licked and *smack*ed her lips. "I've got a secret."

"Yes, you've been acting strangely these past several days now. You know, it's so annoying when you do this, because it always comes out the same. First I'll get tired of waiting, till I reach the point where I don't give a shit. Right now I'm at the point where I'm tired of not giving a shit, but not too tired to remind you that no one ever finds you as cute as you seem to find yourself. You won't have your silly secret by the next exit, I guarantee it. You're dying to tell me, so I'll simply wait. I don't mind waiting." This, of course, wasn't true. Katie had little patience, but she knew she wouldn't be waiting all that long. "Worst case scenario, once we stop this car —" she reached into the cooler for a fistful of cubes "— I'll tickle you until you tell me, or piss yourself, whichever comes first."

Katie began running laps around her track of reason, here a lope, there a sprint. She recalled the past several months, the past couple of years, the greatest moments of her life. Hannah was home and seeming back to her old self—that amazing, fun-loving self before Lincoln Dollar came in and turned everything around. She was back to the time they were two, running extemporaneously without the bother of others in tow. Still, whatever Lincoln had done, he had left Hannah a better person for his kindly efforts; she was even glowing from the experience.

Katie wondered if Lincoln was gone for good, if he had slipped out much the same as he slipped in. Her selfish self wished this was so, while the better part of her missed him. Hannah would be missing him even more, so for her sake Katie tried not to wish him gone for good; because, after all, Hannah was glowing from the experience. *Hannah was glowing?*

Katie's carnal intuition started flashing excitedly in reds and neon purple. Hannah smiled mischievously, B's wheel tight in her hands. "Oh my God!" Katie screamed. Hannah went on smiling, her eyes trained on the road, her attentive driving not so much an effort in traffic etiquette, but more to avert her friend's glare. This was more than Katie could bear. "Pull over, Hannah! Stop this fucking car!"

Hannah went through the motions with the lights and gearshift, rolling slowly to the shoulder. Katie was out of the car before it stopped, pacing the grass on the side of the road, her hands going from her hips to holding her head, back to her hips, then clasped behind her back. She mumbled under her breath.

Hannah sat in the grass, wondering if she should have said something sooner, maybe should have consulted with Katie beforehand? But it was too late now. Besides, Hannah hadn't been all that sure beforehand, and maybe even a bit less sure after the fact.

Katie eventually stopped pacing—she said "Finally!" somewhat under her breath—and came to rest stretched out beside Hannah, asking calmly, "How was it, dear?"

"Certainly the best I've ever had."

Katie was long past excited, coming on titillated. "Tell me everything. *Every*thing."

Hannah recounted the warm afternoon which ushered an even warmer evening. Some special details tried to push their way to the forefront, but she reeled them back, wanting to keep some of it for herself. She was sure Katie could fill in the finer parts of the narrative. Katie was pretty good at filling in.

"I couldn't wait any longer, couldn't wonder any longer, and I don't think he could either. You know I wanted him so. I couldn't even sharpen a pencil in his class without getting all wet. And I know he wanted me. I could see it in his eyes. I could feel it in his ... well, you know. Then everything got all messed up and I didn't know for sure if I would ever see him again." She was close to embarrassed. "I nearly threw myself at him. You would have been proud." Reclining, she added, "It was wonderful. It was so wonderful." She brought her arms behind her head and closed her eyes. "I'm crazy about him, Kate. The way he was holding me, I could actually feel his love. This man I've come to love, loves me right back. How cool is that?"

Katie had the beginnings of tears in her soft, dark eyes. "I'm happy for you, happy for you both. I truly am. Just don't push me out, girl. I can't be no third-fucking-wheel. You know I can't. You know that isn't me." She was uncomfortably close to begging, with her inexperience at begging showing apparent. It was Katie's time to reel it in and change course, change the subject. "How's he going to do that play? With the arm, I mean. The way it keeps going from past to present, and he's supposedly some hot-shot, high school football douche. I've been wondering how he's gonna pull it off."

Hannah accepted the invitation to talk shop. There would be time later to tap out the details of the amended relationship. "He never brought it up, and I didn't think to ask. Must have some good people in makeup."

She'd been so wrapped up in bedding the actor she'd forgotten about the acting. Her ignorance left her in the dark, waiting in the wings, trying to fill production holes and trying to keep all this ignorance from Katie. But Hannah couldn't keep anything from her, not with Katie reminding her of as much with her version of a gentle scold: "Here it is—right here—this is the shit I'm talking about. Right now, behind those gorgeous eyes, you're thinking of how to make Lincoln Dollar playing Biff in New York somehow be about you. So, please, could you discontinue?"

"Okay, I get it, but you don't have to pick on me."

A Delaware State Police cruiser pulled up behind the yellow convertible, its occupants suspiciously lying in the grass. The trooper exited the vehicle and stood at the opened door. She rested her elbow on the frame, her foot on the rocker panel. A shining 357 weighed heavily loaded on her ample hip. Looking over the top of aviator sunglasses at the green license plate, the trooper called it in.

"Busted!" said Katie. "We're going to end up in prison and miss our vacation. And a chick cop—figures! A blow-job's not getting us out of this one. You keep your mouth shut. Let me do the talking."

"Like you don't always do the talking anyway?" Hannah reminded her.

The trooper approached. "Problem today, ladies?" With raised eyebrows, she noticed the half-emptied wine bottle on the back seat.

Katie looked up, shielding her eyes from the sun. "No problems at all, officer," she said, respectfully, shyly, a regression to days when she had more to hide. Were the trooper of another gender, Katie would have been using other tactics.

"Been drinking?" the trooper asked.

Hannah was thinking about walking straight lines, touching her fingers to the tip of her nose, when Katie angelically chimed in, "I've had a bit of wine, officer, but my lovely chauffeur is intoxicated only with the sweet nectar of newfound love." Katie giggled at her own cleverness. Hannah could only nod to affirm. The trooper smiled beneath the mirrored lenses, but with that pang of jealousy which sometimes accompanies the envy of another who has found what one has so desperately sought, however to no avail. "I'd have to dust off the statutes, but I don't think that's against the law in Delaware. Let's just hope you never sober up." By now the trooper was sharing of the infectious intoxication sweetening the air around. "You ladies play it safe out there."

"Thanks," said both in unison. Katie got to her feet, bending to give Hannah a hand. The trooper returned to the cruiser, turned off the flashing lights and continued down the highway. The girls waved as she passed.

Katie pulled Hannah into her arms, kissing her hard on the mouth and squeezing so tightly as to nearly break her wallet. "I'm happy for you. I really am."

Hannah returned the embrace. "I knew you would be. Whatever happens," she vowed, "I'll never let anything come between us. Okay? I'll give up anything—*everything*—so long as I get you. Don't you ever forget that. I want Lincoln, but I need you. Everything else is icing, sweetheart, but you're the cake. You're my Katie-cake." It wasn't enough, though, to feel Katie's head nodding unconvincingly on her shoulder. "Promise you'll never forget that."

"Alright, already, I fucking promise."

"Good," said Hannah, though neither was very convinced.

They were precisely the same height and often stood together with their foreheads touching, looking in one another's eyes. This was their special, familiar embrace, and it was during such moments that the two felt closest and strongest. Energy flowed from one to the other and back. Both felt it, they loved it, and they honored it and respected it. More than mere friendship, what the two shared was an ideal—it was a shared destination which they referred to as *friendship*, but only to have the term for simplicity and flow in the drama, and because they were hard-pressed to wrap it up in any other term. They'd become parts of something larger than their selves, and it was during certain moments, such as when making out on the side of a highway, that they were most aware of all they shared.

A passing car sounded its horn at the sight of a couple of cute girls embraced on the side of the road. Maybe they'd seen a kiss, speculated, perhaps fantasized, but they could never possibly know.

-2-

The girls were three days on the road, moving a bit more slowly and starting to feel a little gamey. While they loved B dearly, they had grown tired of sleeping with her; beside her in a tent on the roadside, the next night inside her, hiding from a pouring rain. When at last they alit on the soft, sugary sands of Virginia Beach, all three needed a break. All three needed to wash.

They played stationary tourists, looking fabulous and acting famous, trying to come off as complex, and all the while radiating a presence. Each morning they watched the sun rise from the sea across the Chesapeake Bay, spending their days sunning on the sand, swapping supine for prone, or stretched on gaudy plastic furniture beside the motel pool. Once the sun was down, they went into the city, gorging on seafood and the local entertainment. The sailors and soldiers from the base at Little Creek made certain the girls didn't want for any attention, and the girls did their USO-best at entertaining the troops.

Many a tall, olive-skinned, clean-cut sailor asked for Hannah's hand, at which she led each one to the floor. "I'd love to dance," she kindly answered, "but we're going to keep all that touchy-feely business in check." And when those same dancing servicemen ventured to punch Katie's card, she just as graciously accepted their advances: "Sure, we'll dance. Yeah, you and me are gonna dance."

No matter how late they played the night before, the girls never missed a morning watching the sun rise out of the bay. At times they arrived back at the motel just in time for the sunrise. Then one morning Hannah was alone to wait for the sun, and not the least pleased with the arrangement, when Katie splashed onto the beach with but minutes to spare. She was out of breath, plopping herself down on the sand next to Hannah. "I hope you weren't worried."

Hannah put an arm around her. "I was more worried for the sailor."

The salty breeze of the bay was on them; soft, like the shells of the crabs, it blew a calming freshness and carried away what few cares and concerns the girls might have imagined they had. B waited patiently in the parking lot, facing east so that she could watch the sun rise, too. A deflector kept her dashboard cool. It made her look like she was wearing sunglasses.

Hannah and Katie arrived late on the sand one evening after having gone to the theater. They had attended a farcical French piece which left Hannah believing she'd been given ample return for her fourteen dollars. Katie was left thinking of the ways her participation might have made the production more substantial, of how she could have juiced up the show with her blossoming theatrical talents.

They were drinking wine and eating fruit from a cooler between them, laid back on lounge chairs they'd pilfered from the motel pool. Hannah was looking out to sea, holding an orange without the heart to tear at its peel.

Young men from the academy at Annapolis were showing off their sailboats, splashing the shallow inland and getting their keels hung up in sandbars and testosterone. A short way down the strand a band of washed up pirates were gathered round a bonfire. Hannah couldn't hear the pirates, but she imagined they were swapping sea stories and singing sad shanties in low and lonely voices. She watched the flames rising from the pirate's fire, dancing with the night, licking at the stars. She could almost feel the warmth.

She rolled the orange around in her hands, speaking of the importance the shad and oysters played in the Chesapeake Bay eco-system. She told Katie she believed the cleanup efforts were paying off, that the bay seemed "fresh and busy."

Katie was only half-listening to Hannah's two thousand-word commentary on the one thousand-word article she had read— something about a pushy guy named Chad eating oysters. She was thinking of something else. "Did you see the audition notice at the theater? For that Russian play?"

The Sand Box Theater had posted bulletins announcing a coming production of *The Cherry Orchard*. The subtitle described the work as *a tragi-comedy of frustrated sexuality and cultural fatality*. Hannah recalled being miffed at the lengthy billing and not bothering with the rest of the advertisement. Her attentions remained concentrated on the pirates round the fire. "What about the notice, dear?"

"It said, *all are encouraged to audition.* Do you think we should audition?"

Lincoln Dollar had introduced them to the theater two years before. Both had been sucked in, way in. Hannah was in it for the lights and the literature, the proscenium arches and makeup, the sets and the scenes and the smells. Katie was in it for the sparkling limelight. For Hannah, the theater was a magnifying glass, a microscope, a telescope and her standard, through which she inspected and dissected and rejected, and against which she gauged all that she was learning of her world. Katie's theater was a mirror—hand held, full length and ceiling-mounted—used for the inspection of herself. The stage was their passion. The theater was their calling. The theater was calling.

"The last auditions are tomorrow," Katie went on. "Do you think we're ready?"

Hannah came from her reclined position to face Katie. Her clear blue eyes were commanding the ocean moonlight with feverish alacrity. "We've had it pretty easy so far, you and me. We've been kept nice and warm, cozy and secure, but I don't want to lean on anyone anymore—no one except you. We've got to find the security we need inside ourselves. If we can do that, we can do anything. We could audition for any play we want." She reached over and took Katie's hand. "Security comes of being whole. I've never felt entirely whole in my life—not until this very minute. I'm feeling whole, Kate. I'm feeling secure."

Katie looked at her with interest, admiration, and a great deal of love. "You get more and more intense every day."

"Think so? Think I'm intense?"

"I do," said Katie.

"Do you trust me?"

"I do," she said again.

"Completely?"

"Yes, I trust you completely."

Hannah rose from the lounge chair, bending to kiss the top of Katie's head. The pirates' fire had grown calmer, the flames now grappling to reach above the passive embers. Some of the pirates were dispersing, the band growing smaller, when Hannah asked, "Would you be willing to do anything to follow me into that cherry orchard?"

Katie's arm was wrapped around Hannah's legs, gripping at her calf. Her voice was muffled in the cotton fabric of Hannah's shorts. "I'd follow you anywhere, for anything. I'd follow you straight the fuck into hell."

"Wow," smiled Hannah, immensely satisfied. "You're such a good girl! And I just might hold you to that, but first we're going to need more wine." She shook the sand from her sandals and strolled up the beach to the motel.

Katie reclined in the chair, adjusting her bikini top, taking time to cup each breast as she arranged it, time enough to leave each nipple a little harder than she found it. She lit a cigarette, staring into the stars, pondering an audition with a professional theater company. Katie wondered if she had it in her. She often wondered if she was good enough. She wasn't sure she was good enough, but she was certain that Hannah was good enough, and that was good enough for now. With Hannah's offer to lead the way, Katie was willing to tilt her own lance at the windmill.

Back in the motel room, Hannah tossed back a spot of vodka, wondering if she was soon to do something silly. She had another spot and wondered if it wasn't downright stupid. After a third she didn't mind how silly or stupid she might appear. She returned to the beach with a chilled bottle of wine, taking a garden rake from against the building on her way past.

Katie was pulling her hand from inside her bikini bottom when Hannah returned. Referring to the rake, she asked, "Did you trade in your broom? That's like going from the Volkswagen to a Jeep—very off-road."

"Witches don't use roads," Hannah returned. "We fly." With that she flew off down the strand towards the pirates, suggesting that Katie join her. "But only when you're done playing with yourself, mind you. I'm going to need your help with something." She was excited to meet the pirates. Perhaps one of them had a hook for an arm. She had a thing for guys with hooks for arms.

Hannah greeted the swashbucklers with a nautical salute: "Fal deral, you rim-dim diddies and rum-dumb dummies." She whispered to Katie, "I got the pirate-speak from dad's Gordon Lightfoot records."

However, Hannah found they weren't pirates after all, but a merry band of young tourists mixed in with some homegrown lads. There wasn't an eye-patch, a parrot, or a rustic sea dog in the lot; and obviously no Lightfoot fans, as Hannah's ahoy was met with only unenthusiastic stares. Nor was the band sipping at rum or grog; rather, they drank Budweiser. *St. Louis Pirates?* Hannah speculated. *Maybe a ball team?* She asked of the merry band, "Who can tell me the difference between flotsam and jetsam?" The question, the same as her greeting, was met with more muddled shrugs. "Definitely not pirates, Kate."

Katie opened an offered beer, opening a conversation with a couple of guys in the group, while Hannah leaned on the rake staring reflectively into the glowing embers. She contemplated the prospect of auditioning for the Chekhov play, staged in that beautiful little theater on the beach. Hannah loved the Russian dramatists, and she was especially fond of Dr. Chekhov. The play would constitute another of her dreams coming true, and she was more than ready to add another to the list. While she may have shared somewhat of Katie's apprehension, she would not take on any of her doubts. She couldn't. One of them had to grab for the bull, so it looked like Hannah was off to the rodeo. She had designs on the horns—*be big!*—but she'd settle for a porterhouse, the balls, or even a little piece of tail.

Charred pieces of driftwood littered the perimeter of the ember bed. "What did you use for the fire?" Hannah asked. "Is it just stuff from the beach? No lumber, nails, glass; no beer cans, nothing like that?"

The faux-pirates looked at one another until one elected himself as representative. "I made the fire. It's all drift from the beach, nice and clean, nothing to fuck up the ozone, if that's what you mean."

"Good," said Hannah. "Your language, however, isn't so good." She offered her hand to the leader of the band for introduction. "And this is my girlfriend, Kate—Katie. Would you mind if we used your fire for a moment? For a little experiment?"

"Be my guest," said he, with an amiable demeanor and a passable bow, reluctant to give up her hand, and unsure if he would ever drop another f-bomb.

Hannah went to the coal bed with the rake and began clearing away the larger charred pieces. She set about constructing a length with the coals, soon evolving into a strip some couple of feet wide and nearly ten feet long; twenty square-feet of neat rectangular fire, eight to ten hot and fluffy inches thick. The stirring invited the coals back to life, to which they happily obliged to over one thousand degrees.

Hannah was not long in the project before Michael realized her intent. Katie sat cross-legged on the sand, nervously sipping her beer. The rest of the group watched on with growing curiosity.

Once satisfied, Hannah addressed everyone present, though her words were for Katie alone. "Fear is the single greatest obstacle in any life, but once a fear's faced, it loses all its power to control."

Katie stared with increased trepidation into the livened embers.

"Fear, once acknowledged, cannot control us. It might slow us down, but it can't stop us, not once exposed for the nonsense it is."

She kicked off her sandals, using her bare foot to etch a line in the sand. "All that we have, all that we *are*, is here." She went to the other end of the fire strip, drawing a circle in the sand with her heel. "Everything we want is *here*: Fame and fortune, peace, freedom and love, happiness and security, God, Allah, Buddha, whoever, whatever, the list is endless. Everything's inside this circle, right here waiting for us, but only if we really want it bad enough, only if we've got the guts enough to go for it."

Hannah returned to the other side and toed the line. The heat licked at her feet. She clutched the bottoms of her shorts and pulled them up the last few inches, lest the fire should crawl up her legs. They were her Columbia shorts, her favorites. Hannah had paid thirty-four dollars for them, and would rather they did not burn—not if she could help it anyway.

Katie stood. "You made your point. You don't need to do this."

Ignoring her, Hannah vowed before the group, "Nothing is ever going to stand in my way again, ever. I'll have what I want, and I'll take what I need." She whispered to herself, "I do hope I understand this correctly."

With a substantial portion of lip between her teeth, Hannah walked into the fire … walked slowly and calmly … until she stood in the circle on the other side. There were only seven steps, taking less than a second each, but still the journey stretched from one world to another. She turned back to face the wide-eyed group. No one spoke.

By this time Katie had moved to the line. She hadn't any choice. Looking across the bed of coals, the red and yellow and orange embers burned in Hannah's shining eyes. A new awareness burned there also. Hannah was gone, gone to a different world, and Katie could not risk letting her get away.

"It's alright," said Hannah. "Trust me, Kate. Come to me. Have faith, sweetheart. Have faith—in *us*."

Katie closed her eyes … and when next she opened them she was in her darling's familiar embrace.

Michael then followed, reasoning there would be an embrace for him on the other side as well, believing it worth the risk to wrap his arms around this pair of lovely young performers on the beach.

Presently the three were holding one another, huddled in the circle in the sand. "Thank you, Michael," said Hannah. "Thank you for the support." She was shaking.

"Tell me you've done this before," he said.

"I saw it on Discovery. Something to do with thermo-dynamics. I figured if those knuckleheads on TV can do it, so can we. How's that for a leap of faith? I can't believe you guys trusted me, you really trusted me. Thank you both so much."

No other pirates dared venture the firewalk. Some stepped farther away from the burning bed, while the rest held their places looking on at the random, impromptu display.

Soon they all looked on as Hannah and Katie returned hand in hand down the strand. But Michael would not have them leave so easily, not after all they'd gone through, and so he called after the girls, prepared to show them and the rest of the world that he could hold his own with the soundest and wisest of swashbucklers. "Um-yes," he said, pausing to clear his throat (*a-hem*); "regarding the flotsam v. jetsam"—he held a hand aloft with the fingers hanging alimp, not so much for Hannah and Katie to see (not in the moonlight and with them now well on their way), but more as a sort of visual reference for his own satisfaction and verification—"I'm quite certain that the flotsams are the ones that hang from the roof of the cave." He then did something with his other hand, coming up under the first to mirror it, possibly—just maybe—trying to convince himself that jetsams rose from the floors of caves to meet these flotsams, forming what could only amount to a nautical spelunker's wonder. Just as quickly, however, watching them walk away, he let the entire business fade.

Hannah waved a smiling *thumbs-up* over her shoulder. "He's a funny fuckin' pirate, that one there."

The girls lay back, staring at the moon and stars. "You're amazing," Katie said at last. "I don't even remember what my life was like before you came along. Sometimes—" She could not finish.

"I know what you mean, my pet. Anyway, fluffy coals and human feet are both poor conductors of heat. Get it? One need only hop on and keep moving. Just don't stop. That's all there is to it. No stinky skin, no *mind over matter* bullshit, nothing paranormal, but it sure does produce some dramatic-fucking-effect, doesn't it? Did you see those guys? That was exciting! Oh! What fun!" Hannah was infinitely pleased with the performance. "Wasn't it? Man, we should have passed the hat after that one!"

Katie did not respond. She held her head in her hands, looking away, the moonlight reflecting in her hair, tears streaming her confused, distraught and overwrought countenance.

Hannah reached over and took her hand, squeezing it for a time. "We'll need monologues for the audition."

"I know," said Katie, recomposing.

"You okay?"

"I will be."

"Good girl." Thinking aloud, Hannah continued with a measure of affection, "I think I'll use one of Hannah's monologues from '*Iguana*.'"

"I'll use one of Anya's from *The Cherry Orchard*," said Katie, in a rare display of practicality.

-3-

Hannah woke the morning after the firewalk with blisters on the arches of both feet. There had been some tingling during the night, but she paid little attention to that. Something or another was always tingling in the night.

She sat on the toilet, using a needle to lance the fleshy bubbles. Once relieved of the clear fluid, Hannah found the feet were none the worse for wear. They were rough and calloused, making her wish the rest of her was so tough. And the blisters were the proof, proof that the firewalk was not part of another dream; but if it was a dream, Katie had dreamt the same, for there was a large blister between the toes of one of her feet. She called out, "I got a problem here."

Hannah came from the bathroom with the needle and a warm, wet cloth. "Let's have a look." She moved in quickly to stab the bubble. "It's not too bad," she assured her, washing the injured foot. Hannah washed the other foot just for the fun of it.

Katie lifted it to have a look. It really wasn't that bad. Regardless, it was well worth it for the experience. "Must be one of the coals got stuck in there. It doesn't hurt."

"That's good," said Hannah, kissing both the feet, "but we'll put some ointment on it just to be sure." She went for the cream in her bag.

"Ointment," Katie repeated with a giggle. "What a stupid word—*oint-ment.*"

"Maybe there was something in the coals. The program said to watch for rocks and stuff. We'll make our own fire next time, make sure it's good and clean." She rubbed the medication into Katie's foot. "I knew in my head we could walk on the fire—anybody can do it—but, push come to shove, my fears tried to tell me I couldn't. Fear trying to override the intellect. I was rather enjoying the conflict."

Katie was wearing a small teddy and nothing else, a teddy which left most of her ass wondering if she'd gone abed wearing anything at all.

She sort of listened, but more watched as the woman lovingly massaged the cream into her foot. Enjoying it immensely, the sensation ran up her calves and into her thighs.

"For heaven's sake," Hannah protested, "put that fuckin' thing away." She slapped Katie's leg. "Jesus Christ! It reminds me of Taco Wednesday at Preston High. Hey, remember that cook with the harelip?"

"Si, señorita," Katie replied, then nearly begged, "One time, Han—please."

"For the thousandth time, *no*." She chastised her good-naturedly, "My, but you're a persistent little slut." Hannah did, however, teasingly walk her fingers up Katie's leg. "And your persistence is only one of the many reasons I love you."

Though she could forego the Mexican entrée, Hannah couldn't stop herself from pushing Katie back on the bed and jumping on top of her, pinning her arms and letting her hair fall in her face. Nor could she stop herself from kissing her dozens of times. "Tell me about your mother. You never talk about your mother."

Katie couldn't avoid Hannah's pressing weight, but she could avoid the pressing of her questions. "What's to talk about? She was a whore who split town." This was as near as they ever got to the subject, but Katie ventured to take it a step further. "Besides, I don't remember much. She was gone before I was born."

Hannah nuzzled her nose in the pillow under Katie's head, next to her neck. She whispered, "That doesn't make any sense, silly. Anyway, I know she left just before we met."

"That's what I mean," Katie returned; "my life didn't even begin until I met you." She was pleased when her comment elicited another kiss. "And I want to remember even less, so let's say you don't ask me about Cathy, and I won't ask you about New York. We'll each have something to keep to ourselves."

This comment elicited a bite, along with a realization for Hannah. "It's getting so I think less and less of that," she said, following with two more kisses. "How about you tuck away that taco, and we'll see if they'll let us play in the Sand Box."

They stood outside the theater with monologues, headshots, a good deal of confidence and a little bit of attitude. Winded with the walk, they had but moments before the last auditions. "Feels strange auditioning for someone else," said Hannah. "Almost like I'm cheating on Lincoln."

They went inside and followed the paper arrows to the green room. They had slipped in, trying to blend in, when the stage manager warmly introduced himself as Charley and put their résumés side by side on the table, at which they sat for an informal interview. He noticed the similarities on the two sheets of paper: Same dates, same plays, same venues.

This was their first experience with a professional stage manager, and while the girls were a bit nervous, they both knew enough of their craft to know that their nervousness, the same as the stagefright they often experienced, would better serve once it was channeled into a more useful energy. Their mutual comfort with the stage manager also aided the interview.

Charley Evans was fifty-ish. He had tired eyes with lines reaching from their corners, as though pulled tight from years of smiling and just as many years of sorrow. He kept what was left of his thinning hair tucked up inside a worn down cap from the old country. The pockets of his vest were repositories for some of the tools of his trade. He smiled tenderly, spoke softly, and had a way of looking into the girls' eyes which made it seem that he was searching behind the words for what had inspired them. Upon first glance Charley might have reminded one of the sketchy uncle who shows up at the holidays, just often enough to remind parents of the importance of keeping an eye on the kids; but upon closer inspection, one might justly conclude that those same children would become better people in the company of silly old Uncle Charley.

The trio kept their voices low, out of earshot regarding others in the room. "These are ambitious plays for high school theater," said Charley, checking them out, feeling them out.

"We were an ambitious troupe," returned Katie, straining to keep her inherent cockiness in check. "We did a few shows during the school year and some summer stock on the green. Best Shakespeare in New England. Kickass stuff. Sets, props, marketing, we did it all. Every show well received, and every one of 'em a money maker."

"Impressive," he interjected, though not impressed—not yet, anyway. "Your friend here doesn't say much."

Hannah finally chimed in, "It's hard to get a word in with her around, Charley. Kate could be in the electric chair and she'd start shooting the shit with the guy pulling the switch; but what she says is true, and she's the best actor you're going to audition, tonight, anywhere, anytime. If you get us cast, I promise you'll have a good show. When the lights come up, the house will be out of their seats. I guarantee it." Hannah was surprised by her own frankness; surprised and wondering if she could ever deliver on such a guarantee.

Now Charley was impressed; so much so, that he repeated, and this time meant it, "Impressive. I'm starting to like you two."

"Wait till you get to know us," Katie returned with her sweetest smile; "you'll like us even more. You get us a shot with your boss in there and I promise, on Hannah's life, we won't let you down."

The stage door opened and a young woman came through. She wore the expression of an actor who had auditioned well, and who had reasonable hopes that those in the audience shared in her opinion. Charley summoned another prospect, escorting him to the stage area. He brought with him the last-minute photo-bios to pass on to the director.

Once they were gone, Katie let fall her self-righteous semblance of professionalism, unable to wrap her head around what had transpired. "We'll either get the leads, or Charley's coming back with security."

This audition represented a crossroad in the journey. The young actors sat at the intersection, staring up at the light, waiting for it to change, engines revving. The two were, and would forever be, a package deal. It was both or neither, across the board. One had to know them only briefly to know that they came as a team, as Charley quietly informed the director of that very thing.

The young actor returned from the staging area with the expression of one who won't expect a callback, of one who knows he auditioned poorly, and who was left without doubts that those in the audience felt the same. Charley followed the actor with the expression of one who had had the misfortune of having to witness the painful audition. He'd seen the young man's headshot land face-down in the *perhaps another time* stack of neglected performers.

"Katherine Pauley," the stage manager announced, "you're up. The boss is center house, a half-dozen rows out. Introduce yourself, your piece, take some time for yourself, then let him have it."

Both girls stood. "Wish me luck," said Katie.

Hannah pulled her close. "You don't need luck. You're brilliant and beautiful, with talent, tits and ass—you're a natural." She reached for a grab of the theatrical assets.

Katie laughed until she reached the door, leaving Hannah and Charley behind. They returned to the table. "Says here you played Miss Julie. What an amazing play. How'd it go?"

Hannah didn't need a stage to begin the audition. "To be honest, Charley, it was a little *dirty*." She kept her cards close to her vest at first, sifting for an approach with this stranger who would soon be her boss. She was confident he was going to be her new boss, though Charley was as yet unaware. Presently Hannah laid her entire hand. "Some viewers of that play might wonder what transpires between those characters once they're behind closed doors. We, on the other hand, didn't allow for any speculation in our production." Hannah rolled her eyes as such that Charley had to hear the rest. "My theater teacher played Jean."

"Go on," he said.

So she did. "The chorus came on with their mandolins and flutes and dancing, and instead of our characters holing-up during the break in the action, we stole off to the pantry to do the deed—if you know what I mean. That fourth wall was like a big window, everyone peeking in like nasty voyeurs. Naturally, I wanted to give them their money's worth; and poor Lincoln, God bless him, he wasn't in any position to back away. Some of those knuckleheads in the audience thought we were really doing it, right on the stage. Caused quite a scandal, me being seventeen at the time, and him my teacher. Needless to say, it'll be a while before I perform up there again." Hannah rolled her eyes again, if only to let the manager know that she was comfortable with being barred from the Preston stage, from any stage.

Charley was grinning, near to salivating. Hannah had a new friend. And though they were alone in the room, still she leaned in close to her new friend, *hush-hush*, saying, "I'll tell you a little secret, Charley. Nobody knows this, not even Kate." She was so close she could smell peppermint gum and cigarettes on his breath. "Every night I did that scene—we nailed five shows before they finally pulled the plug—every night …" She struggled for her explanation, and ultimately it was her trusting the stage manager that allowed her to share her secret. "Let's just say, now, whenever I have … you know, the big 'O,' when I'm getting off … I can still hear those mandolins and flutes."

"You're an interesting woman," said Charley, laughing a bit.

His smile was such, and his eyes sparkling just so, that Hannah believed he genuinely thought she was interesting. She was touched, humbly accepting the compliment. "Thank you, Charley. That's sweet of you to say."

"You and Katherine are pretty close."

"As close as two people can be." But his expression seemed to beg another question, prompting her to continue, "No, no, no. We're not a couple. We're not lesbians, if that's what you mean." She laughed. "We're so much closer than that. She's my best friend. You must have a best friend, don't you, Charley?"

"Yes I do. He's my roommate, and we *are* lesbians. And I can't wait to tell him about you." After a short laugh, he continued, "This show's got some good female roles. I wouldn't be surprised if Carl could find something for you."

There's a foot in the door, thought Hannah. *Uncle Charley thinks this Carl guy can 'find something' for us.* But Hannah didn't want a mere foot in the door; she wanted the door left wide open. She chose her words carefully, looking into his eyes and allowing him into hers, feeling an imminent need to bring Charley up to speed on a couple of things; but gently, without turning him off, without pushing him away or shutting him down. Still, hard as Hannah tried, her words were near reproachful. "I appreciate your help, Charley, I really do, but we don't want simple roles. We need substantial roles, lots of lines, lots of action. We can get plain old roles at the bakery." She reached across the table and took his hand. Her eyes were getting misty. "It wasn't coincidence that brought us to this theater, brought us to you; it was fate, and it's a fate coming with big guarantees, big pay-outs. We walked through fire to get here tonight. Who else has given you as much?"

Charley was sold. "If you're as good out there as in here, I believe you'll get those substantial roles. Is Katherine as … forthcoming?"

"Oh, Kate's the absolute best! And she can act circles around me, but don't you dare tell her I said so."

Thus far, Charley was performing most splendidly with the interview. Hannah had only a couple more issues to cover, one concerning the director in the next room. "I hope there aren't any casting couches to surf in there, Uncle Charley, because we don't go in for that shit. That's *not* how we work."

The stage manager found this especially amusing. "You ladies needn't worry about that, but there was a young gentleman last night who may have piqued the boss's interest."

"Gotcha."

Katie returned from the staging area, closing the door a bit more aggressively that she might have. She wore the expression of an actor who had kicked major ass, and whose performance, she reasonably reckoned, was appreciated for the major ass-kicking that it was.

"How'd it go?" asked Charley.

"Went okay, thank you." Katie was matter-of-fact in speaking to the stage manager, but with Hannah her voice trembled with excitement. "I used the Shakespeare. It just kinda popped out." She put her mouth next to Hannah's ear. "I fucking nailed it, babe. Best ever!"

"Good girl," said Hannah, bringing her hand to Katie's cheek. She was returned from a place new to them both. Katie's eyes spoke more than any words, spoke of how it was and how it would be.

The stage manager watched the interaction, believing that they shared something, some deeply personal secret. He tried to put a label on the secret. *Oneness*, he called it, stopping short of thinking them halves, but conceding that together they made something whole.

Charley was thinking as much when Hannah asked, "May I go in now?"

"Yes, please. Go on in, break a leg." He was torn between going into the house for Hannah's audition, or staying behind to chat up Katie. He decided to stay, reasoning there would be plenty of time to see the other on stage during the next couple of months.

Hannah took the stage, while Katie took a seat, flipping through a back-issue of *Rolling Stone*. After some time, she asked, "When do you post callbacks?"

"Tomorrow, at noon, in the lobby." Charley added, "Hannah said she would walk through fire for a part in this play. How about you?"

Katie looked up from the magazine. "You must have misunderstood her, Charley. We *did* walk through the fire. That's what brought us here." Katie wouldn't have bothered explaining, even if she had the time, which she didn't because Hannah had re-entered the room.

Her cheeks were flushed. Her forehead and temples perspired. There was the glint of stardust in her eyes. She went directly to Katie, offering her a hand from the chair. Hannah turned to the stage manager, offering him the same hand. "Call backs are when?"

Katie answered for him. "Tomorrow, noon, lobby."

"Tomorrow at noon is fine. I'm glad I met you, Uncle Charley. I do hope we're able to work together. I know it'll be fun." She moved to leave.

"Bye, Charley," said Katie following.

It occurred to Charley Evans after the girls were gone that it would have been prudent to have simply given them the scripts and rehearsal schedule, to save having them picked up the following day. He was thinking as much when he entered the house to confer with his colleague. He found the director in the center of row six. Charley stumbled momentarily, his eyes unadjusted, as the only illumination in the grand room was coming from two soft spotlights trained on the center of the stage.

"What do you make of that pair?" the director asked.

"Probably safer than going for a straight."

Carl Thomas was flipping through the pages of résumés, placing discarded lives on the scrapheap of actors on the neighboring seat.

"You do know," added the stage manager, "that was a poker metaphor, as opposed to *poke her*."

Carl often ignored much of what his colleague said, more as a defense mechanism than anything else. "The one with the dark hair, Katherine, she was tough with that court scene from *Merchant'*. Some of the best acting I've seen in a long time. But I don't know about the other one. If she was going for cute, she certainly pulled it off. She's cute as hell, aggressive, impassioned, a real presence."

"It's exciting when they come in off the street like that," said Charley; "exciting, but unpredictable. Still, and you know I'm a penny-pinching bitch, I'd put my money on both of them."

"You saying we should cast them? You willing to accept that responsibility?" The director was holding the women's headshots in either hand at arm's length; Katie posed with a seductive, almost criminal smile; Hannah affecting a near-tragic leer; night and day, Yin and Yang, Martin and Lewis, Cheech and Chong.

"I think we may have our Anya and our Varya," said Charley, however with guarded confidence, "but there's no way I'm taking the responsibility."

Hannah was first to breech the silence which accompanied them back to the motel. "You'll get one, I'll get the other. I love them both, so it doesn't really matter to me."

"Doesn't matter to me either, but what if they want to give us something else?"

"Then we'll let the breeze blow us from the Chesapeake Bay, with our dignity intact, and go someplace else where the sun comes out of the sea." Reflecting briefly, Hannah added, "We were pretty cocky in there, weren't we?"

"Certainly were," Katie agreed.

"I used to think it was cool, but I'm not so sure anymore. I wonder if it doesn't come off as more, I don't know … maybe unbecoming."

"Well, it makes me feel pretty good," argued Katie. "I like being cocky when I got the shit to back it up. I've always been good at using the ginger-peach to get what I want, but with a script I can get what I want by using my head—and of course the ginger-peach, *if* I still need it."

They walked on a bit longer in silence before Katie reminded Hannah of the first time they went on stage, when Lincoln Dollar pre-cast them in *The Crucible*.

"I've been thinking of that. Pre-cast or not, it's good he still made us audition. The practice came in handy. He made us audition so we'd be ready for tonight and for every other night."

Katie felt good about the entire business. "You think this is the way it's going to be?"

"Who knows? It's the way it is right now, and that's all we've really got. We need to milk it while we got the chance—squeeze what we can from the experience. And we'll need a different place to stay."

"I was just thinking of that."

"I'd so love to talk to him right now," Hannah said, seemingly to herself.

Had she been thinking of anyone else—anyone else—Katie would have been insanely jealous. As it was, she was only mildly jealous, just enough to make her notice that she was jealous.

Returned to the motel, they took their places on the beach. It was the end of a kindly September, the warm, salty breeze coming at them from the west. Gentle waves kissed the sand, as the actors stared into the vastness of sea meeting stars in the night. There was no need for conversation, as they listened to the melodious song of the sea, the waves singing of dreams without any boundaries, of endless possibilities, of friendship and freedom, and of many other fun and wonderful things.

-4-

Off in the distant and optimistic east, long across the sparkling bay, the bright red, orange and yellow orb languidly crawled up to begin the day.

As Hannah and Katie were dreaming dreams with building excitement, Lincoln Dollar moved excitedly about New York trying to rebuild his life, while at the same time the V.A. technicians were working to rebuild his arm. He raced between rehearsal schedules and visits to the hospital to have the new hand in place for the show's opening. The surgeons had, literally and figuratively, cut it close.

Two operations were required to connect the artificial hand, made from a mold cast two years before, cast on the day following Hannah and Katie's stage debuts in Preston. Lincoln had been suffering an emotional hangover the morning the cast was made. The process was painful and joyful, mesmerizing, tantalizing, titillating and exciting; that was the girls' performances, of course, not the hospital procedure. The evening when the girls embarked upon their theatrical journey was forever etched in his memory, though he could barely recall the technicians using his hand and a pail of plaster to create the reverse model for its new manmade mate.

Cables ran through the short plastic shell of the prosthesis, attaching it to the muscles of Lincoln's arm. He found the pseudo-fingers moving a novel experience after more than five years without that simple luxury. There was some initial discomfort and difficulty, however, not unlike when he was first fitted with the hook; and the artificial hand was bulky, slow when compared to the functional hook. It was shaded to match Lincoln's flesh, easily passing for the real thing when he was on stage, and getting back on stage had been the strongest motivator for the replacement. He often had to remind himself as much, that he had swapped the awkward appendage out for the stage—for the theater—

and not for other reasons, such as making himself more marketable for far less professional purposes.

With all that vied for his attentions, still Lincoln found ample opportunity to miss his friends. He was in costume and makeup when he went to the phone. Unable to put it off any longer, he had to hear her voice; rather, he wanted to check on the girls' progress, just to know that they were safe, maybe to see if there was anything they might need. Convinced these amended reasons were ripe for making a call, he rang them up at last.

Katie had gone alone to verify the callback listings at the Sand Box Theater. Hannah would play Anya and Katie was cast as Varya; logical choices, the girls playing adoptive sisters. When later they celebrated at poolside, cocktailing with their department store blender and a pre-portioned mix, Katie was excitedly planning the upcoming rehearsal and performance schedule, while Hannah had grown sullen.

"Just call him, for Christ's sake," Katie nearly begged, wearied with the girl's melancholy, self-pitying disposition. Katie took great pleasure in her own self-pity, but found it grotesquely unbecoming in others.

"He's working tonight," Hannah returned, checking the time, adding, "He's on stage this very minute. We should have stopped on our way when we had the chance. We should have stopped in New York. I wish we'd stopped." Her heart was as heavy as the telephone. "Besides, I don't want to push him. And suppose I call and he's with someone else. That would be yucky. I couldn't deal with it right now."

Katie protested, "You're not making any sense. Why would he be with someone else when he's got a little *someone* already? You're a silly actress acting like a silly schoolgirl." Still, Katie hoped for the sake of all that he had not taken up with 'someone else'—not yet, anyway. Once immersed in the production, however, she believed Lincoln's fading away would constitute barely a blip on their fun-filled radar.

Still Hannah brooded, sipping the frosty cocktail in sadness and staring into the swimming pool. The water, illuminated by a single, ghastly, ghostly light, rippled in the warm night's breeze. The eerie reflection well befit her mood. She was reaching for the pitcher of frozen drink when the phone lying next to the pitcher started to sing. Her fingers stumbled over one another in chasing after the call.

Katie watched the pool water lighting her friend suddenly turn a pretty emerald green, absorbed by Hannah's sparkling eyes and returned to the world a lovelier, less intimidating color. Katie watched as Lincoln's words played like music in Hannah's heartsick, schoolgirl-near-prom-night ears. Katie couldn't hear the lyrics, but she imagined that he sang of things like patience and reassurance. The song seemed to have a warming effect, which also pleased Katie, as she needed Hannah feeling warm just now, she needed her friend's cloud lifted. Watching the cloud dissipate, Katie felt as good as though it was happening to her; because, in a sense, it was. When Hannah rose and moved a few steps away to speak with him privately, her whispers made Katie feel even better, so much so that she adjusted her position and rested comfortably, contentedly knowing all was once again well in their world.

Hannah was handing the phone over when the screaming began. *"Ow! Ow! Ow!"* Katie was in a panic. She'd been sucking her straw like a professional when a clogged piece of lime pulp worked free and let loose a sluice of the icy juice which was more than she had bargained for. She squeezed her head in her hands and tried to force the beverage out through her ears. *"Ow ... ow ... ow,"* until it subsided ... *"ahhh."* Briefly testing the waters before letting go a relieved sigh, she said, "That was the most fun I've ever had with my clothes on."

Katie and Lincoln spoke quickly of many things. Before handing the phone back, she told him that she would only tolerate losing Hannah if that loss was to him—to Lincoln Dollar—trying to sprinkle her concession with some humor, and saving her jealousy for another time, such as for when she next listened in on Hannah's continued conversation:

"Me too ... nothing, if you were here ... I know, I wish we could ... I miss you. I ... I ... we'll talk soon."

Hannah finally pressed the button to end the call. She sat staring at the nebula of stars above her, believing herself among them. Hannah blushed with pleasure, struggling for humility, gazing at the sky prickling with a thousand million tiny dots of light, reminding herself that she was but one of those dots, and by no means the brightest of all the thousands of millions. She could no longer afford to visit the center of the nebula. With that belief duly noted, she brought herself back. "I needed that."

"You did. What'd you mean by 'nothing, if you were here?'"

"He asked what I was wearing."

Katie felt somehow relieved. "All the sudden you're risqué?"

"Something I learned from the master."

Katie perked up. "Shit! I forgot to ask—"

But before she could finish, Hannah said, "He got a new hand. Cineplasty, he called it." She went on to explain at length what had briefly been explained to her. "He said when he's under the lights you can't even tell."

"Interesting."

Hannah protested mildly, "Yes, but it would have been nice if he'd said something sooner."

"I know what you mean. How dare he go forth with such a procedure without first consulting his seductress?" Katie agreed wholeheartedly. "He's got some nerve."

"Fuck you," said Hannah.

"If you start trying to control him, you'll end up making a mess, and I'll be the one who gets to clean it up."

"You're right," Hannah conceded, "but be a little patient, will you? I'm still kinda new at this."

"The best thing to do is nothing. He's nuts about you. Just let it happen."

"You think?"

"I do."

"He's happy we're doing the '*Orchard.* Says we'll be great Anyas and Varyas."

"You bet your ass we're gonna be great."

They reclined in silence, the pool light dancing on them lovelier and livelier than before. Hannah wondered of a time when she would be in Lincoln's arms once more. Katie tried picturing Lincoln Dollar with two hands.

-5-

The girls took a small furnished flat close to the bay, a short walk from the Sand Box Theater. Quickly settled, they had six days before beginning the four-week rehearsal period and three weeks of performances; six days of playtime to begin playing at playing. They were cast in substantial roles, with a rehearsal schedule shorter and more compact than they were accustomed to, so they didn't hesitate in preparing, having been trained to show up with their characters well near developed. Together they developed the characters of the Russian sisters, Anya and Varya.

The cast was announced and the crew assembled for an informal read-through of *The Cherry Orchard*. A veteran actor, Emily Rose, was cast as the girls' stage mother. The woman's given name and surname were Emily and Rose, and she introduced herself as such so that it sounded as though the two should be connected; this alone made Hannah and Katie fall for her. Emily Rose was the epitome of grace, beauty and inspiration; she was the woman the girls imagined when they imagined the consummate stage actress, long before they had occasion to know one. She brought credit to the profession and force to the production. An actors' actor, she treated the other actors, regardless of experience, with respect that invited even greater respect in return. Past experience meant little to Emily Rose when viewing the production at hand, with her often reminding casts and crews, "Let's help each other out, people. We're all in this together."

A beautiful woman, Emily Rose had long, flowing auburn hair. Her face was thin, with large, deep brown eyes set far apart, and lashes so full and rich as to seem weighty. Not tall, still she carried herself in a way that added to her natural carriage, carried herself with a sort of paradoxical humble-pride, as such to make women with foresight half her age lift their eyes to take serious notice. Just a smidgen over fifty and gladly admitting to the number, she had spent thirty-five of those years on many stages, from Montreal to Miami—stages real and metaphorical. The consummate stage actress, still Emily Rose maintained a style and dignity all her own, and not a product of her often less-than-transparent profession. Her credentials were impressive, her commitment beyond apparent.

Katie and Hannah would come to spend a lot of time with Emily Rose. They looked forward to the relationship, not only for the friendship, but for the acting experience invariably coming along with it. Listening to Emily Rose read from the script, Hannah discovered a closer connection to her own character. She came to know Anya a little bit better, as daughters often learn about themselves from their mothers, with or without a playwright's script. She was eager to get on stage with Emily Rose. The woman's projection, her eye contact, her waltzing gait and the gentle flowing movement of her hands, the subtle gestures and her lyrics, all these added warmth to the rushing feeling Hannah felt at the prospect of working with her.

Another professional was slotted to play Katie's love interest on stage. The girls found him pretentious, affected, and a general boor. His name was Walter Gordon. Hannah called him 'the man with two first names,' while right off Katie simply referred to him as 'the Gordfather.' Katie didn't much like him, but that was okay; she needed the Gordfather only to get his lines out, and she could take care of the rest. While prepared to do all she could to help him shine, still Katie would rather have had the role of Anya.

Hannah's stage-lover was a young man whom she found two-dimensional, hollow, and perfect for the part. Gabriel Croft's acting ability was adequate at best, but his parents' pockets were deep enough to hold the theater troupe in times of trouble, thus ensuring Gabriel roles in whatever productions the company chose to mount. He recognized Hannah as the woman he had seen walking through fire on the beach, but found her far less mysterious under the florescent lights of the conference room. Still Gabriel struggled over his lines as he sat across the table from her. Hannah took his cues and gave him lines, thankful that Chekhov's script didn't put them in too close a proximity to one another.

Gabriel's older brother was also cast. Michael Croft had some acting ability, but he rarely applied it, except when absolutely necessary. He wasn't putting himself out there for mere community theater, as though he was saving himself for something to come later, or not. What his colleagues in the theater didn't know, except maybe Carl and Charley, was that he held rein on his own talent to allow his younger brother more presence. His self-appointed role was to shine on the sibling, rather than to detract from his light. Michael was pleased to see the girls from the beach sitting across the table at the reading. They were the only people he had ever accompanied through any fire. "Small world," he said to Hannah.

She replied, even cynically, "Until one is saddled with the task of cleaning it up." Deep down, though, Hannah was infinitely happy to have his familiar face in that strange and near-surreal room. Michael helped to connect her to that room, to that beach, and to the play. He would remain forever endeared to her as a fellow firewalker, as one of those whom Hannah said, "walked on gilded splinters," having stolen the expression from a Dr. John song. *Till I burn up, till I burn up, till I burn up ...*

The girls were comfortable with the ensemble, in no small part the result of the comfort they exuded in the group. They found especially dear the fragile, eighty year-old Spenser, who was cast to play the deaf and discontented manservant in the drama. They were hungry and eager to work, and feeling they had the talent to bring it about. The cast and crew were prepared to take their collective skills and ambitions to play in the Sand Box.

October had fallen on the Chesapeake Bay, the autumn a mild friend whom the girls welcomed. They whiled away many hours on the beach in preparation for their parts, their scripts and paperwork trying to fly away on the salty ocean breeze. But they never let a script fly away.

Time finally came for the first physical rehearsal, and no one would deny it was a theatrically memorable evening. The entire cast and crew was prompt and prepared—somewhat amazing in its own right—but the evening's entertainment didn't stop there. Before the night was over the little director would be moved; Charley the stage manager would have a renewed faith in the medium. Some of the veteran actors would be professionally embarrassed, and those novice thespians would end the evening painfully inspired. Others would leave the theater that night with the fears of having to return.

The stage was alight for a scene from the first act when the cast reeled in the anchors, ready to set the sails. Captain Carl was tasked with holding the rudder in the choppy waters of the first rehearsal. Barely out of port, however, the ship threatened to take on water. A lot of water.

Captain Carl Thomas was a slight man, small in size. He was the bastard child of a melodramatic life, full of struggles which he sought to convey by seeming caught up and tangled in artistic high tragedy, with works of such monumental importance that he expected himself to be one day knighted—Sir Vitude or Sir Cumsolar, depending on his time of the month—for the lifetime of great and selfless sacrifices made. And Carl had the artists' temperament, that suffering sensitivity so often expected (and so invariably found) in many regional theater directors. He believed his maroon beret increased the effect of his presence, when really it only detracted from his already diminutive stature.

The director's toughness escaped Hannah and Katie. He couldn't quite seem to pull it off. Also, he was already at a disadvantage in their eyes, as being the second theater director they had worked for when the first was such a demanding act to follow. Still the girls liked Carl, and thought him kind of goofy-cute, agreeing he would be off-the-charts goofy-cute if he wore riding boots and a monocle, slapping out his whiney stage direction on his leg with a crop.

Barely into the first scene, Cap'n Carl inquired after Hannah and Katie as to why they did not have in their possessions their scripts, adding, "being unprepared is a waste of limited and valuable rehearsal time, and shows a blatant disregard for the rest of the cast, the crew, the very playwright himself!"

The last part of the director's angry admonition pained Hannah. She could defend herself against charges of being unprepared if she had to. As for the cast and crew, they could speak for themselves. If she ever showed them any disregard, she expected they would tell her directly, so she could amend her performance accordingly. But this business about showing disregard towards the playwright? Towards Dr. Chekhov? No fucking way. Anton Chekhov was among Hannah's favorite Russians, second only to Catherine, the Second, not the First. Hannah pretty much loved all Russians. She especially enjoyed a good, stiff black Russian. The silliness of the whole affair, mixed with the rise in Carl's voice and intonation, caught her off guard. And coming from the dimly lit center of the sixth row, from where she couldn't clearly see the director, only added to her ill feeling. She did her best to shake it off, saying to the director with forced comfort, "Just tell me where you want me, boss, and I'll make sure I'm there. I shouldn't need to write down my blocking."

It had been some time since Hannah had bothered with any blocking notes. Her former director used to tell her, and rarely more than once, where she was to locate herself during any given point in the action; afterwards, every rehearsal and performance would find Hannah in that same spot. This was the way it had always played out; and, as it seemed to work, Hannah didn't question it, nor did she attempt to modify it. Regarding such an approach, Lincoln had said, "If it works, don't fix it," prompting Hannah to offer her slightly different take: "I have no idea how it works, and I'm too afraid to mess with it." This was how Hannah and Katie were trained to work. They had also been taught to drive through rehearsals with minimal interruptions. Hannah was ready to continue.

Cap'n Carl sifted through her reply until he found a hint of mockery at last, and this on top of being predisposed with a suffering and sensitive artists' temperament. The storm was brewing, further agitated by the young actor's seeming flippancy. All hands were on deck when the director's ego went overboard. Cap'n Carl grabbed for a life preserver, but was weighted further by his delusions of power and control, and by a rising anger, until the director himself rose, coming from his seat to confront this unruly antagonist. Had he been sporting that riding crop, it would have been slapping enough to bruise both his shaking, spindly legs.

"I'm not saying you'll need the script to note your blocking, Ms. Fields. You need the script so you'll know your *goddamn* lines. Christ me! Forty years in, and I'm still working with fucking children!"

Hannah's eyes widened. Her face flushed.

Katie whispered, "Oh shit," while casting a sorrowful glance in the direction of the little director.

Hannah did her best to maintain composure, pondering placating the precarious predicament. She took a long, deep breath and started counting backwards from ten. While many count *to* ten, Hannah employed the count*down* method, not unlike the threateningly ticking timer attached to TNT—the countdown to a reckoning.

The scene was reminiscent of Tombstone. Doc Holiday and Johnny Ringo were at it again. Ringo stood in the darkened theater, both six-shooters having vacated their holsters.

Hannah was not so quick to draw, but she did have the beginnings of a Holiday-twitch in both her pointers. She stifled herself with a reprimand for having become upset in the first place, something she'd been lately trying to keep in check. At the same time, she noticed how sorely unaccustomed she was to being spoken to in such a way. She even managed a smile once realizing how pleasantly unharmed her feelings had fared. She was toughening up some; that was a good thing. Hannah stuck out her chest a bit—what there was of it—and vowed she would never allow anyone to speak to her in such a way again. She decided on the Sand Box stage that she would, henceforth, always be treated with dignity and respect, not only as an actor, but as a person, as a woman. Lastly, and Hannah knew this in her heart, if a similar situation were to arise again, it wouldn't be at the hands of this little shit in the Sand Box.

She moved from under the glare of the overhead lights, to the edge of the stage, to where she could see the little director more clearly. "There's no need to speak that way," she began, her voice soft, firm and sure, "or with that sort of language. I'll have you know I'm a sensitive individual, with feelings easily hurt."

None but Katie knew what would follow. She considered other auditions while melting into the folds of the wings, to a safe distance from where she could view the coming attraction.

"As for the script and lines," Hannah continued, her voice erupting, the blood pouring into her face, "I don't need the fucking script when I have the lines in my fucking head, now do I?! You're lucky I don't have that precious script, for surely I'd smack you with it. I swear to God, you … If you ever speak to me that way again—"

Hannah was livid, even starting to shake. Fat, blue veins were prominently displayed on her neck and temples. Katie looked on with a little bit of worry and a whole lot of proud. Charley watched her from the house, his interest piqued, wondering if the performance wasn't the product of some coaching, some experimental acting experience. Soon the entire group was faded to darkness, leaving Hannah quite alone on the stage.

Johnny Ringo was down and fumbling for a reload. He was seemingly packing only a single shot, while Hannah by now was fully automatic. Then, like it wasn't bad enough to call an actor's professionalism into question, Carl ventured firing a round at her integrity as well. "You can't possibly know your lines. You've had the script but a week!"

Hannah held the wounded little director in her sights. She was nearly paralyzed with self-righteous indignation when she let go, imperatively, "Start reading, Charley. Read my cues from anywhere in the goddamn script you care to start!" She wouldn't take her inflamed eyes from Carl, lest he try to slip away. "Start—fucking—reading!"

The stage manager didn't dare refuse. Thumbing the text, he said in falsetto, "We've waited and waited for you."

"I haven't slept for four nights!" Hannah returned. *"I'm frozen!"*

"Thank God you've arrived. My darling's here! My precious!"

Hannah bit back, *"If you only knew the things I had to put up with!"*

Charley turned more pages. "Yepikhodov, the clerk, proposed to me just after Easter."

Hannah hissed, *"You never talk of anything else! I've lost all my hairpins!"*

"This place smells like patchouli."

"I think I'll go to bed! Good night, Mamma!"

Naturally, Charley had to test her one time, so for the fun of it he mixed up the end of a character's line. "We must first atone for it by suffering, by extraordinary, unceasing exertion. You must understand."

But still there was enough of the cue for the angrily animated actor to follow. *"The house hasn't been ours for a long time! I'll leave it; I give you my word!"*

She was quickly on top of every line, though not reciting them as she would during any performance; her words were sardonic and laced with contempt, tarred and rolled in broken glass, cutting, carving, severing, slicing.

The stage manager, close to giggling, was relishing the scene. He continued reading the characters' lines, randomly chosen from the text. Hannah did not miss a word, not a syllable. The professional actors were fascinated to the point of embarrassment, having barely made a beginning with their lines before rehearsals started. Those newest to the profession, those most desperate to please, still struggled with the lyrics though they slept with scripts tucked under their pillows.

"Give me some more, Uncle Charley. I don't think our fascist little friend is quite convinced."

Rogue laughter tried escaping Charley's nose, but he suppressed his amusement and went on, "Yes, it's wonderful weather."

Hannah was at her apex of attack. *"What have you done to me?! Why am I not so fond of the cherry orchard as I used to be?! I used to think there was no greater place on earth than our orchard!"*

The incorrigible stage manager had to nibble one last time. He couldn't help himself. It was the closest Charley had ever come to falling in love with a woman. "Nature needs beasts of prey that devour everything in their path. You fulfill that need."

The theater grew quiet. The actor was spent. The scene was wrapped. Hannah lowered her eyes to the slatted wood floor, searching for the words, struggling to evoke. Perspiration glistened on her brow. She retreated far into her thoughts, scanning the plays of Anton Chekhov, the plays of all the playwrights trapped inside her swimming head. At a loss, she finally realized what had happened. He was toying with her. Hannah looked to Charley for the first time since the melee began. He was smiling.

Hannah wasn't smiling. "That's not my cue. It's one of Kate's. I'm sure of it."

Charley nodded, still smiling, aching to work with her.

All Hannah's hardness melted away. She glanced around the room as one who has just come out of a dream. She was confused and a little ashamed, barely managing to stammer, "I'm sorry. I'll just go. I have to go."

Katie was coming from the wings to follow when Hannah turned backed to Carl. He was taking careful refuge in row six of the darkened house. There was easy egress from row six. "I only had to answer to you, and I'm sure that's not all that difficult to do; but you, as the director, you have to answer to the playwright, to Dr. Chekhov. Good luck with that, you little motherfucker." Hannah walked off, with Katie close at her heels.

Charley suggested, "Let's everyone take a short break, shall we?" (He reasoned Carl might need a rest.) The group dispersed to vending machines, outside to smoke, anywhere to be away from the not-so-O.K. Corral.

Back in the green room, they hurriedly gathered their belongings. Hannah threw the much talked about script into the trash. The cover read *Fields*. Her character's lines were all highlighted with bold neon yellow; her cues with subdued blue. Hundreds of notes and reminders crowded the borders of the text: Definitions, pronunciations, geographical and cultural references—the entire dramaturgical assessment was tossed into the green room can.

"I'm sorry," said Hannah. "I don't know what else to say."

Katie put her arms around her. "There'll be other plays." She used her sleeve to wipe Hannah's forehead. *"You've got to answer to Dr. Chekhov.* Where do you come up with that shit? Baby, you gave me goosebumps!" Katie squeezed her so tightly she felt her *crunch.*

"I'm so ashamed. I almost called him a cocksucker. Man, sometimes I can't even fucking stand myself."

A prissy voice came from the doorway. "An award-winning performance, honey, if ever I saw one. Or, maybe not award-*winning*, but it's worthy of the nomination. Are you so bitching passionate about everything?"

"Only theater," Hannah replied, "and especially the classics. Again, I'm really sorry. I don't know what came over me. Must be getting my period." All her rage was spent, the tiger turned pussycat, and she was still ashamed enough that she could not face him. Katie stayed close to protect her, and for Carl's protection as well.

The little director cautiously entered the room. He took up the script from the trash, looking through the pages, reading Hannah's notes here and there. "You've all these lines and cues," he said, flipping through the book, "and you know them all?" It was still too much for him to believe. "You've obviously done the play before."

She nodded her head for the question, then shook it for the statement.

"Explain so an old queer can understand, how is it you're off book in six days?"

"I can't explain it, Carl. Please, don't make me even try. It's just how I do. I used to want to be good for myself—I wanted to *look* good—but now there's more to it; now it's about the audience and Kate and you and them, and—this may sound stupid—most of all I want to do right by Dr. Chekhov. Seriously, to write something so beautiful, it would be a travesty if I didn't do everything I could to give it its due, everything in my power."

Hannah lowered her eyes, refusing to let the little director see her tears, going on as best she could, "I'm sorry I'm not better at this, but it's rare that I have to explain myself. I want to act. That's all there is to it. And it's terribly important to me. I can't explain it, but I shouldn't have to. It's just the way it is. And I'm going to act, with or without you and this theater."

The director studied her. He studied her partner. "The same for you, Katherine?"

"Please, call me Katie. Of course I know my lines, but I don't get as fired up about it." She shared a smile with Carl. Hannah, still under the protection of Katie's wing, hung her head still lower, and coiled further with embarrassment.

Carl was forced to a command decision, prompting a stand coming quickly, comfortably, and even somewhat gracefully. "Christ me! We're getting off to a hell of a start. Now get your little asses out there and put this show together." He made for the door.

Hannah was finally able to lift her head. "You still want me after that?"

Carl weighed his words with prudence. "Especially after that, you feisty little bitch. Christ me! I'll have a fucking mutiny on my hands."

Hannah called after the director once more as he left, "Still want me to bring the script?"

He turned back to find her smiling shyly. Carl walked away shaking his head, saying, "Christ me, Christ me," until he was around the corner.

The director had seen what he thought were glittering flakes and dust sparkling under the lights at the audition. During the read-through he detected, unearthed, perhaps a few precious, shining nuggets; now, having witnessed the actors on his stage that night, Carl believed his company had finally tapped a mother lode.

When the girls walked off the Sand Box stage, they might have kept on walking, as far as the little director was concerned. Yes, he wanted them, and wanted them badly, but principles were principles, and especially when casting principals. "Nobody speaks to me like that." And he meant it, kind of, and was firm, or as firm as he could be, what with his suffering sensitivity and all that stuff.

It was then the stage manager stepped in. Far too often Charley had seen his colleague's *principles* stand in the way of bringing quality theater to the bay. As a result, the two were fighting constantly. Both had quit their jobs several times over the years. Twice Carl fired Charley, and twice Charley punched the director in the mouth—the Sand Box's version of a bay area catfight. Now twenty years together, neither had the strength to fight any more. "I don't want to hear about your goddamn principles," Charley told him after Hannah walked away. "If you can't put that fag pride away this one time, I'm leaving with those girls."

Secretly, as often as Charley used such tactics, he was surprised when they still worked.

-6-

Lincoln Dollar's show had let out twenty minutes before. Patrons, a dozen or so, were in the lobby, most waiting for members of the cast and crew, when he exited the backstage door. His dark hair was combed back wet, rinsed of the gel which held it for the performance. His cheeks were flushed with excitement, and from having been roughly scrubbed of makeup. His eyes were tight from hours under the bright stage lights, but they opened wide at the sight of Lauren Stanson coming towards him.

She took his hands, taking also some time to admire him, before moving in for a kiss. Lincoln could not have been happier to see her, yet when next they held apart he could see that her smile was forced, coming slowly and painfully from somewhere uncharacteristically far away.

"This is nice," she said, referring to the new hand. "It feels rubbery—rubberlike, I suppose—but it sure looks like the real deal." She was not the same person Lincoln knew. At one time Lauren was nearly ridiculed for her open contentment, but now she was covered, guarded, tense and weary. "Is it comfortable?"

Lincoln demonstrated the artificial fingers, his rediscovered ability to grip. "I'm getting used to it, though it's not quite what I expected." To change the subject, he asked, "Where's John? I hope he isn't one of those who didn't come back after intermission."

"He's outside, and he loved the show. We both did. Everyone was good, but you, sir, are a gifted actor. I'm so glad you're back on stage."

The compliment was such that Lincoln had to kiss her once more. "It's good to be back."

Lauren spoke softly, and with a sense of forewarning. There was the same sadness in her voice that he had felt in her embrace. Something was amiss, confirmed when she said, "I wanted to speak with you before you saw him."

Lincoln was held fast. "What's going on?"

Again she attempted a smile. "He's not well." Lauren took his arm and started walking the lobby. "He's changed."

"What change? I was with you not four months ago."

"It's been like four centuries." Tears welled in her eyes; tears not for herself, but for Lincoln. Her words were also for him, but just as much to remind herself. "It won't be much longer."

Lincoln wondered if she had come undone. He closed his eyes to clear her away, hoping to open them and find that she was not there, to find the past several minutes were nothing more than a theater-induced, mellow-dramatic blackout. But when he opened his eyes, still she stood before him, wearing an icy cold countenance of affirmation.

Lauren swallowed hard, barely managing to say, "He wanted to see you again, before—" before Lincoln left her and hurried through the lobby, through the foyer, through the doors and into the night, into the throngs of Tuesday night theater strollers. He stood on the sidewalk searching.

Lauren came from the theater behind him, standing in the crowd, watching. She put her hand to her mouth when Lincoln finally found the car. She bit into that hand as he dodged the Manhattan traffic to get to her husband, to get to his friend.

The two marines eyed one another briefly before John found the button to put down the window. Both tried to smile, but both attempts were lost. Lincoln stood quiet, his chest rising in short blasts but not falling. The moisture from years of friendship and adventures came to cloud his vision, but Lincoln could see well enough to know that the feeble shaking of John's head meant that it was long past time for any tears.

With some effort, John got his hand to the window. Lincoln took it. Again the sickly man moved his head from side to side. His voice was hoarse, raspy. "The other one, Sarge. Let me see the new one."

Lincoln put the artificial limb into his hand. The pale neoprene showed all the more artificial once contrasted with John's rich, chocolate skin. Without the sense of touch, still Lincoln felt the pangs coming from his friend. He wished to be away from it. "Isn't it nice?"

he stammered. "It's better than the real—" He choked it off, the real hand moving quickly to his face.

"Make sure you hang onto this one."

Lincoln was wet and miserable in the back seat, as Lauren drove the three through the city full of life. Melancholy silence filled the car, the sort of silence butting against irony and defeat. An obnoxious, sassy rain pecked at the silence, broken by the metronomic wiping of the windshield blades, and by Lincoln's directions as to where Lauren might turn.

"I thought it was just a cold, then the flu." John and Lauren sat across from Lincoln in the cocktail lounge. They'd taken a secluded booth. The customers were few, the music gentle. The candlelight on the table flickered in Lauren's face, casting a shadow on her husband.

Lincoln stared blankly, his mind wandering over past years and recent months. His straw was busy ensuring a consistent scotch-to-water ratio. He had folded over all four corners of the napkin, twice.

"What'd they call it?" John asked Lauren. "Some kind of leukemia."

"Myelogenous," she said, her voice barely a whisper.

"That's the son of a bitch. All over inside—bones, liver, kidneys. Everywhere except my heart, right baby?"

"That's right," Lauren replied, emptily. "There's nothing wrong with your heart."

John tried keeping it light. "You know, I thought it might be stress from all the shit you were causing back home."

"How long?" Lincoln asked.

"How long were you causing the shit?"

"How long do you have?" he clarified, uncomfortably.

"Not sure. Month, week, who knows?" Painfully, he added, "Sometimes feels like any minute. All about the morphine now—patches. Can you believe it? Morphine-fucking-patches? They're delicious! Reminds me of the day you dosed me in the desert. I was higher than a kite. You remember that day?"

"I remember. I hit you twice, not knowing you'd already given yourself a couple." He recalled the painful day. The old pain mingled with the new. "Nothing they can do?" he asked. "What can I do?"

Lauren's eyes were soft and wet in the candlelight. "There was some chemo, radiation and the drugs, but we're past all that. Just trying to stay comfortable now." She broke off, studying herself and studying Lincoln. She looked directly into his eyes. "We've accepted this."

Lincoln took her as meaning he was being asked to join in this acceptance. He tried his best.

"I've thought of it often," she continued, "but never said anything, because I always considered it a sort of silent understanding between us, but it's because of you that I had the time I did with this man. They've been the best years of my life, and I'll always be grateful for that." Her tears were heavy enough now that they began the descent to steal a watery path down her glowing cheeks. She quickly brushed them away.

Lincoln drank largely from the glass, wishing the whiskey was without water. He wanted it to burn. "You folks have been a big part of the best years of mine," he may have heard himself saying.

"Check on my friend once in a while," said John. "Make sure she's okay. And be good to yourself. Keep it safe, like we agreed."

"I'll do what I can," Lincoln replied, though he hadn't any idea what he would do.

John was running low. "You were great on that stage tonight," he managed. "That's my buddy up there, I said. That's my friend playing Biff." Then trailing off — "that's my friend."

The three held hands around the table, and in the briefest flicker of a moment Lincoln sat with himself at the bar, hollow and alone, as Lauren and John went through the tunnel into Jersey, into the nighttime journey north to Vermont, back to the Preston Valley. Lincoln knew that he would not see the man again, this man who had touched upon his life so profoundly, but it was not that which troubled him; what hurt so badly was to see John in such pain. Pain such as his had no place in any life, let alone in the life of Captain John Stanson. Such pain was beneath John. He was too good for it.

Lincoln quietly closed the door of the phone booth, resting on the makeshift seat. In the darkness and solitude of the compartment his emotions came unfettered. He was holding the receiver near his face to create the impression of being on some business, when a mechanical voice suggested that he either hang up or make some sort of call. He opted for the latter. Not planning for it, still his fingers found the buttons to ring her up.

Hannah wiped the crunchy sleep from her eyes. "This is a nice surprise. Everything okay?"

Lincoln apologized for waking her, attempting an explanation.

"Do you need me there?" Hannah hoped he did. "Hold onto yourself till I get there, just as soon as I can."

Lincoln said he was already better for having spoken with her. "It'll work out," he said, though trapped in the lonely telephone booth he was hoping she would not accept his protestations.

Hannah didn't. "It'll work out better when I'm there."

Soon he was sitting back at the bar. The attendant introduced him to a shorter style of glass, adding only a small pair of cubes. The bartender had occasionally seen the guy, same barstool, same scotch, and made as not to notice the change in the customer's usual carefree demeanor since his friends' departure. His towel went round, methodically removing nonexistent spots from a martini glass, before going once more to top off the customer.

Lincoln considered gripping the glass with his new hand, but abandoned the idea as premature, with potential for causing a spill. He had become, however, adept at removing cigarettes from the package with the new south paw.

The bartender struck a match and noticed for the first time the artificial hand holding the smoke.

Lincoln saw the guy eyeing the hand. "Brand new," he said, turning it over a couple of times for both to inspect. "Got it shot off in the desert."

"Amazing, the shit they can do these days."

"Sure is," Lincoln agreed.

Neither man knew the other by name, but the bartender knew more about his customer than most everyone else.

-7-

Lincoln stood on the hotel balcony. The snows of November had come early and found their way into the collar of his shirt. Automobiles slid noisily by on the shiny highway. The lights of the small city flickered through the heavy, wet flakes, the weather providing a suitable setting for the day's later requiem. Nearly six years before Lincoln had fought at the man's side. He later returned to work at the man's side once more. He was now returned to bury the man.

Lincoln had been awake for what felt like weeks, yet still he felt no need for rest. The damp cold on him felt good. It felt fresh, numbing him, keeping him alert and apprised, reminding him that he was alive, albeit painfully. He was leaning on the railing when Hannah's arms encircled his waist. Her inviting voice wrapped around his chilled wet neck. "Come inside and get some rest. It's going to be a long day."

John's passing invited loneliness, but turning to find her helped to keep that loneliness at bay. Lincoln allowed her to lead him through the sliding glass doors, into the room, and away from the murky, mournful night.

Hannah had been waiting in his Brooklyn apartment only hours after receiving his call, on the first direct to LaGuardia once clearing the exigency with Carl. She had called the director early in the day as she watched the sun rise over the bay. "I need to speak with you."

"So speak."

"No," she corrected herself. "I need to *see* you."

As Hannah seldom asked for anything, Carl did not question. He told her to be at the theater in twenty minutes.

She had planned all the logistics beforehand. There would be some scrambling, but she'd miss only three rehearsals if she hurried back by Saturday, allowing time for travel, some time with Lincoln, and nearly a week left before the show's opening on Friday next. Still, it struck Hannah as fantastic that she was ready to debut in her first professional theater performance, but was now planning a clandestine meeting with the director to ask to be excused during the peak rehearsal period. She had determined that Katie and Charley would have to cover for her. That's all there was to it; no way around it.

Carl was waiting in the office when she arrived. It was six in the morning, leaving the rest of the cast and crew still several hours away. He had stopped to get them coffee on his way. Hannah had also stopped for coffee.

"We've plenty of beverages to wash down your latest drama," said Carl. "And this had better be good, sweet-cheeks; I was up most the night with costume changes and lights." He leaned back in his chair, putting his feet crossed on the desk, looking over the set designer's sketches, and over his reading glasses at Hannah.

She was fidgeting, seemingly trying to get comfortable, but more as an effort to disguise her nervousness. The two had become good friends during their working together. Carl was directing Hannah effectively, which alone made him especially dear to her. Hannah was shining brightly on his stage, which, among other reasons, made him adore her. The evening of their showdown was long since in the past. Carl may have revisited the night periodically. Hannah never gave it another thought.

She looked to him warmly and intently. "I have to go to New York."

"On Broadway, or off? Christ me, darling, be patient. At the rate you're going, you'll get to that nasty street of dreams soon enough."

"You don't understand. I need to go this morning. I need to go right now."

Carl's feet came down from the desk, taking some sketches with them. He canted towards her. "Excuse me? We open the orchard in nine days—*nine days!*" He looked to the calendar for unneeded verification. "Nobody goes anywhere!" he cried. "Christ me! Nobody! Anywhere! What are you even thinking?"

"Please, Carl. I'm desperate. Just till Sunday, I promise. We have to make this happen." She held in her breath, while the director looked on incredulously, then launched into the cause of her petition, the first glimpse Carl had had into her personal life. He knew only the facets of the theater, often wondering if there were any others.

Hannah presented her rehearsed version of the dilemma. She came across as straight-forward, candid, and even bordering on valid. For extra measure, she padded her request by hinting that the Sand Box might even owe her this one small favor, that the Sand Box might owe as much to Lincoln Dollar. "If it wasn't for him, I wouldn't be here right now. And I don't mean I wouldn't be on your stage; I wouldn't be *here* here—period. I owe my life to him." She leaned in close to her director-friend. Hannah began an explanation of feelings, but quickly decided it would take too much time. She didn't have a lot of time. "He needs me, Carl, and I don't want him alone just now. He deserves better. Please, please don't deny me this."

The director could deny her nothing. "I'll have Charley walk through your part."

Hannah was able to breathe again. "I'll want to check with him first."

"You know as well as I—Christ me!—that he would stand for you on opening night if you asked."

Hannah smiled at the thought of Charley standing for her on opening night, smiling gratefully because she knew in her heart that he would actually do it. "I'll check with everyone. I won't go if anyone has a problem with it." She put this last contingent out there only because she believed her absence would be collectively forgiven, that she might even take along her friends' blessings and support. Once it was firmly in her head she was going to New York, she was finally able to relax.

"We appreciate all you've done for this production," said Carl, softening, "and I know I speak for everyone." But he quickly reeled himself back in; as a little, suffering sort of guy he couldn't allow too much a show of softness. "Besides, I'm the goddamn boss around here, and I'm telling you to go to New York. I'm ordering you to go—just get back as quick as you can." He caught himself and questioned, "You're not taking Katie with you?"

"Of course not. We can't both go." They had already worked this out. "She'll cover my scenes she's not in."

"The little starlet could even cover the scenes you have together. So go, go to New York, do what you have to do. I'm sorry for your friend, and for his friend."

Carl was already missing her before she was off the grounds. *A special sort of girl, that Hannah,* thought he, *Christ me.* Both girls had brought a fresh, new energy to his theater; youth and talent, commitment and ambition. They reminded Carl that live theater was still alive, that it would never die, and the dramatists would never die, not with players the likes of his present cast. *Christ me,* thought Carl, *it's a thing to behold.*

Katie was sleeping when Hannah returned. She was already packed, her bag waiting by the door. She leaned in to kiss her flatmate on the way.

Katie's arm came from under the covers, to around Hannah's neck. "I'll get up and drive you," she said, her words slurred, tangled in a yawn.

"I already called a cab. Go back to sleep. I'll call you when I get there."

Katie's head was on the pillow, her eyes opened just enough to register. "Give him my love. I hope things work out for Mr. Stanson. He's a good guy." Her eyes were closed again before she finished speaking.

Hannah adjusted the covers and kissed the girl again. Only once since the two got together had they spent any time apart. "Be good while I'm gone," she said in a maternal whisper, then put her bag over her shoulder and went quietly into the fresh, salty morning.

The bay was alive with fishermen after stripers. Seagulls trailed the chugging out-rigged boats, cawing, begging for the refuse of fish not yet caught.

Later that day Hannah let herself into Lincoln's apartment on Prospect Park. She was comfortable in his bed, rolling in the sheets, inhaling of his scent, impatient for his arrival, when the phone rang. A woman's voice was on the other end. "May I speak with Lincoln?"

Hannah's heart grew a little heavy. "He's not in. Is there a message?"

"Is this Hannah?" the voice inquired.

As Hannah listened, her heart grew heavier still. "I'm so, so sorry, Lauren. I admired your husband very much."

John and Lauren had pulled into Preston four hours after leaving Lincoln in New York. So much had been said during the past months that they made the trip in near silence. The end was nigh, and neither cared to discuss it further.

Lauren pressed the button to open the garage. Once inside she turned off the engine. They sat with their hands clasped over the console. The rest of John's strength was leaving him, off to join that already gone. A new and renewed pain came to occupy its place. "It's getting bad."

Lauren nodded. "I understand, John."

"It's real bad," he reiterated, a plea for understanding in his broken voice.

"I understand," she said again.

"You go inside. I'll be with you shortly."

Lauren leaned in to kiss him. She wanted to say so much, but there was really nothing left. She managed to whisper, "I've always loved you, since the day you came to me. You've given my life such joy and friendship and meaning. We'll be together forever my precious friend— my dear, sweet, precious man."

She left the car and climbed the stairs to the house, moving through the darkened rooms. Coming at last to the den, Lauren curled into a corner of the sofa. In the moonlight she could make out the shapes of picture frames on the mantle. She could not see the photographs, but imagined the reproductions of a life together. As memories of the life played, she was able to smile once more through the tears.

Lauren's smile faded to resigned acceptance when she heard the motor of the car restart. Ever searching for the silver lining, she was presently thankful for hearing the car, for she knew John's handgun was in the glovebox. "My dear, good man." She leaned back and pulled the pillows in close, tightly over her ears.

Lauren would have felt terrible calling at such an hour, but she knew no concept of time. With the arrangements pre-made, it was agreed she was to call any time, at any hour, whenever John was ready.

Arlin Prescott was not at all surprised to find Lauren on the phone as dawn crept upon the crisp autumn day. Arlin had assured the Stansons that Prescott Memorial would handle all the affairs. Arlin assured Lauren as much again over the phone. Lastly, he suggested that she leave her place on the couch, as the gas would soon fill the garage and begin seeping into the lonely house.

Hannah wrote out the service information, then called Virginia. Not daring to call Carl, however, she had first to listen to her own voice on the machine before leaving the message for Katie. "Change in plans. Mr. Stanson has passed away. I'm going to Vermont with Lincoln. Be back for rehearsal on Tuesday. Tell Carl I'm really sorry."

Hannah hadn't any real plans, but rather the assumption she would be going to Preston with Lincoln, when she dressed and went down to the busy street, hailing a taxi for the ride to Manhattan; up Flatbush, over the bridge to Chinatown, through the Bowery and into the concrete and asphalt jungle. She was accompanied by the rushing feeling of seeing him again, however mixed with dark memories of the setting, and with the pain of the circumstances bringing about the reunion. Tipping the hack at the theater, though, she chanced to see her lover's face on posters in the windows, and Hannah thought that was kind of cool.

The usher wouldn't disturb the house, but once she told him who she was to meet, he ushered her quietly to the lighting booth, from where she could watch the remainder of the performance. With misty eyes, Hannah looked on as an amber-gelled, five hundred-watt lamp lifted it from the stage and tossed it to the booth with a semi-sheen reflection.

She did not like it.

She tried to ignore it, but it fought to steal her attentions. It seemed alien and not a part of him. Hannah did not like it, because it was alien and not a part of him, but she was hoping he did.

The play's end was the mourning for a man who never knew who he was, a man who chased the wrong dreams, a man who could not remain right-sized. It struck Hannah how they would now mourn another man, but a man who chased good and noble dreams, a man who knew who he was. Hannah had not been especially close to John Stanson, but she felt deeply for Lincoln, and for all those who were. Hannah felt for a world having lost one of its better players.

She fought her want to applaud at the end of the performance. Rather, when Lincoln bowed under the lights, first by himself, then with the rest of the cast, she gratefully whispered, "Bravo."

Soon the stage was empty, save the abandoned set—a doll's house once its occupants are neatly tucked away in the chest of toys, to be taken out again later, played with another time. The house lights were up. The crew had left the booth.

Hannah had to navigate several patrons in the lobby before finding a door reading STAFF ONLY. "Close enough," she said and entered, moving through the halls until she found the men's dressing room.

She was met by a busy scene, brightly lit on three sides with personal stations, members of the cast moving about in various stages of dress and undress. Hannah searched each of them—a couple more than once—before finally finding her own. He was seated at one of the stations, inspecting tired eyes in the mirror, when his colleagues' cat-calls and comments came to rouse him. Lincoln saw her standing behind, looking with longing into the glass, and was immediately in her arms—speechless, unlike others in the room:

"Nice of you to invite your daughter to the show," one jeered, with seeming jealousy.

"Fuck you, Arnie," Lincoln returned. He never took his eyes from Hannah's.

"Yeah—fuck you, Arnie," Hannah reiterated, her arms wrapped around Lincoln's neck. She kissed him so hard and deep and wet and long that the others in the room had to give up on them. When at last he needed oxygen, Lincoln held her away. He could tell something was off.

"Lauren called while I was at your place."

"What did she …?" he began, but stopped. "It doesn't matter. He's done suffering, and you're here. That's all that matters. How'd you get away?"

"Oh, it wasn't a big deal. I actually do this all the time."

"I'm really happy to see you. I can't even tell you."

"I was hoping you would be," she returned. Hannah could tell he was relieved, but it was nice to hear it just the same. And, as for herself … "Get this stuff off your face and I'll take you out for a drink."

Hannah waited in the lobby, discussing the show with a stooping couple who remembered, proudly, albeit vaguely, the original New York production with Lee J. Cobb. Hannah had to fight the urge to tell the seniors that her boyfriend was part of the show. *Boyfriend?* She thought about it and liked the way it sounded; she actually loved the way it sounded, after which she had to share the information with the couple. She tried not to sound boasting, but couldn't quite pull it off. The old folks didn't seem to mind.

Hannah was three days in New York, a city of brutal memories and glorious dreams, chockfull of pain and possibilities. She went to Lincoln's play every night, and every night the show was different. It was this spontaneity and unpredictability which, for Hannah, was the beauty of live theater, something her new boyfriend had often impressed. She now understood what he meant, and she had to agree.

At the Sunday show, on a stool in the lighting booth with her feet up, Hannah's memories brought her back to *Miss Julie*, to the warm, hushed melodies of flutes and mandolins. But they were memories cooled by a splash of jealousy, because she was not presently on the stage with him. They were now a team and should not be performing in two different productions in two different states. But without the patience, energy, or nerve to project further on such thoughts, she did her best to remain secure within the lighting booth for only that performance, for only that day. After the show they left the city and drove through the night to Vermont.

It was four a.m. Lincoln stood in the snowy rain on the hotel balcony, reconciling the coming day with everything past. He tried preparing himself to be back in Preston, back on the shallow, hollow stage of collective intolerance, back in the courtroom of public opinion.

Hannah's breath was on his neck. "Come inside. Let's get some rest." She dried the cold from his face and hair, undressed him and led him to bed.

There was comfort in her warmth, but still the sleep would not visit Lincoln. Monday was his one day of rest, the one day when the theater was dark; but on this Monday the rest eluded him and only the darkness remained. He closed his eyes and tried to force it, but myriad memories kept the images swimming in the colored dots and flashes of the darkness, until at last he gave in. Lincoln surrendered to the past, allowing it to take him adrift, to take him to the Middle East, back to the Syrian, back to where he was always taken when he surrendered to the past.

It was February, 1991. The leathernecks and Allied Arab Forces had crossed the border to Kuwait, moving fast in small strike-groups, following the Euphrates northward, on towards Iraq, towards the capital at Baghdad, driving the enemy back as they advanced, inflicting casualties and meeting little resistance. The 100-Hour War was right on schedule. It appeared the mission wouldn't take very long.

Among the eighty pounds of gear that Lincoln carried was his indifference; a hundred hours or a hundred years, the rifleman didn't care how long it took. He didn't enjoy it, nor did he dislike it, but rather wanted to keep it as simple as possible. The desert sun glared, windswept sand burned his eyes, acrid smoke from the burning oil rigs filled and scratched at his lungs. And engulfing it all was the stench of ironic defeat; they were a rapid deployment force, employed to protect the oil reserves and other interests in the Middle East, but still the oil and the interests were burning away. Their rapid deployment was not rapid enough. The window had been missed, but at least they had liberated tiny Kuwait, and were presently driving the bully back home.

It was the third day of the hours-long battle when Captain Stanson's platoon met, face to face, hand to hand, the Republican Guard. The platoon was entrenched, getting hit with big guns, small arms and mortars. John's men were in the front, first to stop the bullets. While allied planes were quick to disperse the Guard's guns, they did not fly in quickly enough for the young captain's men. They'd already been hit.

There were craters in the sand as large and deep as swimming pools—big, sandy pools dotting the desert, all too devoid of water. Sand was flying and bodies scattering. Lincoln couldn't remember any of the sounds, any noises in the desert, but he supposed there must have been many. He was looking about for those still moving, and at those who would never move again, when he spotted Captain Stanson dragging himself along on his elbows, his weapon cradled in the crook of his arms, his lifeless lower body following sadly behind. Rifle shots splashed around the captain like a nebula of tiny starbursts. Trying to ascertain how many times the man had been hit, Lincoln finally settled on *several*, then left his cover to go for the fallen man.

He sprinted over sand that only moments before had swallowed his every footfall, but now felt as sure and solid as the ground beneath a track meet, his combat boots having sprouted cleats. With the wounded man and their weapons gathered up, Lincoln dashed back across the sand. The man over his shoulder was an awkward package; one of his feet faced away, while the corresponding knee was facing in; the other leg moved comically about the femur.

Lincoln rested the captain on the sand, away from the shrapnel and bullets. He hit each of the man's legs with a morphine injection. Opening a third packet, he noticed the captain had closed his eyes. Rather than waste the hypodermic, Lincoln reached around and stuck it in his own ass, and was quickly on the sweet honey end of the bee-like sting.

He peered over the mound and saw Perry, his fellow *boot* from the island. Once again he ran across the sand, firing his weapon at an enemy he could not see. He didn't bother telling Perry *help is on the way*. He didn't tell him *hang on, we're going to make it*. Lincoln could only hold the young marine and watch him die, deciding that when his own time was at hand, he would prefer he was alone.

Lincoln laid the man gently in the sand, then helped himself to the magazines from Perry's pouches. He fired at the unseen enemy with Perry's bullets, until he came upon one of the new guys. With this comrade over his back, he heard the *twpt, splash, crunch, twpt* of a bullet crashing through the kid's leg. It ripped the young man's uniform, tearing at his flesh, muscle and bone. The blood splashed Lincoln's face. In his anger and contempt, his eyes tight and teeth clenched, Lincoln pivoted atop the dune and fired another thirty rounds at nothing.

Reloaded, running, shooting and searching—dead, dead, dead— "Hey Pappy! Let's get you outta here." Lincoln pulled his friend onto his back, picking up his M-16A2 and scrambling over the sand. Once more atop the dune, he lost hold of the rifle; then reaching to retrieve it, he discovered the hand would not pick it up. A violent, spinning bullet had torn through his forearm, crashing, crushing, ripping and ricocheting, leaving an ugly, bloody mess in its wake. The useless appendage remained barely connected by the thinnest strips of ragged flesh; it dangled, like the conversation in a melancholy Paul Simon song. Lincoln grabbed up the weapon with his other hand. With Pappy lying across his back, he went for safety behind the dune.

The rest of the day came through like clouds in foggy, misty bits and pieces. It might have been Private Burleson who harpooned him into senselessness—like Richard Speck, like Queequeg in chapter forty-eight—*once, twice, thrice* ... darkness.

Lincoln turned into that frightful, lonely, sandy darkness and reached out, gently alighting on the warm, soft skin of Hannah's hip. She was faced away from him in the bed with the moonlight over the green mountains coming through the glass doors and getting tangled up in her hair. He nuzzled his nose in the moonlight and kissed her shoulder. "I love you."

It had slipped out, a hushed confession for her tender sleep. Lincoln marveled at the sound of those words rolling past his clumsy, sandy lips. He ran his hand secretly along her thigh, over her hip to her waist. He thought to try those words once again, and to have another go at the shoulder kiss.

Hannah smiled, biting into her lip, pretending to sleep. The cloudy moonlight danced in her eyes. Moonlit thoughts danced about in her head. *I knew it,* thought she; *thank you, thank you, thank you.* Her moonlit eyes were finally able to close.

The alarm clock sounded two hours before the funeral. Lincoln turned it off, scarcely aware whether or not he had slept. Water was running in the bathroom and coffee was dripping in the pot—coffee so strong, black, rich and delicious as to bring to mind a beloved writer;

this was Lincoln's second thought of the day; the first was in the next room.

Her face was washed and sparkling, her blond hair brushed and alive with the morning, when at last she appeared. Hannah had not heard the alarm and was pleased to find him awake. Without words, with only a whisper of expression, she let her robe fall to the floor and sleekly crawled into the sheets on top of him. She laid her head on his chest, listening to the beating of his heart.

Hannah Mae Fields had never loved any man. She'd never given any call to suspect that he might be loved by her. She was sure of it. She had kept it in check, always too precocious for puppy love, as yet too young for commitment, held in a never-never land of impertinent abstinence reinforced by a levee. But now that levee was compromised and replaced by a bridge.

Hannah positioned herself on top of him, brushing his cheeks with her lips, letting her hair fall in his face, looking into his eyes, into the eyes betraying everything he could not say. He could keep no secrets, not from her. Slowly, steadily, she moved over him, the melodious tunes of paired metal strings and wooden cylinders sounding in her head. She held him tightly, for fear he might want to get away. She would not let him get away.

"There's going to be a good deal of whispering today," she eventually said. "We'll be sure to turn some Preston heads."

"You're always turning heads."

"How sweet of you to say. And you're often the subject of whispering; but I mean *we*, as a couple. How do you feel about that—the whispering, the hypocrisy, the bullshit?" Hannah adopted a mock-tragic tone, furrowing her brow and pouting her lips. "We'll be criticized, ostracized, crucified, possibly burned at the stake. If they threaten to stone us, we can tell them we're already stoned."

"What we have is between us and the people who care about us. Those who matter don't mind, and those who mind don't matter."

"Yeah, thanks a lot," said Hannah. "I'm looking for support, and you're quoting Dr. Seuss. I'm stressing out, and you give me the relationship equivalent of green eggs and ham. Just make sure you stay close-by today."

Meanwhile, Katie was in Virginia, inhaling deeply, first through one nostril, then the other. Melting into the overstuffed chair, she reclined her head back to allow the chemical to run down her throat. The white horseman galloped down her spine and traveled her nervous system. He rang the doorbell at each vertebra, stopping long enough to say *hello*, though declining all invitations for tea. He curled down around under her ass and sleekly up between her legs, giving her a *smack*, as though to say, *You're it!* before running down around the insides of her thighs. Once reaching her toes, the equestrian began the return travel, a straight shot north, sending Katie back further still.

She danced a horny jig at the crossroads of Shangri-La and la-dee-dah. As much as her head wanted to say *no* to the stuff, the intense euphoria was too enjoyable to cast aside. The sun was set, the red neon lights of the retail strip flashing in the darkened room.

The extended-stay motel flat was the girls' new home until the end of the production. Sparsely furnished, it came with the chair in which Katie sat, the sofa-bed presently shared by the brothers Croft, and a small table between the two. There was a dinette table and chairs for meals, and Monet prints on the walls—or perhaps they were Manet; Katie couldn't tell the difference. White-knuckled, she gripped the arms of the chair once more as the horseman rushed on.

Michael Croft was darker than his brother, older by three years and harder by thirty. Under dark, mischievous eyes, his aquiline nose rested askew from petty street battles, many of them in defense of the younger Croft.

Michael enjoyed performing in the bay area plays, although he did not share his sibling's passion for the craft. Michael's acting was a hobby and little more. He claimed it kept him sharp and helped to while away the time. "Keeps me out of trouble, for the most part," he'd say to the guys on the beach, adding that the theater was also a "great place to score pussy."

Michael could have played a formidable Hamlet, but instead maintained an acting indifference. His stage was a safe haven, a place to meet women and an extra two hundred dollars a week in his pocket, about enough to keep the tank topped off. Mom and dad covered the balance of his expenses, provided he direct his life in a somewhat forward direction—they weren't concerned with pace—and keep watchful eyes on his mother's favorite son.

Gabriel was less imposing than his brother, his demeanor gentler, with hair the sandy fairness of the beach he played upon. His passions for the theater were intense, with secret—and some not so secret—dreams of a theater life; but his talents and range lagged in the wake of his ambitions, prompting local directors to cast him in roles requiring a soft presence and not many lines. But still they worked to build him into larger parts, if only because he was a kind and decent sort of chap, and because his parents were generous patrons.

The brothers had a go at the white powder on the table, with a little extra for the courage it might give them with their company. The younger Gabriel was forever losing out to his older brother, always in the front seat at the drive-in, always dribbling J.V. in the shadow of Michael's varsity, always playing at tertiary roles while his brother got the leads, the lines and leading ladies. But he sensed his luck was changing. False courage and security were better than none at all. He thought that Katie had tossed him a quick glance which held a certain longing, not knowing that Katie looked at nearly everything with a certain longing.

Hannah was off with Lincoln, leaving Katie to find her own way in Virginia. She was the third wheel of the triune and starting to feel like that wheel. The seed had been cultivated—the seed Katie saw planted on the lawn at Preston High, on the morning when she saw the dreamy look in Hannah's eyes. Katie was being pushed into loneliness, but she would not be alone, not unless by her choice, and the brothers Croft were one of those choices. She hadn't counted on the dope, and let them know that Hannah was not to hear of it. "She doesn't mind a pull off a joint now and then, but if she knew I was doing this shit, I'd have hell to pay."

"Where'd she take off to?" asked Gabriel.

Katie's head remained at ease over the top of the chair. She spoke as though addressing the alfresco ceiling. "Soon as she got to New York a friend of ours died, so she's going up to Vermont for the service.

Supposed to be two days, but now she won't be back till Tuesday's rehearsal. Carl's gonna be so pissed. I can't wait to tell him."

"You girls are pretty tight," observed Michael. "I used to think you were a couple."

Katie brought her head erect and looked squarely at him. "Silly actor. One woman is more than enough in any relationship. Besides, we both dig on men, not that that should concern you."

"The look on Carl's face the night she laid into him," continued Michael, smiling at the recollection, "I'll never forget it. That was classic. Someone needed to put him straight. He hasn't been the same since."

"That's my girl," said Katie a little proudly. "She's the sweetest, most selfless lady on the planet, till you cross her. I could tell you stories that'd make your tongues hard, but I'm not going to. Do mom and dad have any more of you little angels at home?"

"Not just angels—archangels. I am the great prince which standeth for the children of thy people."

"My father's name is Michael," said Katie. "He's a great prince, too."

The younger brother chimed in, "And I am Gabriel, that stand in the presence of God and am sent to speak unto thee."

"Luke, Chapter One," said Katie; to his brother, she said, "Michael and his angels fought against the dragon. Revelation, Twelve."

Michael was showing some interest. "You know your bible?"

"I know all sorts of stuff."

Now he was really interested. "Like what?"

"Like, I know you've been gawking at my tits since I met you; your little brother too, at the risk of being obvious."

For the first time since meeting Katie, the guys found something else, anything else, to look at, humming and hawing before she rescued them, leaning towards Gabriel. "I need you to work hard next week. You're going to be part of some real powerful stuff. These rehearsals are one thing, but when Hannah's got a house to play for ... well, you'll see. Stay close to her and get your lines out, give her cues like you mean it, and I promise she'll make you a big fucking star."

Gabriel was set to argue that he was already doing all he possibly could. "She's hard to work with. She's a good actress, but she's distant. I kind of get the feeling she doesn't like me." At his brother's instruction, he leaned in to cut more lines of the dope.

Katie offered a knowing smile. "She's just being selfish, but Hannah's selfishness is paradoxical, in that she'll focus entirely on herself, but only so she can be her best for everyone else—if that makes any sense." It made perfect sense to Katie. She was getting high. The dope made her loquacious. "Don't think that she doesn't like you. I happen to know she cares for you a great deal, but she'll find you questionable until you prove yourself. You'll get your chance on Friday night. If you treat her right, she'll be your best friend in the world. She'll do anything for you. But if you screw her over, well—just don't. Carl went for her and you saw what happened to him. She'll put you in your place. She'll humble you."

Again the powder swam through Katie's head. She was excited. Things weren't perfect, but they were still pretty good. She was feeling alright. She missed Hannah, and Lincoln for that matter, but had recently decided that she should start finding ways around it. The relationship was changed, something she would have to accept, but she'd be able to accept the change more easily under certain circumstances—her circumstances. The brothers Croft were circumstantial.

"Get the cork out of the other bottle. I'm going to slip into something a little more comfortable." It sounded like a line from a b-feature flick, but neither of the guys minded. They didn't really seem to notice.

Michael moved to work the corkscrew while his brother brooded with boyish desire, drinking in all of Katie's movements as she left the room. The older said to the younger, "I'll slip out of here after I see what she slips into." He poured himself another short glass of wine.

Katie stood before the bedroom mirror removing her clothes. Energy coursed through her body at her own hungry touch. Inspecting herself, she whispered, "Eindrucksvoll," the only German she knew, to honor Dr. Grafenberg, whom she thought the sweetest of all Germans.

She pondered the guys in the other room, considering the choice and how it might be brought about. She found them both kind of cute, each in his way. It's a tough call, she conceded, deciding Michael would most likely take her for a ride, but that it might be fun taking the little brother for his own trip around the world. She'd made sure to leave the door ajar, watching them in the mirror watching her.

Katie finally came from the room. She put alight three wicks of a lavender candle. She wore a short black wrap, struggling vainly to restrain her, the smooth silk draping teasingly over her ass, barely touching at her thighs. Her shiny dark hair spilled on her shoulders, framing the intense, black Irish beauty. Her lips were sweet and pouty, begging to be kissed and licked and bitten.

Katie enjoyed the obvious effect she produced. She adored the adoration. She was in the driver's seat, at the helm, the Sun Queen, the boss. She *sizzled*. Katie didn't want any love, no promises, no commitments. She wanted only to control and be controlled. She wanted to touch and be touched. She wanted to hold and be held, all the while biding the time she would need to reorganize her world.

She lowered herself on the coffee table facing the brothers. The silk of her robe failed in its duties by exposing the whole of one breast. Katie crossed her legs, modestly tucking a swatch of the silk between her quivering thighs, first looking deeply into one pair of lustful eyes, then the other. *A tough call, indeed.*

"Do you want me, Michael?" He was standing behind his brother, keeping watch and watching. Katie did not give him time to answer. "Maybe your brother wants me?" The candlelight from the table sparkled in her hair. "Which of you is going to make love with me? Which of the archangels wants to fuck me?"

When neither could answer promptly, she suggested they flip a coin.

Michael reached into a pocket grown tighter. "You want a coin toss to decide who sleeps with you?" he asked, thankful he was still in the running, and rather enjoying the fifty-fifty odds.

Katie slid into the growing lap of Gabriel. "I want you to flip to see who goes first."

-8-

Lincoln and Hannah stayed with Lauren in the front near the podium for the benediction. Lauren's veil did well to shade the mourning, but failed to mask the sweetly abrasive odor of her Scottish breakfast. Lincoln held her gloved hand throughout the service.

There was a collective relief once all were out of doors again. The sun had waited courteously for the procession, bringing with it a slight breeze, just enough to stir the naked trees; then an angry cracking of weaponry shattered the late autumn silence, the color guard from the V.F.W.-Preston Post sounding a salute to their fallen comrade. The banner was lifted from the casket, folded, and presented to Lauren on behalf of a grateful nation.

Hannah stood greedily close to Lincoln, her arm intertwined with his. Both were dressed all in black, making it difficult to discern where one ended and the other began. He was stoic throughout the service, lost behind dark glasses, but at one point she caught a glimpse of him smiling to himself.

"What are you thinking about?"

"The day I met John," he returned, his smile growing broader as he fought it for its inappropriateness.

There was reference at the graveside to the effect that *God cares*, and that they "need not grieve for the man." There was something about *a better place*; Lincoln found this last part easy to believe, as the casket strained against the nylon webbing lowering it into the hole. He moved forward, kicking away a muddy top layer to expose the drier dirt underneath. He took a handful and slowly let it fall on the polished maple box, staring intently, as though to etch the image on his memory forever. "Semper fi," he whispered, and walked away from the grave, away from John Stanson. On his way past the widow he leaned in close. "I'm sorry," he said, for he truly was.

John's friends and colleagues and former students were gathered at the Stanson home, Beth Bronson having handled the arrangements, her eyes wet the whole time, not only because she had lost her boss and one of her best friends, but because Beth had a tendency to lapse into melancholy anyway. Jennifer Novak and Cyndi Partlow represented the recent student body. Saddened with the occasion, still they were excited to see Hannah and Lincoln again. They were rich with stories of their work in the theater department at the University of Vermont. Cyndi bragged of Burlington's thirteen theater companies, and touted the city as one of the country's most gay-friendly.

"It's perfect," added Jennifer.

Lauren had a lot to drink, but managed it well. She played the gracious host, moving about to ensure the comfort of her guests. Lincoln watched her in and out of the rooms, wondering how she would fare once the group was gone, regretting he wasn't able to stay longer. He was thumbing a photo album when Lauren finally came to him, perching herself on the arm of the chair. "How are you holding up?" she asked.

"I was wondering the same about you. I wish I didn't have to leave so soon."

"Don't be silly. The theater calls. John would understand."

"What will you do?" he asked.

"I've postponed classes at the studio and I'm taking a leave of absence from school. I'm going to do some traveling. I like traveling." She had begun the grieving process long before John's final breath, but still she was far from acceptance, still closer to anger. "We were supposed to grow old together, Lincoln. I hate it when my plans fall through. I fucking hate it! But I know he wouldn't want me sitting around crying all over myself." She leaned in close to Lincoln's ear. "I don't believe I need to ask what your plans are," she said, tossing her head in Hannah's direction. "I bet they're right over there on the other side of the room."

Hannah was chatting it up with Beth over cosmopolitans. Pretty drinks and pretty strong, Beth enjoyed them immensely, and was enjoying herself even more for having abandoned the resentment she had held for Hannah. Beth topped off their glasses, thinking such things shouldn't be bothered over, and especially on the day of her boss's funeral.

"She's good for you," Lauren continued, "and it's time you settled down anyway."

Lincoln was preparing to argue that he was far too young to settle down when Hannah approached them with fresh drinks.

"Sit with us a minute," said Lauren.

Hannah bent to embrace her and to leave a kiss on top of Lincoln's head. "I'd rather you two spend this time together. I can find someone else to bother, but I'll be close if you need me." She addressed her last comment to both.

Once Hannah had left, Lauren continued, "Here you are, at my best friend's funeral … and … Jesus, I think I'm starting to get a little buzz." Lauren paused. "Nope—I'm certain of it. I *am* getting buzzed." She breathed deep, sobering up enough to say, "Now you're looking over old photos with a devious smile. What is it about my man that's making you smile so?"

"The day I met John down in North Carolina; it sure was an unforgettable day." He began to recount the story, the same as her husband had done many times before, but Lauren stopped Lincoln in the tale, doing her best to steady herself on his shoulder.

"Hold on." She set about addressing the room and those rooms adjoining, gathering the attention of her guests. She let go an ear-piercing whistle, unladylike and unLaurenlike, until the house was hushed. "I want to thank everyone for coming here today to celebrate my husband's life. A wonderful man, he loved you all very much."

There were murmurs of "Hear, hear," and "He was the best." Jennifer let go a hearty, "Fuckin' right, sister," to the malicious glare of Mable Green.

"There are people here today who knew John most his life," Lauren went on, "and others at various stages—so many years, gone so quickly—but my friend, Lincoln, was with John in times and places the rest of us know precious little about, so I've asked him to share some of those memories with us, provided, of course, he keeps it clean."

Lincoln was shocked at the insinuation, insisting, "All of my experiences with your husband are squeaky clean," though he was shaking his head as such to let her know that this wasn't necessarily so.

Hannah began inching still further away from her man. Negotiating the crowd, she moved back until she was against the furthest wall, as far away from him as she could be while remaining in the room, to a point from where she could take all of him in.

Lincoln's mind had played the scene a thousand times, but he had never attempted any articulation of the events. Those days were now more akin to feelings than to any actual happenings. "At the service this morning," he began, "I started thinking about the day I met John. It nearly got me to laughing, how that day showed no promise—not even a hint—of any sort of friendship.

"He somehow got himself assigned to our unit—a brand new lieutenant, fresh out of Quantico. I'd heard he had some prior service, but I knew it couldn't have been with a bunch like us. We had a bit of a reputation in those days—a rapid deployment unit, anywhere in the world in twenty-four hours, boots on the ground, ready to fight. I was pretty gung-ho, a corporal at the time, been in a few years.

"When John arrived we were gearing up for a mass-tactical airborne gig, dropping all kinds of supplies—weapons, jeeps, troops—a real big deal jump. John no sooner got to camp before he had the 'chute on his back. We called the new guys *cherries*, made them wear a yellow helmet for their first jump with the unit, with cherries painted all over it. A sort of hazing, I suppose, a ritual, rite-of-passage. It was John's cherry blast and he didn't seem very excited at the prospect. I didn't know at the time he was to be my new boss.

"We were loaded on the tarmac. It was a pitch-black night. John looked like he was walking straight into hell. I gave him a big *thumbs-up*, then made the sign of the cross. He didn't look well.

"Finally we were on the plane. It was dark and loud, hot and cramped, a really busy scene. John was next to me on the bird. All I could see of him were his big, white eyes. I was sure it was the closest he'd been to a parachute since jump school, and just as sure he'd never been on a jump like this, so I thought to have a little fun with him, try to build his confidence. I used to love those night jumps, with the moon and the stars, the gear and the guns."

Silence, like Seattle fog, had settled in Lauren's den. None but Lincoln could hear the whining engines of the C-141 Starlifter. No others felt the steady vibration as the aircraft demanded altitude. None smelled the acrid jet fuel exhaust fumes blowing in the blast of the whirring, turbine motors. Lincoln alone was one thousand feet into the dark skies over North Carolina, when he continued, "The red light came on, time to hook up. John was in front of me, so I'd have to follow him out. The doors opened—wind, noise.

"The green light came on, and everyone pushed for the doors. We always spilled both doors, both sticks, forty or fifty guys, nine to ten seconds tops, but it looked like John was going to hold us up. Rather than wait, I wrapped myself around him and we left the plane as one. I lost my grip when we bounced off the tail. Choking in tangled lines, I had all I could do to kick out the twists, hoping John was kicking, too. It's a hairy ride with twisted lines. Once settled, I couldn't help but start laughing. I was so relieved. I couldn't see John during the descent, but I knew he was close. And I was pretty sure he wouldn't think it was as funny as did I.

"Once returned to terra firma, I was gathering up my gear when he found me. I could tell it was him coming by the glint of that yellow helmet in the moonlight. I'm assuming he's pissed, as was well within his rights, so I snapped to attention and sounded off, 'The marines have landed, sir! The situation is well at hand!' Then, all the sudden— *pow!*—he nailed me in the face, almost knocked me out. I was lying on the ground, still in my harness."

Lincoln's neoprene hand brushed at the place where John's fist had made its connection those years before, feeling for any remnants of his now departed friend and comrade. "John was screaming, 'What did you say on that plane, corporal?' It was a few minutes before I was able to get up, then a few minutes longer wondering if I dared.

"I said, Semper Fi! Sir!"

"'Bullshit,' he says. The lieutenant wanted to know what I had said, and I thought, what the hell, he's already going to take a stripe or another swing, or both, so I told him, 'I was telling you to get the fuck out of my way, sir! You cherry son of a bitch! Sir!"

"'You damn near killed us both!' he said, and I suppose he was right. 'But I didn't, sir! We're on the ground and ready to fight! The situation is at hand! Sir!'

"That was it. He walked away from me. I figured I'd never see him again. After a long march back to the main post to turn in the gear, I saw him again in the hanger, and still wearing that yellow helmet. I tried avoiding him, but he spotted me. I'm thinking he's coming over to give me my walking papers, but instead he gave me his hand. Didn't say anything, just stood there shaking hands. He had really big hands. And I remember feeling like he was looking inside me, looking to see if he could trust me, and giving me the acknowledgement that he could, and that he did. It was strange. Something about the new lieutenant seemed out of place; the whole experience screamed of incongruity. It was one of the most powerful experiences of my entire life. An hour before I wouldn't have pissed on the guy if he was on fire, but after a simple handshake he was ever after the most honorable man I've known."

Lincoln's thoughts went contrary to parachuting marines, lifting, floating upward, dissipating in the night sky. As the fog began to lift, someone had to make a move, prompting Hannah to come from across the room. "Are you okay, sweetheart?"

"I suppose so," he returned, somewhat startled.

She smiled, relieved. "You were going to tell us about the day you met Mr. Stanson?"

Lincoln shook the rest of the fog clear, even more startled to find everyone in the quiet room studying him. He was reminded briefly of the recurring dream where he's in a play and doesn't know his part. An actor, though, he improvised, groping for a line or two to paste in the script. "I've loved him ever since that night, and I always will."

The words *ever since* and *always will* remained in the air like the crisp clouds of the late autumn day. Hannah returned to the others. Lincoln remained a while longer in the moonlit North Carolina evening.

Hannah watched through the rain-streaked glass at the misty arrivals and departures, wishing hers was not so soon to leave. She was all too good at saying goodbye, and pained at having acquired the skill so quickly, so easily and proficiently. "What are we going to do?" she asked without looking at him.

Lincoln also watched the airplanes on the tarmac. "How do you mean?"

"How I *mean* is, I'm going back to the beach and you're staying here, and I have no idea when I'll see you again, or even if I'll see you again. It's your nature to act randomly, so I'm willing to make some concessions; but I don't want to spend a lot of time wondering if something solid's coming of this, or if we're just gonna get together every few months, to get laid then go our separate ways, like we're some kind of biannual fuck buddies. I'm like a carnival girl to you, is that it? A good time when I come to town; but, once gone, forgotten? Is that what this is to you? Am I your carnival girl? Should I be making other plans?" Hannah faced the tarmac. She wouldn't let him see into her lying eyes. While her mouth could speak of *making other plans*, her eyes would reveal an entirely different take on the situation.

"The other carnival won't run past the holidays. We'll be done by Christmas at the latest. I'll wrap things up downtown and maybe we can get together before you go to Louisiana. Soon you'll be busy enough, without much time for anything else."

"*Busy enough*?" We'll *get together*? Where do you get off? When I signed on for this relationship donut, it was my intention to be the custard or the jelly, or at least the glaze, and not just another hole—if you know what I mean. Everything I do is with *us* in mind. I'm fighting off sailors and soldiers and actors waiting for you, all the time busting my ass, hoping and waiting for us to be together." She didn't want them to, but still the words escaped her mouth. "Don't you trust me?"

"I like donuts."

"Why do you wait until I'm asleep to tell me you love me, when those are the words I want most to hear? Why is that so hard for you to say?" Hannah's patience and itinerary were both worn thin. She quick-like searched his eyes for confirmation—to be sure she wasn't just another donut hole—and was pleased at not needing long to find it.

"Here's an easier question, and you're going to answer this one before I get on that plane. What can I do, today, to make this work? I need to know that you're in my life before something else gets all fucked up and it's too late. What will you have of me? I'll do whatever it takes. I'll be your carnival girl."

Now it was Lincoln's time to search. "Are you sure that's what you want?"

"More than anything, I want you. I love you. I really do. And I need you—you, me and Kate again, like the old days." She kissed him so hard that airport security gave them a second glance. "Besides," she spoke sweetly and seductively, though loudly enough to warrant a third glance from security, "I *gave* myself to you. That must count for something."

It did count for something—glances four and five. "I'll finish up the show and go to New Orleans with you. I'll be close, should you need me or want me. I hope it's both."

The entire dialogue had gone too easily. Hannah thought, *he gave in way too much, and way too soon.* "You were planning to go all along. You little sneak! You were planning to go all along."

"I was hoping all along. I know a place downriver from the city, in the bayou. I'm going to hide out there for a spell, see about writing a play."

Hannah liked plays. "What about?"

"Something to do with pirates, I think—the swashbuckling, whore-mongering pirates of Barataria Bay. I didn't expect this to happen, Hannah, and now it's too late. I wanted to be content to love you from a distance, but all the time I wanted you closer and closer." He kissed all over her face, close to her smiling eyes. "I loved you when I wasn't supposed to, but now it's happening so easily, I'm just going to let it happen. I don't know what else to do."

If ever you don't know what to do, then don't do anything. Her knees begged to weaken, if only for a moment. She looked at the schedule. Everything was right on time. *Spot-on.* Her fellow passengers were boarding.

She had furrowed her brow, nipping at her lower lip, when she finally returned her eyes to him. She was wearing the lecture's-coming leer that she usually saved for Katie. "You're not the only one taking a chance here. All I have to go on is instinct. You're my friend, my mentor, my lover and my inspiration, and I have to trust you're not going to leave me. Considering the way I feel about you, you'd be crazy to leave—even crazier than I already know you are. I'm an alright person, right? I'm cute, am I not? And I'm smart and I'm kind and I'm yours. As long as you want me, I am so, so yours."

She reached into her bag for the tickets. "Carl's gonna be pissed. I hope he hasn't replaced me. I really enjoyed your show. It was powerful. Made me think, made me feel. A father-son piece that asks a girl to understand, and it's the only play I've ever seen four nights in a row. I always learn a lot from watching you work. Next to Kate, you're the best actor I know, and I've been around for a while. Speaking of which, it's too bad you can't see the little tramp in the cherry orchard. She's amazing, totally big." As her thoughts went from Lincoln to Katie, Hannah's happiness was such as to nearly overpower her. "Oh," she said, righting herself. "What fun!"

This is the final boarding call for ...

"My winged chariot awaits. I'll see you soon. And make no mistake, that was a statement, not a question. I *will* see you soon. We're good enough now at saying goodbye; I want to start saying good morning more often."

Hannah kissed him once again and began skipping down the gangplank. She had not gone far before he called after her. She turned back, barely slowing her gait. "What is it *now*?"

He held up the new hand. "You never said anything about this."

Hannah shrugged. "I suppose I'll get used to it. Honestly, though, I kind of liked the ol' backscratcher, but I'll work around it." She gave her own ass a sharp slap for his benefit, then disappeared around the corner.

Lincoln was still watching after her as the wheels of the plane were pulled up into the belly and she sailed away over the dark and cloudy skyline.

-9-

Scant applause met Hannah when she burst running through the door of the Sand Box Theater; more she was offered *where the hell have you been?* snobbery. Considerably late for rehearsal—days late—she vowed to give more of herself to the production to atone for this wanton neglect. She would somehow have to find more of herself to give.

The cast was in full dress when she spilled into the room wearing khaki pants and Birkenstocks over wool socks. Some had considered giving up on her, having taken little comfort in Katie's mild insistence: "She said she'd be here, she'll fuckin' be here. Get off it already."

Hannah glided through the sixth row with embraces and apologies for Carl and Charley. Without waiting for responses, such as "You're fired," or "Great to have you back," she flew over the remaining rows to her place on the stage, high-fiving Katie and patting Emily Rose on the ass along the way.

Katie smugly addressed the cast: "Told ya."

Little else now mattered. She was relieved, refreshed and satisfied. Everything settled, all that remained was to meet up with a mismatched group of characters in a cherry orchard in turn-of-the-century Russia.

Hannah enjoyed watching through the curtain as the seats filled. The first time she tried this back at Preston High the pressure had nearly killed her, but she had come to get off on it, to embrace the energy, the titillation. She especially enjoyed the Friday night crowds, the end of the week theater-goers, who had been out for dinner and cocktails, and were eagerly arrived for a spot of cultural entertainment. That's where Hannah came in; it was her new job.

She peeked through the curtain, trying to judge the audience's mood and expectations, and was often envious of them, as they were able to see the show, something that she could never ever do.

"There's an ass in every seat," she reported to the cast. The group was assembled with an intense, nervous energy embracing the room. Tchaikovsky seeped into the greenroom through the sound system to signal the ten-minute call. Presently the stage manager's voice came in on top of the music: "Ten minutes to curtain everyone. If for any reason anyone's not ready, kindly get yourself that way." Charley's voice was gone and the Tchaikovsky returned.

Cap'n Carl entered the room, more humbled than he had in the past. Carl had entered the same room on many nights, minutes before the curtain, only to find actors who had forgotten their lines, or lights that were not working, sound system shortcomings, poor sales, missing talent, a host of mishaps. But none of these mishaps were present that night at the Sand Box Theater. Carl was as pleased as a suffering, little artist-director could possibly be. "This is the soundest ship I've ever had the pleasure to sail. We've weathered some storms along the way, and even came close to never getting out of port"—he sneaked a glance at Hannah—"but we're now safely asea, safely guided by all of you, the stars." He avoided looking at Hannah. "I'm twenty years directing in this theater, and I've never been happier. Thank you—every one of you. I love you all."

Extending the nautical metaphor, Katie added, "I say, chips ahoy and avast ye fuckers. Y'all can hang out in the hold, or come along topside with me, up onto the promenade deck." With still more private sailor-talk for the archangels, she continued, "And mates, the poop deck's gonna need some more seamen." She blew the guys a kiss, and another for the deflating director.

The girls had their heads together. "Lincoln's writing a play," said Hannah.

"What sort of play?"

"Something about pirates."

"Interesting. Too bad he got rid of the hook." Then, having avoided asking until now, "What do you think of the new hand?"

"I liked the hook."

But Katie was not listening. "I am terribly psyched for this show," she said, her excitement apparent. Hannah could see it in her eyes. Katie's bosom heaved. The muscles in her neck quivered.

"You're licking your teeth," said Hannah. "You always do that when you're fired up. I so love working with you."

"I know. Me too." She tucked in a strand of Hannah's hair. "Oh, don't start. You'll fuck up your makeup. There's muses in the room tonight, Han. I can feel 'em. This is going to be a magical evening."

The Bay Players are staging Chekhov's, The Cherry Orchard, *now playing at the Sand Box Theater. Do not miss this show.*

Katie enjoyed reading about the production, and herself, in the weekend arts supplement:

Mixing New England and New York talent with some local favorites, Director Carl Thomas has assembled a cast and crew unrivaled in Norfolk memory. The resulting concoction is delicious!

Emily Rose, of the Boston Roses, is captivating as Mme. Ranevsky, the flighty owner of the doomed orchard. Her character blindly floats between a blissful past—now an all-but-forgotten memory—and the denial of an unimaginable future, making it difficult for us to laugh with *her, and, sadly, far too easy to laugh* at *her.*

Hannah Fields, a young actor visiting from Vermont, plays the daughter, Anya. Her scenes with her mother, as well as those with on-stage love interest, Trofimov, are among some of the program's more memorable moments. However, the actor to watch on opening night was another from Vermont, Ms. Katherine Pauley. As the love-torn Varya, she brings passion to the role seemingly flying above this already soaring cast. Her segues from the comic to the tragic are as imperceptible as a blink of her beautiful eyes, and just as natural. Katherine Pauley is the face of contemporary theater.

The rest of the cast serves well in supporting these major players. The brothers Croft, Michael and Gabriel, familiar to bay area audiences, perform unusually strong in their roles. Gabriel Croft, playing opposite Fields, has reached the point of real acting distinction, obviously having picked up something since last we saw him.

Thomas' set, wonderfully minimal, acts as a canvas upon which he's used watercolors to portray this poignant story of cultural fatality. At play's end, these watercolors, as though left in the rain, run and fade, melting into pools of gray and black. As the area has come to expect, costumes, lights, and Thomas' choice of musical accompaniment serve well to compliment this classic Russian tragic-comedy. If The Cherry Orchard *and this cast of the Bay Players portends the future of area theater, the Chesapeake Bay is in for a welcomed treat.*

The production runs until Thanksgiving. Do not miss this show!

This was only one of a few local reviews, but it was by far Katie's favorite. Every night filled every seat in the Sand Box. Charley was said to have looked through the ledgers, rumored to have put away his red pen for the black. Night after night saw the show build in intensity. The group turned the play upside down and inside out, they tip-toed through the lyrics, sifted through the nuance, and turned Chekhov's orchard into a beautiful and successful piece of pre-Revolution real estate.

Hannah was sitting at her station one evening near the end of the run, carefully wiping the cold cream from around her eyes, when Emily Rose approached. She sat at the station next to Hannah's.

"You were wonderful tonight," said Emily Rose.

Hannah turned to her. "Thanks to you. That thing with you and the Gordfather is so powerful. It's tough coming in at the end of such a scene every night, like some huge energy field I have to break through just to deliver those few lines. I love it. I absolutely love it. I feel so blessed being out there with you guys."

"Your magic scene with Charlotte got quite a laugh."

"Yeah, it was fun," Hannah returned.

She continued with her makeup. Emily Rose sat reversed in the chair, her arms resting on the back. Her chin was on her arms. She spent some time quietly studying Hannah, so much so that the young actor began to find it disconcerting, before finally asking, "Is there something wrong, mother?" Hannah liked to carry the maternal relationship with her from the stage.

Her admiration for Emily Rose was profound. The woman had devoted a lifetime to this art which Hannah found so moving and important. And she was also a mom away from home, of sorts, when needed. Emily Rose reciprocated the strong affection for Hannah, and for many of the same reasons, however she liked to think of herself as more of an older sister, of sorts.

A seasoned performer, no prima donna, Emily Rose was tough, hardened by a demanding career and a precarious life. A large part of her labors was spent in keeping an actor's vanity in check, in staying right-sized, something she had learned to do, but this was not always so.

Emily Rose began her career with the noblest of intentions, but once caught up in the limelight, the pleasure of bringing the literature to the stage was trumped by the increasing need to be recognized for doing so. Ashamed with the change, she sought to quit the theater before the theater quit her, but she frightfully found that she had no other place to go. Or so it seemed to Emily Rose. She then rearranged her priorities, accepting what she believed was her lot. She began trying to keep others' needs ahead her own, be they actors or the audience. In returning to the stage to work this new strategy, Emily Rose was brought to the sands of Virginia Beach, to the Sand Box Theater.

Finished removing the makeup, Hannah turned to the woman. "What is it, dear?"

"I'd like to take you for a drink."

"But I don't have ID," said Hannah with feigned innocence.

"You don't need identification, sweetie. Everyone knows who you are. Come with me, just the two of us. It'll be fun."

"It does sound fun. Let me tell Kate, and I'll be ready in a few minutes."

Hannah finished preparing her station for the following performance. Emily Rose continued watching her new friend with professional admiration. She had seen many actors barely out of their costumes before they were out of the building, leaving whatever mess behind, put off for some other time. But Hannah's makeup and accessories were returned to their places, her costumes brushed and hung in the order she would use them for the next show. Another actor might have accused her of anal-retentiveness, but Emily Rose found

Hannah professionally and charmingly well prepared. The veteran actor nearly melted when Hannah explained how the vanity station, the same as any talent she may or may not have, belonged to the public—the audience—as much as it did to her, so she did whatever she could, within reason, to treat it accordingly. Hannah did allow a couple of personal indulgences at her station: There was a vase of flowers left by a gushing young sailor, seeming able bodied, but who had still gone from predilection to love in a mere two hours, and from three rows out; there was also a small photograph of Lincoln Dollar, his headshot from a New York playbill.

Hannah received Katie's permission to go cocktailing with Emily Rose. "Run along, love. I've got the archangels to keep me entertained."

The two actresses walked arm in arm down the street to a pub. While she was no stranger to alcohol, Hannah had but little experience in drinking establishments, and was mischievously excited at the prospect of skirting the law.

The place was smoky loud, with customers playing at bar games, and others sitting at the bar watching sports on television, or looking at scoreboards in the bottoms of highball glasses. Emily Rose and Hannah bellied up and took a pair of stools. The air was cloudy with dusty beer and disinterest.

"Hey, handsome," said Emily Rose to the barkeep. "What do we call you?"

"Friends call me Nic. What can I get you?"

"I'm Emily Rose, Nickolas. This is my daughter, Hannah, and we'd like two of the driest martinis you've got back there."

He reached for the shaker. "The Nic is short for Nicodemus." In went the ice and gin, with vermouth as barely an afterthought. "Daughter?" he smiled. "I'd of guessed you were sisters."

"You just fix those drinks." She said to Hannah, "Our new friend is sticky for tips," just loud enough for the server to hear.

Hannah lit a cigarette, passed it to her friend, and was lighting another when Nic put down their drinks. The barkeep was smiling. "I thought I recognized you ladies. You're in that show at the Sand Box. We went a couple weeks ago. It was a great play, a wonderful show."

The more Nic let loose the compliments, the more star-struck he became. He didn't meet a lot of actors. "Wait here. I gotta get my sister. She's still talking about that show."

Emily Rose was warmly pleased with his excitement. "Go ahead. We'll wait right here."

Hannah believed the bartender's words among the sweetest she had ever heard.

He quit his post and hurried across the dance floor, to a room housing a pair of billiard tables and a row of video games, soon returning with his sister in tow. She was carrying a personalized pool cue in one hand and a customized margarita in the other. Chunks of salt were falling from both.

Carla's eyes lit up when she saw the two. As though they had grown up together, she wrapped her arms around Emily Rose and kissed both her cheeks, with an excitement not born solely of tequila, though it must have surely helped it along. Carla then made a move for Hannah. "Anya!" she shrieked, embracing her tightly. "You were amazing. So real. And the other girl, with the dark hair, I wept, she was so wonderful! I'm trying to get my boyfriend to take me to see it again, but I may as well be asking this pool stick. He's all about action flicks." Carla motioned toward the other room where the action flick fan was leaning on a stick and watching the game.

Hannah fished her cargo pockets for her wallet, for a couple of comp' tickets to the show. She'd had them for weeks with no one to give them to. She *boogied*, in her fashion, across the dance floor and passed the tickets along to the unsuspecting gentleman. "I'm inviting you and your lady friend to the theater tomorrow night. Wear a sport coat, please, and a tie would be nice, and please don't be late." She returned to the bar, leaving the guy resigned to a plan of attending the theater the following evening. Hannah left him wondering if his jacket still fit, but he was still on the fence concerning any necktie.

Carla thanked Emily Rose and Hannah once again, and thanked her bartender-brother for a fresh cocktail. She then walked her pool cue to the other room, enforcing her sweetheart's resignation with a sloppy Cuervo kiss.

"Be careful," Emily Rose warned Hannah. The juniper berries were tickling the young actor's nose, bringing tears to her eyes and a flush to her cheeks. "It's best to let the olives marinate a while."

Still Hannah bit into the glass once more. She *smack*ed her lips, then sent herself spinning seven hundred twenty degrees on the stool, before coming to a stop once again facing the bar. The bottles stood like soldiers at crystalline attention. Smoke hung in the air at eye level. There was an ivory-against-ivory *clack* of pool balls on the felt, with the happy ringing of bells and the flapping of flippers in a well lubricated pinball machine. Hannah took some time to admire the handsome bartender, and lastly a moment devoted solely to her colleague. She was happy—and a little dizzy—when she finally spoke. "I love the stage. When we left Vermont, I wasn't sure what I wanted to do. Thought I'd find something to study, maybe do some acting on the side. I suppose I'm kind of good at it, and it's a lot of fun, but I always thought of it as more like a hobby. These past several weeks, though—working with you and Carl and Charley, even the Gordfather—have got me to thinking; that is, I've been thinking, but just now, that thing with Carla, I want in. I definitely want to be an actor. Who knows? Perhaps I was meant to be an actor." She took another greedy swallow from her drink, winced, and smiled with sweet adolescence for her dear Emily Rose. "When I grow up, I want to be just like you." Sure, it sounded juvenile, but Hannah was getting buzzed enough so she did not care.

Emily Rose was entirely charmed, but still felt ethically bound to dissuade. "Be careful what you wish for. Don't sell your pretty soul to walk a mile in these worn-out mules. Three failed marriages, a kid in college on the west coast who thinks I'm a nut job; he won't even speak to me. I'm never home, always waking up next to someone different. My entire life is voice, tits and hair, but I'm stuck, the same as you'll get stuck if you're not careful. And still there's nothing else I'd rather do.

"I finished my degree decades ago," Emily Rose continued. "I could've walked off the stage—at any time—and gone right into a classroom, and made a lot more money doing it; but I just couldn't make the leap, couldn't get out from under those lights, couldn't get away from that dream of making it to New York. I've been dreaming of

Broadway since I was a little girl, but as it's turned out I'm just an old yo-yo on the finger of regional theater. It always snaps me back. Seems almost silly now."

Emily Rose waved a couple of fingers for Nic's attention. Her eyes were wet. Hannah watched as the woman's girlish dreams tried to get away, and she watched as Emily Rose fought to call them back. "It's incredible, really, to think of all I've sacrificed to get within a few blocks of that street of dreams. I believe I was born to play the stage, the same as you, but it's a hard life. It's mean and vindictive, unpredictable, and once all is settled the pay works out to about sixty cents an hour. And one is forced to work with some of the most nightmarish people on the planet—no names, of course. But one thing's for sure; I've never prostituted myself in the theater. I'm not saying I haven't spent a good deal of time on my back, but I've never done anything that I didn't truly believe in. Maybe I've got some talent; I don't know and I'm long past caring, but at the end of the day I feel like I've done what I was meant to do. From the page to the stage, Hannah, that's my job." She hit her drink once more, hard. The girls were getting high. "Sometimes I get in my Prozac moods and wonder if it was all worth it. I get to wondering if this whole thing wasn't all one huge vocational error. That's where you come in."

Hannah was misty listening, lost in the woman's story, each word bringing her closer and closer until she wore the veteran actor like a comfortable wrap, like a soft cloak of satin, theater and gin. *Where you come in* was tying up the sash when Emily Rose went on, "I'm forever going to look back on this production and I'm going to think of you, and I'm going to know in my heart it was worth it—worth every minute of it."

Hannah's tears were now flowing freely. She lit another cigarette, though she already had one burning in the ashtray. Emily Rose had floored her—Emily Rose and the gin. *I've inspired my inspiration,* she mused; *give and take, quid pro quo.* Looking into the woman's sparkling rich, deep chocolate-brown, almond eyes, Hannah could see herself. Looking past the foregone nuptials and estranged children, she saw the devotion, the dedication and the passion. All that Hannah saw stirred her.

"We'll get there," she said. "We'll get to Broadway, Em. By God, we'll get there." As the words left her mouth, Hannah believed what she said was true, that it was going to happen. She could feel it. She felt something. It might have been the gin.

Emily Rose found tissue for both, though not nearly enough.

"Excuse me," said Hannah. She turned one hundred eighty degrees and dismounted the stool. In the ladies' room she splashed cold water on her face, inspecting herself in the mirror. Her eyes were rimmed red from tears and liquor. She even looked a little buzzed. Accepting herself for what she was, she said, "Oh, well," toweled herself off and went to the telephone.

Hannah's mother was in a tired panic once she finally found the phone on the bedstand. "What is it, Hannah? What's wrong, dear?" Connie fumbled for the lamp switch. Hannah's father mumbled incoherently, something about needing more of the comforter. He turned away and buried his head in the pillows. "What's happened?" Connie asked. "Are you crying?"

Hannah could barely get her words out. "Nothing's wrong. Nothing's ever been so right. All you guys have done for me, all the love and support and understanding, it's all paid off, just this very minute. I love you so much, both of you, and I just wanted to tell you. Kinda goofy, huh?"

It was eighteen years and a few months since the baby invaded, uninvited, the home of the young, professional couple. Their credo had been the enjoyment of life, not the creation of it. Connie was amused at seeing her husband with the blanketed bundle squirming in his awkward, untrained arms, unable to tell which end was up. Connie named the baby Hannah, lest there be any confusion from left to right, right to left. Now the palindromic baby was a woman newly come into her own. Gone back and having returned, Connie found no regrets in her travels, so she thought herself a pretty good mom. She put down the receiver, allowing the satisfaction to flow into her peaceful, sleepy eyes. She leaned in to kiss her husband, to him from Hannah, and gave him another quick peck from herself.

Emily Rose was pleased when Hannah returned, though the bartender was not, having lost his monopoly on the woman's attentions.

"Christ me, I was starting to worry about you," though she had been watching her the entire time in the mirror.

"I had to call my mom."

To the bartender, Emily Rose said, "Be a love and settle us up."

Nic came to the end of the bar, not bothering to hide his disappointment. "You're not leaving already. I'm getting off in a little while."

"You don't know the half of it," said Emily Rose, quietly to herself, rummaging in her purse. "After I've seen my talented, young friend home, I'm coming back for a little nightcap with you."

Sunrise found Hannah's tongue wearing a sweater of cheap wool. She could taste lingering olives and junipers for much of the morning, but all the produce was totally dissipated by the two o'clock matinee.

During the three-hour break between performances, the last of the performances, Hannah rested, planning to pull out all the stops, planning to go into the last show as raw and unbridled and impassioned and intense as she could be; which is to say, Hannah was going into the show much the same as she had gone into the twenty before. She might have gone in with even more, had she known who would be in the audience.

The stage manager moved from the ticket booth to the green room, from the lobby to the backstage area, from properties to actors, to sales, to crew. Lincoln could spot a stage manager from a mile off—the most harried of the group in the minutes before the curtain—but, coupled with Hannah's description, he only had to use about twenty-five feet to spot Charley Evans.

The manager was whistling one of Mary's songs from *Jesus Christ Superstar* as he went about his business, pleasantly happy though frenzied. These were the last of Charley's responsibilities after an all-out, three-month stressor. He checked the clock on the wall to make sure that it coincided with the one on his wrist, looking forward to the final curtain call three hours away. As there was no one yet to work the box office, Charley added those to his duties, approaching the man in the lobby. "How may I help?"

"You must be Charley."

"Depends. If this is about me trying to play photographer at the *Playgirl* swimsuit shoot—" the lobby guy looked like he might have a sense of humor "—I can explain."

"My name's Lincoln Dollar. I hear you've got a couple of my friends in your show."

Charley beamed, grabbing at his hand with both of his. "You really do exist. They never said you were coming, the shits. I'll get them."

"They don't know I'm here. I'll wait and see them after. I've been looking forward to the show."

"As well you should be. What a run! I'm glad you could make it." He was giddy at the prospect of the girls' surprise, and happy that Lincoln would have the opportunity to see his friends working in the orchard. "But if you plan on surprising them, you'd better stay out of the house until the lights go down. Hannah likes to peek—but you must know that. Of course you do. And you'll come with us after the show? Of course you will. Cast party, you know."

"We had ours a couple nights ago. Almost as taxing as the production."

"How was the run? *'Salesman*, right? You played Biff?"

"Second chance at the part," said Lincoln. "Less about the character, more about the play." He urged the stage manager away. "I don't want to keep you, Charley. We'll talk later."

With forty-five minutes left before the curtain, Lincoln left the theater and found a pub down the street. The bartender was crisp, closely-shaven and kempt, his shirt ironed to razor-sharp creases, held closed with a tight Windsor knot. Lincoln thought the server a bit over-dressed for such an establishment and on such an evening, not knowing that the crispness was for a certain actress whom the bartender hoped to meet with later on.

Impatiently, Nic drew the guy an ice-cold draft.

An early May morning was playing in the hushed darkness of the Sand Box. A thin layer of frost blanketed the orchard in Russian opaque, accentuating and teasing the beginnings of the cherry blossoms.

A businessman and the house servant waited in the parlor, waiting on the train, the Moscow Line. It was not a question of, *Will it be late?* but rather, *How late will it be?* Then there was a carriage ride—still more waiting—from the station to the estate. At last there were the sounds of irritated horses pulling up to the house. Guests and staff rushed about excitedly in preparation to receive the returning family. Commotion began building in the adjoining rooms, growing louder, until he finally heard her voice, and Hannah appeared before him; rather, she appeared before the audience, wearing a flowing satin gown, the transparent blue of sapphires, the same blue caught and emitted by her moist, shining eyes. Her hair was pulled back tight, showing the curves of her neck and head. Her hands were clasped at her abdomen with weary gaiety. Standing stiffly straight, she was a young woman acting exhausted with travel; she was a woman acting happy to be back home after years abroad; she was a woman acting.

Lincoln watched on, pushed into his seat, thinking of laying her on the set's divan, imagining kissing from her neck down to the low of her back, smelling her, feeling her. He grew lost in the singsong melody of the lyrics, in the lighting, the sparse setting and lavish costumes. His thoughts wandered to a point later in the evening, to when she would hover above him, laugh with him and love him. And just as quickly he was returned by the sound of Chesapeake Bay applause.

The women weren't threatened by Charley's presence in their dressing room. Another guy would likely have been shown the door, but the stage manager was like one of the girls. There was a hollowness in the air now that the show was over. The cherry orchard was in foreclosure. The production was a wrap. Time was near for all to go their separate ways.

Charley found Hannah at her station, telling her excitedly, "I've got a surprise!"

Hannah was performing her post-production toilet, removing the Anya from her face for the last time. She was dressed only in underpants and a Yankees ball cap, flip chapeau, with a towel over one shoulder; the other shoulder and one breast were exposed, the pointed nipple still sharp from her recent curtain call. "I've got a surprise for you, too," she returned.

"You first."

"Looks like we're staying on for *Scrooge and Marley*. Kate wants to play that little Tommy what's-his-name, and I'm going to play the Ghost of Christmas Sucks. Won't that be fun, Uncle Charley? We can all stay together on the beach for the holidays—if you'll have us, that is."

"You're not teasing me?" he asked.

"I haven't the equipment to tease you."

Charley put his hands on her shoulders, looking over her head at her face in the mirror. She was a good girl and a good friend, and he was thinking as much when Hannah asked, "So, what's your surprise?"

"Oh, I almost forgot," he said indifferently. "Someone wants to see you in the lobby."

"More soldiers and sailors looking to get their dicks autographed? No, thanks."

"Not sailor, nor soldier, but seems like a nice enough guy just the same. I think he's got a rubber hand."

Hannah's mouth was agape. Her eyes were wide with skeptical surprise. "You're fucking with me, right?"

Of course he wasn't, he couldn't, he wouldn't dare.

She jumped, threw the towel at Charley, and rushed about looking for something to cover herself. Nearly ready to say, 'to hell with it' and go ahead without, she finally settled on Emily Rose's robe, tying it closed as she ran out the door and into the hallway. Her bare feet slapped at the floor with hungry anticipation.

Hannah found her man in the lobby. She approached him running and jumped into his arms, slamming him against the wall, smothering him, moving closer and closer until they melted into one. "Kiss me, kiss me, please," she begged, hugging him violently.

The commotion had taken the attention of everyone in the busy room. As much as Hannah had come to enjoy performing for others, still she shied away from personal public displays, so she quickly composed herself, backed off and settled down. "Awkward," she said. "It's a pleasure to see you again, sir, and I'll look forward to meeting with you presently." Still, unable to restrain herself, she fell back into his arms, putting her mouth close to his ear. "I'm so, *so* happy you're here. Man, I sure do love you. Lemme get Kate." She returned with forced dignity to the backstage area.

Hannah was only seconds gone before Katie burst through the same door, going for Lincoln, going straight for the new hand. She grabbed hold of the prosthesis, turning it, inspecting thoroughly. "Not bad," she said, half-approvingly, full-condescendingly, "but it feels kind of funny, like—I don't know, almost feels familiar." She kissed him hard on the mouth. "It's good to see you, and you look so good." She kept a tight hold on the neoprene hand.

"You were wonderful tonight," said Lincoln. "Chekhov would be pleased."

"He would be more pleased with the guy who taught me everything I know." Katie redoubled her hold on the new hand and stepped away. Her face dropped. "I know what this thing reminds me of."

"Do I dare ask?" he wondered aloud.

Her smile was sheepish. "Suffice to say, I keep mine in the drawer beside the bed."

"Amazing," said Lincoln, shaking his head, unable to respond otherwise.

With another hug and a snicker, Katie left a smudge of makeup on his lapel. "I'm happy to see you. How'd you get away?"

"We're done. Couldn't sell another ticket. It was fun, but I'm glad it's over. Time for another adventure."

"The pirate play?"

"Maybe."

"Crazy fucker. Why pirates?"

"Because pirates are cool. You've lost some weight."

"From chasing around after your girlfriend, but that'll be your job now. Let me finish getting ready. We're going to party." There was another hug, and still another kiss. "It really is good to see you, Lincoln. I've needed to see you."

At his leisure, Lincoln loitered alone in the lobby. Others in the room were waiting to see what other pretty lady actors would sail through the stage door and into his arms, but no other pretty lady actors sailed through.

Nic was beyond pleased when the cast and crew of the cherry orchard filed into the pub. This would not be a typical Sunday night. The procession took some time in entering, with Emily Rose purposely picking up the rear. The bartender had waited at the door for her entrance, sidling close. "How was the show?" he asked.

"Nothing compared to your performance last night. Christ me, I can barely walk."

Soon the crisp and cockstrong Nic was moving to put tables together to accommodate the growing crowd. His sister entered soon after with her man-friend in tow. Upon Hannah's invitation, he had gone to the theater, he had arrived early, and had even worn a jacket, but he didn't wear the tie, because he didn't like people telling him what to do; nor did he know the night before that he'd be thanking Hannah for a theatrical experience, but he immediately found himself doing just that. He and Carla joined the group. More chairs were wedged in.

Between mixing the drinks and lusting after Emily Rose, Nic had his hands full. Charley and Carl were leaning in close to one another, guzzling wine like flappers and making plans for the Christmas show. Lighting techs and stagehands lined the bar to see who could stomach the most tequila. Katie sat at center table like a lusty novel, with the brothers Croft as her personal bookends. She was ready to play with the brothers again in the coming Christmas show, while at present she played with them under the table.

The only actor not attending the cast party was Spencer. The octogenarian had had his fill of such parties. "Too much drama," he protested, more than content to celebrate his last stage appearance alone at home watching *The Golden Girls*. He thought Bea Arthur was a real cut up.

Hannah was close to Lincoln, struggling to hear and be heard over the boisterous crowd. "Let's get out of here," she finally said, initiating an exit that went nearly unnoticed, save by Katie who saw them out with lazy happiness, her hand gripped tightly to the inside of Gabriel's thigh.

The evening was cool, November on the Chesapeake, but the salty breeze of the bay whispered warmly through the streets. They were walking hand in hand when Hannah told Lincoln of the change in plans to keep them in Virginia longer than expected. She didn't want to go to Vermont for the holidays. "It isn't home. It never was. My home's with you and Kate. Mom and dad can come and visit us."

Lincoln made no mention of reservations for three on Paradise Island for the holidays, though the brochure had been burning in his pocket for weeks. A Christmas production at the Sand Box easily trumped any plans of getting to the beaches of the Bahamas. When the theater called, one had to pick up the phone.

"Do you miss teaching?" Hannah finally asked. She'd hooked her arm in his as they walked along, watching their feet moving over the pavement, staying as close to him as she could. "Did you enjoy it?"

"I did for the first year, but then it got rough, and mostly because of you."

"Because I was such a terrible student?"

"Exactly."

"But you're glad you stuck it out?"

"I am."

Hannah held him closer still. "You'll stay with us on the beach, right? Hang out and write the pirate play? We can all go down south together." She rested her head on his shoulder, walking along, waiting for an answer.

"It doesn't matter to me. I can do the writing anywhere." He stopped her, held her and kissed her a couple of times. "Would you rather go back to the pub, or to my cheap hotel?"

"We live just a few more doors down," Hannah answered. "Let me show you the place. There's something I want to give you before we go back—a little something I picked up hanging out with the soldiers and sailors of the Chesapeake Bay."

"Lovely."

As Hannah got him nearer the flat, she asked, "You got roles for us in the pirate play? For me and Kate?"

"I hadn't really thought about it."

"Pirates need chicks on the boat, you know," she suggested, putting the key in the lock. "It must get boring on the briny when there ain't no ships to plunder."

Act Four

-1-

The broad beams of the headlights struggled to cut a path through the fog which hovered over the bayou like a misty tropical steam. The twilight was still and quiet on the marshes and tributaries of the mighty river, with a bright full moon highlighting the haunting landscape, and shadowing the long-hanging, grayish tendrils of the Spanish moss dripping from the arms of the oak and baldcypress trees. The last sun of October was but moments gone. The coolness of the night tried to settle on the bayou, but the heat of the past day remained in the sticky hands of the thick vegetation, casually released to warm the dawning of a bayou November.

There were many sounds of the night on the river, though coming together they made little noise. Frogs could be heard stealing a dinner of crickets, at the same time the fish were sneaking up on the frogs; pelicans splashed in the distance, bucket-loading scoops of the fish, and teetering at the top of the bayou foodchain, the alligators waited patiently for the large birds and for anything else; but still the total of the hungry voices was quieted in the sound of the silent darkness.

Art Fields was bounding, determined to see the rental vehicle live up to its title of 'Pathfinder.' Thus far it had served well, finding several paths, and some of them barely beaten. With all four wheels engaged, he pounded the twisting, marshy roads, all the while having a grand time of the adventure. Once finally returned to second gear, he turned on the overhead light and unclasped his appointment book to thumb the directory. The sandy, swamp roads made for an arduous task, but he succeeded at last in making a connection.

The noises of the night were hypnotizing. From the river's silence every so often came the faint sounds of automobiles in the distance, mostly lost tourists, those unfortunates who had strayed from tourist-beaten paths. In the thick of the bayou mist, many were lost indefinitely; many were lost forever.

Lost in that same silence was Lincoln Dollar. He was swinging in a chair which hung from the porch roof of the cabin, his feet resting on the railing, when the insidious ringing of the telephone shattered the night's illusion. As it was most often Hannah who was calling, however, the illusion-shattering was generally worthwhile. He rubbed the dreamy solitude from his far-away eyes, shaking the tangled thoughts from his mind. He was surprised to find that it was Art on the line. Hannah's father had called but three times in the four years since they'd met.

"How are you?" Art asked.

"Not bad for a swamp recluse, but it's a while since I've been off the place. I'm seeing gremlins running about. Last night they stopped in for cocktails."

"You need help, and I just might be your guy."

"Where you at and what do you have?"

"How about you get rid of the gremlins and have a cocktail with me? Look outside, see the headlights? Start pouring."

Indeed, Lincoln looked out the window and saw the Pathfinder's headlights pull up alongside the cabin. He rushed to greet him, greedily grabbing for his hand. "How'd you find the place?" He was close to ecstatic at seeing Hannah's father. Any company at all was cause for holiday-like excitement, but Lincoln was especially fond of Arthur Fields.

"The kid gives good directions." Art stretched to shuffle the four-wheeled tension in his back and neck. "What do you have to drink? I've been on the road most of the day."

From a large kettle of water steaming on the gas stove, Lincoln ladled some into a smaller basin and set it on what served as the cabin's table. "Freshen yourself up. I'll hit the liquor department."

Art moved to wash the road trip from his face and hands, inspecting the room and its surroundings as he toweled off. "How can you live down here? It's got to be the gloomiest place on the planet."

Lincoln was quick to disagree, to defend. "Not at all. Like this scotch, the rolling prairie's an acquired taste. Far from gloomy, it's passionate and moody, strange and warm, sweet and mysterious, a little scary, a little lazy, and incredibly sensual. It's beautiful, really. It's … well, it's an acquired taste, I suppose."

In his own opinion, Lincoln might just as well have been describing Hannah as the bayou, but he was happy he'd kept the comparison to himself when her father promptly replied,

"You make it sound like a high-end whore." Kindled and refreshed, Art added, "Let's ride to the city, see the girls. Hannah doesn't know I'm in town."

Regarding Hannah, Lincoln spoke mostly to fill any voids that might allow other feelings and motives to escape, those he believed were best kept to himself. "That'd be great. It's hard to believe they're in their forth semester already. They did some Ibsen a few months back, some of the best theater I've ever seen anywhere. How's Connie? It's nearly a year since we were up north, last Christmas."

"Everything's the same. Lauren looks forward to seeing you at the holidays." Letting briefly go the small talk, Art added, "We're glad you're down here, Lincoln, close by. Makes it easier for us, and we appreciate it. If there's ever anything we can do—"

"Instead of driving to the city," Lincoln interrupted, "we'll go up the river. There's a good moon tonight. Tomi can bring us up in the boat. It'll take a little longer, but it's a nicer ride, and I'm sure he won't mind the fare. I'll ring him up."

Art expected Lincoln would go for the phone; instead, he went to the porch, cupped his hands, and yelled into the swallowing darkness. Returned with the screen door slamming behind him, Lincoln said, "He'll be over in a minute. He'll get us up to the city. Tomi knows the Mississippi better than Mark Twain." He directed Art's attention to some watercolors hanging about the room. "These are his."

Art barely inspected the paintings, but went to the window, looking at the night sky and at the floating, pulsating field which served as a tributary to the mighty Mississippi. He could not help voicing his concern. "It doesn't look like very friendly sailing tonight. You sure this guy can steer us through these swamps and islands?"

"Not swamps and islands," Lincoln replied; "bayous and chenieres."

Lincoln moved about the cabin preparing for the river excursion, eager for the adventure. It had been two months since he'd left the property. His only cause to leave the delta was to visit the girls in the Garden District of the city—twenty miles off as birds fly, close to thirty when negotiating the bends of the river, and nearly forty on roads seldom paved—but Hannah and Katie often came to visit him, making his trips less necessary. Lincoln's travel schedule was based solely on the university's theater program; when the girls were on stage, he went to the city. It was a simple arrangement lasting two years so far. In the meantime, he was content to hole-up in the bayou cabin, scribbling stories of local color, as well as other writings depicting strange and wondrous scenes.

While Lincoln less-than-fastidiously tended to his hygiene, Art went to the watercolor paintings on the walls. One showed the bayou outside the cabin door. Another was the marketplace at Cathedral Square, a small combo sweating jazz in the Bourbon Street heat. Another was a row of shotgun houses in the Quarter, another a cemetery in the Garden District. Art knew little of art, but still found himself studying the works—twelve of them—with an eye of appreciation for their detail. They treated their subjects kindly, each seemingly holding secrets to which only the artist was privy. There was also something delicate, almost effeminate, in the works, enough so that Art would not have believed them of a man's hand had Lincoln not told him this was so. All were framed and displayed with care. "These are quite good."

Lincoln continued to tidy himself up. "I'll say. He's given me one every Christmas since I've known him. Tomi's self-taught, never had any formal training, never sat in any classroom. The bayou was his classroom, his forefathers the teachers. And, in a sense, Tomi's been a teacher to me.

"There's a magic in these people, Art, and they take it pretty seriously. They claim to see something in Hannah, like she's possessed of something, and it must be something good, as they seem to take a sincere interest in her. Good totem, I suppose. Good mojo. They'll think you're pretty special for having made her."

Art was suddenly feeling pretty special, inhaling deeply of the thick, mossy surroundings. It was a rich, dark, and earthy world. "What do you do with yourself all alone down here?"

Each of the walls had one window, no curtains. The floor consisted of two-by-six planks tacked to a shallow frame which rested on the earth. Sparsely furnished, there was a table with three chairs in the middle of the place, seeming a boundary between living and working spaces. There was a small sofa, sorrowfully sagging with years of bayou abuse. There were many books, old, new, classics and the esoteric, and two desks piled high, a mass of confusion to anyone but their owner. The kitchen consisted of a gas stove, gas refrigerator, a half-dozen cupboards and some cabinets. There were no dirty dishes in the sink. There was no *dirty* anything. The place was beat up and cluttered, but it was clean; in camp-like fashion, the cabin was rustic. A small generator hummed outside allowing for the sparse lighting, electronics, and occasional music. Telephones were cellular.

"It's difficult to see at night, but I've actually got quite a few neighbors. Most have been living here as long as the river. They don't usually let outsiders in, but I suppose I've been coming long enough that my motives are no longer questioned. I don't know what I'd do without them."

Art sipped at the scotch. "How's the writing?" he asked, reading the spines of the books: Sontag, Moliere, Hansberry, Henley, Shakespeare, Pirandello, Shaw—*plays,* thought Art; *never cared much for plays*. "Hannah tells us you're working on a play—some pirate thing." Having finished looking over the books, he scanned the papers strewn about the desks. He saw no mention of pirates, swashbuckling or otherwise.

Lincoln backed away from the subject of the pirates of Barataria Bay, backed away from the subject of writing altogether. "Everything's right on schedule," he said, leaving it at that. "Tomi's real Creole, Art. They've lived here for four hundred years. Never been farther north than the city or farther south than the gulf, but he knows this stretch of the Mississippi better than anyone. He'll get us up to New Orleans, and there's no prettier way to travel—especially tonight. It's All Saint's Eve. Folks'll be on the river, conjuring the souls of the dead." He grew increasingly excited at the prospect of the river journey. "The more I think about it, the more I like the idea. I'm real glad you showed up. It's a nice surprise." He raised his glass to Art's on his search for some sort of a change of clothes.

Art was demurred with the idea of the swamp tour, still skeptical, but slowly growing willing. "Want me to call the girls, or should we surprise them?"

"A bunch of college kids on Halloween?" Lincoln reminded him; "it's more likely we'll be the ones who get surprised. But we'll wait and call them once we're ashore. Hannah'd be nervous if she knew we were on the river at night. No sense worrying her."

Lincoln's neighbor rapped on the cabin door and let himself in. Tomi was a dark bear of a fellow, with centuries of African, European and Spanish blood coursing in his Creole veins. His worn clothing was homemade of plain patterned cotton, save a tired and tattered tan fedora and knee-high black rubber boots. His shirt was sleeveless, revealing arms like tree limbs, with the broken lines of scars from both shoulders to the wrists; scars a shade or two darker or lighter than his own nightly skin, scars speaking of a life marked by difficult and dangerous labors. Strong and smooth, soft and sweet, Tomi was a cross between Huckleberry Finn and an elderberry wine. In the darkened cabin, he was darker still. His deep, heavy voice dripped the local patois.

Most are self-proclaimed, either to add romance and adventure to reclusive bayou existences, or to cash in on the tourism trade, but Tomi was a bona fide descendant of the corsairs and privateers of the Barataria Islands at the mouth of the river. They had referred themselves as privateers, entrepreneurs who left homes and families in the city to search for riches on the seas; the rest of the world called them pirates. Tomi's relatives had sailed under the charters of the brothers Lafitte.

His home lay just south of Lincoln's place, through a dense thicket of cypress trees and muscadina vines, all choked in purple hyacinth. It was a small, clapboard dwelling he shared with Celine and their four young children. Both mothers were now gone, and the fathers had long since been taken by the mysterious waters, the same as many bayou fishermen before them. There were complexities of necessity in the bayou life kept simple by those born into it. Laws and regulations were enacted and repealed, the prairie flooded and the prairie dried up, generations came and generations went, and the Creole shrimpers keep shrimping through and around it all.

For threescore years Tomi's family had leased the right to live in the dilapidated cabin, sending monthly payments to some white Southern Baptists up in Lafayette. The lease was barely within reach, but always still nearer than any mortgage. Lincoln's right to dwell on a similar small tract was granted by the same fat man in Lafayette, though under even less generous terms. They were neighbors going on thirteen years, although Lincoln's residences were sporadic and varying in length. Tomi kept up the place when he was away, free of the bayou vermin, vegetation and squatters wanting to move in. He kept the cabin in serviceable repair, bayou-style, always at the ready for the next sporadic return. He always returned.

Lincoln left the bayou one day nearly seven years before and was gone longer than his usual, giving his neighbor cause to miss him. Finally, Tomi heard the one-lunger chugging near the shore. Mista Lincoln was returned. He rushed to meet the river-taxi, reaching with enthusiasm to assist the man and his luggage from the boat. "Welcome home, Mista Lincoln," he said, then noticed the missing limb.

Lincoln waved away the man's hand and struggled with his bags; but this waving away offended the Creole—this seeming embarrassment, this feigned independence—as an insult to bayou life, to the bayou spirit. When again Tomi offered, or rather strongly suggested, Lincoln put the hook in the large hand and allowed himself to be pulled from the craft. He did not attempt any explanation, nor had the big man asked for any. They would discuss it another time, or perhaps they would not.

The Creole entered the cabin heavily, holding his hat against his stomach, happy to have seen Art's vehicle pulling up. Lincoln having company was the same as Tomi having company. Few visitors came so deep into the bayou.

"Evenin Mista Lincoln. Evenin sir." Tomi nodded to the stranger. "Y'all be wantin to go up river." His was not a question, but rather a statement of past experience.

"That's right. Tomi, this is Arthur Fields, Hannah's father."

The Creole took Art's hand like a pump handle, like one who seldom made new acquaintances. "Ah! Miz Hannah's a fine woman, yeah. Celine say Hannah gon be big one day." He spoke excitedly. "Y'all be wantin to go to Nawlens den? Go see Miz Hannah?"

Art was caught off guard by the Creole's explosive friendliness. Having met the vessel's operator, he no longer concerned himself with the dark river cruise. Tomi appeared an able-bodied skipper. "Yes, please, if you're available. We'll go up that big ol' river tonight, up to see Hannah."

Addressing both men, the Creole suggested, "We go soon den, so I git back. We conjur big spirit to-ni. Dey magic in dat bayou to-ni."

Quickly wrapping up preparations for the trip, Lincoln told Art of the Creole custom to celebrate the night's holiday. "They'll be honoring their deceased at their resting places, along the river, in the cemeteries, exciting stuff."

"Sounds like a bunch of hoodoo-voodoo to me," Art opined.

"Oh, no. That's a whole different ballgame."

The chenieres were bright in the moonlight, the rich, dark green leaves of the trees, black in the night, casting floating shadows on the rolling dark waters. A breeze blew warmly and sweetly from the mouth of the river, carrying the flavors of orange and lemon blossoms, chamomile and jasmine. Tomi stood at the helm, concentrating a sailor's focus on the narrow passages. His speed was slow, constant and sure.

Closer to shore the alligators *splash*ed and *thrash*ed at the disturbance of the boat's raspy motor, but once the craft was safely by they settled back into their predatory lethargy, with only their feral, hungry eyes and suspicious nostrils above the murky surface.

"Are we hunting tonight?" Lincoln asked the skipper, his voice barely audible, blending with the myriad sounds of the starry night. He sat near to where the 30-06 was tucked up under the stern, at the ready with a cartridge chambered.

Tomi's eyes were on the water, his hands lightly resting on the wheel to feel for any changes in the course. "No hunt to-ni."

Poachers have all but spoiled the alligator hunt for the natives of the river, adding the creature to an ever-growing list of endangered; but Tomi's family still depended on the meat for much of its sustenance, and he could still fetch a good price for the hide with the city's black marketeers. It was a risky dinner procurement when Tomi had one of the great cigar-shaped beasts in his sights, when he was forced to consider who would provide if he was apprehended in his lawlessness; however, Tomi's faith in God and Justice usually allowed the gumption needed to fire the single round.

Art had taken to peering over the side of the craft into the dark water. He was humming an old Doobie Brothers song when something jumped. He started back, scrambling to brace himself, quickly feeling about his face to ensure that nothing was changed. The event ended with Art not finding the experience nearly as amusing as did his traveling companions, and with him commenting as such as he moved to a seat nearer the center of the craft. The journey continued in silence.

Arthur Fields was enrapt in the night, captivated—nearly hypnotized—by the sights and sounds and smells of the journey, until at last they came to the great bend in the river, to where the Crescent City shined brightly and festively in the night. Throngs of tourists and hucksters moved about under the spotlighted spires of the Saint Louis Cathedral on Jackson Square.

Hannah's father returned from the trance and shook the dreaminess of the journey from his mind. He stretched his arms and legs, thinking himself a nautical sort of fellow for having weathered the river excursion. One thought led to another, until he said to his daughter's friend, "Tell me about the pirate play."

Lincoln was moving about with the rigging and working the lines. One of the loosely coiled lengths was gripped in the artificial hand. "I haven't started it yet. Maybe in a few more months."

"But Hannah told us … she said you've been working at it over a year."

Lincoln was forced to admit, "Yeah, I told her that's what I've been doing."

"Interesting." Once thinking that some of the incredulity was removed from the question, Art asked, "So you're lying to my kid—already?"

Tomi guided the craft toward the pier while Lincoln sat on the starboard edge, alternating his glances between the dock and Hannah's father. He had allowed the lies to pile for more than a year, the whole time justifying them as small and white. He was now satisfied, without finding fault, and tried to explain as much to Art. "I was trying to steal myself a little time, but now Hannah's gone way past nosy. My time is running out." He kept an eye on the coming pier.

"It was awhile back that I decided to write the play—the pirate play—but then I met your daughter and everything changed. I've been a basket case most my life, Art. It's been ugly at times, mostly a fucking mess really, always digging myself deeper and deeper. I ended up in Preston as a sort of last resort, even an act of desperation. I didn't know what else to do at the time. Then everything changed; I started seeing things differently, doing things differently, feeling things differently, and your kid had a lot to do with it—she had everything to do with it, and Katie, too." He smiled a moment, then shook it off. "Katie—she's like a kid sister—she's gotta be the most entertaining person I've ever met in my life. And Hannah …"

Lincoln prepared the mooring lines, double-checking, continuing, "I decided, instead of the pirate play, I would write something for her, something she could stage. I've written a few one-acts, three-quarters of a shitty novel, but I've never tried anything like this, and I didn't know if I'd be able to pull it off, didn't know if my feelings for her would get in the way. I didn't know if I was being delusional about the entire thing, tilting at windmills again, caught up in more wishful thinking. Now, regarding the *untruths*—my lying about the pirate thing—I had to tell her something. I didn't want her to think I was doing nothing but sitting on my ass and fishing in the bayou."

If no one else, at least Lincoln was satisfied with the explanation. "So, there you have it."

Art was satisfied, too, as well as curious. "You think you can pull it off? Are you going to write this play for my little girl?"

Lincoln was again awash with the same excitement that had poured over him, two weeks back, when he penned the last lines of the manuscript. The excitement ran up and down over his skin. It leapt in his chest as he faced the approaching pier. "I'll know more in a month, but I kinda like it; and, more importantly, I think Hannah's going to like it. But let's you and me keep it to ourselves for now. As far as they know, it was the pirate play I sent to the editors."

Lincoln tossed a bight of line over the cleat. He pulled it taut and tied it off. He was hungry to catch the streetcar over to St. Charles, wondering how he was going to find some time alone with Hannah. His thoughts were delicious thoughts, and mostly sweet thoughts—mostly—but they were tainted by the guilt of having been thought in the company of her father.

He hoisted himself to the pier and extended his hand. "All ashore, Mr. Fields. First stop, Bourbon Street—where, I reckon, we'll find the makings of a happy Halloween, indeed."

-2-

Hannah closed the spiral-bound manuscript, glancing about while covertly wiping her tears, lest anyone should see her crying in the park, and at such a nonhuman hour. She didn't have to worry, though, for she was very much alone, save the uniformed attendants on their way to work at the zoo. The animals would be waking soon and looking for some breakfast.

She sat on her favorite bench in Audubon Park. There were rarely any visitors so early in the morning, making these early morning hours all the more attractive to her. It was Hannah's place, her space, her time away from the university, away from the theater, away from Katie, away from life. It was the place where she thought of her lover, dreamt of where they were going, of what was coming next. Never sure of what was coming, Hannah was at least comfortable knowing that Lincoln would be there when it came.

The sun was new on the park, the fresh dew glistening on the green, and along the grass of St. Charles Avenue separating the park from campus. The oak trees shined in the day's new light. *How beautiful,* Hannah thought; *how perfectly and honestly beautiful.* She was referring to the manuscript, not the morning, though she would have held the same opinion of the day were she not so enrapt in her reading. Once again she opened the manuscript and began reading anew. The lyrics washed over her even more lovely and lively than the first time through. Again she could not put it down before weeping over the last tragic lines.

"Oh, this is good," she said aloud. "It's very good." She ran her fingers slowly, gently, over the title page, like a newly-blind person with guarded eagerness to learn her braille. Back and forth over the words she read, "*The Awakening*. I like it. I love it." Like a new mother holding her long-awaited child, Hannah brought the manuscript up to rest over her heart.

The St. Charles streetcar passed by, again and again and again, noisily rocking on the thin rails, coming to sudden, jerking stops at every other block, picking up and dropping off the early morning riders, their hands full of coffee cups and electronic devices, briefcases and backpacks, portfolios and inky copies of the *Times-Picayune*.

Hannah was well into a day she knew would be like none before. She sat for some time on the bench with her head in her hands, weeping and wondering and laughing. She wished to put one foot in front of the other, to do what felt right, but her feet were suddenly very heavy. Confused, she would have to figure it out on her way to … to … she didn't know where she was going. Still, as heavy as the feet were, they started moving. They took Hannah to the university theater department. The doors were locked.

The director of theater operations finally opened the doors from the inside. Hannah flicked her cigarette into the shrubbery, and, in one fluid movement, upped her ass and slid off the half-wall upon which she'd been sitting. She handed him the envelope with the manuscript enclosed.

"This was due a week ago," the director scolded while receiving the parcel. "I'm taking points off this time."

"It's not my paper. That's still not good enough for you, but *this* is. I want you to read it, read it now, and promise you won't let it leave the office."

Hannah left him and sprinted across the quad. Most of the dorm was still asleep. Once inside the community room, she rang up Lincoln.

"You're my favorite person in the world."

"I bet you say that to a lot of people," said he, not at all surprised that she should find him before any alarm. "You got the package, I take it. What'd you think?"

Her hands were shaking with nervous confusion. "I gave it to Brad. I didn't know what else to do. What should I do?"

"Start by settling down. Everything else okay?"

"You wrote me a play!" She was nearly screaming. "Pirate play? You weren't writing any pirate play."

"Do you like it?"

"I love it. You knew I would." Hannah was giddy in her excitement.

"You'll try to get Brad to stage it?"

"Oh, I won't *try*; we *will* stage your play."

And now he corrected her. "That's your play. It belongs to you. After a couple of years, I'm totally out of the loop. You figure out what to do with it."

"It's one of the most beautiful plays I've ever read. It really is. How were you able to do it?"

"Inspired, I suppose. The rest is simple mechanics."

"Christ me, I don't know what to do."

"Do what you can to make it work for you," said Lincoln.

"No, no, no. It can't be about me. I've learned from a reliable source that I can't afford to let that happen."

Hannah remembered Emily Rose's decline as the result of putting her own needs above those in the audience, the result of letting go of the art to chase after the applause. Hannah did not judge, nor would she ever venture to compare, but she could identify with Emily Rose, and she was grateful for her having learned the lesson for them both, hence saving Hannah that painful experience. "This cannot be about me— ever."

"You're a good kid."

"Thanks, I guess. But what's the trump card? In case he won't buy it? Tell me something good."

Lincoln paused in his return. The last time she wanted to be told *something good*, he had only to tell her to *be big*, but now she had accomplished that *bigness* as such that he could not use the same advice again. However, it did not matter what Lincoln might say, for she was already off and running. Hannah had given the manuscript to Brad. She knew what she had to do.

"Tell him if he doesn't want it, you've got someone who'll put up the money so you can stage it yourself."

"Is that true?"

"Not really. It's a bluff, but it's a pretty good one. I don't think Brad's going to pass." When she was silent, he asked, "Why did you give it to him in the first place?"

Hannah hadn't yet considered this. "I don't know. I mean, he's my director, my friend, and he's done a lot for me and Kate. It's only fitting we should do something for him. Right?"

"Kind of makes me proud of you."

Though she could hear the kind sentiments in his voice, still she found the compliment condescending by present tastes. "Like I'm your good little student? You're a fine teacher, Mr. Dollar. Is that what you need to hear?"

"What I mean is, I'm proud to be your friend."

"That's more like it," she returned, "though pride's a terrible thing. What else?"

"I guess I like hanging out with you."

"Again, good. What else?"

He appeared to be thinking of something more, but had finally to give it up. "I believe that's it."

"Then that's good enough for now. I'm going to owe you big-time for this. You really *are* a good teacher, and you're an amazing writer; you're a wicked good actor and a pretty good piece of ass. All in all, you ain't half-bad. A *keeper*, that's what you are."

"So keep me," he challenged. "I double-dog dare you."

Hannah sighed. She tried to say something, but her smile wouldn't allow the words passage. She managed only to whisper "double-dog."

"That play belongs to you. Don't be afraid to talk about money."

"Are you serious?" she asked.

"It's worth a try."

"You know, it's coming up on five years since you crashed into me. I've been in love with you a whole quarter of my life. And I know you love me. You must. I knew we'd end up together, and I know we're together for a reason. I totally believe that. One day we'll find out just what that reason is."

Her musings had raised cause for pondering on both ends of the phone. It was much too much to handle at present—Hannah had other things to do—so she came in to rescue them both. "That's too deep for so early in the morning, and I'm sure to start crying if I don't stop right now. We'll have to get together, work this out. What are your plans?"

"I believe I've done my part. The rest is up to you. I'm going fishing, but I won't be far." She was silent for a time, prompting him to ask, "You still there?"

"I'm here. Thanks again. Thank you, my friend. I'm going to do everything I can to bring this to life for you."

"For them. Bring it to life for them. And I know you will. You already have."

Katie didn't share Hannah's fondness for the early hours; Katie's was reserved for the French Quarter, where she'd recently taken to trading her mornings for evenings, now frolicking later and later into the night. Hannah left the Quarter to Katie and Katie to the Quarter, as she found the downtown spectacle barely tolerable, something she could take only in small doses, not unlike radiation and with much the same effect. She sometimes felt that Katie enjoyed the old Quarter of the city a little *too* much, that it had the potential to fester into something one day coming between them. But Hannah wouldn't let that happen. Besides, in spite of Katie's reckless behavior, she was always available when needed. And, after all, Hannah lastly surmised, to reassure herself if nothing else, Kate always was a tart.

She roused her roommate none too gently, "Get up and get ready. We've got a big day."

Katie languidly complained, without expending the energy to open her eyes, "I'm off today."

"You're not off anymore. Get up. I'll tell you all about it."

"Tell me about it later." She pulled the covers over her head.

Hannah was quick to pull the covers back. "Up, Katherine—*now!*"

Katie mumbled something through gritted teeth, something she didn't really want Hannah to hear. Reluctantly, she rose from the bed and dragged herself toward the bathroom. She turned the water on hot.

Hannah followed. She sat to pee, then began excitedly, "It wasn't any pirate play."

"Wash my back," Katie lazily demanded. "What are you talking about?"

Hannah fastened herself up and fumbled some soap onto a sponge. "Lincoln's play, it's got nothing to do with pirates. It's for us, Kate. He wrote a play for you and me. And it's beautiful—it's so goddamn beautiful! I just gave it to Brad."

Katie turned on her. "You gave it to Brad? What about me? D'ya think I might want to see it?"

"You can see your own copy through the little window on your mailbox, if you got your lazy ass down there once in a while." To make up for the insult, she added, "It may be lazy, but it's nice."

"Yeah, I know. So, tell me more."

"He wrote the play for us," said Hannah, "and it's perfect—simply perfect." Her arm was wet to the shoulder. "Get out of there. I want to be at the theater when Brad's finished. Man! Wait till you read it!"

Katie finished quickly as instructed, as it had been some time since her friend was so excited. *Come to think of it*, thought Katie, *the last time was all about Lincoln Dollar, too.*

The girls had recently begun their fifth semester at Tulane, just into their third year, but already they were eager to put the college experience behind them. They wanted to be back on the road. They wanted to act. Both were getting a lot of stage time at the university, but they were hungry for more direction, different sets, changes of scene. They had swallowed their theater instruction whole, while barely nibbling at the core classes—reluctantly, and with turned up noses: marketing, economics, statistics, science with a lab. Outside her theater work, Hannah discovered that she had affinities for literary theory and history. Katie discovered she could trade sex for term papers. But now the theater classes were over and the remainder of their undergrad experience was sure to drag on. Katie was determined to get the degree; Hannah didn't care one way or the other. Higher education was playing less and less a part in her plans. She felt she knew what she needed to know; mainly how to work an audience by using her fail-proof approach: Make 'em laugh, make 'em cry, and make 'em wait—but not too, too long. She truly believed it was all in the timing.

Theater Director Brad Gooding sat on the edge of the main stage in the building he had managed the past four years. Behind him was the partially constructed set for an upcoming Oscar Wilde play. Hannah and Katie had leads in the production, another of Brad's projects. He was holding the script Hannah had given him, tightly enough so the tension showed in the muscles of his wrist.

Having taken all four of the department's directors for test runs, Brad was the girls' favorite. Time under his direction was proving time well spent. He was a skilled artisan who wasn't afraid to take risks, as he believed the two went hand in hand. Brad encouraged his students to take these same risks, and was afforded the satisfaction of watching them grow into their crafts. Katie and Hannah were growing into their crafts. Brad had watched the two hone their skills as such that there was little doubt they would achieve a measure of success once released from his menial charge.

"Where did you get it?" asked the director.

Hannah hopped up on the stage to sit next to him. "It was a gift." She worked her pitch, while Katie sat in the front row of the house reading her mailbox copy of the manuscript.

"From your friend with the fake hand?" Brad asked, though he was already pretty sure of the source. When Hannah didn't entertain him with particulars, he continued, "What do you want me to do with it?"

"What do you think, you knucklehead?" The junior looked at the director as though he were a freshman. "Didn't you read it? We need to do it—*now*."

"Who's *we*?"

"Us, me and Kate, and we need you to direct. I'm playing Edna. Kate's playing Adèle." Hannah then added, though as the words ran from her she already knew they were too forward, too direct; but, by the time she realized this, it was already too late, so she had to run along with them; "You can decide the rest."

"I appreciate that," was the director's humble reply. "To think I've only spent twenty-plus years in this business, now the head of this fine department, and already the students are allowing me to make some of the decisions. My life's devotion is finally paying off."

"Alright, alright. I'm sorry." It was Hannah's time to get humble. "We can't do this without you. I'm asking for your help, as a friend."

It was a shame Katie was so involved with the script, as she would have enjoyed Hannah's approach.

Brad, on the other hand, was enjoying it less and less. He had the entire department to consider, many of the students paying hefty tuitions to study theater; students who, rightly so, expected to have their own acting egos tickled. He continued along this same line of reasoning. "You know, I've been through your work. Neither of you has ever acted in any tertiary role. You were little girls when you were cast for leads in *'Crucible,* and the roles have only gotten bigger since. Most of us have to start at the bottom, work our way up."

Hannah then had to restrain herself or there would be no awakening; she had to restrain herself or there might be bloodshed. "Don't you dare imply we haven't worked to get where we are. It's from working my ass off that we're even having this conversation. If I was drilling for oil and struck it rich, would you expect me start turning wrenches on the derrick? It doesn't make any sense. It's not even fair." Hannah was pissed, though also infinitely pleased with her oil rig analogy, however sorry her partner had missed it. She made a mental note to tell Katie about it later.

Brad, still on the other hand, was unwilling to draw a connection between black gold and prima donnas. "You've got the leads in *'Importance.'* You can't have all the leads, Hannah. I've got fifty other students auditioning."

"I can appreciate your situation, but this play is mine. It belongs to *me*. If you're worried about me taking all the leads, I'll pass on *'Importance'* and do this instead." (Of course, this wasn't true; Hannah would never pass on anything to which she was already committed. Brad knew this as well as she did, but he saw no point in calling her on it.)

Katie remained lost in the script, in an awakening of her own. She paid no attention to her friend and the director.

Impassioned and on her own, Hannah continued, "Haven't I always been there for you? *'Streetcar', Hamlet, 'Doll's House, 'Seagull, Twelfth Night,* all those one-acts? I've done shit for you I didn't even want to audition for. (Of course, this wasn't true, either. Hannah never missed any audition, regardless of the production, the role or the position. She would have gladly cleaned the other actors' stations, if instructed; anything to bring her closer to any show. Brad knew this as well, but, again, he didn't see the need to point it out.)

Hannah's excitement increased. She had him. As for Lincoln's advice to suggest taking the play to someone else, she tucked it away to save for another time. Certain that she had him on board, she went on with the particulars. "I'll need a couple of things, in addition to your artful directing. We would prefer that the author remain anonymous, to hide what might look like any conflicts of interest. And Kate and I have a say in who gets cast—all under the radar, of course. We need to know who's going into this with us. And we want it in the black box, up close and intimate, to score a real connection with the audience."

She paused for a breath, and for the chance to toss around some numbers. "And whatever the average take is on black box shows, I want anything over that to go to some charity—whales, literacy, jungle kids, something like that." Then, if only to cross any lines still left, and with her own fingers crossed, Hannah told him, "This is non-negotiable, Brad, but if you help—and I give you my word—I will not forget you, and you know I'm good for it."

Brad wondered if she was finished.

Hannah was almost finished. "Give it some thought. Remember everything we've done, and think of what you know we can still do. Think of where we've been and where we can go. You're a wonderful friend and an even better director, and I have faith you'll do the right thing."

With affected nonchalance, Hannah slipped off the stage and hit the floor with bent knees. "Please, do the right thing," she reiterated, patting his leg and gently prying the script from his reluctant hand. On her way to the door, she said, "I'm going for a cup of coffee. We'll talk soon."

Brad called after her, "Would you bring me a cup?"

Giving herself over to a spontaneous notion, Hannah replied, "It's going to be awhile. I'm having my coffee in the bayou."

The door closed. The director remained sitting on the edge of the main stage. He watched Katie reading the script, but his mind was not on her; rather, it was on the one who had departed. He regretted that she had taken the script. Brad wanted it. He wanted it very much.

In his theatrical mind he could see the story unfold on the black box stage—*up close and intimate*, like Hannah had said. Brad liked the sound of that. And while he found her overly demanding and overbearing with her 'non-negotiable' terms, he could find no other problems with those terms. He reasoned that, rather than wait for Hannah's return, he would borrow Katie's copy to make others for the department. She said, *We need to do it now*, and Brad was on the verge of agreeing. His imaginings of the advertisements hanging in the windows of the downtown shops added a special touch.

Katie never lifted her eyes from the pages, nor did she hear any words other than those that came from the pages. She didn't hear the door close when Hannah left. She paid no attention when Brad left shortly after. She did not notice for some time that she was alone in the big, hollow room, not until she turned the final page of Lincoln Dollar's play. It was an adaptation of one of Katie's favorite novels. The ending made her eyes sweat.

Though Katie fought thinking along such lines, at times it was more powerful than she. This was one of those times. *If only he hadn't shown up*, she thought, *but then we wouldn't be here, but we'd be someplace else, just us two*. And, just as quickly, Katie reprimanded herself for entertaining the thoughts again. *Get over yourself. Be happy for them. You selfish, little bitch.*

Her tears fell on the final page, blurring a portion of epilogue.

-3-

Brad Gooding was New Orleans bred, raised on Prytannia Street in the Garden District, a son of the Big Easy. He took his degree from the university a half-dozen blocks away, and wasn't long looking out from the stage before discovering that his forte was rather facing that same stage, conducting others in the theater crafts. The limited perspective of the individual actor wasn't enough for Brad; he preferred looking at bigger pictures.

After twenty years he landed back at the university, another arc in his circle: St. Louis, Santa Fe, a space in Montreal, three in Manhattan, then a return to the city of his birth. Not a lot had changed in New Orleans while he was away, but there were many changes in him; most notably, he was now the boss. Brad was in charge, and provided the world trusted in his artistic vision, he found little that could trouble him. His only current problem was an uppity and overbearing young actor.

He passed copies of Lincoln Dollar's play to his colleagues in the department. It was decided that the costumes would be period and lavish. The set designers and technicians offered a cyclorama splashed with mood-enhancing lights; subtle and warm as a prominent theme; hot, cold, or crisp when the scenes required. In the background would be the ever-present whispering of the sea during the first act, the songs of birds and waves, the music of Chopin; act two would ring with the noises and bustle of the city: Streetcars, horse races, dinner parties and dancing. With two distinct worlds to create, the staff collectively agreed that the project would be challenging, though technically and economically feasible. It would be no walk in the park for the crew, though some of the characters would be blocked, in the second act, scene 3, for a walk in the park.

There was some disagreement regarding the small, black box theater, and whether it could accommodate such a production. When Brad suggested they take the show to the main stage, into the *big room*, an all-or-nothing endeavor, the staff greedily agreed. The director also suggested substituting Hannah's complicated financial requests with a straight percentage of the take. The department thought highly of the philanthropic angle, if only for the advertising and marketing value. "Without royalties, it more or less balances out," was the economic consensus. The afore-planned production of *Crimes of the Heart* would wait for the following spring. Lincoln Dollar's play would premier after the summer break.

All this and more was decided before Hannah returned from her visit downriver. The impromptu vacation cost her three days of classes, but it returned three quiet mornings, three sticky afternoons, and three starry bayou nights spent in expressing her gratitude to a playwright for his playwriting efforts. She wanted to stay longer in the bayou, forever even, but in *'Earnest* she made a reluctant return.

-4-

Hannah lay awake waiting, looking nervously into the darkness of the dormitory room, the same as she had done on now far too many nights. This nervous waiting had become a problem, now getting in the way of what should have been some important and pressing business. Hannah made up her mind to put it all to rest before it was too late, if it wasn't too late already. She cursed herself for letting it go on for as long as she did.

The girls were nearing events well beyond their wild young dreams, but the friendship had lately turned down a precarious path. Hannah was stalled between the path and the dreams, but fiercely certain of the direction she was going. If forced, she was willing and prepared to travel alone, but she wasn't going solo without a fight—even knock-down, violent and bloody, should the split come to as much.

The sun wasn't yet over Audubon Park when Katie's weary key found its way into the lock. She threw her coat over the back of a chair and the rest of her clothes into a corner. The lighter for her cigarette broke the darkness in the room, broken once more when she opened the refrigerator to pour some wine from a box. Katie drank the glass off in one breathless gulp, then went into the bathroom and closed the door.

Hannah could hear the girl crying. She heard the *flick* of the lighter for another cigarette. Soon she heard the *tap, tap, tap* of a razor blade against the porcelain of the vanity, followed by a period of quiet. She imagined Katie was looking for a straw; Hannah had already found the last one.

Katie came out at last. Lonely, quietly, she slid into her bed, biting the saddle of her hand to stifle her crying. Even in the darkness, Hannah knew the girl was biting into her hand. Katie often did so, and more so of late. Though faced away, Hannah could see the girl's face as clear as if she was looking into her eyes, until finally she could stand it no longer.

The lazy dawn was beginning to wash the twilight from the room.

Hannah swung her legs over the side of the bed. "Why are you doing this?"

"Not now, please," said Katie to the pillow. "Let me rest."

"Fuck your rest! After all we've been through, we've finally got our chance and you're a fucking mess!"

Katie bolted upright. "*I'm* a mess? You self-righteous cunt! You haven't drawn a sober breath since we left Vermont. This isn't *our* chance, Hannah; this is *your* chance. It was sweet when he showed up with that script for *us*, but it's *yours,* and *yours* alone. That's your little baby, *baby*. I'm washing my hands of the whole fucking thing!"

"Listen to you!" Hannah raged. "I don't even know you anymore! All I wanted was us together again, like it was in the beginning, the three of us."

In an angry outburst of tears, Katie's volume grew. "What planet are you on? It hasn't been the *three of us* since farmer Dollar started plowing the fields! I've only been in the way. I should've stayed up in Virginia." She began slowing down, wearing herself down. "You don't need me anymore unless you want someone to hold the camera. That's not me. I thought I could handle it—you know I tried—but I can't do it anymore." Building again, she added, "And now I'm sick of trying. I wish you both all the best, I really do. Seriously, give my fucking regards to Broadway." And again she was down. "I love you both, I really do. I love you both, but I'm tired. I can't do it anymore. I just can't."

"Don't you dare do this to me!" said Hannah, nearly screaming. "I swear, Katherine, I'll never forgive you. I can do this alone—don't think I can't—but I don't want to, and I'm not going to. I'll get so far away from you and him, just to spite you. If it's not the three of us, it's *none of us!* I didn't think you had it in you, but you ruined us—ruined *us!*—you miserable, fucking wretch!"

In their five years together, Hannah had never spoken a word in anger to Katie. She'd barely raised her voice. It now left her feeling empty, bitter and petty, but it couldn't be helped and it couldn't be taken back. The time for holding back and taking back was past. She was angrier still for letting it go so far as it did. Hannah wasn't herself and Katie was not Kate, and the strangeness of it all frightened her as such that she was convinced she had to bring it back together, and in this very moment. Hannah had to rid herself of the fear, or surely it would mean the end of her dream. She couldn't allow anything the power to stand in the way of the dream. Not now, no way.

Katie was again faced away. Tears flowed freely from her sad, tired eyes. She had been slipping away, falling off, fading. By the time she herself realized where she was, Katie found that it was right nextdoor to lost. Aimless again, she took refuge in the gutters of the city. In with the Quarter regulars and the drunken tourists, Katie was able to shine brilliantly, helping to inflate an exhausted and failing ego.

So wrapped up in herself, Hannah was not attuned to the gradual descent, not until Katie had fallen so far that attempts at retrieving her seemed monumental. Lincoln had suggested that she keep an eye on the girl. "She's into something," he'd warned. "Probably coke. I hope it's only coke." Whether it was the dope, or Lincoln—or both, or neither—causing the split, Hannah was determined to either put an end to it or hasten it. She was lonely standing alone, stalling, cowardly.

"This is nonsense, Katherine! It's like some silly Alanis Morissette song, and I'm not putting up with it any longer!" She stood and aggressively walked the three steps to Katie's bed. Hannah got in, roughly pulling the covers over them both. "My dear, dear Katherine, I love you more than anything in the world—forever. That'll never change. I told you in the beginning that I wouldn't let anything ever come between us, and that still goes. If I have to choose between you and him, between you and the theater, between you and anything, everything, I'm still gonna choose you every time. Let's not complicate it, dear. I was nothing when I met Lincoln Dollar, and I can be nothing again, so long as I'm nothing with you." Hannah could feel the girl relaxing in her arms.

Katie found a measure of safety and security under Hannah's touch, managing to speak through her choked sobbing. "I don't want you giving your love to anyone else." She was whimpering. "I'm deathly afraid of losing you. I'm so lost without you." Katie rolled over to face her. "I know it's wrong, but I can't help it. I loathe myself for it, but I still can't help it. He's taking you away from me."

Hannah cried a few tears of her own. She pulled her t-shirt over her head, using it to wipe them all away. She brought Katie closer, kissing her mouth and her hot, salty cheeks. "You'll never lose me, Kate. I promise." She ran her hand along the relaxing curves. "You're as much a part of me as I am."

Katie melted under her touch. "Hold me close. I need to get away from the Quarter. I need to get out of this city. I want to go back to Carl and Uncle Charley and the archangels." There was a fresh outbreak of tears from both.

"Just a little longer, please," Hannah whispered. "Be patient. Good things come to patient girls."

With gentle hands and a loving mouth, she dismissed the rest of Katie's tears and fears, taking her away, if only for the moment.

-5-

Jordan Sinclair let the proposal fall on the desk as such that Lincoln could read it from the other side. Nearly everything having to do with theater in New Orleans eventually fell on Jordan's desk, such was his passion for the medium, but his passion was of a business sense: Bookings, tours and festivals, SROs and profit margins.

Bustling tourists scrambled along in and out of the shops on the Riverwalk beneath the office windows. The paddlewheel of the Dixie Queen slapped happily against the Mississippi as she left the pier for an afternoon dinner cruise.

The two men knew one another from their undergrad studies at the university on the other side of town. Jordan had been the only student on campus with a theater minor to complement a business major. Playing no small role in his concentration choices was his family's owning and operating the Crescent City Production Company, the hub of the New Orleans entertainment wheel. Jordan's father had strongly suggested it prudent to gain some knowledge of the product the son would be selling. He even hinted that there might be a new Corvette on the other side of those studies, provided they were taken up in earnest.

An unlikely coupling, the students were paired when an instructor assigned Jordan to assist Lincoln on the final project for a directing class. Close to wrapping up the minor, Jordan agreed to the project with his one-armed classmate. He needed only those last two credit-hours. All that stood between Jordan and the Chevy was the class project and Lincoln Dollar.

The assignment was the staging of a one-act piece from start to finish: Conception, assessment, auditions, casting, sets, costumes, lighting and marketing. Lincoln was mired in a lackluster semester at the time, and grabbed at the project with hopes of rejuvenating a fading scholastic interest. Rather than limit himself to one-act choices, however, he applied the work to a full-length drama, intending to use a self-supporting scene for the presentation.

With the waters of the school's talent pool scarcely rippling, the one-armed, one-act director recruited two bartenders and a server from The House of Blues in the French Quarter, who agreed to work pro bono, for the theater, for the team, and for their one-armed customer.

Jordan did his best to stay out of the way. He kept himself available and did what was asked of him, but he had little interest in the direction of plays. He did, however, come to enjoy watching his classmate. Lincoln seemed to have a flair for the work that Jordan could appreciate—an aggressive mix of pseudo-professionalism and passion. Jordan sat in the wings of the set and tossed numbers around—work for which he had a flair of his own.

The project was time consuming for the scant fifteen minutes of performance on the university stage. Lincoln and Jordan received satisfactory grades for their efforts and were shaking hands, preparing to part after the two months' preparation for the brief gig. Lincoln was going into his final semester. Jordan was hopping into the Stingray for the short drive to the Riverwalk, to where a desk awaited him at his grandfather's production company.

The budding executive's head was scheming, swimming with numbers, numbers, numbers. He still had Lincoln's hand in his when he suggested, "You know, Dollar, we've got the actors, costumes and set; we'd just have to find a deal on some lighting and sound equipment. If I could get us a small stage in the Quarter, how would you feel about running this thing a while? Maybe make a little money—know what I mean?" He rubbed his thumb against his index and social fingers in the international hand signal to signify greed.

The only times Lincoln had ever associated cash with the theater were those occasions when he couldn't afford the admission price. He had never connected the stage with money, and with decades of interest vested in the medium, he was left feeling naïve for having overlooked so obvious a coupling.

It was the fall of 1994. The scarring on the end of his arm was calloused. He wore the plastic, leather and steel prosthesis, waiting for the Veteran's Administration to phone him up with word of technology to relieve him of the impractical appendage, though he wasn't holding his breath. In the meantime, he gained a certain infamy as being among the more nontraditional students in the theater department, and as being the only guy on campus who could roll a joint with one hand.

Lincoln listened to Jordan's pitch. The salesman had a dreamy, faraway look in his eyes—a look Lincoln often saw in the eyes of people associated with the theater—but Jordan's young dreams were already of the financial order.

"Better still, why not keep it on campus? There's nothing in the black box for the next couple of months. I'll have my grandfather set it up. That's a hundred and thirty seats, maybe ten bucks a head, for, say, twenty or so shows, less the room, less wages, less miscellaneous expense. You get those actors from the bar and I'll take care of the rest. We'll split it down the middle, Dollar—something like twelve, fourteen grand apiece."

Everyone was pleased with the production arrangements, except the manager at The House of Blues who was pushed to cover the combined ninety-plus shifts his employees would disrupt with their stagebound moonlighting.

Ashlee, Brendan and Caitlin had found their ways to New Orleans with starlit hopes of working in the theater, but, as occasionally happens, there proved a lot more jobs in the hospitality industry. By necessity they were forced to push their acting plans to the rear burner, focusing their energies instead on paying the rent and utilities. With some patience and a bit of theatrical irony, however, it came to pass that those acting opportunities found them at the club, and all quite suddenly one evening over cocktails with the one-armed guy from the university.

Lincoln persuaded the tight-fisted Jordan to loosen up a bit, thus securing a better wage for the actors, assuring the young executive that he would have plenty of opportunity later in his career to "fuck over the talent;" after all, strong was Lincoln's opinion that all performers should be well compensated for their work, and especially Caitlin, Brendan and Ashlee, for they kept him generously in his cups, and so he wished to remain in their good graces.

The show was laudably received, bringing a lot of traffic to the campus and running for an unexpected twenty-six performances. Lincoln Dollar exchanged his fistful of dollars for westbound travelers' checks, while Jordan Sinclair invested his share of the profits in the Crescent City Production Company.

Jordan looked out the office window as the passenger ferry to Algiers slowly shied away from the pier, having given Lincoln time enough to look over the proposal. "What a great show. I couldn't believe it when I saw your name in the program. Lincoln Dollar back in New Orleans." Referring to the change in his friend's anatomy since last he saw him, Jordan added, "Used to be giving someone a hand meant offering applause, but as usual you take it to another level." He thought his play on words was clever.

Lincoln had been paying little attention, but when he heard *hand* he referred to the prosthesis contemptuously. "Yeah, this thing's not working out. Thought I'd be able to do more shows, but now I don't want to do the shows, so I went back to the V.A. They went nuts when I told them I wanted the hook back, like they were insulted or something. Said they couldn't find time to accommodate the procedure. But when I chatted it up with my congressman, Purple Heart-this, sacrifice-that—duty, honor, country—they set up the appointment." He finished scanning the proposal and placed it back on the desk facing Jordan, prepared as much as he loathed it to talk a bit of business.

"We really should open this at *Le Petite*," said Jordan. "I mean, it's a no-brainer."

"If I had it my way, we probably would, but I don't have my way. It's Hannah's deal and she wants out of the city."

"What's your connection to her?"

"Friend of a friend, long story, but she's leaving and I'm going with her. If you put the money behind this thing, we'll invite you along, too."

"I'm going to be honest with you—"

Lincoln cut him off. "Don't, Jordan. Whenever I hear, *I'm going to be honest with you,* I get myself ready for a load of bullshit. Please, please, don't drive us away."

"Not with you, man. We got history." Jordan tried his business-best to sound convincing. "You helped me out, so I'll be straight with you. Sure, I'm in it for the money, but I also want to see this thing happen. Hear me out." He poured a pair of neat bourbons and returned to his desk. "It took some selling before I could get anyone down here to look at this. They don't want anything new, only stuff with guarantees. And they never, ever look at anything premiering on a campus. If it wasn't for those reviews in the *Times-Picayune,* we'd be opening and closing this show right over these drinks, so we owe those people over there—big-time."

He picked up the proposal and ran down the list of venues. "Seven states, seven months, about fifty shows. This one place—Preston, Vermont—took me half a day just to get them on the phone. We'll see what happens after that. People from New York'll check us out on the road. Who knows?"

The informal, pre-contractual offer, written in Jordan's pen, had the same dripping, southern drawl as its author. Jacksonville, Atlanta, Charleston, Winston-Salem, Norfolk, Hartford, Boston; *for a limited engagement* was underlined, referring to two shows as part of the new City Arts Summer Series in the sunny Preston Valley. This last venue was Hannah's idea, a graceful effort at burying the hatchet with the city she said she'd never play again; still, one might be left wondering if her intention wasn't to bury that hatchet deep in Preston's collective skull.

"I think it stands a chance," Jordan continued, "and I want to get behind it. Course, I'm a sucker for anything that smells of the south, but this is a really good play. It's fresh. It's real—a period piece that's not dated. It's fun, and it's for a good cause, and that alone is going to sell us some tickets." He let his professionalism take a backseat to the friendship they had shared during their college years. "Sign me on, Lincoln, with an option, of course. I want a part of this. I really do."

"You'll go to Hannah with this? She's the boss. She's got friends in Virginia she wants. I know them. They're good people, good at what they do."

Jordan agreed with Lincoln's terms, and just as much with Hannah's. "I'll work with her myself. We've got Katherine Pauley and a couple others, but I won't take anyone else from the university. I still have to live in this town. My people will re-cast whatever's left. Everyone gets paid scale, right across the board, above the board, an all-equity show. We'll divvy things up at the end. If we can make some money, great; if not, at least we'll be doing our part to entertain the groundlings. It's a great new play. We'll get it out there."

Still, Jordan could keep the professionalism at bay for only so long. "And we *will* make some money."

Assuming the business end was put to rest, Lincoln suggested, "Let's go over to that revolving bar for some of those eight-dollar martinis. I'll tell you about Hannah playing Strindberg in Vermont."

"You're out of the loop," said Jordan. "Those eight-dollar martinis are now fourteen-fifty."

In the elevator to the top of the International Trade Mart, Lincoln told Jordan of Hannah's recruitment of her former colleagues. She first got hold of Carl Thomas and Charley Evans, both of whom had enjoyed marginal success since the blockbuster summer three years before. Carl immediately signed on to paint Hannah's production with the watercolors of his suffering, sentimental, temperamental artistry. She was eager to have his perspective brought to the work, building on the foundation already laid by director Gooding.

Hannah next sent the script along to Emily Rose, asking would she please portray the stately Madame Lebrun. Emily Rose suggested instead that she play the old spinster, Mademoiselle Reisz, leaving Hannah feeling foolish for having suggested any other role.

Excited to get back into rehearsals, fresh and anew with a cast of old friends, Hannah then invited the archangels to bestow their blessings on the production. The brothers eagerly hopped on board, ready to work, ready to play. When eight hopefuls auditioned to play Robert, Hannah saw that the role went to Gabriel. Michael Croft was cast as Léonce. One of the archangels would play Hannah's husband, and the other her lover, and she adored them both for these commitments; once off the stage, Katie would be able to play with the angels, and Hannah adored them even more for taking on that tactical commitment.

Jennifer Novak and Cyndi Partlow, newly graduated by the University of Vermont, were on their way to New Orleans to work the tech end of the show, hungry to launch their pro careers, and thrilled at the prospect of seeing their old friends. "I knew we'd all work together again," said Jen as she went over the contract. Cyndi accused her of waxing sentimental, calling up Jen's squealing reply, "No, really, I just knew it!"

Time came for the final show of the Tulane run. Friends and colleagues were gathered in the audience at the university's main stage.

Three hundred mouths were quiet as the gentle lapping of the waves whispered through the theater sound system. The stage lights were dimmed with blues and ambers to create a sun setting on the sensuous ocean gulf. Hannah stood alone at the shore. As Edna Pontellier, she bent to loosen the straps of her sandals. As Edna, she let go the sash of her peignoir; it held to her naked body but briefly, before falling from her shoulders and onto the beach.

Perhaps the audience was taken aback by Hannah's character dropping all veils in the final scene, but it could not have been more so than the cast and crew, because during every rehearsal and for all the previous performances Hannah had modestly worn a body-stocking to cover her nakedness in the closing scene. During the last show, however, the robe fell away from her natural nakedness beneath. She no longer wanted to hide. There was nothing left for her to hide from.

Katie watched from backstage, biting her hand, tears rolling down her cheeks, as Edna—naked, beautiful, torn and alone—walked determinedly into the chilling waters, slowly swimming the expanse to the last of her strength, leagues past the point of any return.

The stage was blackened and blued. Not a soul or voice stirred, the whole of the room waiting on young Edna's return; but Edna wasn't coming back. A stagehand in the auditorium began to softly clap, slowly building in intensity, to inform the audience that Edna was not coming back. Once cued, all six hundred hands came together to join in the celebration.

Hannah covered herself in the wings. Her heart was pounding. She breathed deep the energy of the applause.

With a curtain call, the cast bowed one last time, then broke left and right to exit the stage. Hannah stayed a moment longer, shielding her eyes from the overhead glare. There was more applause, and graciously accepted, though more applause was not what she sought. In time the room quieted, growing nearer to silence, as Hannah looked out over the friendly hall. She said quietly, part question, part wishful thinking, addressing only the one person, "Are you here? ... Emily Rose?"

Whispers passed from patron to patron, until at last the soft and familiar voice called from the house, "I'm here, my friend, my dear, dear girl." Emily Rose left her seat and moved with eager dignity down the aisle. Hannah met her in front of the apron, grabbing for her with hungry arms. They sobbed in one another's embrace, the house once again lifting with applause, though it seemed to them that they were the only two in the room.

"The show is magic," said Emily Rose. "This is the one, I know it. This play's going to take us to the street of dreams." She broke from the embrace, excusing herself from the scene, from her beliefs, from her dreams, and from all the overwhelming emotion it was bringing on. She found escape through a fire exit, stage-right, fleeing just ahead of still greater applause.

It took some doing, but Hannah finally pulled herself together; with still more effort, she pulled herself onto the apron. She sat facing the audience while an over-zealous lighting tech used the opportunity to wash her with a hot, white spot. Looking up at the catwalk, Hannah shielded her eyes. She was unable to see her tormentor, but she knew he was up there. "Shut that thing off, will you? I'm getting a tan down here."

The spotlight was extinguished by the main booth, and more house lights brought up until Hannah could finally look comfortably out into the room, into all the familiar and friendly faces. It was a *home*y feeling, like she was at the intersection, and the whole of the moment quick-like reminded her of why she was where she presently was. It sent a chill up her spine.

Katie was tingling as well, shaking with the excitement of the scene, as she crossed downstage to join her partner. Her reappearance was met with applause, but Katie paid them little mind. This night was not about her. She sat on the stage's edge, taking Hannah's hand, prepared to do everything she could to support her, the same as Hannah had done for her so many, many times, the same as they had always done for one another. The rest of the cast joined them on the apron.

Projecting to the back row and beyond, with eyes shining and bright, Hannah said, "Ladies and gentlemen"—she gestured halfway up one aisle—"the man who wrote the play, Mr. Lincoln Dollar."

The writer reluctantly rose, waving self-consciously to a small piece of the room. Theater-goers turned about with applause and cries—"author, author"—while the author remained looking long and hard on the actor. He gave her a short nod before sitting, having used what was left of his faculties to keep from running to her. He wanted her so badly just then, without the confines of the theater and the people. He wanted her all alone, all for himself.

"I love you," Hannah confessed in front of a packed house.

The room was soon quiet, the patrons settled, when she continued, her words heartfelt, chockfull of appreciation and farewell, "It's gone by so fast, these three years; so many shows on this beautiful stage, in this amazing city; and all the familiar faces here tonight make going away even more difficult." She was getting misty, but fought it away and gathered herself up. "It's been a gift bringing this beautiful little novel to life under these lights—except, of course, that one light up there." She pointed him out, waving to the technician on the catwalk.

"I can't thank all the people who've put this night together. I won't even try. But it's been an amazing journey, with so many friends. Lincoln, Emily Rose, Uncle Charley, Carl, Brad, Jordan, mom, dad …" Hannah's heart put such a stranglehold on her tongue, it allowed her to only whisper Katie's name, more squeezing her hand instead. "Let's just say there's a lot of love in this room.

"We're going to take this show on the road, hoping to spread the charm of this city, and hoping to make some money in the process, money to help some unfortunate people, people who've got it rough because of some of the messes we've made. We can't count on those knuckleheads in Washington to help us out, so we've got to do it ourselves, people like you and me; republican, democrat, liberal, conservative, black or white, jazz or opera, Saints or Bears, it doesn't matter. We're trying to open our hearts and minds, and to take a good, honest look at what we've done, and at what we need to do to make it right. Something special has brought us together tonight. In the spirit of that same unity, let's stay together and work together and try to make this planet a better place for everyone—for *everyone*."

Applause began again in the room, but it was gentle and restrained, perhaps an action to occupy hundreds of hands while considering a larger position.

Hannah looked into the faces of the theater-goers, all of them recently returned from a journey one hundred years past, returned and seeming grateful for the experience, many with souvenirs from the trip brought back with them, and some with ideas perhaps applicable in the present and tomorrow.

The cashier from the bodega on St. Charles was in the front row. She often sold Hannah black coffee and red wine, cigarettes, magazines and tampons. She waved. Hannah waved back—"Hi, Maura. Thanks for coming"—and then it hit her. The feeling returned. It came to give Hannah a quick slap, just a gentle reminder that the night was not about Hannah Mae Fields; it came to remind her how the lone actor is but a small part of the larger drama. She was but a supporting player at best, and only when at her best. With Katie at her side, their nails biting into one another's hands, Hannah felt strength enough to redouble an already committed effort. The tour would be an amazing journey. It would be an important journey.

She lastly told the packed auditorium, "We've refreshments in the lobby, courtesy of the university theater department. Thank you for your support and for all your kindness. None of this—" She engulfed with both her arms all that was without, and for herself everything within "—none of this happens without all of you." She put a clenched fist into the air. "Viva New Orleans!"

The audience was on their feet, applauding, echoing, "Viva New Orleans!"

The ensemble stood and formed a line, dress-right-dress, across the stage. With clasped hands held high, they bowed one last time before breaking at the center and retreating to the wings. The audience made an exodus of their own.

Lincoln Dollar hadn't yet seen a performance of the play. He had played the drama thousands of times under the proscenium arches of his imagination, but on such a temperamental stage it had always been lacking, always missing something ... *something*. Lincoln now realized what had been missing was her. Hannah gave the piece life and meaning; the rest of the players gave it soul and humanity and the flavor of realism.

Lincoln's instinct asked that he pick apart the work, deconstruct the literature, dissect the performance. He was compelled to look for faults in creation and construction, compelled to question: *How? Why? What if?* But he was able at last to decline all invitations for the compelling search, the chase, the quest for faults; therefore, he could not find any. What he found was beauty and friendship and reality, with kindness and honesty. He had wanted it just so, to allay the fears and doubts that had pestered him in the process. Everything had gone into the work, all that was him, the largest part of Lincoln Dollar. His fear was the wondering if it would be enough. He now believed that all he had put into it was returned ten-fold. Finally, a sound investment.

He did not stand as the crowd was leaving, but remained seated, looking through the departing bodies at the darkened set on the stage below. It was the same set he had envisioned, the same he had struggled to get onto the page. It *was* the beach at Grand Isle. Lincoln had wanted it just so. He needed it just so. And, because it was all that he wanted and needed, the night's show had left him a pretty happy guy; happy enough, but still kind of wondering, trying—struggling—to steer clear of any premature excitement, expectations or speculation. But he couldn't help himself, nor could he deny, not after seeing the performance, that it was big, bigger than he ever imagined it would be. Almost disturbingly big. And Hannah was big, infinitely bigger than he had imagined when, back at Preston High, he suggested that she hop up on the stage and *be big*. Suddenly everything was bigger.

The theater troupe was scheduled to take its collective bigness up the east coast. From Jackson Square to Herald Square, theater-goers were going to know the name, Hannah Fields. But were his opinions too subjective? After all, his lover? In the play he wrote? Were his views even valid? Again, Lincoln shooed away the questions, concluding, with all the honesty and humility he could muster, that if anyone else had penned the script, he would have held the same opinion. He knew, from a technical standpoint, that the work was sound; he liked that, that it was *sound*. There was no denying that *The Awakening* was a good play; but regarding the actual physical performance, Lincoln was far too close to have any objectivity there. That closeness brought him closer still.

When at last he was alone in the theater, he stood and moved down the aisle. The beach at Grand Isle beckoned, drawing him to the stage and into his imagined world. Lincoln stood alone on the Gulf of Mexico, breathing the salt water, the sea grass, the lichens and abalones. He felt the waves breaking at his feet, could hear the indolent gulls circling aerial reconnaissance.

Hannah stood in the darkness of the wings, smoking a cigarette held cupped in her hand with extra caution; having decidedly pushed Brad far enough with the production as it was, she didn't want to burn down his theater on top of everything else. She'd been eying Lincoln since she left the stage, watching him through parts in the curtains, trying to imagine what was happening in his head.

Hannah quickly fell into the role of Edna Pontellier. She went into rehearsals with a disregard for whatever talent she may or may not have had, following instead the notion that Lincoln had written the role with her in mind, so all she really had to do was get on stage and be herself. Provided she knew her lines and cues, there was virtually no way she could screw it up. The comfort and confidence which came of knowing she couldn't fail then followed her to the stage. If pulled over along the way, Hannah was prepared to show her poetic license and registration. "Just being me, officer," would have been the reply, her performance having been ordained by forces beyond her control, and far beyond any supposed attributes or principles; talent, ambition, role-playing and love were all relegated to the background. Then, when her license met this same disregard, the magic began; however, this meeting passed unknown to Hannah, as by now she was locked in a feedback loop, having found that the more she gave of herself to the role, the more control she had over it.

And this same loop suggested that she keep from looking too far ahead. The loop bade her be content with the dates and venues on the schedule, nothing more. But every so often she thought of … *shhh* … New York, those silly theater dreams with lots of lights, nice clothes and pricey shoes. Hannah no longer thought of being raped in alleyways, as such thoughts were without power inside her loop.

After sixteen shows with the university she was aching to hit the road. The girls still had a few required classes, but those could wait until they returned. Hannah opted away from Jordan's advice to premiere downtown at *Le Petite Theatre*; three years in New Orleans was "quite enough for now, thank you very much." She wanted Katie out of the city, away from the Quarter. ("Some time apart might do you all some good.") It was time to freshen up, begin anew, and rebuild on an exciting new foundation; time to strike while the dramatic iron was hot. Five years earlier, she and Katie, bored, restless and discontent, sat on a park bench formulating dreams. Nothing in those dreams hinted at becoming actors and embarking on a theatrical road trip, but in retrospect the current course would have made the most sense. In light of all their pubescent craziness and self-importance, the girls had made a pact on the park bench; whatever dream they decided to chase, they were going to chase it together. True in their friendship and somewhat true to themselves, the journey was far from anything they had expected, just as journeys worthwhile often are. The dream continued until there was no turning back, and now a large part of the dream was standing before her, her presence unknown to him.

She had no sooner shared vows with Katie in Memorial Park when Lincoln Dollar stumbled into her life. Hannah then exploded with the love she felt for both, soon coming to crave their love in return. Hannah, who thought she needed nothing from anyone, began to live as such to get everything that Katie and Lincoln had to offer. This quid pro quo approach helped her to develop a self-love which she was able to tend and nurture, while at the same time keeping it in check, keeping it small, discreet and valuable. With this love came honor, a bit of dignity, some self-respect and a certain measure of grace. Granted, Hannah had to work especially hard for the grace; and finally believing she may have acquired some grace, she initially thought it was all kind of neat, but quickly decided that people working to acquire such qualities as grace probably didn't refer to them as *neat*. Hannah was, and would always be, a work in progress.

Lincoln was on the stage, lost in a dream in which she went to find him. But rather than take him from the dream, Hannah wished to join him in it. "Is it everything you hoped it would be?" Her voice was quiet, though it sounded loud and carried in the hushed and hollowed hall.

"More—so much more," He was turning a full circle to take in the entire set, the entire theater, 360-degrees, from the catwalks to the stage floor. "I can't believe you guys used real sand."

She was happy he was pleased. "The boards needed redoing, anyway. One of Kate's penises refinishes floors, said he'd give us a deal."

"The asides worked well for exposition and contrast."

He makes it sound so technical, she thought. But if he wanted to talk shop, she would oblige him. Her curtain call was over. This was Lincoln's time. "It's a good vehicle to impart information quickly. I already told you it was clever." He was the star of this present scene.

She wanted to spoil him. Hannah wanted to stroke his ego, as well as the rest of him. "I haven't seen any numbers yet, but I think we did okay at the box office."

Lincoln stretched his muscles a half-dozen different ways to realign himself after more than two hours in the auditorium seat. "What do we do now?"

"Vacation, finally" She began inching her way nearer to him, examining bits and pieces of the set along the way, each of them offering one memory or another. "Once finals are over, everything's going into storage. We'll meet up with the new cast in Florida next month. I've got a bunch of time off and I'm spending every minute of it with you." She was getting closer still. "I recently decided I'm going to spend my life with you—just a couple minutes ago, actually—so I thought it'd be a good idea if we got to know one another a little better, if that's alright with you. It is alright, isn't it?"

When at last they met on the sandy beach of Grand Isle, Lincoln asked, "Will you come with me to the V.A. tomorrow? Just for a couple of days?"

"Going to see the doctor?"

"Sort of."

She took hold of the artificial hand. "Getting rid of this?"

"Yeah, I want it off."

"Then so do I."

"You'll come with me?"

"Why not? It'll be fun. Along the way you can tell me about the day the mean old tiger shark ate your arm."

"I was kidding about the shark. It was actually a bullet took the arm."

Hannah rolled her eyes. "Yeah, I figured as much." She put her hand on his face and kissed the side of his mouth. "I once thought you were the only person in the world who could hurt me, but I know now that the only person with the power to hurt me is me; and I believe you're the one person who's going to keep me from hurting myself. I need you, Lincoln, I really do. Now more than ever, more than you know."

"You'll have me."

She rested her head on his shoulder, safe, sure and secure. "You're a saint, to put up with me the way you have."

With his hand at the small of her back, he pulled her closer. She was warm from spending the last two hours under the hot theater lights. Her sweat was on his cheek and neck. She was wet beneath the thin cotton robe. "It's been a gift."

The *humm* of her words vibrated on his collarbone. "That's not true. I know better than anyone how difficult I am. Shameful, really. If I was a good friend, I'd have warned you against me. *Stay away from her*, I would've said. *Spoiled, self-serving, self-centered, little twit, that one.* I was just learning those little games when I met you, games where I was so much smarter than the rest of the players."

"If they're your games," Lincoln reasoned, "it only makes sense that you're the best player. We all play our own games, Hannah. You're the most selfless person I know."

She shook her head on his shoulder. "No, I'm not, but I'm trying to be. And now, after all you've done, I still have one more favor to ask. Typical, right? Me, me, me. But just this once more, and I'll never ask you for anything else."

Lincoln knew she didn't like her ears kissed, but he went ahead and did it just the same, enjoying it enough for them both. He tried once more, but Hannah turned and offered her lips instead. "Anything to make you happy," he said.

Hannah squirmed from his embrace and went into the wings. There followed the electrical *pop* of the theater's twelve speakers. She moved the control forward and some musical notes entered, circling to fill the void in the expansive room. Hannah didn't recognize the tune, but as it was soft and slow and loaded with strings, she was pleased at having chanced upon it. Considering the circumstances, she couldn't help but notice there weren't any mandolins in the selection, but Hannah knew whence she could call them up. She could even conjure a flautist or two if needed. She was good at conjuring. She moved more controls to turn down more of the lights. "Come dance with me. We've never danced, and I want to do everything with you—everything, always."

In one another's arms they moved across the stage, up and down the streets of the city, in and out of alleyways and gardens, through the weathered cottages of the island, up the steps and across the verandah of the main house. Awash in blue lights, they danced through *The Awakening*, to the sandy, moonlit beach—dancing further and further into the folds of the curtains, into the blue shadows, into the darkest recesses of the stage.

Hannah looked around to ensure no one watched, though she cared little if anyone did, as one of her hands worked on her clothing, while with the other hand she began exploring him. She kissed him down to his chest and back. Fired, Hannah was determined to fire him, to light him up. Making an ample start, she *tee-hee*d with hesitation, guiding the prosthetic hand between her legs. "Can I? Since we're getting rid of it? Just this one time, for me, for the fun of it, only so I can say I did."

Hannah had often felt the touch of the hand, but it had never touched her there. She found it warm enough, room temperature, though it was not as warm as his other. And it was soft enough, though not as soft as his other. "That's it," she said, slowly lowering herself, stirring and purring, rocking. The couple of artificial fingers were fine in their way, but they weren't as good as the others.

Hannah undid his belt and brought him near. Reaching high into the thick fabric hanging from the catwalk, she pulled herself up until her feet were off the sandy stage, inviting him to move to where she hovered above, pressing against him. She slowly let herself down, and the more she lowered, the more she opened, the more she let herself down. With her hands full of the draperies, she raised and lowered herself over him, slowly and quickly, the whole of her body supported by the curtains and Lincoln's pelvis.

Hannah looked up to the catwalk, at the frame holding the curtains, wondering if it was going to stand the stress. From her stagecraft classes she knew that each of the O-rings at the grommets was rated for thirty-five hundred pounds, yet still she wondered if the curtain was coming down. Hannah didn't care if it came down. She wanted to bring the curtain down. She was cursing to make a sailor swoon, praying to make a pastor blush, growing bolder, louder and faster, until her limbs had burst afire, until she could stand it no longer. "Let me down! Let me down! My arms are killing me." Once her feet were back on the stage, her exhausted limbs fell to his shoulders. "Make love to me on the beach," she said, "on this beach you made for me."

"Oh!" she said, presently surprised as she lay on her back on the sandy stage floor, her robe opened wide, her legs even wider. "Oh," she said again, pleased at how well they worked together. "Ohhh," she repeated once more, then, "Oh, oh—oh shit, honey. Stop for a minute." Hannah pushed him away. "I've got sand in my cooch. Can you feel it? (And I can't believe I just called you *honey*.)"

Sure enough, honey agreed, the cooch had grown gritty.

"What do we do?" she asked, though she well knew what was needed. "You'll have to get it out if we're to continue. Can you?"

"I can try. Anything for you—honey."

"Can you do it without using your hands?"

It took some time and a bit of doing—with a good deal of patience and attention to detail on both their parts—but between them they extracted every grain of the Grand Isle sand and sent them individually back to the beach. When both were certain the job was successful, still they allowed the search to continue awhile longer, just to be sure.

Later that evening, as they negotiated the narrow bed in Hannah's dormitory room, she revisited the predicament of beach in her vagina, of sand grains caught in her *cooch*. "What do you think would happen if we couldn't get it out?" she asked. "I wonder if I'd work like an oyster and keep coating it and coating it." She propped herself on an elbow to better gauge his reaction. "The way you juice me up, if I had a cunt full of sand, I could turn it into an entire string of pearls. I could give *you* a pearl necklace."

Lincoln gazed at the ceiling. He gave her a wider berth—as wide as he could on a bed four and a half feet across—and pulled the covers up closer to his chin. "Those are profound musings, and put forth with fine language. Cultured—like your pearls."

-6-

Direct from New Orleans, the show was aptly billed, *for a limited engagement.* This announcement was made after the seasonal programs had been printed at the Jacksonville Arts Center, so an addendum to the schedule was promptly mailed to subscribers.

Soon after the opening, Jordan Sinclair telephoned the troupe, talking to Lincoln. "There's no way to get bigger halls at this stage in the game. The only way to sell more tickets is to do more shows, and that's only if the venues have the open space. Of course, that'll mean more scrambling for the cast and crew, less time off. See what Carl wants to do, but don't push it. We don't want to fuck this up. You know I'm all about selling tickets—more the better—but we need to play this right. A little patience, some prayer, a little bit of luck, and this thing might just pay off.

"Put the understudies on for a night or two," he continued. "Give the principals a break, keep them fresh. Spoil them, Lincoln; kiss ass, do whatever it takes. We've got some important people coming to see us. We've got to be top-shelf."

Lincoln had been feeling that the entire drama had the potential of getting out of control, out of his control; but at the same time he was wondering why he felt he needed that control, especially when the control should not be his, and in light of the fact that he didn't really want it. He was an ex-marine, a part-time actor and a failed teacher; he had a bad arm, a bad back, and most times a bad attitude; he liked to read and go fishing. In fact, Lincoln Dollar had so little business on the set of a touring theater company, he finally decided he would remain another stagehand in the background. When it became increasingly likely that the show would run a little crazy, he decided to simply run along with it. And when it got a little whacky, he had only to lob it back to Jordan. "The ball's in your court, but I wonder if we might be getting a little too big for ourselves."

"I'm counting on you to keeps things together. Carl and Charley—God bless 'em—they're a pair of pussies. There's not a backbone between them. I need you to stay alert, stay focused, and keep your crazy girlfriend in line. My wife wants to put an addition on the house and you're the only thing standing in my way. How's she holding up, anyway?"

Lincoln had been enjoying watching Hannah fly about the production. She was constantly going to Emily Rose for advice, to Carl for direction and to Uncle Charley for vindication and motivation. Her hands were into everything, first to offload the truck, first with the drill gun to strike the set. She ran lines with colleagues on the bus, in restaurants, in bar- and hotel rooms. She maintained her own props, brushed and pressed her own costumes. She was having fun, and was bent on making a wonderful time of the experience, not only for herself but for everyone else. Having the time of her life, she flowered, fluttered and flew about the production in a state of perpetual gratitude; everything was *please* and *thanks so much*. A stranger might have found her behavior affected, even disconcerting, but those who knew her needed only to consider the silly source. Of course, Emily Rose thought she was adorable, while Katie found her sweet enough, though sometimes lapsing into pretentiousness. Carl was content only to be needed and Charley to be wanted, and the rest took Hannah's gratitude as the reaction of one who was happily thankful. Lincoln stayed in the back of the house with the other stagehands; he sometimes shared their hotel rooms.

Their last night playing Florida was moody and dreamy. After the show, Hannah was lured outside the theater by a dark, unwholesome appearing character. Inked and leathered, the stranger had lightning bolts cut into his whiskers. Hannah ran to catch up, following the man to the parking lot, close on his heels, where he stopped at a large, black motorcycle—a bike even more sinister looking than the man's facial hair. He turned with a fight or flight instinct to ascertain who followed, his hand slowly moving to his hip of its own accord, and was pleasantly surprised to find the cute actor behind him. "Good show," he said. "Thanks."

"It was fun. I'm glad you liked it. You think you could you take me for a spin? Is that what you call it? A spin?"

The biker mounted the machine and pressed the starter, roaring the bike to life. "I'll take you for a ride, little lady."

Hannah raised her eyebrows at the double entendre—hoping it was, in fact, some double entendre—as she mounted the gleaming, steel horse. The sinister stranger and she flew from the parking lot, sans helmets, sans cares, while Lincoln stood dismayed at the theater door, watching the taillight move further and faster away. He would have preferred that Hannah not ride without wearing some sort of protective headgear, and he would have preferred that she not go off on the motorcycles of strangers with sinister sideburns. Meanwhile he waited as patiently as he was able.

It was nearly twenty minutes before Hannah and the biker returned. She held two handfuls of his jacket when they pulled up to the theater. Much of her hair was still on the highway when she dismounted. Hannah gave the biker a high-five and kissed his cheek before he and his lightning bolts thundered into the night.

She was recovering from the trip, smoothing her wind-blown and tangled locks when she went to Lincoln, taking his cigarette and eagerly puffing it. "That was amazing! I'm gonna get me one of those, for sure. The speed, the wind, and *ooooh* the rumbling—if I was wearing underpants they'd be soaked. I definitely want a motorcycle."

The following day Hannah went to Florida's Department of Motor Vehicles and picked up a sample test. She went to the bookstore for a bagful on safety, operation and maintenance. Hannah lastly visited a dealer in downtown Jacksonville, where within the confines of the parking lot she test-drove a few models. Beginning with two hundred cubic centimeters, she worked her way up to six-fifty. With her checkbook in hand, though little money in the account, Hannah thanked the dealer and left, sure of two things: the Japanese bikes didn't offer the *rumm*bling she had so thoroughly enjoyed; secondly, she would be needing more than six hundred and fifty cubic centimeters. She wasn't quite sure what the *cubic centimeter* thing referred to, except that it had something to do with the motor, but she was certain she would be needing several more of them. But Hannah wanted to think on it some more, and by the time she had returned to the hotel she'd shoved most of the idea into a crowded corner. She asked Lincoln, "What's your opinion on this business with Kate and the archangels?"

"As long as she's happy, and no one's getting hurt—too, too bad—I try not to have an opinion."

"Me, too," Hannah agreed, adding, "they do make a rather handsome threesome, though, if you ask me. Kind of a *ménage à yummy*, don't you think?"

"I believe they do."

Six months on the road found the theater troupe having played six states. The Empire of the South hosted the players in Atlanta, Macon, Albany and Savannah for a total of fifteen shows. When the troupe began referring to the lead player as *Savannah Hannah*, Lincoln was ready to push north.

Traveling through the Palmetto State, the actors worked in Charleston, Columbia and Greenville. Scheduled stops in North Carolina included Wilmington, Charlotte and Raleigh. Jordan arranged for the group to play for the marines at Camp Lejeune, and although live theater wasn't terribly high on the leatherneck list of entertainment, once Hannah made known that the play was conceived by one of their own, the show received a hearty *Semper Fi!* Many of the jarheads especially appreciated the ending of the drama which afforded the opportunity to "check out the cute blonde's little tits." Lincoln treated Hannah and Katie to a tour of the post, introducing them to some of his former haunts. There were so many, many men hovering about, Katie reasoned she'd died and gone to heaven. Drinks were on the house.

On a fresh, sunny afternoon in May, the troupe opened a matinee to a packed house at the Sand Box Theater on the Chesapeake Bay. The brothers Croft reconnected with some old friends, while Emily Rose spent the evening connected to a young bartender.

The troupe finally reached New England, playing Hartford, New London and the Foxwoods Casino before moving on to Boston for three shows on the waterfront and two in the park. Connie and Arthur drove to the city to meet them.

Jordan called again to check in, speaking with Lincoln. "How's everything going?"

"We might have a little problem," the stagehand returned.

"What sort of problem?"

"There was a Partridge Family marathon on cable the other night. You remember the show?"

"Sure, I remember. What about it?"

"After a couple of episodes, Hannah got to thinking the Partridge bus was kind of cool."

Jordan's eyes were awash with dollar signs. "Tell me she didn't paint the bus."

"No, no. She didn't paint the bus."

The producer sighed.

"But she does have everyone else painting it. They're out in the parking lot now. She's selling space on the rig, charging by the square-inch or something—giving the money to charity, or so she says. People were lined up around the block when I'd had enough. I didn't want any part of it."

"You're joking, right? I'm renting that fucking bus! This'll cost me a fortune!"

"And you'll take it up with her, I'm sure. As it stands, the Celtics, the Red Sox and the Bruins are all represented, all with team colors; and … let's see … there was something about snowboarding or skateboarding, something about Boston terriers, the side door says *Katie hearts Boston creampies* (whatever that means), and the back door reads *Back Off*, with some other smaller print now bowdlerized."

"So much for keeping an eye on her. I'm hanging up before I say something I'll regret." A bit perturbed, Jordan Sinclair then put down the phone. He removed his glasses and rubbed his eyes. Soon after, with his elbows on the desk, he was running his fingers through his hair and laughing aloud and alone in his office on the Riverwalk.

The Boston shows were wrapped and the cast and crew agreed that the city would be a good place to settle down, to rest up, with the guys going in one direction and the gals in quite another. Hannah, with her mother, Aunt Patty, Katie and the rest, found leisure at a local lounge which advertised a *ladies' night*, where those ladies wrapped currency up in strings until the wee-wee hours.

Lincoln played a gentleman in a gentlemen's club under the watchful eye of Hannah's father. The brothers Croft, under no watchful eyes, made impulse buys in the club's back room. The crew's gender split, however, was not complete; Charley had stayed on with the women, blushing the entire time and thinking of how he was sticking it to his unruly sweetie back home. (Oh, if that bitch could only see me now!) Jennifer and Cyndi had followed the guys on their quest for breasts and butts. Later that evening they slept in separate beds.

Jordan called once more, to check in and check up, and to let Lincoln know that he was "still disappointed over the bus painting incident," before going on to say, "I've got good and bad news. What do you want first?"

"Give me the bad, boss." Lincoln preferred the bad first.

"I hope you're not too comfortable up there."

Lincoln was actually lying on the bed of a Boston hotel and feeling as close to comfortable as he'd had in some time. He moved to sit on the edge of the bed.

"I scheduled four shows in Montreal, at McGill, before we go into Vermont. I've been there. It's a great space. And we're opening in three days, which means your vacation ended a few minutes ago. End bad news."

"We knew the job was dangerous when we took it," was Lincoln's cagey reply.

Jordan was happy the bad was done. The weary group was apt to shoot a messenger with anything remotely taxing, with Lincoln Dollar leading the mutinous charge. Jordan was now ready, if he were cornered by the feral mob, with the promise of all news being good from here on out.

"What else you got?" asked Lincoln. "Tell me you found us a little room in New York. Get us anywhere close to the island and you'll have a bunch of grateful actors on your hands."

Jordan regretted that he was seventeen hundred miles from his oddly-matched group of artists. He desperately wanted to wrap his arms around the lot and give them all New Orleans kisses. "Where's Hannah?"

"She went down the hall to get some ice. We were celebrating our time off, before you called and spoiled it. Hold on, she's coming now." Lincoln didn't bother holding his hand over the mouthpiece. "Jordan's on the line. Says he got new news. You want to speak with him?"

Hannah replied, with forced carelessness, "He's always calling with some news or other," but still her heart jumped every time he called. Even his bad news was fun. She went on, striving for casual, "Tell him if it's not news of New York, then I don't really need to speak with him. And I don't want more news of the New York Yankees." Jordan had used this trick once before.

Lincoln relayed to Jordan, "You heard?" He then held out the phone to her. "You might want to take this one. It's … well, it's got nothing to do with baseball." He could have added, "except we may have hit a homerun," were he not downing the nearly four ounces of whiskey without waiting for the ice.

Hannah took the phone. She stood close to Lincoln, so that his face was level with her tummy, where he was pressed tightly against her, to a point where he could not properly breathe; but Lincoln presently had little use for breath, and probably wouldn't have known what to do with it anyway. Thankfully, Hannah reasoned he'd need the air and backed away. She held the phone in one hand, the bucket of ice in the other. "Where ya at?" she asked, an expression she'd stolen from New Orleans.

When asked what she was up to, Hannah figured there was some reference to the bus painting, as she had yet to receive any proper sort of reprimand. "Well," she answered, "I may be exercising some rather poor judgment, but at least I'm exercising. How's my favorite-ever producer?" Jordan was her only-ever producer.

She could not have been sloppier than she was, though she was actually even sloppier earlier, before having *freshened up*, in her fashion, to go down the hallway for the ice. She and Lincoln were into a second pint of whiskey and a third game of Triple Yahtzee when Jordan called. Neither had given any thought to showering for the past two days. Hannah's grey sweatpants were baggy, sagging, drooping in the ass, worn through above one knee and stained in several places, with coffee and red wine among those identifiable. Her t-shirt was two sizes too small, riding high and advertising maliciously carefree nipples. Her unkempt hair was hidden beneath a hastily tied bandanna that one could scarcely be sure had been washed since it was last used for less hygienic purposes. She hadn't bothered securing the straps of her sandals over her heels—not for the simple task of going down the corridor for a bucket of ice—so that they *flip-flop*ped as she moved about. In all her sloppiness, Lincoln was nearly ill with the love he was feeling for her.

Hannah saw that the man was eyeballing her, prompting her to stick out her tongue. When this didn't garner the desired effect, she held the phone with her shoulder and lifted her shirt, thus prompting two responses: first was an affirmation that she was still among the most immature and obnoxious actors of any tour in the history of live theater; second was seeing a man's passion nearly leak from his pores. More than satisfied, Hannah teasingly put back down the shirt and continued with the producer.

"The best things are done already. We've given new life to the novel, which is really cool. And I talked to Jody a few days ago, and she said some of the money's already making it into the coffers for the Southeast Asia project. Ain't that the least we can do? God gave us two hands for a reason, right, Jordan? Am I my brother's keeper? Yes, I am, I surely am.

A recent *National Geographic* article had gotten Hannah to thinking about—of all things—landmines. It was an article of about 10,000 words, though she used well over that in describing it to anyone who would listen. In Hannah's twenty years, she had never once buried any landmines, ever, anywhere; still, upon embarking on the tour, she got it into her head that she was going to start gathering up some mines, those unexploded and discarded. Back in New Orleans she applied the statistics from the magazine article to the time she spent on stage. In the same two hours during which she acted in any given performance, five people were either killed or maimed by landmine explosions; five people, somewhere on the planet—her planet—every two hours, all day, every day, prompting her to say, "This is unacceptable."

Though professing a near inability to look at big pictures, Hannah knew that it was unconscionable that children at curious play or a farmer tilling his field should have the limbs blown from their bodies. "It's just not right," she said then, and she still says it today. Some of the proceeds from the theater tour were going to providing assistance and education to landmine victims, as well as towards the training of mine-sniffing dogs. Before the tour had reached New England, news came of a child having been fitted with a prosthetic limb, allowing for the troupe to hold their collective head a little higher. Off the record, Hannah referred to the road trip as the *St. Michael Tour*, telling the older Croft it was to honor his angel, 'the great prince which standeth for thy people.'

"So, make my day, you sweet Cajun king, and tell me you got us a little spot off-off." Hannah gave her boyfriend another wink—before her eyes grew wide. Her breathing stopped. "Not *off*-off? Oh, goodie! Well, then … just how far off are we?"

Hannah let go a gasp. Her lower lip trembled. The bucket fell from her hand, hitting the carpet with a resounding *thud*, the cubes leaping from the container like shattered glass. Presently the telephone fell from her other hand and she ran for the bathroom. From the tiled room came the dry-heaving sound of gut-wrenched, porcelain-echoed disbelief.

Lincoln was some time before finding the wherewithal to retrieve the receiver from the floor. "You there?" he asked. "It seems you've made my partner ill—violently ill, from the sounds of it."

Lincoln could hear the hollow screaming of the Mississippi riverboat steam whistle mixed with Jordan's words, along with Hannah's muffled sobbing coming from the next room, but beyond those couple of sounds he hadn't so much as a clue as to what was going on around him. He had to let Jordan go. Somehow he managed to press the button to ring the front desk. "Please, connect me with Carl Thomas." He took another long pull from the short bottle of whiskey on the bedstand. By the time Carl picked up, Lincoln had forgotten who he was calling.

Hannah sat on the floor in the bathroom, leaning against the tiled wall. She looked up at Lincoln in the doorway. Her eyes were puffy red. "We made it, just like we said we would." Her crying began anew.

Lincoln sat on the floor beside her, letting his head fall on her shoulder. "Just like *you* said."

Hannah took the hook so tightly in her hand, she nearly bent the metal.

Back in New Orleans Jordan Sinclair leaned far back in his chair. He put his feet on his grandfather's old desk and tossed the headset. He wasn't taking any more calls. On the wall above the bookcase there hung a flattering portrait of the old man, Cyrus Sinclair, the artist having generously captured the bayou tycoon with roughly applied oils. His pose was debonair, old Cyrus supported by his signature, narwhal tusk walking stick, his strong age-bitten hands wrapped atop the gold handle. Jordan had loved the old man dearly.

Too bad you're not around for this one, he thought—imagining the old boy's reaction when the company he founded opened its first production on the Great White Way. He knew that Cyrus would have been pleased, though the old man hadn't been a big fan of the New York strip in his later years. "The theater's dead," he used to say. "Broadway died in the thirties, and it was that son of a bitch Gene O'Neill who killed it—that christless son of a whore."

Jordan could picture the hard and crotchety Cyrus, slamming that narwhal cane against the cobblestones of the dark streets of the old Quarter; he then juxtaposed the same man against the neon backdrop of Broadway. The resulting image was incongruous, a near oil and water mix, which made the grandson long to take hold of the old man's gnarled hand just once more, to walk with him down the bustling starlit street of dreams. He imagined asking the patriarch, "What do you think, granddad?"

Among the evening gowns and skateboards and prostitutes, immigrants in tuxedoes and tourists in plastic shoes, taxi horns blaring, cameras flashing, homeless vets and millionaires, junkies, Jules and Jims, Jordan would have asked, "Still think it's dead, old man?"

Cyrus would squeeze the grandson's hand as he looked around at all the hype that was the Great White Way. "That O'Neill was a third-rate son of a bitch," the old man would have said.

-7-

They moved through the streets of Boston on their way to Logan: Art driving, Hannah shotgun and Lincoln in the back. Lincoln was returning to New Orleans to sign more of Jordan's documents and to check on the cabin on the river. He'd also been tasked with getting B from storage and driving her up to Vermont. He would meet up with the troupe for the last show at McGill University, after which they would all return to Preston together.

"This Montreal appearance will make us an international hit," Hannah said. "It's true. And by the end of the year we'll be a Broadway smash. That's true, as well. Isn't that something, guys? Imagine it." She was giddy, Lincoln preoccupied and Art driving.

Hannah went on, "You know why the show's so popular? I mean, apart from the talent? It's because I get naked at the end. Isn't that why you put that in there? What do you think about that, daddy? How do you feel about this so-called writer exploiting your daughter? Don't you wanna fuck him up?"

Art turned up the radio. The louder Hannah spoke, the higher he put the volume; but she finally gave up, as did the music as they pulled into the airport terminal.

She carried her boyfriend's bag until they reached the lounge, where Lincoln suggested, "I could use a cocktail." He looked at his watch and checked the departure schedule. "Unless I'm wearing a parachute, these things give me the creeps."

He and Art took a booth while Hannah went off to take care of some minor business. Art ordered for the three and waited for the server to leave. "Is there something we need to talk about?"

"Why do you ask?"

"I suppose we get a hunch when these things are coming."

"Which *things* are you talking about?"

"You tell me, and I'll tell you if I'm right."

Lincoln shuddered. "I feel like I'm fifteen,"

The server brought some reprieve along with their drinks.

Lincoln next spit out, "I'll take her off your hands—if she'll have me, that is. I wanted to run it by you first." Lincoln hit the whiskey sour hard. "This is nearly as awkward as I imagined it would be."

"You got a ring?"

Lincoln dug one from his pocket. It was a plain setting; no diamonds, but rather a couple of the lesser-known stones and a bit of lint. Though there was no engraving, still it said *Hannah and Lincoln*.

Art approved, pondering briefly. "You'll have her mother's blessing, I'm sure. She thinks you're an all right guy. She'll suppose the kid could do a helluva lot worse." He showed his own drink the rope-a-dope. "Son," he said with a chuckle; "that's gonna take some getting used to." Still caught up in the chuckling, he pulled a thick envelope from the inside pocket of his coat. "Look this over when you've got some time. Let us know what you think."

Lincoln put it into his bag.

When Hannah returned, Art rose to leave. "I gotta piss."

"You would not talk like that if mom was here."

Once her father was gone, Hannah began pawing at her friend. "It seems like forever since I've been alone with you. Let's do it right here, quick, before he comes back." When she was met by such little response, her advances seeming spurned, she gave way to pouting. "Don't you like me anymore? How come you won't do me in the booth?" Still she got no response. "What's on your mind now? You got something you wanna say?"

He grabbed for her hand with the hook, managing to negotiate the ring on her finger before she found chance to pull away. All he could say was, "Will you?"

There seemed to come a short nod; she may have said *whoa*, or was starting to say *what*.

Lincoln hadn't any words prepared, attempting to ride only on what he was feeling. "I'm not trying to change your name or your plans. I like what we have and I like you, and I want to keep it with you. So, let's."

Her eyes never left his. She dared not take them away. "I'm forever yours." When at last Hannah could look at the ring, she said, "It's beautiful. It's the second—no, third—most beautiful thing you've ever given to me. Now having considered your proposal, I'm prepared to accept the offer."

Art returned with fresh drinks.

"Look, daddy." Hannah flaunted the ring. "Electra's flying the coop. Aren't you jealous? Don't you have to kill him or something?"

When her father wasn't as surprised as she had expected, Hannah was taken even further aback. "You already checked with Arthur? You actually asked my father for my hand? So, so chivalrous!"

"I'm happy to be rid of you," said Art, "and your mother's going be pleased."

Hannah visited a memory which made her blush. She said, seeming to herself, "I once wrote *Hannah Dollar* inside my notebook. My God! How pathetic!"

Lincoln's departure was near. "Keep an eye on Carl. He's been as white as Vermont since Jordan called. Get him to rest up, go back to the beach or something. He's not doing anything anyway. We'll need him when we get to New York—Charley, too. And we'll put some understudies on in Preston, make sure they're ready."

Hannah looked again at the ring on her finger. "Any more orders, bossy-boss?"

He stood and put the bag over his shoulder. "Just keep everyone in line, including yourself."

She handed him a list. "Here's the stuff you're to get from storage. Remember, B's trunk is in the front."

"I know the trunk is in the front. I'll see myself to the gate. Be sure to leave a tip." Lincoln thought, at that moment, that she had never looked more beautiful. "I'm glad it's only for a few days," he said, kissing her forehead and mouth. "I'm going to miss you."

"Yeah, whatever. You just be nice to B. She's a sensitive car, and I know how you drive."

As he gave his hand to Art, Lincoln thought to try it on for size, if only one time: "See you soon—dad." He had never in his life referred to any man as *dad.*

Lincoln turned and walked off toward the concourse, his bag bouncing on his hip. There was something of a change in his pace and direction of which he was aware; for it was not long before that he had walked across an entire desert without any direction or care, yet now he barely made twenty steps before having to stop and assess all that was about him. He turned back to Hannah and her father.

She had moved to the other side of the table and was nearly prostrate in Art's lap, watching Lincoln as he walked away. "We're going to New York!" he yelled across the distance, raising his hooked arm in a victory salute.

Hannah and Art waved in return.

It was sunny and warm outside the airport, but still a chill ran through the terminal. Hannah didn't like it. It wasn't any product of air conditioning, but rather something she felt was meant specifically for her. It settled near to her heart, seemingly suggesting that she keep right with herself. She whispered a gentle plea under her breath. *Bring him back safely to me*, but ended the prayer by cursing her selfishness, believing that God would surely look down an omnipotent nose at such prayers, paying little mind to Hannah Mae Fields' petty wants and wishes. So, rather than lie in a cocktail lounge booth asking that God bring her boyfriend, her *fiancé*, safely back to her, Hannah revised the prayer as such to suggest that He bring him back for the benefit of others; because, according to the prayer, the world needed people like Lincoln Dollar. *Now, who am I to tell God what this world needs?* Now she was getting somewhat antsy. *Alright, just keep him in this world, for Christ's sake—oops! —Your world, that is, to help in Your work, and according to Your will.* Much, much better. Lastly, she added, *And please bring him back to me, so that I'm at peace and better able to help You in serving my brothers and sisters. I humbly ask your guidance and complete cooperation. Thank you God. Love, Hannah.* It would have to do for now, and it did actually help to get rid of some of the chill, helped to lift some of the weight. She whispered, "Hannah Dollar," listening for any music there might be in it, but resettled on Hannah Fields and smiled at her defiance. She whispered, "Lincoln junior?" and then there was music, or so she thought, smiling at such projections. She had to tilt her head back to look up at her father. "What do you think, Arthur?"

He was running his hand through her hair. "I trust you're safe with him, and that's all I'm asking from this world."

"Cool," said Hannah.

The flight attendant put Lincoln's third drink on the tray, marking a check in her book. With a hand on his shoulder, she asked, "Is there anything else?"

"Pinch me."

"Excuse me."

"Pinch me," Lincoln said. "I might be stuck in some crazy dream."

"It's usually the passengers pinching the crew," she returned, taking a couple of fingers full of his cheek. "But even if it is a dream, you don't have to wake up till Atlanta."

Lincoln pulled away the elastic tie holding closed the envelope Arthur had given him. There was another envelope inside, upon which was attached a sticky note from Hannah's mother: *To be sure our daughter always has a home …*

The return address read Lafayette, Louisiana. Inside Lincoln found the deed and bill of sale for the property Tomi shared with his family on the bayou, covering the tract of land from the river to the road and a fair stretch on either side, a stretch upon which sat Lincoln's humble home. The paperwork named Lincoln, Hannah, Tomi and Celine as co-owners of the estate.

The big Creole was the only family Lincoln had known before the people of Preston came into his life. He would have struggled, possibly perished, in the bayou had Tomi and his family not steered him around the chenieres and the solitude. Lincoln must have said as much to Art, must have told him he'd have done anything to relieve the timeworn burden of his kin. He must have told Art how Tomi would never accept a neighbor's gifts, that the pirates of his past would never have allowed it; but a gift from his one-time northern acquaintance, from Hannah's father, was something Tomi and the pirates could welcome. They could honor such a gift, as well as the circumstances bestowing it upon the family.

When Lincoln later offered Tomi and Celine the deed, along with the best explanation he could, the grateful Creole wiped his eyes with his hat and said, "You yankees iz sum strange peepoles."

Strange, indeed.

-8-

Hannah's steamy southern drama played well in the Canadian summer. The *Montreal Gazette* suggested that its readers not miss the show before it left for New York. Attendance suggested that few of them did.

The play's author-slash-stagehand rolled into the city on the northbound Amtrak, pulling up to the back door of the theater in a taxi just in time to help the crew load the set into the trucks.

Lincoln had taken care of arrangements with Crescent City Productions in New Orleans, then rescued B from the storage lot, filled her tank, and filled her front-trunk with the girls' belongings. The pair then went further south to the cabin for a short visit before making a beeline back north. Neither B nor Lincoln was nice to the other along the way. He pushed at the old girl's mechanics just enough to piss her off; she retaliated by crawling on the hills and cutting the radio in and out. Hannah was sure to hear of the abuse; B was certain to tell her that Lincoln referred to her, for nearly two thousand miles, as a *sloppy German bitch*. In the driver's eagerness to return north, he decided he would simply have to take his chances with B, and again with the mistress, should it come to as much.

Once they crossed the Massachusetts border into Vermont, both had had more than enough of one another. Lincoln pulled Frau B into Preston, wishing her a ta-ta, guten tag. After dinner with Lauren Stanson, he went to the Fields' house, where at last he was able to stretch in Hannah's bed. He was spent, weary with travel, and just all-around tired. Making matters more taxing, his lying in Hannah's bed was making him horny as well. He called her in Montreal.

"You made it," she said, happy to hear his voice.

"So far. How were the shows?"

"Best yet. They love us in Canada. How'd it go with B?"

"Oh, we got to know one another. A pleasure for us both." It was just as well she could not see his expression. "How are Katie and the rest?"

"Happy and well fed," Hannah replied. "I bought myself something. Wait till you see it. Well, my father bought it, but I'm going to pay him back. It's sweet!"

"What'd you get?"

"Come up here and you'll see. Where you at?"

"I can't drive another mile, and right now I'm in your bed. It feels so nice I'm going to stay for a bit. I'll come up on the train in the morning. We can come back together."

"You're in my bed? *Oooh!*" At first Hannah was a little jealous, then worried. "Don't you dare read my journal!"

"You shouldn't have said anything. Now I'm curious."

"No, you wouldn't do that; and I don't even care anymore. No more secrets."

Lincoln was curious, not about her journals, but concerning her purchase. "You like me wondering, don't you? I've heard women do that."

"Don't you lump me in with the rest. I'm special." Hannah gave him some time to let the *special* fact settle, then made a push to bring him from his curiosity. "I was reading about phantom limb pain. Do you get that shit?"

"Pseudesthesia—I used to, but not so much anymore; maybe a little—I try not to think about it. Tell me what you got."

"You'll find out tomorrow," she said teasingly. "Just get your ass up here. Technically, I'm kinda *your* boss, and I want you here for work. So, no more dilly-dally, chopity-chop." She let go an uncomfortable sigh. "I don't like the thought of you with that pseudo-stuff. I don't like the thought of you hurting."

"It can't be aqua toys and donuts all the time; besides, a lot of people have it a lot worse, like the people you're working to help. Now, tell your fiancé what you got."

"My husband. *Husband!* Kate was so excited, and more than a little jealous, I'll bet. She wants to know how big the wedding's going to be. Only a few of us, right?"

"I'll see you in the morning," he said.

"You're going to sleep in my bed?"

"I am, and it feels pretty good."

"Be sure and make it after. I have to have my bed made. I'm funny like that."

"See you in the morning, funny girl."

The beach from Grand Isle was being packed into the transports when the Fields pulled into the theater parking lot. Arthur and Connie were in the Lexus; Hannah followed closely—wobbly—behind, atop a shining Harley-Davidson motorcycle, a 1200 Custom. The bike was orange and black and unadorned, save chrome crash bars to protect the power plant and leather tassels hanging from the levers. Hannah tended the machine slowly, gingerly. One could well see that she was new to the experience, but one might also sense that she wouldn't be inexperienced for long. Her entrance, not surprisingly, was loud. She was covered in black leather: a jacket with the collar snuggly closed, along with chaps, boots and gloves. She wore a tiny helmet with goggles. Her blonde hair spilled behind.

Hannah brought the machine to a stop and turned it off. She put down the kickstand and slowly leaned it against the pavement, seeming unsure if it would support all six hundred pounds. The gloves and goggles went into the helmet which she hung from the handlebars. Hannah remained on the bike, giving the others a moment to experience the new persona. She smelled of fresh leather and smiled brilliantly.

The assembled group collectively looked to Lincoln for his response. All noted that it was one of disbelief which soon melted into resignation. He was shaking his head as he went to her.

"What do you think? Pretty nice, huh? Twelve hundred cubic centimeters (whatever that means). And look at this." She showed him where her name was etched on the chromed gas tank cover: *Hannah Mae Fields.* "I'd let you take it for a ride, but I don't want anyone taking it for a ride."

"What were you thinking?" Lincoln finally asked. It was all he could think of saying.

To tell him what she was thinking seemed, to Hannah, a drawn-out tale. She had been walking down St. Denis in Montreal when she passed the Harley-Davidson dealer and saw the bike in the showroom. She went in to have a closer look and decided that she had to have the motorcycle, that particular machine. Regarding what she was thinking, she could have added that she had decided long before that she was going to have everything she wanted; from motorcycles to the stars, Hannah was going to have it all; but at the same time she vowed she wouldn't ask for anything unreasonable. Hannah didn't think the motorcycle was unreasonable; but by now any explanation of what she was thinking had proved beyond unapproachable, so she simply said again, "Pretty nice, huh?"

Lincoln took a minute to get over his astonishment. "It really is, and so are you. And I love the colors, on both of you. Got a license for that thing?"

Hannah brushed this off as "a minor technicality. I'm good for the written test. A few days' practice and I'll be ready for the road test."

He had also to ask, "Are you comfortable on it?"

"I think so. The guy at the shop pretty much showed me how it works."

"The extent of your riding lessons were in the dealer's shop?" As valid as Lincoln believed his question, still he knew it would end with his losing any debate.

Hannah could see well enough his backing off, so she began the demonstration. "It's a motorcycle, not the fucking space shuttle. This thing makes it go and this one makes it stop. Throttle, brake, clutch, lights"—illustrating each one—"gears, wheels, not much to it really." She tooted the horn. "They tried to sell me a bunch of stuff to put on it, but I kind of like it like this." She caressed the side with a display of tender affection. "Isn't it nice? I love it." There was a smudge on the tank. She wet a finger in her mouth to wash it away.

"Did you know that motorcyclists all wave to one another when they pass? I didn't really know what was going on at first; thought they were just being nice, or they thought I was cute. I haven't been waving back, but only because I don't dare to take my hands off the grips. I hope they don't think I'm stuck up. I try to give them a toot instead." She hit the horn again. It sounded a little like saying *hi*.

When Hannah dismounted the machine and stretched, Lincoln leaned in to have a look at the odometer. Eleven-point-six miles. "Living on the edge."

"You got it, sport. Anyone not on the edge is taking up too much space." Hannah reached into the pocket of her new leather jacket. "Got something for you, too." She quickly slipped a ring on his finger. "Wrong hand, of course, but we'll have to work around it. Now you're mine, right?" (After a second kiss, he nodded in the affirmative.) "And I can have any motorcycle I want, right?" Hannah kissed him once again, just to keep him at bay, and from the bay Lincoln nodded once more.

She took the helmet and gear from the handlebars. "I'll meet y'all back in Preston. You look so beautiful to me. I wish I had my camera."

Lincoln mildly protested one last time, for anything it was worth. "I wish you were coming back with us, instead of on that quarter-ton dildo."

"I know you've been on a bike or two. Did you enjoy the vibration as well?" She put the gloves on the seat, the goggles around her neck, and what there was for a helmet on her head. It was but a half-helmet, not much bigger than a kippah, barely covering her crown. A small label on the back read HELMET LAWS SUCK; always the rebel. Hannah remounted the iron horse with Don Quixote-like flair, striving for the insolence of a Hell's Angel, but coming off more like an inept, leather-clad seraph.

She turned the ignition switch and kicked the gears into the neutral position. "Come, Kate. Give me some sugar." Hannah kissed Katie so hard it made her father cringe. "Can I trust you to keep your hands off my fiancé in the car, or do I need to separate you?"

"Too old for me. Besides, I can't picture him with anyone but you." They held one another closely. Katie breathed deep. "Yum—I love the smell of leather."

"Godspeed, family," Hannah told them all, as though it was a journey of a hundred thousand miles, rather than the hundred it was. "I'm so looking forward to this ride. I could use some time alone."

Art moved in for a kiss and a hug. "Your mother wants to do some shopping, and we'll probably stop to eat. Take this in case you get hungry." Hannah adjusted herself so he could tuck a twenty and a ten into the pocket of her jeans. "You'll be careful? You're not so grown up that I can't still take away your toys."

"I know. I promise I'll be extra careful."

Hannah hit the starter button. A spark ignited the fuel mixture, causing an explosion inside the shaft—an explosion so powerful that it forced the fat piston down, just as it forced up its twin, again and again and again, until the two danced up and down to the song of a Wisconsin composer, increasing in power and frequency until the song sang out that Hannah and the bike were ready to go. It was a rough and tough, throaty, sexy sort of song—kind of like a John Hiatt ballad.

She put the goggles over her eyes. They made her look like an insect, like a pretty, blonde bug. Hannah slowly released the clutch, inched a bit forward and … stalled, thus ending the song. She shrugged her shoulders and smiled. "Going to take some getting used to." Hitting the starter once more to replay the song, then listing to one side and the other, Hannah rolled away from the parking lot and onto the main street, the blue, new motor exhaust puffing from the gleaming chromed pipes. She hit the horn twice. It sounded like John Hiatt saying *See ya*.

It was well into the afternoon as Hannah was flying over the Jacques Cartier and looking down on the mighty St. Lawrence, the motorcycle rumbling beneath as she leaned into the wind. She turned the throttle toward her so close and so quickly that the machine made as though to go on without her. *Whoa!* she bit her lower lip and let go the grip, finally catching up to the bike. *That's okay, that's cool, that's how we learn.*

-9-

Little Stevie Hazzard had shared the summer literature class with Hannah and Katie at Preston High. In light of dismal scholastic achievements in the past, Stevie did alright with his second attempt at American literature—got kind of yellow wallpapered and caught up in the rye for part of that summer—but was at a complete loss by his senior year.

He was an odd sort of child, always sitting as far away from the teacher as he could, and always with a dreamy, lost look in his hollow eyes. "It's a pity he does not apply himself," was the collective opinion of the teachers at Preston High. A couple of them believed little Stevie had the potential to tackle nuclear fission, but most expected to find him atop Saint Mary's clock tower one afternoon with an automatic weapon and a few thousand rounds. He was the sort of boy who could have gone either way.

The caption below his yearbook photo read *Motorhead*, while the yearbook staff secretly voted him *most likely to perish in a fiery car crash*. Furthermore, little Stevie had a passion for alcohol unrivalled by his peers, aptly summed up by his yearbook motto *If I don't remember, it didn't happen*. Preston High finally gave him the diploma and a pat on the back, showing him the door, happy only to have him gone.

The unfriendly little boy inevitably grew into a disgruntled young man, and a rather large one at that, but still everyone called him *little*. He sweated his forty hours at Miller's Garage on the corner of Main and Thirteenth, and when the gas pumps were turned off he went racing through the streets, leaving the stench of burning rubber at various intersections. Little Stevie had not the least control over any aspect of his empty life until he got behind the wheel, where he was suddenly and magically in charge, finding his increasingly needed power surges by flying over the highways and byways of the sleepy Preston Valley.

Hannah found it easier to keep the new motorcycle under control once she was on the open road and away from traffic, away from the constant stopping and starting so blatantly advertising her riding inexperience. Once on her way, she was better balanced. *Like riding a bicycle,* she mused; *a huge bicycle that flies like a rocket.* She was loving her new toy.

She pulled up to the customs station at the Canada-Vermont border with some concern, lest she have to show more paperwork than she currently possessed. She carefully balanced the bike while speaking to the agent, her crotch off the saddle, her feet flat on the ground—barely, and only with the help of her thick-soled boots.

Hannah had proof of ownership for the bike, her conventional drivers' license, but nothing more. To her pleasure, the agent questioned only her citizenship and destination; she proudly answered the first, but became somewhat confused as to the second. Hannah caught herself telling him she was headed for *home*; then her gloved hand instinctively went for the cross dangling from her neck and she amended her report: "My parents live in Preston," and she was on her way again without having turned off the machine.

The open American road of I-89 South was friendlier to the new rider. She kept the bike at sixty per, though her mind was moving much faster. Hannah had all she could do to keep from thinking ahead to the New York opening, still three months off, her anticipation and excitement beginning to prove distracting.

She was getting herself worked up. Hannah had to abandon all else and bring it back to the here and now. She had to keep it in the *now*, which meant remaining content and enjoying the ride. It wasn't prudent to ask for more.

And what a ride! She kept her speed steady, smiling contently, until something large and wingéd splashed her upper lip—it might have been an owl, or an angel. Thankful her mouth was closed, Hannah wondered if the windshield was such a bad idea after all. She wiped the intestines from her lip to her shoulder, checking for remnants with her tongue. Finding none, she continued riding and smiling, having a wonderful time of the day. But she was starting to get a little thirsty, thinking a whistle-wetter might be in order.

By now Hannah had been voting for a few years and cocktailing for a few more than those. She knew she enjoyed the booze more than was her share, but always allowed herself a little leeway, some wiggle-room to skirt any problems arising with her justifications. Sure, she may drink a lot, but so did so many others, and more than those did so much worse; plus, she *never* used drugs; and she worked hard, so she reserved the right to play hard; she wasn't hurting anyone, kind of, and she was keeping it under control, for the most part. So what if there were a few nights that ended hazily. They were extenuating circumstances and special occasions—okay, so there were a lot of special occasions. Finally, when the justifications themselves grew a little hazy, Hannah fell back to the main reason: She drank because she wanted to, and she had long since grown accustomed to doing exactly as she pleased—encouraged, even—and besides, she was assaulted, nearly killed, and might well be to blame for …

Everything she had read suggested that she keep the drinking in check, and she did for the most part. She tried to, anyway. She had long since dispelled the vision she once held of the alcoholic as a dirty, down and out, uneducated and forlorn bindlestiff, lonely in a crowd and living under the bridge near the railroad tracks. When a bit of curious research brought her to a meeting of alcoholics in Florida, Hannah found that the face of contemporary alcoholism was much the same as that of contemporary America. Those attending the meeting reminded her of the alcohol awareness posters hanging in the halls at Preston High, public service announcements challenging her to choose from among the many faces—doctors, businesspeople, athletes, actors and stay-at-home parents—who was alcoholic. Hannah had been surprised to learn they were all alcoholic, and remembered thinking at the time how cool it was that they were all kind enough to get together to pose for the public service photograph. For the fun of it she used to like to imagine Katie's face on the poster; before long she began inserting her own, and this wasn't nearly as fun.

All the thinking about drinking made Hannah think about a drink, and she would stop for that cocktail soon enough, if for no other reason than to keep from ending her cocktailing streak. She wasn't very good with numbers, but the math wasn't all that difficult. Beginning just prior to her sixteenth year, Hannah had taken to cocktailing each and every day, and was now into it two thousand days gone with no signs of the cocktailing streak ending anytime soon—or even letting up for that matter; contrary, she'd lately been going in the other direction.

After a few laps around a few blocks, Art finally found parking on Ste. Catherine Street. Katie was in a foul mood, enough so that, when looking up at the street sign, she cursed the entire city of Montreal as *idiots* for misspelling Catherine, with a *C,* the same as her mother misspelled it. They agreed to meet back at the car in an hour. Arthur, Connie and Lincoln went in three different directions to shop. Katie went into a gentlemen's bar.

The doorman wanted a cover charge, but relinquished when Katie told him she was "looking for someone. I'll only be a moment." She ordered whiskey with soda, scoffed at the price and took a seat near the stage. Katie was the only woman in the room not dancing.

In her pocket was a letter from her father saying that Maddie was coming up for the show in Memorial Park, and excited at the prospect of seeing her baby sister, and this on top of her father's own desire of having the family together again, at least those three of the four. The letter hinted that he might have done more to bridge the familial gaps, and that he would have had he not put all his time into the market; he added in his defense that the store was doing well and that he hoped for a time when they could all share in the success. Katie ached to see her father and Maddie again, if only for a month, or a week, or an afternoon. And she was looking forward to getting back on the Preston stage. It was there she would receive her redemption. Katie was the bad girl made good. She knew it, and she wanted everyone else to know; but on close inspection she had to admit that she didn't care if everyone else knew or not; anyone save her father and Maddie. The smallest part of her wished that her mother could be in Preston to see the play; but when this thought reared up, it was only briefly before Katie put Catherine with a *C* in the *everyone else* category. There was little connection left regarding her mother, but that which she felt toward her father and her sister, and even towards the town of Preston, Katie wanted all of that again, before it all got away from her for good.

She still harbored some jealous resentment, but Katie had come to harbor it well. She had always viewed Hannah's relationship as her having a *steady*, while Katie herself played the wider field; but now, although it was Hannah who was locked in with the ring, it was Katie's field seeming narrower. Granted, she had her archangels, but they were going back to Virginia to await the New York opening. She would eventually have to make a plan regarding the brothers, but she didn't have to do it tonight. Not even in the next several months. Everything was fine for now.

Katie felt that she was changing, wondering if she might finally be growing up, or at least finally acknowledging the importance of acceptance and patience and other grown-up principles that had not long before escaped her. *Growing up?* Katie stirred the whiskey and soda with a vengeance, vowing to put off growing up. She didn't have to do that tonight either. She wondered if someday she might get married, perhaps lure the archangels to Utah? *Is that even legal?*

Katie motioned for the dancer, taking the performer away from obviously more interested clientele, but only long enough to tuck a folded bill into the couple of threads serving as the woman's work clothes. She sucked the rest of her drink through the ice and went to the bar for another. Once again the cash register prompted her Americanism: "You're shittin' me." With little time, she quickly drank it off, leaving another folded twenty under the glass.

Passing the doorman again, he asked if she had found the person she was looking for. "Not yet," said Katie, "but I've got a better idea where to look."

She was sitting with Lincoln in the back seats, welcoming the effects of the quickly pounded drinks. Connie was in the front with her husband. The music was low, the conversation lower. Katie had hold of the steel at the end of Lincoln's arm, staring from the window for several miles at nothing. She shook the hook and had a look at him. "Thank you, for everything." There were tears in her eyes. "You're such a good friend." She shook the hook once more, facing back to the window.

The rest were silent as Art verified their nationalities and explained their business in Canada. Once returned to U.S. soil, the rolling green mountains of Vermont opened before them to offer the safest of passage.

As much as Hannah enjoyed the wind in her face and the motor between her legs, by the time she came upon Preston from the interstate she had been on the bike quite long enough.

There was a fat, black cat sitting atop the guardrail at the exit ramp. It licked its paw and rubbed at its brow, waving to the blonde on the motorcycle, as though to say "Welcome to Vermont, now go home." Hannah began to quiet the loud, shaking machine.

She rolled down the main drag because she wanted to see the set construction in Memorial Park, and because she absolutely had to roll down the main drag. Those four summers before she had played with Shakespeare on the same stage, but Hannah was now obliged to another playwright. If forced to choose between the two, she was prepared to take Dollar. He was only ten years her senior, while the Bard had her beat by four hundred. *As gamey as Lincoln can get at times, old Shakeshaft must really reek.* Smiling at the thought, she rounded the corner. The next logical stop was the Stansons'. Hannah had a new bike and a new ring to show off, and she was certain that Lauren would appreciate them both.

Lauren heard the motorcycle coming a block away. She had been watering the plants in front of the house; at the sight of Hannah's face beaming under the half-helmet, she went on to water the mailbox and two windows before letting go of the trigger.

They pitched chairs on the edge of the lawn and sat to catch up. Hannah declined an offer of iced tea, suggesting something *a little stiffer* instead. Lauren laughed at the size of the bike, said it was imposing and exciting, Hannahesque, that her brother once had one, but John would never dream of ever …

As Hannah listened, she tried to hold her drink as such that her ring finger remained in Lauren's sightline.

The motorcycle was one thing, but the engagement set Lauren completely back. "Thank God, but I saw it coming." She took hold of Hannah's hand for a closer look. "The day we gathered for John's funeral, I knew you'd be together. What I saw in the two of you helped me through that difficult day." Lauren was excited. "How could you not love that man, Hannah? And I know he loves you. I've known it for a long time."

Lauren was pleased as one who has seen what is divine come into fruition, coupled with the satisfaction of one who had had seen it coming. When sadness tried to cast its shadows on her satisfaction, Lauren would not let it, save admitting to Hannah, "There're times I miss John more than others, and this is one of those times. He would be so happy for you—happy for you both."

"You've always been there for us. You always understood. And I'll never forget that it was you and Mr. Stanson who brought him into my life.

"He told me what happened in the Middle East," Hannah continued; "rather, he's told me some of it, and the more I'm with him the more I understand the stuff he doesn't talk about. Can you imagine, Lauren? I'm grateful they had each other over there. I barely knew your husband, just what I saw of him at school, but he turned out to be one of the most important people in my life. It's amazing, really, the interconnectedness of us all. It humbles me, keeps me from discounting anyone. One simply never knows."

"As John used to say, it's hard telling not knowing." Lauren smiled in her reflections. "He would be happy for you. He loved Lincoln so much it nearly pained him. Those marines all call one another *bro*, but my John genuinely thought of Lincoln as a brother; Lord knows, they often argued like brothers. And neither had siblings, so in a sense they were blessed to have found one another. In a lot of senses, I suppose."

Hannah still waded in the amazement of interconnectivity, of brotherhood and sisterhood. "We have to look after one another. All of us, we all need each other. I used to think, if I was forced to, I could go it alone, but that just isn't so. It never was."

The philosophical ramifications were making her sleepy. Hannah blamed it on the motorcycle. She begged off, telling Lauren how exhausted she was, that there would be plenty of time to catch up later, and they'd do just that once everyone was back, perhaps a get-together and dinner after the shows in Memorial Park.

"*The Awakening* read well," said Lauren, walking with Hannah to the driveway. "I'm excited to see it performed. The whole town's talking about it." She paused, taking Hannah's hand. "And if there's ever anything you want to talk about, anything at all, I want you to know that you can always come to me. Regarding anything, Hannah— always."

Hannah wondered if she referred to the drinking, or to a night years past when she was witness to the killings of three men. Perhaps Lauren referred to neither of these issues, these problems currently weighing so heavily upon Hannah. Perhaps it was both. Regardless, she tucked away the invitation, grateful to have it, grateful for the friendship. She was near certain they would take it up later on, but for now she returned to the subject of the theater as she donned her riding gear. "I know you appreciate a good play, so I don't think you'll be disappointed. A lot of people worked really hard on this."

As the Preston summer sun toyed with the idea of setting, Hannah was once again on her way. Her own eyes were toying with the idea of closing as she set a course for the house on Maple Street.

At last she could see B in the distance. Hannah revved the motor as she pulled into the driveway up close to the Volkswagen. Once she had put down the stand and got off the bike, she gave B a big kiss on her headlight housing. Imagining how silly it must seem to the neighbors and passersby to see her kissing a car, still she kissed B once again and gave her what might have passed for a hug.

Hannah ran her hand along the canvas roof with a loving caress. She spoke in a tender voice. "I want you to meet your new baby sister. We're gonna call her H-D, for obvious reasons, and I expect the two of you are going to get on just famously." There was enough of a tone of preemptive reprimand in Hannah's voice that both B and H-D immediately resigned themselves to the fact that they would simply have to accept one another, whether they liked it or not.

Once inside the house Hannah checked herself in the hallway mirror, stripping away the leather, eying her ass in the chaps. Dale Evans, eat your heart out. *Hot little cowgirl*, thought Hannah, *sans the blues*; contrary, she was tickled.

The jacket, vest, chaps and boots weighed in at no less than twenty pounds, though they felt closer to a hundred and twenty. Hannah'd been feeling rather light in general, and especially light once the gear was removed, and lighter still after a hot shower and another tall drink.

She changed into something passing for pajamas, and was pleased to find Lincoln's scent mixed in with her bedclothes. She inhaled deeply of the prospect of sleeping with him in that bed, and of memories of nights past when she fell asleep to dreams of sleeping with him in the same bed. "Who says dreams don't come true?" Hannah asked aloud, her voice muffled in the sheets. "I challenge anyone who says they don't." She spent some time rolling in the sheets, dreaming more dreamy dreams, before slipping back into her discarded pajamas. She whistled a tune on her way down the stairs.

Hannah fixed another drink. On her way to the couch she hit the button on the stereo; an invitation, as it was, for Gordon Lightfoot to join her in the den.

> *To all you gentle strangers who by nature do not smile,*
> *To everyone who cannot hold a pen,*
> *To all you heavy rounders with a headache for your pains,*
> *Who dread the thought of going round the bend ...*

Hannah was pleased with the selection, and even inclined to agree with the gentle folk performer;

> *Bless you all and keep you on the road to better things.*
> *Heaven can be yours just for now.*

She pulled the comforter from over the back of the couch, wrapped herself up and stretched out. She closed her eyes, allowing herself to drift away, taken by the water, taken to the bay of Monterey, a little girl again.

In oceans, lakes, rivers and gulfs, Hannah swam them all, floating on her back, floating face down, swimming and floating over the sandbars of Virginia Beach, trailing a sloop in the Gulf of Mexico. She tasted the salty spray splashing in her face, the waves bringing her further and further until she was on the beach at Grand Isle. The stars above prickled and shined, the moon was full and bright, as Hannah undid the tie and let her wrap fall to the sand.

The beach was deathly quiet, but for distant melodies of flutes and mandolins mingled with the seductive rhythm of waves kissing the shore. The water called to Hannah, begging her to wade forth; she ceded, heeding the beckoning, unable to refuse, so warm and inviting, so mixed up with life and the night. The water wrapped around her calves, her thighs, between her legs, kissing with gentle lips at her stomach and breasts. Without choice or care, she let the water take her, inch by inch, enveloping, caressing and welcoming. When it finally touched her shoulders she gave way completely, kicking, reaching into the expanse with outstretched arms, grabbing for passage without any return.

-10-

There was a *lip* on the railroad tracks at Cedar Crossing, on the outskirts of Preston, the result of built-up asphalt bordering the west side rail. Just below the lip was a *dip*, the result of Connecticut River Valley topography. The lip and dip together constituted what passed for something like a ramp. With the passing of time, what began as an oversight by the highway department turned to a discrepancy over whether they or the railroad should be responsible for the repair. Eventually, with the passing of enough time, both parties lost any interest they may have initially had, and traffic signs were posted suggesting that motorists slow down at the lip and dip. Cautious drivers heeded the signs.

There were other drivers, drivers like little Stevie Hazzard, with Wright-like bravura and ambitions, who enjoyed seeing just how much *air* they could experience by flying over the ramp at the lip and dip. Little Stevie was always alone when it supposedly happened, but he bragged about hitting the bump at sixty-five and clearing nearly one hundred feet of pavement on the other side. "Raises all kinds of hell with my suspension," Stevie used to say, "but I put her back together at the shop." All kinds of hell, indeed; little Stevie, hard-pressed as a mechanic, had yet to advance to swapping out shock-absorbers during his six-year apprenticeship at Miller's garage.

The guys at the bowling alley accused Stevie of "talking shit," which was, of course, exactly what Stevie was talking, but he had talked his particular shit for so long that he had actually convinced himself that he could clear the hundred feet at sixty-five. In the past he had flown maybe ten feet at thirty-five, but everything was bigger in little Stevie's eyes.

He'd had his young man's heart set on meeting up with Stephanie after he closed the garage that sweet summer evening, late-June. Relating his plans to the guys at the bowling alley, Stevie was certain he was "gettin' laid," casually letting on that this was on par for the sweet summer evening's course. In actuality, as Stevie was laid so infrequently—never, in fact—his excitement was near to epic proportions. He had all he could do not to giggle in front of the guys.

Little Stevie was washing the dead bugs from a customer's windshield a couple of hours before the big rendezvous when he saw Stephanie drive by on Main Street with an unidentified male passenger. Stevie knew nothing of the guy, other than he stood in the way of his date for the evening. It turned out little Stevie wasn't gettin' laid after all. This caused him to forcefully jam the squeegee into the bucket. "Fuck him," he said, referring to the guy with Stephanie whom he did not know. With Stephanie out of the picture, he reasoned he could make just as awkward love to a quart of bourbon in her stead. "Fuck her," he said, referring to Stephanie. And when the windshield detergent splashed his shoes and coveralls, Stevie said, "Fuck me," referring to little Stevie Hazzard.

He was carded buying the whiskey, which made him all the angrier, an anger he exhibited for the door of the liquor store and the door of his car. The inside of the vehicle smelled of motor oil, Jim Beam and self-pity as he squealed away from the parking lot.

In need of an outlet, the energy Stevie had hoped to release through sexual fumblings with Stephanie went directly to his accelerator foot. *I'll show her*, thought he, as he headed for the lip and dip, vowing to break the Cedar Crossing ramp record. He took the bottle from between his legs and had a good, long swallow, muttering, "Fuck it," referring to everything. He then tipped the bottle once again and allowed another large gulp into his throat. That last drink was little Stevie's last drink.

He was drunk and flying over Cedar Road. The speedometer said eighty-five, but Stevie cared nothing about numbers. However, he did notice that the world was passing him by more quickly than usual, now much too quickly for his whiskey-impaired vision. His head somehow transmitted this same message to his foot, but the foot was slow in moving to the other pedal. Stevie managed to drop it down to seventy-five, but by then he was already on the tracks. He'd hit the lip and cleared the dip. Brake lights followed the Caprice into the darkness. He would never boast success at the Bowl-a-Rama again.

Stevie was pressed into the vinyl seat for the flight, paralyzed by g-force and Clermont bourbon. Had he been at the helm of an airplane or boat, he might have had some control over the vessel; but pinned into the rudderless, one and a quarter-ton chunk of airborne Detroit steel, little Stevie had none. He was, much the same as he had always been, completely out of control. If Stevie's foot had not wandered clumsily to the brake pedal, the feat in all likelihood might have been marginally successful; however, he did hit the brake, and as soon as he did he knew he'd made a mistake—a huge mistake—the last in a lengthy series of huge mistakes. And now having changed his tune, and finally finished *fuck*ing everything, Stevie whispered, "Please, God ... No."

With a seemingly choreographed melding of distance and timing, unforgiving fate introduced his car to the top of the Lexus sedan traveling east on Cedar Road. In passing, the undercarriage of Stevie's Chevrolet connected with the roof of the oncoming car and disturbed what might have been a salvageable descent. This coupling of automobiles sent the Chevy into a forward roll, causing it to strike Cedar Road roof first.

The top of little Stevie's car was crushed. This fact had but a moment to register before his head made contact with the asphalt. Pressure from within worked with the vehicle's continuous sliding to grate little Stevie down. Beginning at his crown, the car didn't stop until his head was worn past his ear lobes in a line parallel to his jaw. The little skull that remained was void of any brain matter, and the morticians, both of whom had known Stevie for most of his life, later joked with one another while poking around at the young man's insides that there probably hadn't been a whole lot of brain matter in there to begin with.

Arthur Fields saw the high-beams coming over the tracks. He hadn't any place to go and no time to get there. The top of his car, and most of his torso, meshed with the bottom of Stevie's car. In passing over the back seat, his limp and severed body fused with the young woman sitting behind him, just long enough to shatter her, to kill her, to lift her from the seat and lay her on the trunk. Every part of her was broken: the pretty, sharp-featured face, the slender neck, the large bosom, the larger heart—everything lay broken on the trunk, broken beyond any repair. The coroners later found seat fabric, clothing and skin from the driver's back gathered behind her broken teeth. The driver's blonde hair was fused to her broken face.

The woman in the passenger seat had been sleeping, exhausted from an afternoon of Canadian shopping and Chinese food. With eyes closed in peaceful sleep, she never opened them again. What had once been so beautiful was spilled in an ugly mess to cover the floor of the sedan. Her future son-in-law in the seat behind her was splayed in the open air of the newly-made convertible. The patterned mark of a tire tread ran over his battered forehead.

Little Stevie's upturned car finally came to a stop in the middle of Cedar Road, its wheels still turning, an eerie mist rising from the engine compartment. Then there was quiet. There were no more sounds in the night, as there was no one left to hear. A librarian's *shhh!* had pressed upon the entire valley, as the survivor was transported to the emergency room at Preston Medical. Once stabilized, the one-armed man was taken by helicopter to Dartmouth-Hitchcock on the other side of the river.

Lauren Stanson was whiling away that sweet summer evening, sitting on the deck at her home. She had heard the crunch and scraping of crushed steel. She'd seen, above the treeline, the festival of lights at Cedar Crossing. It was a dangerous road. There were often festivals flashing over the treeline.

Then Lauren heard the sirens which invariably accompanied the lights. She habitually followed the festival with a prayer; however, this time she stopped in her prayer and thought—but only for a moment before she shook it away. Her breath stopped. "It can't be," she whispered into her hand, but something in that sweet summer evening whispered back that it could be—it could well be, and it very well was.

With a flashlight to find the footpath through the trees to the railroad tracks, Lauren followed the tracks to the crossing. The air was still, the town was quiet, and the night was stifling, gloomy and lonely.

Early next morning as the sun was rising over the green in Memorial Park, Preston City Arts workers sullenly removed the lights and sound equipment intended for the weekend shows. The advertisements were stamped, *Cancelled*. They might have read, had those in marketing been more creative, *Due to tragedy, there will be no tragedy*.

Act Five

-1-

Hannah woke from her terrible dreams to find herself on the set of *The Awakening* in Memorial Park, in Preston Vermont. The set was abandoned. She was very much alone. The night was dark, without any moon.

She was some time in trying to realize where she was, then some time longer ascertaining why she was there. A half-emptied bottle of dark rum was by her side. Near the bottle was her father's 380 Browning pistol. Hannah's head swam achingly; her mind was muddled and confused, her body was listless. Her chest was bruised and sore, her movements slow and pained. She was several moments more trying to remember why she felt the way she did.

She took a long, burning drink from the rum. Thick and sweet, it erupted when it met the acids in her stomach. She readied herself to throw it up and try again when she noticed a stirring on the monument a few yards away. The noise came from the spot where she would be in the second act of that forgotten play. Oh, if only she could return to that life! Away from the dark performance on this life's painful stage!

All the world is a stage, a stage upon which Hannah cast herself in the role of a forlorn and beaten character reaching for a gun. She struggled to remember her firearm lessons as the sounds in the darkness came nearer. She pulled back the slide and let it return; it *snap*ped and *click*ed as the bullet was chambered. Hannah checked to ensure the safety was disengaged. The gun was heavy, her shaking hands wrapped tightly around the walnut grips.

In response to the gun's metallic action, a voice came out of the darkness. "No one's going to hurt you. Don't you be afraid, Hannah. I'm all alone. It's just me, and I'm a friend. Everything's okay."

"Stay away from me!" Hannah was cat-like, heightened, startled and perplexed. "I mean it, stay the fuck away!"

"Hush now. I know who you are, Hannah. I know why you're here. No one's going to hurt you. Just you and me here. Everything's okay." The voice in the darkness was maternal, soft and gentle.

Giving up, giving in, Hannah leaned against the constructed flats of the stage. With her forearms resting on her knees, the pistol in one hand and the rum in the other, she began to cry like never before.

The woman slowly came nearer, walking on her knees. A weary and weathered backpack scraped along on the stage floor behind her. She came to a stop next to Hannah and sat with her back against the same flat. In the darkness the woman was beautiful, like an angel; but she was dirty and she smelled rather sour. Hannah knew this dirty angel.

She was a woman named Patricia, whom the city of Preston referred to as *homeless*, or *the bag lady*. She was a woman who moved throughout the shadows of the city, in and out of alleyways and dumpsters, amid children's taunts and adults' intolerance. A tiny scrap of a creature, she was homely, with grey lips and a sharp nose, and long, unkempt hair, dirty and thick with oil. Patricia coughed continuously, raising a phlegm she either swallowed or spit, dependent not on her whereabouts, but on her mood. She habitually groaned, and had sharp, malicious eyes looking upon nearly everyone and everything with loathing distrust. Hannah was among the few exceptions.

Soon after moving to Preston, Hannah had begun leaving foodstuffs and bags of returnable bottles in places where she knew the bag lady would find them. Later, when Hannah was about seeking mischief with the youth of Preston, the teens often looked to the homeless woman about Memorial Park for help in procuring alcohol. The sour woman often acquiesced, provided she was satisfied they wouldn't be riding in cars around the valley. Patricia knew what she did was wrong, but reasoned if she didn't help the kids they might resort to more desperate measures. *Lord knows I did,* she thought. *Bad enough they gotta ask the bag lady.*

Hannah had been afraid of Patricia, but now, cloaked in a tragedy of her own, sitting with pulled up knees on the floor of an abandoned stage set, she understood why the woman had bothered her so; it was because Patricia seemingly had so little, while Hannah had always had far too much. The bag lady was but the personification of her own gluttonous shame; but now Hannah had nothing, and the playing field was leveled. She no longer feared Patricia.

Hannah had always sought to portray herself as among the more fearless of her mischief-seeking peers. As a result, she was often enlisted, often voluntarily, to act as go-between for the money (her peers) and the booze (the bag lady). Once grown comfortable with the transactions, Hannah began asking Patricia to get her "a little something extra," something she wouldn't necessarily have to share with her friends. A little something extra for Patricia, as well, established that the bag lady could keep a secret. Initially the extra was something Hannah shared with Katie alone, kept secret from the rest; before long, though, the little something extra was kept secret from Katie, too. It had become Hannah's little secret. She half-jokingly justified, *If Victoria can have a secret, then so can I*; but what was once funny no longer made her smile.

It was not Patricia's intent to rescue the girl on the abandoned set; rather, she encouraged Hannah's crying. "That's it, honey. Let it out. Get it all out."

And Hannah did. She weaved in and out of convulsive sobbing, clutching the alcohol and firearm. Tears and mucous dripped thickly and freely to the stage floor.

"That's good, honey. It's good to get it out." The sour woman slid a bit closer. "But unless you're going to shoot me, let's put the gun down. Your old friend, Patricia, she don't like guns." Hannah allowed her to take the weapon. She moved the switch to the *safe* position and gently put it on the deck. "You got a cigarette?"

Hannah gave her the package. "I can't believe you remember me. I was a kid when I was bothering you."

Patricia lit one of the smokes. "But you're a modest woman now, like you were a silly child then. Everybody knows who you are. Big shot actress returned to Preston. Everybody's been expecting you, and now all this."

"I don't know what to do," said Hannah, choking on her sobbing. "I don't understand what I'm supposed to do."

"How about you be a good girl and give Patricia a swig off that bottle, and we'll see if I can help you." She took a long pull from the rum, wiping her mouth on a dirty sleeve. "Your parents are dead. They're gone, Hannah. And your best friend is gone, too. And your boyfriend with the hook is in the hospital, and you, my young friend, you got a broken cope*r*. You're having trouble coping, so let's see if we can fix up your cope*r*, then we can talk about losses and being lost."

Hannah retrieved the rum and tipped the bottle back.

"First things first, honey," continued Patricia, "the last thing you need right now is more booze," and once again the bag lady had control of the bottle.

Some days before, the doorbell had wakened Hannah from her seaside dreams. The comforter dragged behind as she went to answer. There were bright, flashing lights on the quiet street. Lauren Stanson was standing on the stoop. Her large brown eyes were full of tears. She was shaking her head. Her lips were tight as she struggled to find the words she would have rather kept back.

Hannah stood looking at her. She even smiled momentarily, mostly out of habit, but also because—deep down—she thought that one of her coy, cagey, famous and phony smiles might help to quiet the whirling lights, maybe lessen the business about. All the more confused, she pulled the comforter tighter around herself. Fear came to her eyes as she waited impatiently for the woman to say something, anything, but at the same time she did not want her to speak. Hannah wanted to scream for her to remain silent.

"Your parents … Katie … Lincoln …" She didn't need to say more.

Hannah fell to her knees, listing to one side, held up by a shoulder against the wall. Her hands and arms were tangled in the fabric. "Mom?" she asked with disbelief. "Daddy? Katie?" she questioned, getting louder. Hannah struggled to her feet. "Lincoln? Lincoln!" she screamed. Each name struck her like a fist, the last blow hitting her hard, head-on, and sending her backwards. Hannah bounced off the wall, continuing, striking her head against the table. The carpet swallowed the blood as quickly as it ran from the angry wound. The world went to black.

Preston P.D. crawled down Maple Street, moving slowly as the reluctant bearers of dreadful news. To move any slower, they would have needed the cruiser in reverse, so they were easily overtaken by Doctor Hart. With lights atop the jeep flashing, it seemed the doctor's vehicle was afire as he passed the cruiser and finished the last furlong of Maple Street over curbs and across the neighbors' lawns.

Doctor Walter Hart—'Doc' to those who knew him, and to many who didn't—was a legend in the valley, famous for dramatic entrances. Whether a dog bite or a heart attack, Doc was sure to show on the scene with lights aglow and sod falling from the toothy tires.

An old CJ-6 with all-terrain wheels, a lift-kit brought Doc's vehicle nearly three feet above its standard counterparts, with rollbars and crashbars—not to mention a portable bar—configured as such that the machine encaged itself. Spotlights, floodlights and emergency lights kept the rig at the ready for Christmas or the Fourth of July. Reserve fuel tanks were strapped to the rear. The spare tire cover was emblazoned with the insignia of the International Red Cross, though it was often mistaken by casual observers as an advertisement for Swiss Army knives. There was a winch on the front; during winter months it wore a plow. The vanity plate read *Doc Hart*; it was the extent of Doc Hart's vanity.

He had seen the same lightshow as did Lauren Stanson, the commotion above the treeline at Cedar Crossing. Doc was quickly on the scene, however the total of his services was far too little too late. He stayed with the lone survivor until the paramedics arrived.

Doc was parked half in the Fields' driveway and half on the lawn when he stopped. He wore a battle-wearied travel vest, and carried the same worn leather surgical bag he had carried through nearly six decades. It was custom-made in Italy to his specifications, with pockets and compartments for his many tools, and, what he liked to call, his potions. He referred to the satchel as his *kit bag*, his *surgical bag*, or his *bag of tricks*, dependent upon whom he was addressing and upon the bag's current application. An old belt and contact cement were used to patch the worn spots where his tools and potions poked through.

As an army captain, Doc swam the beaches of Normandy. He was with Patton's corps chasing Rommel through Africa. As a colonel he treated the Americans and Chinese in the Korean conflict. Doc still walked with a noticeable limp, his souvenir from that conflict; he'd been hit by a bullet from a Chinese rifle while, he'd say *ironically*, tending to the wounds of a Chinese soldier. He then spent part of the sixties at Cambridge with Dr. Leary, and the rest of the sixties leery of what next would come down the pike. Physically, morally and emotionally incapable of mopping up after another war, Doc set up shop in the Preston Valley.

An interview of the inhabitants of the valley might turn up ten people who didn't love and respect the old man; but subjected to a closer scrutiny it would be discovered that nine of those people owed the doctor money, and the tenth would either be new to the valley or a relative of Erwin Rommel. The lives he had saved were numbered in the hundreds, while the lives he had touched might well have been measured in millions.

Preston's finest were relieved when they were overtaken on Maple Street, pulling up behind the country doctor. From the walkway Doc could see through the opened door, Lauren sitting in the hallway and cradling Hannah's bleeding head. Addressing the approaching officers, he said, "Thanks for coming gentlemen, but Mrs. Stanson and I will take care of things here."

"Sure thing, Doc," replied one grateful officer. "Call if you need anything," added the other, and just as pleased.

It saddened Doc having to call on Hannah. With a sympathetic heart he applied valium to her nerves, and his deft, old hands applied the sutures to her scalp. When he leaned in to kiss the young woman's forehead, the blood no longer flowed from the jagged wound. Unconscious, Hannah was moved to the sofa and made as comfortable as presently possible. Doc knelt on the floor close to her, running his tired fingers through her matted hair. "My poor young friend. What are we to do?" Wondering aloud, he repeated, "What are we going to do?"

He looked up at Lauren, who was standing by and waiting for a prognosis. "Let's round us up a pot of coffee, Mrs. Stanson. We'll need to figure this out."

"Who's left?" Doc asked, once sitting across from Lauren at the Fields' dining table. "Who's going to take care of her?"

"Her mother's got a sister in Boston, but she and Hannah have never gotten along." She stared into the steaming mug. "I don't know of anyone else."

"If someone doesn't come for her, I'm certain we'll have to lock her in for her own protection. The strain of this will be more than she can bear. It'll put her over the edge." Doc paused, sipping the black coffee and scratching his wispy, grey locks. "Here's where my younger colleagues start hiding behind things like doctor-patient confidentiality, and all other sorts of textbook nonsense, but we need honesty here, Mrs. Stanson. Besides, I've really nothing to lose. By the time I was called to the carpet for any violations, I'd be long gone, so I'm asking for your help. And you must help. All things considered, I don't know where else to go."

"What will you have me do, Doctor Hart? Anything at all."

He related how he'd come to know Hannah Fields, first as a patient, then as a friend. During lapses in the conversation they could hear her in the next room whimpering on the sofa in pained and fitful delirium.

Hannah's mother had brought the girl to see the doctor shortly after they moved to the Preston Valley, regarding "a minor girl problem," as Doc gently put it. Not long after this visit the mother called the office once again, asking to speak with the doctor and managing to catch him between patients.

"Hannah wants us to set up a visit," Connie had told him. "Is it possible you can get her in?"

"Of what does she complain, Mrs. Fields?"

"She's not really complaining of anything, per se. She simply asked that I call and get her an appointment. I'm not quite sure what it regards, but I suppose that'll be between you and her. Mind you, I'll remain available should you need me." She lastly added, "I think it's safe to say it's not an emergency—no ambulances, ERs, anything dramatic like that."

Doc said he'd be happy to give Hannah a note to get out of school. "I'm sure she wouldn't mind the morning off from classes." He told Connie she could pop in anytime the following day.

So Hannah popped in, browsing old magazines while waiting for an opening.

Over smoking mugs at the dining table six years later, Doc Hart said to Lauren, "I've come to admire that girl a great deal. She's a model patient for one thing, and she's honest, almost to a fault, never complaining of imaginary ailments. It was around the time you folks were doing that Arthur Miller play, the one about the witches. She was nervous about being in the show."

The Preston Valley listed but a handful of reasons why sixteen year-old girls would want to see Doctor Hart under the parental radar. Doc reasoned before Hannah arrived that he would have answers to her questions at the ready. He had only to wait patiently for their asking.

"Nice to see you again, Doctor Hart," said Hannah when she entered the examining room. She shook his hand and dropped herself in a chair. "I'm always seeing you tearing up the roads in your jeep. You don't mess around with that thing."

Doc knew she wasn't in the office to discuss his driving habits, but he let her continue just the same.

With more attempts at small talk, and perhaps some stalling, Hannah asked, "You want to take my blood pressure or something?"

Doc obliged.

Hannah was on the table, pleased to find that her blood was flowing within the acceptable range, when the doctor asked, "Are you sexually active?"

"Kind of, but I'm still a virgin, if that's what you mean."

"Do you have a boyfriend?"

"Kind of, only he doesn't know it yet." After a moment, she added, "Why? You interested? Ha! Just kidding." She really was only joking.

He was taking off the cuff when Hannah said, not joking this time, "I think I've got a problem and I don't want to worry my parents with it just yet."

He *shhh*'d her while listening to her heart and lungs. All three were seeming present, so he removed the stethoscope and took a stool next to the table. He took one of Hannah's hands into his. "So, young lady, what's the problem?"

Hannah had felt at ease with very few people. They had come and gone with such frequency, a sea of bodies and faces often causing her head to swim, that she hadn't the opportunities to get comfortable. However, after just the one prior visit she felt comfortable with Doctor Hart. He was the epitome of all that she believed was right and just. He was kind and intelligent, and she was warmed by the sparkle in his knowing eyes. Fighting tears and confusion, she looked for his wisdom.

"Whatever it is, we'll get through it together, you and me." He gave her hand a squeeze. "Tell me what is it, Hannah."

"I'm … I've …" she began—stumbling, struggling, grabbing at the first thing coming to mind—"I'm thinking about a boob job."

Doc Hart slowly shook his head to let her know that he wasn't buying what she was trying to sell.

"Alrighty then. I'm … it seems I have an affinity for the drink, Doctor Hart. I think I'm an alcoholic."

Hannah immediately felt a measure of relief having voiced it. "I'm actually pretty sure I am. Everything I've read, about the progression and all, I'm sure-as-shit alcoholic. And I know enough about it to know I'm probably here right now hoping you'll tell me I'm not, but I know in my heart I am, and I'm wondering what to do about it; that is, I think I know what to do, but it's the matter of doing it. And because I consider you, like, my doctor, I guess I thought you should know about this … this flaw in my makeup. I haven't been able to tell anyone else; not yet, anyway." Hannah considered reminding Doc that anything said should be kept in confidence, but just as quickly she decided that he wouldn't need reminding.

"What do you plan to do about it? Should we consider a treatment facility?"

"No, no, no," Hannah had not yet considered such an option. "Nothing like that. I'll try and keep it in check for now. It doesn't seem as bad since we started working in the theater. Maybe the trick is to keep busy. I read that I'll probably never shake it, but maybe I can fight it." Hannah gave him a light poke in his shoulder. "We're tough, right? We'll fight it." She then asked, now with timidity, again looking for comfort, "Maybe you can help me fight it?"

"I'm glad you came to see me today."

"Me too." She hopped off the table. "I thought you should know, and I so needed to tell somebody. You're the only person I could think of. I … I trust you." Hannah offered her hand.

"I trust you, too." Doc walked with her to the door. "You know, there's therapy, support groups, meetings and the like, if you think that might be the way to go."

Hannah shrugged her shoulders. "I'm still not sure. Like I said, I'm going to try and keep busy."

They were standing at the opened door between the office and waiting room when Hannah gave him another light poke, this time in his ribs with her elbow. "Who knows? Maybe it'll pass." She added a wink to the poke.

"We both know it's never going to pass."

Eyes in the waiting room looked over the tops of magazines at the recipient of the eavesdropped prognosis. It wasn't polite to listen in, but they couldn't help themselves; the wise and stern old doctor with the fragile and terminal young girl was too tasty a bone not to chew.

Both Doc and Hannah saw the others' interest. He lowered his voice and asked her again, "What are you going to do?"

Hannah raised her voice in reply, "I'll keep my fingers crossed and pray my ass off." Ensuring that her response was processed by those in the room, as well as the receptionist, she added, "Prayers that aren't too, too selfish have a better chance of being heard, so I'll find some way to approach this so it's not all about me. The more I stay out of myself, the better my chances are. Maybe I'll get that from the theater."

Hannah hadn't thought of it before, but now she wondered, *What better way is there to stay out of myself than by working on stage? I can forget about me by pretending to be others. After all, it's playing Hannah that seems to be the problem.*

She was suddenly relieved now that she had what she believed was a course of action, albeit haphazard. She didn't know what else to do. She did, however, need some sort of vindication, some validation to let her know that she might be on the right track, so Hannah was even more relieved when Doc roughly rubbed his old hand in her hair, doing his darndest to muss it up. "I think that's a pretty good plan—for now."

The old country doctor hadn't chance to finish the mottled memory of what had drawn him to the profession those many years past before Hannah moved in and gathered him in a large hug. She kissed his weathered cheek. "Thank you again for taking time out of your day to see me. I feel much, much better." She left him and walked through the patients out of the office.

The receptionist asked Doctor Hart, "How should we bill Hannah's checkup?"

"Don't worry about that. She just stopped in to say hello. Hannah stopped in to check up on us."

Six years later Doctor Hart considered Hannah's situation aloud as he sat with Lauren. "I always hoped the acting would keep her away from the booze, and I suppose it has to some extent; but I also believed that it was only a matter of time before the bottom fell out. The thing is, Mrs. Stanson, this disease doesn't wait around patiently for one to take some time off to address it. It grows, it feeds upon itself, and eventually it rears an ugly head. I believe that time is now at hand and I'm terribly worried for the girl."

Doc left Hannah in Lauren's caring hands, also leaving in her hands varying strengths of sedation. "Be careful with the medication when she's in the drink." Lauren would have her caring hands full.

Hannah teetered between hysteria and lethargy. She did not eat. Her short spells of sleep were fitful. As though sleepwalking, she scuffed her bare feet across the carpet past her father's empty recliner to where the liquor was kept.

It took great pains for Lauren to dress Hannah in black and take her by the arm to the church. Two caskets, side by side, held those who had brought her into a cruel and painful world, those who had given her heartbreaking life. She was angry with them and lost without them. Only with Lauren's constant physical support was Hannah able to remain upright for the service. The room resonated with the strains of her anguish, her sadness and fear. In angry, childish confusion, Hannah cried out for them, but for the first time since she had the breath for pleas, Constance and Arthur did not rush to answer her call. The coffins were closed.

Carl Thomas, Uncle Charley Evans, Emily Rose, and the entire theater troupe were gathered for the summer service. Hannah did not see them. She couldn't see them. She did not know them. All were strangers apart from Lauren and the two up front. Otherwise she was right next to alone.

In the same church the following day, a lone coffin was parked parallel to the pew at which Hannah sat once again, now even closer to alone. Lauren once again on her arm was all that connected her to the painful world. Again Hannah saw the unfamiliar faces of those she might have known in another time. Emily Rose weeping next to the angry archangels; Carl and Charley, Jennifer and Cyndi—they were all strangers, characters from some forgotten tragedy upon which the curtain had long since fallen.

Hannah reached out for her partner in the drama. "Katherine!" she tried to reason, hissing at polished wood. "We had an agreement! Goddammit, we had a deal!" She raised her eyes to the ceiling, certain that nothing up there listened any longer. "You back-stabbing son of a bitch!" Hannah stood. She wanted revenge. She wanted to reclaim that which had belonged to her. She wanted to present herself and take back that which was rightfully hers, but her flight for fight was short-lived. She came crashing back, everything once again fading to black, as she lay in the aisle of the oppressively hollow room.

The next thing Hannah remembered was her awakening in Memorial Park, with no recollection of how she came to arrive on the abandoned set.

"It's too much to handle all at once," said Patricia. "These losses got to be dealt with individually. One by one, you need to let them go, but only when you're ready. You'll know when you're ready. Embrace them and set them free. You can do it, Hannah, and you must. God knows, you must move forward. You got others need you now."

Hannah could not dry her tears of grieving under the auspice that everything would be *okay*. It would never be *okay* again. There was such pain on her—like a sickness, like animals—but the dirty, homeless woman applied a sense of solace helping to bandage the spiritual wounds. At the mention of God, Hannah's ears and heart opened. She knew the words Patricia spoke were true, but still she had to traverse the minefield of her grief if she was to get to Lincoln on the other side. He must need her, but he was so far, far away. She could barely see him through the misty distance. Hannah could barely remember him, and was unable to picture his face, but she knew she had to get to him. Mom, dad and Kate were in her way. She had to get past them if she was to get to him. And Hannah had to get to him, had to get to this one she could not remember.

"You used to leave me things when you were a girl," Patricia told her. "You used to leave me food, and one time you left a coat and some mittens. You remember that? And you left me some money—twenty-four dollars and eighty cents." Patricia pulled a worn and tattered envelope from the pocket of her coat. It had her name on it, the same as

Hannah had written it six years before. She shook the envelope to jingle the coins, as Hannah's long-forgotten currency muffled the jingling sound. "Why did you leave me these things? Why did you sneak to those hiding places when your friends weren't watching?"

"I thought I was helping. I always want to help, but it seems the more I want to, the less I'm able."

Patricia seemingly understood. "It's difficult to care, isn't it? You thought I needed your help because I'm an old girl, down on my luck. I didn't need that stuff, Hannah; I didn't need it, but I sure got a kick out of watching you sneaking around doing all those nice things. Your little friends thought nothing of stepping over me in their rush to get to the shopping mall, but you, you care about people."

Patricia slid a little closer to Hannah, to where they were shoulder to shoulder. "When I read about the work you were doing, I wasn't surprised. No, sir. I expected as much from you, from someone like you. It's been fun watching you grow from that scared little girl into the kind and caring woman you've become—and such an important woman, too. What you're doing is important, and it's especially important for you to continue, now more than ever; but you gotta be careful, careful of the inside of your head. It's gonna be like a bad neighborhood in there until you get yourself right with all that's happened. If you hang out there long enough, you're gonna get hurt. Trust me, little girl, you don't want to hang out in that neighborhood. It's a dangerous place."

"Now you're confusing me, and you really kind of stink." Hannah wiped an eye on each sleeve and slid a few inches away from the woman, to where they no longer touched. "How do you know so much about me? How could you possibly know what I'm going through?"

"I don't know what you're going through, but I know about loss. I know what it's like to lose everything. All but a memory now—like a bad dream—but between the time I punched out from work and arrived at home, everything was gone. I lost it all, and I lost myself in the fallout. It was only with the help of some special folks that I was finally able to accept what happened. And it was the belief that more would eventually be revealed that helped me to get through it. And I still believe that. It's what keeps me strong."

Hannah desperately begged the question, "Do you think … is God testing me?"

Patricia stretched her legs and took another drink of the rum. "God doesn't *test* us—that would be mean and petty—but I believe He prepares us, and not at all randomly. God has a plan for you, just like He's got a plan for me, and what's to say you're not part of my plan? Funny, all the secret booze I used to buy for you, and now here we are"—she passed the bottle, watching as Hannah took a long drink—"here we are having us a secret little drink together. Funny how things turn out."

"I don't think it's the least bit funny," Hannah replied, wiping the burning rum from her lips, "but I'm starting to understand what you're saying."

The homeless woman brought to light a newspaper clipping from the same tattered envelope containing the twenty-four-eighty. She carefully unfolded it. The heading from the *Preston Valley Messenger* read, 'Local Women Acting to Ban Landmines.' "Maybe this is your God's plan for you. Maybe your plan is to go to that hospital, to the man with one arm, and not just for him, Hannah, but for yourself."

"But it hurts so much," she said, her head falling to the woman's shoulder.

"I'm sure it does, but it'll get easier, I promise. Remember, Hannah, God controls the pain, but it's up to us to control the suffering."

Hannah considered what the woman said as best she could, believing it might be true. It was simple enough to be true, and Hannah desperately needed simple just now—simplicity and truth. After basking briefly in the truth of Patricia's words, she said, "You really need a bath, you know?"

"I suppose," Patricia replied. She took Hannah's hand. "Tell me something: A few summers back you and the one-arm schoolteacher went missing—had the whole village in an uproar. At first I was wondering if he killed you and ate you and picked his teeth with your bones; then I got to hoping that the two of you run off together. I couldn't decide which story I liked better."

Hannah angrily started back. "What the fuck?! Like things aren't bad enough, you gotta bring that shit up? Thanks a lot, Pat."

Now the other started back. "The name's *Pa-tricia*, thank you very much. Do I look like a slab o' butter to you?" The woman gave her a friendly shoulder to shoulder urging. "C'mon, what'd you do to that nice man, to make him run away like he did?"

Some muddled memories finally pushed their way to the front. "I think I told him I loved him."

The woman tipped back the bottle. "That'll do it, for sure."

-2-

Hannah brought in a tall stool to complement the low chair next to Lincoln's hospital bed, not wanting a limited vantage forcing her to always look up at him; there would be times when she needed to watch over him. She also thought it a good idea to vary positions and maximize her comfort, for the prognoses suggested that she make herself comfortable. The physicians agreed she would be keeping watch for some time.

Into the first week she brought pillows, blankets, changes of clothes and toiletries. By the second week she developed a disregard for visiting hours, and into week three the hospital staff had developed a disregard for her, save their greetings and good wishes. If she was wearing scrubs, Hannah might well have gone about entirely unnoticed, except by those who would have sympathized with her having to work double and oftentimes triple shifts.

Hannah's patient was not much for company, but still she logged the hours at his bedside. She rarely went anywhere else; only periodically for cocktails and to smoke. To give herself more time with the man, she eventually began keeping a bottle stashed in the cabinet, where Lincoln's clothes patiently awaited his release.

Hannah bathed her patient daily. She tended his nails and kept his face cleanly shaven. She coaxed a stylist in to cut his hair. She sought his help with the daily crossword. "Four-letter word for *departed*; begins with *g*." Hannah looked up from the newspaper with a feeling of neglect at not having received his usual smiling assistance.

She read to him, some books among his favorites, but mostly favorites of her own. She read plays, trying her best to distinguish the different characters with different voices. She read letters from *Penthouse Forum* and passages from a bible she'd found in the bedstand drawer. She read stories she'd written since beginning their tour, and shared notes for others that would never be written. Hannah confessed to him that she wished he hadn't inspired her to write, for she didn't think herself a worthy wordsmith; at the same time, she did thank him for inspiring her to act, for she did fancy herself proficient enough on the stage. "The theater's my tree," she told him one late evening in the quiet, sterile room. "I should be a good little monkey and stay in my own tree."

Hannah kept up strong appearances during the days, but once the lights were dimmed she cried through the nights. And all the while she kept herself in the drink.

"I brought some more books," she told him one afternoon, having just returned from the library and putting something into her stomach, as well as having resupplied at the liquor market. Hannah was disheveled, spending more time taking care of the patient than herself. She'd grown thin. "But no more Anne Rice; I'm all vampired out. I got … let me see … Frost and Dickenson … and London; I know you like those goofy Klondike stories. And I've got the *Tales of a Thousand Nights and a Night*. We'll ride this out together."

Hannah adjusted his pillows and tucked the covers under his arms. She kissed the fading mark on his forehead and kissed him hungrily on his mouth, holding his face as to kiss him properly, hoping to wake the sleeping man.

With her cheek against his, the tears began anew. It happened every time she rested her face next to his, when there was no way he'd be able to see into her eyes if he was to open his own. "I'm doing the best I can," she said, trying to convince him as well as herself. "I'm just so depressed." Hannah dried her eyes and reached into the pile of books. "Let's read this one again."

She turned out the lights, leaving only the one by which she read. Hannah settled into the chair, pausing a moment with the worn book unopened in her lap. "I don't know what to do. I could really use you right now. I'm sinking fast and you're the one person who'd know what to do. I'm so afraid." Fighting back the customary second round of tears, she went on, "I'm afraid like never before. Wake up and help. Wake up and help." She tried everything; she tried loving him more— maybe that would work—and she even tried her best to hate him, yet nothing would open those eyes.

The darkness of the outdoors tried stealing in, barely kept away by the soft florescent glow of the fresh, white room. Hannah gathered breath enough to carry her into the little novel, but before she had chance to begin a nurse making rounds checked in on the couple, whispering her greeting from the doorway. "Visiting hours are over, and there's a new super on tonight. I'm going to close the door a bit, just in case she comes by."

Hannah thanked her.

"How's he doing?" the nurse asked.

"Same."

"How are you doing?"

"I'm okay," Hannah said, though she was far from *okay*.

"Hit the button if you need anything. I'm on all night." The woman put the door ajar and continued on her rounds.

Hannah began reading from the novel: "A green and yellow parrot, which hung in a cage outside the door, kept repeating over and over, 'Allez vous-en! Allez vous-en! Sapristi! That's all right!" Her calm, trained, methodical voice marked time with the slow and steady drip of intravenous fluids, and fell in with the monotonous mechanical action of the respirator; the one feeding precious life as the other struggled to sustain it.

The story brought Hannah aboard a small sloop on the Gulf of Mexico. She was topless, sunning her breasts, watching as Lincoln worked the sail. She could not see the shore, but the seagulls overhead reminded her of land nearby.

Her sailor was topless as well, with Hannah's smiling eyes full of approval. *Were it not for the missing bit of forearm*, she thought, *he'd be pretty close to perfect. Much nicer than the boy-sailors on the bay.* She let her eyes close and lay back on the deck. The gulf was silent, except for some playful waves slapping and tapping at the hull, making feebly mischievous attempts to rock the little boat, though not quite pulling it off.

In the silence, Hannah could feel the sailor's eyes burning into her; while she was enjoying the burn, eventually it got a little too warm. It got downright hot. "What are you looking at?" She waited, stretched out, eyes closed, for his answer. When none came, she said, "I pray you haven't gone overboard. I don't know how to steer this thing."

"I'm here. Are you happy?"

"Things have never been better."

"I appreciate what you've done with the play—all of you. It's past anything I could have imagined."

"You did most of it. We just filled it in, gave it some voice. Of course, Brad helped a lot, and Kate's especially close to it. She knows how you feel about the book."

"You've really done it justice."

"Just doin' my job. From the page to the stage, right?"

"That's right."

"We make a pretty good team, you and me."

"We seem to work well together," Lincoln agreed.

"How about working this lotion with me?" she suggested, wiggling out of her shorts.

The waves bouncing against the side of the sloop grew stronger, more aggressive. They were sweaty waves, salty waves, hungry waves, now steadily and powerfully rocking the small craft … and soon the seas were calm again. The sloop remained adrift in the night.

The night supervisor cleared her throat.

Hannah opened her eyes to see the shadow of the woman standing in the doorway. The florescent light of the corridor shone from behind as such that the woman looked near heavenly. "I'm sorry, but visitors were supposed to be out a while ago. If you're a relative, we could make an exception."

Hannah shook her head clear of the Gulf of Mexico and love making, of seagulls and sailors and kind memories past. She rose from the chair and kissed her sleeping man once more, bringing down a lock of his hair to cover the bruised forehead.

"You are a relative of Mr. Dollar, aren't you?"

"I almost was. I'll just be another minute with him, please. And thank you for checking in."

Once the heavenly image of the graveyard shift supervisor was gone, she said her farewells to the sleeping man. "I need help, Lincoln. I need it bad. I need some sort of answer." However, as much as she caressed his face and pleaded, he would not provide any answers.

Hannah moved to put the small novel in the bedside drawer. It was a shorter work, a novella, set on the Gulf of Mexico. "The gulf! The bayou! Tomi!"

Her feet pounded the tiled floor of the hospital corridor. The entire city block shook when she fired the motorcycle. Hannah aimed the machine at the interstate and worked the passing lane of the southbound route, the pavement inches from her feet and moving swiftly beneath.

-3-

The Creole was mending nets when he heard the earth rattling roar of the Harley-Davidson. Tomi had long before felt the vibration of the bike in his feet, had felt the change in the bayou. Change was riding into the bayou.

Hannah dismounted the bike outside Lincoln's cabin. She was most of a day and a half on the road, stopping only for fuel and to stretch her worn-down frame. Barely able to walk, she met Tomi halfway through the thicket, her tears pursuing her into the brush and finally catching up as she collapsed in the big man's arms. Tomi carried Hannah the rest of the way, to where Celine waited for them at the door.

They put her in the children's bed in a darkened corner of the room, letting the netting fall around her. Hannah was asleep before the woman could remove her zippered boots.

As they watched the girl's broken sleep, the couple speculated on the circumstances bringing her back to the bayou, back into their home, knowing only that it was no social call. The curious children watched and listened as the young woman stirred and mumbled in the semidarkness, until their mother finally had to shoo them away. "Passez! Adieu!"

The following day Celine wrestled Hannah free of the rest of her riding gear and into some clothes she'd found at the cabin nextdoor. She washed and scented the girl's face and body, relaxing her, freshening her and cooling her. Hannah gave over to being handled, welcoming Celine's care, welcoming the love, when so long it had been since anyone had touched her nicely and kindly. Barely able to open her swollen eyes and dry mouth, Hannah whispered, "Thank you, Celine. Merci, mon amie." She was fast asleep once more.

Celine moved the hair from Hannah's forehead and tucked it behind her ears. She let the net fall back round the wearied sleeping beauty.

With four days' rest under her belt, Hannah moved over to Lincoln's place and, there, sitting in the privy on the side of the cabin, was reminded that it had been some weeks since she'd had her period. "Could this get any more fucked up?" Hoping for bleeding hope, she spent another day weeping over Lincoln's belongings, looking for anything that might offer even the semblance of some direction.

A watercolor painting was on Lincoln's desk, not yet framed and hung with the others. It beheld the artist's rendition of the stage at Tulane University, his recreation of the final scene of Lincoln Dollar's play. Hannah recognized herself on the beach as the painting's subject, unaware that the artist had seen the show, or if the image was created from Lincoln's description or from Tomi's imagination. Hannah looked over the painting for what seemed like hours. A single tear fell onto the paper, washing a few grains of sand back into the gulf.

Hannah and Tomi were idle in the skiff, floating on the rolling prairie. Still feeling a bit queasy, she had to have him secure the bait to her hook. As instructed, Hannah let the line into the water on the side of the boat. The top of the river was still, though there was a vibration below the surface. Hannah felt a *hum*ming in her feet through the bottom of the boat as she told the Creole of all that had happened, of all that brought her once again to the cabin on the river. Hannah told Tomi everything.

She explained, as best she could, what the doctors up at Dartmouth had explained to her. Deep within she found the strength to tell Tomi that his friend would not be returning to the bayou. Mista Lincoln was not coming home.

The Creole listened and fished and listened, not venturing any question or comment until Hannah was long past finished. "Mista Lincoln, he on da bridge," he finally said. "No here—" he gestured with his large hand to show that *here* was the sticky and mysterious bayou— "an he not dare," implying *dare* was a welcoming resting place. "He on dat bridge, Miz Hannah. He need hep crost dat bridge. You his wife, mon chere. You git him crost dat bridge."

Hannah well knew that Mista Lincoln was on *da bridge*. She had known as much when she mounted the motorcycle in the hospital parking lot, and had accepted as much during the long ride back to the bayou, hoping every mile that Tomi would verify what she already knew had to be done.

Though it was not yet hurricane season, still Hannah was caught in a tempest of hurricane proportions; but just as quickly as it came, it subsided, leaving in its stead a peaceful feeling washing over her. Hannah had found her vindication, and right at the same time something found her hook. Pulled under the boat, the pole was bent nearly in half.

Tomi took the wrestling tackle while throwing in another suggestion—another coming packaged in unconditional Creole love. "And, mon chere, you sho gotta git off dat alca-hol."

Resigned, tired, unable to argue or defend, Miz Hannah could only reply, "That seems to be the general consensus."

Not quite sure of her meaning, the Creole wondered if *General Consensus* was one of the officers Mista Lincoln had served with.

-4-

It had been so long since she last spoke that she had first to clear her throat before beginning, "I want you to marry us, Padre. I need Lincoln Hannah-mated."

She was sitting on the stool next to Lincoln's bed, somewhat pleased at having rediscovered a seeming lost sense of humor, even as the sterile room smelled of nasty sadness. She let go a small laugh, but if the priest thought she was funny he certainly wasn't letting on.

The man of the cloth was making his rounds of the patients in the hospital. He prayed over Lincoln each evening, though Hannah didn't care much for his brief presences; but while she couldn't ascertain any direct benefit from these visits, at the same time she couldn't see any harm. She was certain of one thing; the priest would not be in the room if the choice was Lincoln's.

The dark haired night supervisor once again cast her shadow into the room, but finding Hannah in conversation with the priest, again she went away. The same nurse often looked in, but always without venturing further. Hannah found the behavior strange, but also strangely comforting—peaceful, and kind of load-lightening.

"I can't," said the priest. "It's my belief you want to marry Lincoln only to end his life support, and I can't be a party to that, nor will the Church condone it. I suggest we pray together instead."

She was near whining. "But you have to."

"I can't do it," was his theological reply.

"You mean you *won't* do it?"

"I'm afraid not. Let God's will be done."

"If you won't, I'll find someone who will."

The priest crossed himself, preparing his leave. He put his hand on Hannah's shoulder. "I'll pray for you both."

Hannah shook the hand away. "Go fuck yourself," she said, without much feeling. The priest never returned.

She was away from the hospital only to go to the lonely motel room where she washed and napped. She stopped at the liquor store to restock Lincoln's closet on her way back and forth.

Two weeks and a conversion ensued before Pastor James would finally agree to unite Hannah and Lincoln on paper. It was all she needed, as they'd long before been united on the etheric plane.

Once again, the same as many times before, the night supervisor looked in of a dark and lonely evening; and as always she remained but a shadow in the doorway without entering the room. Hannah wondered if the woman sometimes came in, but only when Hannah was not there. "Do we know you?" she had finally to ask. "How are you familiar to me? To us?"

And at last she came, slowly, even reluctantly, from the shadows— this lovely woman, shapely, well featured, uniformed so purely in the traditional white. Her hair was rich chestnut cascading, and her large eyes dark and deep almost to vacancy. *Those eyes,* thought Hannah; *beautiful, and painfully familiar*. This heavenly vision of purity was the bearer of still more pain to come.

The nurse held a small stack of books—well-used leather bound volumes—one brown, one red, two of them blue. The books were also familiar to Hannah. "My father wants you to have these."

Hannah was certain that she herself had purchased two of the four books. She took them, opening the first to be sure, though she already knew what they contained. She knew the handwriting as well as her own.

Suddenly angry and confused, Hannah began interrogating, threateningly, "Where did you get these?" Then she looked at the nurse's badge. Under the title of *Night Supervisor*, the name read, 'Madeline Pauley.'

The tears came so heavily that Hannah could no longer see the woman, but only a hazy, white outline. She closed her eyes tightly to squeeze them out "I'm so sorry," she finally said, standing and taking hold of her. "I loved her so much, Maddie. She was my best friend. Kate was on her way home when … She was coming home to see you. I'm …" Hannah fell back in the chair, distraught, overwhelmed.

Katie's sister got close to Hannah and remained there. Dressed in white while she was working and in street clothes off the clock, Maddie told Hannah of all she remembered of Katie's childhood, while the other told the story of Katie's life since, with both sides inspiring a great deal of crying and just as much laughter. When Hannah did the talking,

Maddie's eyes were wet with imagining her baby sister on stage, enrobed in a happiness she'd never expected to see.

Hannah read everything in Katie's journals, then she read them all again, and from those writings she grew closer to Katie than she had ever been before. A soft, friendly light was beginning to shine.

Katie's sister poked her head into the quiet room, the same as many times before. "Hey, you. How's it going?"

"Hey," Hannah returned, "I was just thinking about you. The lawyer called, says we might be able to work something out. When she started citing the *Universal Declaration of Human Rights*, I knew she was a winner. We really appreciate your help."

"She'll know what to do. It's going to work out. I know it will." Maddie then asked, "Would you mind an extra visitor tonight? There's someone here I want you to meet."

"More the merrier, I suppose, though I'm afraid I'm not much for company."

Maddie held open the door. "Come on in, sweetheart."

The visitor slipped into the room, under her mother's arm. "Hannah, this is Chelsea. Honey, this is the lady I told you about, your auntie's friend."

The little girl went to Hannah with obvious delight. "Hi," she said happily, offering a folded construction paper sympathy card and a flower to her new friend. "Mommy says you're a act-triss. My mommy was in plays, just like you and Katie. I'm gonna be in plays when I go to school."

Maddie corrected the girl. "Honey, your mom did some plays for fun. Hannah and Katie are professionals."

This distinction, however, was lost on Chelsea. "Mommy says maybe you can be my auntie now. Is that true?"

"I hope so. I'd really like that, Chelsea. I'd like it a whole lot."

"Cause my auntie died," the little girl further qualified. "Do you got any kids?"

"Do I *have* any kids? Not yet, Chelsea. I haven't any children—yet."

"Good," said the girl. "I got pictures of Auntie Katie. She's really pretty. Are you sad cause she died?"

"I have been, very much so, but it's starting to get a little better." She attempted a smile which even young Chelsea knew was contrived. Hannah bit into one of the same lips that attempted the contrived smile.

The girl looked to her mother, unsure of what to do. After receiving an *it's okay*-nod, she moved close and put her arms around Hannah. Her hands came together just below Hannah's butt, her face pressed into the woman's hip. "Don't cry, Auntie Hannah. It's okay."

Hannah found that the less she fought her emotions, the more control she had over them. She mouthed *thank you* to Maddie and brought the little girl closer.

Chelsea noticed for the first time the man lying hushed in the hospital bed. "Who's that guy? Is he your husband?"

Hannah lifted the girl and turned with her to face the bed. "He's not my husband yet, but he's going to be real soon. This is Lincoln Dollar, Chelsea. He was a friend of Katie's. We were all really good friends."

Finally face to face with Hannah, the little girl scrunched up her nose at the odor of liquor on auntie's breath, but with displeasure seeming minor enough that Hannah did not believe it warranted any response. The girl continued, past Hannah's hundred-proof exhaling, "He was with Katie when she got hurt, and your mommy and daddy too. That's what mom told me. Is he sleeping?" Her voice became a whisper in Hannah's ear, careful not to wake the man. "Uncle Lincoln. I never had a uncle before."

Hannah cleared her belongings from the motel room, strapped the parcel to the motorcycle seat and went to stay with Maddie and Chelsea. Soon after the relocation she was dabbing herself and found some spotting on the tissue. Saddened and gladdened, she cried and laughed; she remembered and imagined, accepted and prepared—all this and more before she buttoned up her jeans. Hannah might have stayed longer and been taken even further, but of a sudden she felt it was high time to check in with Crescent City Productions.

It was a new morning in New Orleans, just as it was in New Hampshire. The sun was bright on the crescent of the Mississippi outside Jordan Sinclair's office on the Riverwalk.

"It's time we got everyone back together, Jordan. I've been stuck inside myself quite long enough, doing the very thing I said I wouldn't do with this production. Let's get ready for New York. Let's put this show up."

"Who's going to play Adèle? Should we start casting?"

"I want Maddie to audition for the role. She lit up when I suggested it. And she's got some experience; not a lot, but anything lacking she'll make up for in ambition. She'll shine once she's up there, I know she will. And she wants to get away from the hospital, from the bedpans, chasing old folks around the wards. After all she's done … I need her, Jordan. I need her on that stage with me. Anyone else in the role … I don't think I can do it with anyone else."

"I don't believe that, but if you want Maddie, we'll give her a chance." There was a pause in the conversation, a shift from Jordan's professional approach to another more personal. "What's happening with Lincoln?" he finally asked.

"We're getting married this afternoon. I'll have to get a new cover for my gas tank. *Hannah Mae Dollar*—rings nice, don't you think?"

Jordan agreed that it did in fact have a nice ring.

"Maddie's the maid of honor, Chelsea's got the rings, and Dr. Goldman's giving me up—away, I mean; he's going to give me away." There was another period of silence.

"Congratulations," Jordan finally said. "I'm happy for you." He fought his want to question, *What then?* but he didn't have to fight it long.

"Once we put those rings on, I'll be within my legal rights to end the life support, and that's what I'm going to do, right after the wedding." She gave her plan a moment to register. With no response forthcoming, she added, "He's not coming out of this, Jordan. All the scans show near-zero activity. Goldman and all his golf buddies, and all their golf buddies, are certain that the little activity there is is only a result of the pain, and it's likely it's a lot of pain. *He feels just enough to feel pain.* That's not right. That's not Lincoln."

She put her hand over the mouthpiece, her chest heaving, convulsing; but of late the crying had come and gone so often, Hannah knew it would not last for long. Jordan waited patiently.

"Putting it off is only cause for more pain and I can't stand the thought of that. I trust these guys, and I trust science and my conscience. Lincoln wouldn't want it like this. You know the sort of man he is. He's a hundred percent kind of guy, and this is the best he's ever going to be? I can't have it. It's breaking my heart. And Tomi, he knows better than anyone, and he's given me his blessing, and I'm convinced it's the right thing to do. I have to do this. And I don't have to justify it, not to anyone, not after this afternoon."

"You don't have to convince me. You're doing the right thing, and I believe it's what …"

It was Jordan's time to cover the mouthpiece. He loudly cleared his throat, much better at stowing his emotions than Hannah, though not so proficient that they couldn't travel the sixteen hundred miles to connect with a place deep within Hannah's heart. "He's lucky to have you … in his corner … to help him with this."

"He'd do the same for me," she replied. "I've been looking for a sign, Jordan, something to tell me for sure that I'm doing the right thing, and though I've yet to pinpoint it, I believe one day it'll be revealed to me. One day this will all make sense. Everything'll make sense. I'll know I did the right thing, and I'll know exactly why. I'm certain of it, just the same as it was with mom and dad and Kate. It'll all come together, if only I can hold out, if only I can make it."

"Let me know what you need me to do," said Jordan. "I got your back. I need you to know that."

"You've done so much already." Her gratitude tried to overpower her, but Hannah fought it away. "I'm so stupid. *Pull the plug* is just a figure of speech, you know; they actually just turn off the machines." She was able to laugh at herself. "I thought I would have to, like, pull a cord from the wall socket or something. I'm so fucking naïve sometimes—most times really. What we'll do is give him a bunch of drugs through the tube, then I'll turn off the machine. I've got it in my head there'll be one more blast of pain, but then his suffering will be over forever, and I will have helped him with that—if I'm able to, that is; Maddie and Goldman will be there, so I think I'll be okay. I just hope the last of his pain isn't too, too bad."

Hannah inhaled deeply, and with the incoming air came a sense of equanimity filling her so full of peace that she nearly burst into tears of joy; with the exhale went all little hangers-on of question and doubt. "We're doing the right thing. I know we are. And we're going to open this show, on Broadway, on schedule, and on budget, just like Lincoln would want it. So get the gang together. Tell 'em Maddie's coming with us. She played Stella at UVM; if she can do Tennessee Williams, she can do Lincoln Dollar. And I know Chelsea'll love it, too. She wants to know what Auntie Kate was all about. This way she can find out firsthand."

"I'll set the meeting up close to you," said Jordan. "We'll shoot for the pre-Christmas opening like we planned. I love you, Hannah, and not only because you're making me money. You'll always remind me of the whacky one-armed guy I went to college with. Thanks for keeping this together."

"It wasn't me. We all did this together, and we need to keep it together, especially now—now more than ever—for Lincoln and for Kate, for mom and dad, and for you, and for the audience. The show goes on, right boss?"

Before she put down the phone, Hannah heard the happy blast of the River Queen's steam whistle. It startled her into a smile, and it left Hannah certain that Jordan had held the phone near the window to achieve that very purpose.

Contrasting with the hearty roar of the river boat, Hannah also heard some early morning stirring coming from the next room. She found Chelsea with her feet hanging at the edge of her bed, stretching little arms, and rubbing the crunchy sleep from her eyes.

"Good morning, sunshine."

"Morning," Chelsea mumbled, caught up in a yawn.

Hannah sat beside the girl, putting her arm around her. "We've got a real big day ahead. There's big change in the air. It's time we went back to work."

The little girl enjoyed being held by her new friend, having taken quite a liking to her. "Hannah," she said, without looking up, her head resting against auntie's chest, "do you miss your mommy and daddy?"

Hannah pulled the girl closer. "I sure do. I miss seeing them and talking with them and laughing with them, but they're still with me, really close, inside me. They'll always live in my heart, just like Auntie Katie does." Hannah smiled and teared a bit at the thought; it was a comforting thought to welcome the beginning of such an important day. "How about we make some breakfast for your mom? We'll make her some pancakes. Won't that be a surprise?"

It would be a surprise, indeed, as all Hannah's food preparation was surprising. She wasn't quite sure what a spice 'rack' consisted of. Hannah had never in her life made a single pancake, nor had her companion. "Then you can help me get ready for the wedding. Auntie Hannah has all sorts of fun stuff for us to do."

Though the cooking aspect of the proposition didn't carry much weight, the girl perked with exceeding interest at the mention of "all sorts of fun stuff."

"You're a pretty cool kid," said the auntie.

"So are you."

Giving the girl another squeeze, Hannah wondered if her new little friend wasn't taking on some of her own ways, her mannerisms, her commentary, perhaps her goofy sense of humor. But Hannah thought this only briefly before realizing that the little girl was more cast of the same mold as her real auntie. The little girl had grabbed at Hannah's heart and squeezed it, massaging it and warming it, much the same as a younger Kate had done some years before. *I only hope she's not too much like Kate*, thought Hannah; deciding then and there on the little girl's bed that once Chelsea hit puberty, Hannah would not let her out of her sight—not for a moment—lest she have to hunt for the girl under gymnasium bleachers and in the back seats of cars.

Hannah tried to remember the kind of September when life was slow, and oh, so mellow—where the grass was green and the fields of grain were yellow—while in this late September she made the last in a series of vows to Lincoln Dollar. She gave him her never ending love, though it was more an affirmation, as she'd given him that love long before. In exchange, she took his name.

Her sash read *Just Married*, and though Hannah had to admit it was silly, she didn't really care how silly she looked on her wedding day. This natural lack of caring was heightened when one of Dr. Goldman's hypodermics found its way into her arm. Hannah received the shot a few moments before the more powerful needle was set up for the patient's push. Maddie lit a pair of candles.

With the bride and groom thus sedated, the wedding was a relaxed, quiet and subdued affair. No one threw any rice, no tin cans were tied to the bumper, *and no one wept except the willows …*

The wedding party left the decorated room, leaving Mrs. Dollar alone with her new husband for the first time, for the last time. The room was eerily silent without the incessant, mechanical pulse of the ventilator.

Hannah kicked off her shoes and climbed into the bed. She breathed in deeply the moisturizing balm she had massaged into his shaven face that morning. "I'm sorry Kate never got to know her niece," she said to her husband. "She's a special little girl, and she couldn't have come into my life at a better time. I thought you and I were going to have a little one of our own, but I guess it wasn't meant to be."

Unless, she thought …

No. Hannah fought the urge to restart the machine, fought the urge to *push* the plug. Her head rested in her hand, her elbow propped on the pillow, as she ran her fingers through his hair, caressing his neck and cheek. "You couldn't have come into my life at a better time either. I've so much to be grateful for, so much to lean on when the pain is difficult. It's been such an adventure, such a wild ride with you and Kate, always fun, with feelings so intense. That summer morning on the high school lawn, when you grabbed me with the hook—I was never so embarrassed in my life, and on my birthday no less. What a gift I'd received—heaven sent, this birthday present to me—and I was blushing a dozen shades upon receipt.

"I've always been able to slip into any role on any stage, but that performance behind the school was the most difficult I ever had to play. I thought that you, the whole class, the entire world could see through me for the stupid, lovesick schoolgirl I was, right from the start. I even looked at your other hand to see if you were actually available, and somehow I knew it then, with never a thought that it wasn't going to happen. Arrogant and immature, selfish and self-centered, I always had everything I wanted, and I wanted you, my birthday gift from God.

"I convinced myself you'd love me back, given time—so convinced, I even looked for hints of it. Then one night it was there, Christmastime on the stoop. It was ten degrees outside, but I was still sweating. That was the night I knew it for sure; I knew that if you didn't love me already, you were at least heading in that direction. It was the single greatest moment of my life. And I'm going to have lots more of them, enough for both of us. And there's gonna be a big part of you in every one. Wherever I go, I'm taking you with me.

"Thank you for everything, my dear man, my jarhead, my teacher, my actor, my love. Thank you for bringing the meaning into my life." Hannah let her head down on the pillow. "Rest now, my friend. I'm sorry if I've caused you any pain."

With her arm draped over her new husband, Hannah felt the beating of his heart for the very last time. Her eyes were sparkling wet, happy and free.

Maddie and Chelsea had a lunch of sandwiches, potato chips and milk in the hospital cafeteria, allowing the newlyweds some quiet, private time. Once finished, they rode the elevator back up to Critical Care and returned to the candle-lit room. Hannah Mae Dollar was fast asleep. Lincoln Dollar was dead.

Maddie called for her colleagues before waking the bride.

Hannah's hand immediately went under the covers and fell on her husband's chest. She let go a protracted sigh. Satisfied, she got out of the bed. She fixed the covers around him and leaned in, unsteady with a smidgeon of valium hangover, and kissed him one last time … and whispered one last secret.

"You okay?" Maddie asked.

"I am. I believe I truly am. Next to my life and your sister, Lincoln was the greatest gift I've ever received. Now, as not to squander any of these blessings, it's time to move on. It's what my husband would have wanted, and that's really all I've got to go on right now." She went to Maddie for comfort and found all that she needed. "It can't be any other way. As it's all I've got, it's gotta be enough."

On their way back to the apartment, Hannah asked to stop so she could buy some inconspicuous stationary. One sheet and one envelope would have been plenty, but she had to purchase an entire box of fifteen.

Still in her wedding dress, Hannah addressed the envelope to the New York City Police Department. *On the night of April 23rd* … it began, and ended with the request, in the form of suggestion, that they allow the case to grow cold, like their wet, dark alleyways. And though

Hannah had never watched a lot of television, still she'd seen enough to convince herself she should wear disposable gloves while handling the stationary. She scribed it entirely in block letters, on top of her plan to place the correspondence in an out-of-town drop.

It was the shortest missive she had ever written. Barely a paragraph, still it closed a chapter.

"He's gone, Jordan, and I believe he went peacefully. As his wife, I want to thank you for your friendship. I know Lincoln thought highly of you, he admired you and respected you." It was all Hannah had to say about that, even going so far as saying, "That's all I'm saying about that. Maddie and Chelsea are ready to join us in New York. Maddie's nervous as all get-out, but excited, as am I. When can we get together?"

"How much time does she need?"

"Just enough to get in with the cast. We're already running her lines. She's gonna be great. I'd never dare say so to Kate, but her sister's going to give her a run for her money."

Hannah realized once again that, although she was on the threshold of acceptance regarding her parents and Lincoln, letting go of Katie was going to take a bit more doing. She would eventually release her, as Hannah knew she hadn't any choice, but it was going to take some time. Probably a lot of time.

"Everyone's ready," said Jordan, "and we're excited to meet Maddie, and Chelsea, too. With some planes and trains, we can all meet in Burlington in … let me see … in about three weeks. That gives us," again he checked his calendar, "about nine weeks to get ready. I'll book the Flynn for rehearsals and a couple of shows before we go to New York. How much time do you need?"

Consulting a calendar of her own, she returned, "I need more time with Tomi. Can I have three weeks?"

Preparing for another return to the bayou, Hannah got to wondering … She went to Maddie, asking, almost pleading, "Can Chelsea come with me? If it's okay with her? Please? I could really use the company."

Maddie's eyes were alight at the possibility of such a dream coming true. "Are you serious? You don't mind?" She imagined, excitedly, *Three entire weeks!* But after some consideration, she did have to ask, "You don't mean on the motorcycle?"

"Of course not." Hannah let go a laugh at the prospect of such a ride. "Neither of us would handle that very well. I'll go up and get the car. We'll take B; rather, she'll take us. Kate used to love cruising with B, riding with her top down—both with their tops down. I bet Chelsea'll like her, too."

Maddie was still processing the offer. "You know I love that girl with all my heart, but the thought of some alone-time sounds pretty attractive right now. In four years, we've had exactly *zero* nights apart. It'd be good for both of us." Still she felt she was imposing, having forgotten in her excitement that it was Hannah who initiated the offer. "Are you sure you don't mind? You're sure it's okay?"

"It'll be good for all of us, and it'll be fun. I need some fun right now. A couple of amusement parks and beaches would come in handy, and I don't want to be alone, not right now, not yet. I promise we'll call every day, and I'll bring her back safe and sound, one way or the other."

"If I didn't hear from you the whole time I probably wouldn't be terribly upset. No offense. But you're still here? Please, go, before you change your mind."

"I was worried, but I'm better now knowing that we'll be together, the three of us. If it wasn't for you and the kid, I don't know where I'd be." Rather than dwell on where she'd be, Hannah grew animated at the prospect of a traveling companion for this important journey back to the bayou. She was going home, and was unable to wait enlisting her young friend. "Let's see if she's into it."

Then Maddie became hesitant. "I need you to do something for me first, because we're living together now and working together—we're sort of like family." She was having a hard time of it, but she needed to be heard. "I know you're going through a lot, and I know you know we love you, but—"

But? thought Hannah, having never known a love coming with conditions. *But?* But she had run up against a lot of things lately with which she had little experience, so she urged Maddie on. "What is it?"

"Well … it's the drinking. Could you cut it back some, please, at least around the kid? I don't want to be prudish or anything, but would you do that, for me? You know, for the obvious reasons, and … well … I'd rather she didn't see you like that. I don't want her getting hurt, and I sure don't like watching you hurt yourself. Does that make any sense?"

It made far too much sense. Hannah had often wondered who would finally step up to spearhead the intervention. Never in her wildest wonderings did she imagine it would be Katie's sister. She was always pretty sure it wouldn't be Katie herself, as she rarely had time out of her own life, with all its issues, to take time to address the shortcomings of others. Katie had had all she could do to acknowledge her own. Hannah never believed her parents would step up, for reasons similar to Katie's, and because Arthur and Connie had long before strayed from reproving any of their daughter's actions. She always guessed it would be Lincoln who would comment on the cocktailing one day, so she kept a series of rebukes stashed away, handy, at the ready: *But, but, but*—but Hannah no longer needed *but*s.

She hugged Maddie, appreciative for the honesty. It was a difficult pill, but Katie's sister made it easier to swallow. "I'll be more conscious of it," said Hannah, thanking her for her caring. "I'll try, Maddie. I'll try my best."

"And while we're on the subject, I got something for you. I hope you don't mind." Maddie went to the kitchen table and came back with a bag. "We use this at the hospital sometimes. I don't want to seem too forward. It's only because we care." She pulled a book from the bag and gave it to Hannah. It was the fourth edition of *Alcoholics Anonymous*—what dipsomaniacs call 'the Big Book.'

She thanked Maddie once again and hugged her again still tighter than before. "I'll try my best."

What Hannah didn't tell Maddie was that she had already read the book. In lieu of any potential worry such an admission might carry, Hannah instead vowed to give the text another go. She did admire its approach to matters spiritual, and had to concede that she had not read the volume as closely as she might have.

-5-

Chelsea and Hannah tore down I-95, laughing every mile along the way. The driver adjusted the child's seat to allow for a clear view of the roads and all they passed. B had a grand time of the trip as well, grateful for the company, and for the chance to blow the dust from her fenders and bumpers. The car's gratitude, however, was marred by fast food wrappers on the floor in the back. Chicken *nuggets*?! Yuck!

With a warm, Chesapeake Bay breeze trying to push them back, still they forged on until they reached the Sand Box Theater. "This is where your aunties used to work."

Chelsea looked at the salty theater and said nothing. Nor did Carl Thomas' car in the theater parking lot mean very much to her. Hannah, on the other hand, had been driving on eggshells from New Hampshire to Virginia, nearly overcome with her desire to see the director. She was in desperate need of direction, and had phoned Carl the previous day, asking that he meet them on the beach. Chelsea played in the sand while they waited.

"Christ me! I've missed you so much!" said he, once arrived. "You amazing woman! I'm so proud of you, my little starlet, my jewel of sweetness. You're so strong!"

Hannah sat with Carl on the sand while Chelsea returned to constructing a castle of ostentatious architectural design.

"I'm not feeling so strong, and I'm certainly not any jewel. It's been rough, that's for sure, and I'm tired, I'm confused and I'm lonely. I'm trying to do the right thing, trying to move on and all that shit, but I get so fucking sad it wears me down. I'm exhausted with the sadness."

Hannah looked out over the bay. The whispering waves reminded her of happy times with Katie on that same beach. One wave spoke of treading *gilded splinters*, and another sought to humble: *You thought you were pretty special back then, full of yourself, all bulletproof and immune*. And another came near to taunting, teasing with stern but friendly advice: *You miss them, of course you do, and her and him, as well you should, and you wonder where to go, when inside you already know. Keep doing what you're doing. Do the next right thing, it's as simple as that. You look for answers in waves when you need only listen to yourself. Silly girl with your stages and roles and crutches, always running, always running, always looking for answers from without when everything you need is already within.*

Chelsea continued building a castle of her own, higher and higher in the air. She erected ramparts and parapets, moats and walls of impenetrable defense. Inside were kings and queens, ladies-in-waiting and court jesters, banquets and orgies, murder and laughter. But the little girl eyed the approaching waves with the beginnings of nervousness, watching as they came nearer and nearer. Chelsea looked to Hannah for direction, but she was busy with the funny little man, looking for a direction of her own.

Carl was happy to have Hannah with him again, not going lightly with this one he'd come so to admire. That she now had this child with whom she could experience the joys and pains of vicarious parenthood was not lost on him. "Your new friend is adorable. Christ me, she looks like Katie—like a little Katie."

"She really does," Hannah agreed. "I've pictures of Kate as a girl. One would be hard pressed to tell who's who."

"Blessed are the children. I talk about adopting, but that selfish son of a bitch is all about dinner parties, Martha Stewart and porn. He's not the motherly type, nor am I, I suppose, not after…"

It had been a matter of time, now Carl was first to broach the subject. "A big piece of me died with Katie. Christ me, she added twenty years to my life when she came in, then took that and more away with her when she left. There's never been such a painful void in my fucked up, crazy world. All the envy I once held for parents died as well, once I knew the pain that comes of losing a child."

Hannah could not discuss Katie. "After the accident I missed my period for a few weeks. What a rollercoaster that was. On top of everything else, the thought of being knocked up was way too much. I didn't know what to do. Boy or girl, though, I was going to name it *Sand*." Hannah let go a laugh, mostly because she felt she had to.

"When I realized I wasn't pregnant, it was even worse, thinking I could never have any children."

She lowered her voice, leaning close to Carl, lest Chelsea should hear and make sense of what she was telling the funny man (though the adults could barely understand it themselves). "Swear you'll never tell anyone," Hannah whispered. "I tried a couple more times in the hospital, but it just wasn't happening. I couldn't get him, you know, ready. I didn't take it personally, mind you, as I certainly never had any problems there before."

"Hannah! You're so bad!"

"I know. Crazy, right? I thought because Lincoln's gone—that's it—I'm never having any kids. I've never been with another, and it never occurred to me that someone else might come along some day and knock me up. Then enter Chelsea and Maddie and I forgot all about that business, at least for now. It's just as well, as I really need to get moving, and that would be even harder than it already is with a little Lincoln underfoot. Instead, I'm saddled with a little Kate. I love her, Carl, and her mother too. I'm nothing without these people in my life, people like you."

When the director tried to look away, she made a grab for his sandy hand. "How's Uncle Charley?"

"Oh, he's a mess, as usual, but even more so since—well, you know. Christ me! And he's still angry about that motorcycle! 'I don't like motorcycles,' he says, 'and especially big motorcycles with Hannah Fields on top of them.' He's excited to go to Burlington next month, to get back to the theater. It's all he's got, you know that, right love?" Carl pondered a moment. "And it's all I have. This moment, right here and now, is all any of us will ever have."

"I'll take Uncle Charley for a ride when he comes up. Once he gets a taste of it, he'll make a good biker bitch." They shared a laugh at the thought of Charley Evans on the back of Hannah's motorcycle. Both imagined tears in his eyes, holding fast with white knuckles and little girlish screams.

Presently the comical images faded and Hannah's tone found more serious air. "Kate's father gave me her journals. I'm trying to come to terms with a lot of it, and now that the fog is lifting, things are starting to make more sense." Again she took hold of his hand. "I won't go into the details, not now, but you should know that Kate cared for you very much. She had huge respect for you and for what you stand for. She really loved you, Carl—very much—and Uncle Charlie too, like family."

"Thank you, thank you," the misty director replied. "Christ me, it means so much to hear you say that."

Hannah looked up and down for signs of pirates and bonfires, white wine and cotton candy sunsets, soldiers and sailors, friendships and dreams and love. It was all still alive on the beach. There was love enough to coat every grain of the sugary white sand. She stood and brushed the sugary sand from her jeans, calling to her traveling companion. "You ready to get rolling, kiddo?"

By now the waves had reached the castle. Water flooded the moat. Correspondence was left with the drawbridge keeper bearing news of a temporary truce. The king and queen released Chelsea from their charge, thanking her for service to the realm. "Ready, Auntie Hannah," the castle constructor returned, running to them and carrying upon her all the sand a castle constructor could possibly wear.

"*Auntie Hannah*," Carl giggled. "That's precious!"

"I know. Ain't it something?"

Carl took both her hands in his, smiling happily and helplessly. "But there's something else, isn't there? For an actor, you haven't much of a poker face."

Hannah's thoughts rippled and splashed. She paddled out to them and away from them, like a surfer looking for the ideal opportunity. During the past two months the waves had been coming and going, ebbing and flowing. At times she was atop the one that she thought would carry her in, only to have it crest ahead and pass her by, leaving her all the more adrift. Hannah now knew that there was no perfect wave, and she knew she could no longer afford to await its coming. She had to take what wave was presented, or risk being forever marooned in a sea of questions. She had to get her feet on dry land, and the best place for her to do so was back on the bayou.

Chelsea took Hannah's hand, more than ready to leave and go somewhere else to play. Hannah's other hand was in Carl's as the three trudged the sand to the boardwalk. Hannah brushed the girl clean before helping her into the car seat, then turned back to Carl. "There is one more thing, and you're the only person in the world I can trust to do this for me."

A flock of petulant seagulls flew into the scene, selfishly vying for the director's attentions and making it difficult for him to hear. Hannah would not repeat herself, nor did Carl really want her to, for it was as terrible a request as any he had ever heard, and as perfect as any he might possibly imagine. It was as pure as one he would expect from her, and to it Carl agreed, and with so little reluctance that he surprised not only Hannah but himself.

He watched the girls pull away from the parking lot, away from the Chesapeake Bay. He loved Hannah a little bit more than he had earlier that day.

She always left him so.

Christ Me.

-6-

B's motor hadn't time to cool before Hannah and Chelsea went to work fixing up the cabin on the bayou. It was Hannah's cabin now. Her home. Hannah's *home*. Tomi's children were pleasantly taken with their new friend from New Hampshire, more than eager to help the yankee girl with her part in the renovation labors. Chelsea was just as excited about her association with the Creole siblings, and just as quickly was led away from those same labors, lured to more enticing adventures on the mysterious river.

Hannah remained in a constant state of worry over the girl's playing so near the water, as such that it cut into her time for cabin improvements. Her tendency was to hover over the child while trying not to smother her. Hannah wondered if the struggle had been the same for her parents when she was at that same age and playing in the Pacific. Still, Hannah's fret was anything but pacific.

She was working in the new flower beds early one morning when she heard the earth shattering, heart piercing screams of the child. Hannah cursed herself for allowing the girl so near the shore—*damn that fucking rolling prairie!*—and with all that was in her she ran to find the little girl, the whole time dreading what she might find, and hating herself for such wanton inattentiveness, for being such a piss-poor excuse for an auntie!

The sobbing, frightened girl met Hannah halfway between the cabin and the shore. Running hard and fast, Chelsea leapt the final twenty meters and landed in Hannah's trembling arms. Her breathing was short and strained, her eyes wide with confused terror.

Hannah asked demandingly, in a panic, "Where are you hurt? Show me, now! Show me where you're hurt!"

Finding a measure of safety in auntie's arms, the girl's spasms lessened. Her subsiding fear soon moved on to anger, then to a boldness barely containable in a four-year-old frame. "Big … *sniff* … crocodile … son of a bitch … *sniff* … tried to eat me."

Hannah's fear then moved to laughter, which she tactfully kept to herself. "Now, now. There's no need to curse."

Tomi's children were close behind, coming one by one from the brush, happy to see the girl had found her solace, stifling giggles of their own, vainly struggling to mask the amusement of their new friend's yankee naïveté.

"There, there. It's okay. He's gone." Hannah continued to hold the frightened girl. "You know, kiddo, it must have been an alligator who tried to eat you. There aren't many crocs around here. They're a lot bigger and a lot meaner. Aren't we lucky we don't have crocodiles here on the bayou?"

Chelsea could not presently appreciate the distinction, thank you very much, nor did she care for any impromptu lesson regarding the different reptilian orders. "His mouth was … *sniff* … so *big*." She wiped her tears and nose on Hannah's shoulder.

Auntie squeezed the girl tighter, also helping to suppress her own laughter. "Alligators like flowers. He probably thought you were a flower and wanted to see you up close."

Once more Chelsea expressed her condemnation of all reptiles: "Big … *sniff* … mean … *sniff* … son of a bitch"—and ever after she swapped the shores for the chores, forced to relay to her new friends, and even with an air of professionalism, that she could no longer afford to play along the bayou, as her help was much needed about the cabin. It was, after all, the right thing to do. The Creole children weren't exactly sure what an *auntie* was, but they reasoned it was a title important enough that they, too, should be helping with the labors.

All hands were on deck, and on the porch and in the garden. Hannah fixed the broken railing. She hung curtains in all four windows. Everyone worked at weeding, planting and painting. Though Hannah was initially hesitant in allowing the children free rein with the brushes, she came to appreciate the character their small hands brought to the work. All five children, as well as a good part of the grounds surrounding the cabin, were adorned with this same appreciable character. The place was shaping up nicely.

Chelsea called her mother every evening with full reports of the days' events. Maddie was pleased that the girl was having such fun, and each night reminded her to be careful near the water, and to mind her Auntie Hannah. The water advice was easy to follow, and minding Hannah was even easier.

With difficulty and a lot of tears, the widow Dollar set about sorting through Lincoln's belongings. Much of his clothing she would eventually use, however cinched and tucked.

She dusted the books, returning them neatly to the shelves in the same order she had taken them down. She cleaned the glass and frames of the paintings, rehanging them decidedly more strategically on the freshly painted walls. The entire cabin interior was scrubbed, rinsed and scrubbed again. She boxed and labeled Lincoln's personal papers, putting them into B's front trunk. Hannah wanted to wait until more time was passed before sorting through those.

They were almost three weeks into the renovation-vacation when Hannah was pleasantly reminded of the fleetingness of childhood desires. Chelsea professed one starlit evening as they rocked together in the porch swing, seeming sincere, "I want to stay with you on the bi-you forever and ever;" the very next morning the little girl said, "I miss mommy. Can we go home?"

Hannah agreed that it was time. "We'll pack right now and leave in the morning."

Tomi's family saw the pair off, with the Creole lastly reminding her, "Dis yo home now, Miz Hannah. We always be yo famly."

-7-

Those three, Chelsea, Hannah and B, crossed back over the Connecticut River and drove straight to the hospital. They met Maddie with open arms and gifts from the south. Chelsea excitedly, exhaustingly, explained the entire excursion from the minute they had left, leaving Maddie exhausted from so verbose a recounting. She sensed her daughter was a different girl than the one who had left barely a few weeks before. She sensed also that Hannah was a different sort of woman; gone were the shadows under her eyes; she laughed less and smiled more.

As Hannah watched Chelsea sleeping later that evening she reminisced of their adventure, and of all past adventures with the little girl's aunt. In the cool painful light of all that came from her remembrances, Hannah was able to enjoy where she was. Some difficult decisions had been made and some old dreams put to rest. The return to the bayou—to Tomi and the family, to the alligators, the pelicans and baldcypress, to the Spanish moss, the French patois and the American south—had answered most of the questions still holding her. Katie's journals had answered all the rest.

She called to verify her reservation at the Sheraton in Burlington.

Maddie and Chelsea promised they'd be only minutes behind, leaving Hannah with hugs and kisses to hold as collateral until they arrived. "You'll never know how much this means to me," she said to Maddie, "you being a part of this."

Maddie was glad she was going, hoping along the way to find the answers to some questions of her own. "We'll do this for Katie, and for Lincoln, and your parents. They deserve it. You deserve it." Rather than stand around crying, she made herself ready to leave, telling Hannah over her shoulder, "We'll see you up in Burlington."

Hannah and B drove to the other side of the river, back to the theater, back to Carl and Uncle Charley and the brothers Croft, back to Emily Rose, back to the real world.

Carl met her in the lobby of the Sheraton Hotel. Hannah had only one small bag, politely refusing his offer to take it. "Is everyone here?" she asked.

"Not necessarily in the building, but scattered about the city." He added, with a theater director's passion, "The Flynn is beautiful!"

Hannah wasn't so much thinking about the new venue. Her next question was more pressing. "Is *she* here?"

"In the lounge. Come, I'll introduce you."

Hannah followed. When they were just inside the door, the director pointed to the woman at the bar. "That's her. That's Billie."

"She's beautiful, but isn't she a little older than the part?"

"That's why God invented makeup, love; the same makeup that makes you look older."

"Is she better than me?" Hannah asked, only a tad curious. "Is she bigger?"

"Nobody's better than you, or *bigger* than you. Is that what you want to hear, my pet? Christ me! You actors are fucking nightmares!"

"She's beautiful," Hannah said again, then kissed the director's forehead. "Thanks for doing this. Can I have her alone for a minute?"

Hannah made way to the bar. She put down her bag and offered her hand. "I'm Hannah Fields," she said, however quickly correcting herself; "I mean, Hannah Dollar, Hannah Mae Dollar. It's a new name—gonna take some getting used to."

"I've heard a lot about you. I'm Billie Reynoso—Billie *Mae* Reynoso."

"Oh no!" said Hannah. "Mae-day! Mae-day!"

She took the stool next to Billie's and said to the bartender, "Um … club soda … with lemon, I guess."

Billie was as perfect as she was pretty. She *was* Edna Pontellier. She was Kate Chopin and Cleopatra, Mother Teresa, Mata Hari and Marilyn Monroe. She was Susan Anthony, Susan Sontag and O-Susie-Q. Billie was Tess Durbeyfield, Scarlett O'Hara, Scarlett Johansson and *The Scarlet Letter*; she was Queen Elizabeth, Queen Latifah and the Dixie Queen—Eve, Joan of Arc and the Latina girls in Herald Square, Nikita and Bonita, Virginia Wolfe and Virginia Beach and *The Vagina Monologues*; she was Aphrodite and Nefertiti, the bayou and the mountains, the rivers and the sea, the stars and the song, the script and the stage. Billie Mae was woman. She was *the* woman.

"I can't imagine what this must mean to you," said Billie, "but, upon my honor, I'll be true to this work, true to the author, and to the director. I'm a southern girl, Hannah, southern-trained, and I'll treat this play with the respect it deserves. I'm just thankful y'all are giving me this opportunity. I'm honored and inspired; I truly am."

Once Hannah knew the role was safe, protected and respected by Billie Mae, the last of the heavy weight fell away. Lincoln's play was safe in Billie Mae's loving southern hands.

The reunion at the Flynn was joyful and tearful. Plans were rearranged and courses altered. Hannah was a different sort of actor; more professional, less playful, with her shoulders back and head high.

Maddie's introduction was met with collective confidence, but it was patently clear that Chelsea was the new star of the show.

Billie's introduction was met by a confused and protracted silence. No one had known anything of Billie Mae Reynoso, but everyone would soon know her well.

The silence was finally broken with an eruption of questions. Hannah directed them all to Carl. It was more than she could deal with, so she simply—and at times not so simply—didn't. She no longer wanted to act as hub of the production. Hannah no longer wanted to be the star in any show.

Emily Rose watched from the opposite end of the conference table. The room was sounding with the searching of twenty acting souls, yet in all the chatty din and excitement, she was able to quietly reflect upon her young actress friend, who was seeming everywhere and nowhere, absorbing all in the room, breathing in all the excitement of the live theater, but now from a safe and comfortable distance. Emily Rose herself was still riding the yo-yo dangle, resignedly, however contentedly, and remaining at the ready for the imminent recoil. The other had severed the string and hung up her wings.

Hannah was sitting tall and straight in the high-back chair, her arms on the rests, her hands clasped and resting on her stomach. She looked long about the room, content now that everyone had someone with whom to make their plans. Out of utter defeat, here was the lasting victory. Hannah was a different sort of woman. She would always be different.

Her roaming eyes finally met those of Emily Rose, now so far, far away. The two women shared a knowing smile. "Good job," said Emily Rose with a misty nod.

Hannah could not hear, but she read the woman's lips, figuring that Emily Rose referred to the collective efforts of the cast and crew, of management and production; that she referred to the writers and the teachers and editors, and to every actor in every company, and to even the critics, and especially and most importantly, to everyone in the audience—and even more especially to those who had paid the full cover price. She could only nod in humble agreement with her darling Emily Rose.

-8-

Billie Mae Reynoso strolled through the sand in front of a packed house at the Flynn Theater, as Hannah and B were driving back to New Orleans, back to Tulane. She returned to the theater department to finish the degree after her academic advisor suggested she was too far into the major to switch.

Hannah was reading favorable reviews of her husband's play at the start of the summer session when she moved over to the history department to begin her graduate studies. Regarding those lessons of the world unobtainable at the university, she sought them further downriver, from Tomi and his family—her new family.

Graduation day was sunny and warm. Lauren Stanson flew to New Orleans to watch Hannah walk in the ceremony. The pair then continued walking downtown to the Army/Navy surplus store. Both were amazed at the selection of cargo pants, the different colors, and all with berets to match. Hannah was especially pleased to find the pants and hats in purple, suspecting they were the surplus of an army spearheaded by an obnoxious dinosaur formally known as Prince.

Her next post-graduation stop was at the building of government offices. The halls were crisp, hollow and cold when compared to the softness of the Louisiana summer outdoors, but Hannah did not plan on staying for long. She poked her head into the Marine Corps recruitment office and let go a hearty, "Semper Fi," adding what passed for a salute. She said, "Ooh-rah!" as she walked past the Army, Navy and Air Force offices.

Hannah went into the Coast Guard recruiting office, but only by accident, before finally finding the office for Peace Corps volunteers. She formally accepted her assignment, there latching onto another silly schoolgirl dream.

Her mission brought her to the northern shoulder of South America. Beginning at the mouth of the Demerara, she worked her way down to the village of Enmore. The fine print of the two-year contract was explicit; she was to 'promote further growth by developing and broadening the skill set of the work force through literary education initiatives.' *Whew!* thought she of such a windy mission statement. Able to put it more simply—she wanted to keep everything simple—Hannah was going to teach. Rather, she had signed on to go down to Guyana to teach, but Hannah discovered, just as soon as the plane touched down, that she was once again the student. She would forever remain the student.

Hannah went into the jungle with plans of teaching her sisters and brothers to read and to write, the same as she'd planned in her schoolgirl dream. At the time it had been a dream of paramount importance, but that was before she was sidetracked into another. Once living the dream of Lincoln and Katherine and the theater, she had to put all of her other dreams on hold.

The theater dream came to her true and the theater people even truer, but it had played itself out. The dream had pushed its way into her life, and just as aggressively it was gone. This new dream had a planned beginning and a definite end; it was a two-year dream, start to finish.

Not a part of the original dream, still Hannah watched as the planning of local contractors, with the hands of local labor, raised the modest, eight-classroom, octagonal building. The school, going up in direct proportion to Hannah's resources going down back home, opened on a courtyard in which the well was drilled. She and her neighbors had to enter the building for their water, and a good many of them, once inside, decided to stick around and see what it was all about.

Two years to the day of Hannah's arrival, the school children, the same as every morning, were outside her window: "Buenos días, Señora Dollar."

Hannah loved the sound it left in her ears. There was just enough of the local dialect to oxygenate the second syllable—'Doe-*lair*;' she liked to imagine a couple of soft, fuzzy fawns with the doe in the lair. But on this day the señora did not answer. Having developed an aversion to all types of farewell, Hannah had quietly stolen away in the night and was on her way back to the United States.

Seven hundred and thirty days after her arrival she left her South American friends and returned to the bayou cabin. She had a couple of months to spend with her family before reporting for her next assignment.

Hannah Mae Dollar traded her flutes and mandolins for rock & roll music. Her scarlet letter began waxing earthier tones. She gave up tank tops, khaki pants and Birkenstocks for pressed slacks and sensible shoes, and started wearing blazers and vests—separately, never together. She swapped the house on Maple Street for a one-bedroom close to Lauren's, and stopped by nearly every morning for coffee on her way to work.

The first day back was awkward, as Hannah expected it might be, but in later describing it to Lauren, she said "it felt fresh and really real," the worst of it being her short heels sounding an annoying *click, click, click* on the tiled floors. The halls at Preston High were filled with friendly faces, though few of them were familiar, and that was okay. There were also plenty of kind greetings and words of encouragement:

"Good morning, Ms. Dollar."

"Welcome back."

"Good job, girl."

In another time, another life, Hannah had graced the same hallways with a backpack full of sand and chewing gum wrappers, worn down books and colorful pencils and schoolgirl dreams in a made up world. She now carried a satchel of red pens, essays and tests, and a book of memories that she helped to write with the love and support of many others. Not all of the memories were good, but all of them were real—they were really real—and Hannah carried the scars from them as proof. She went way out of her way to avoid the railroad tracks at Cedar Crossing.

While the book of Hannah's life thus far didn't always read happily, it did at last evolve from a work of dreamy fiction into a fact-based narrative. She would forever after refer to her book as a *creative-nonfiction, work-in-progress*.

All Hannah's world was still a stage, and at last she was able to humbly accept the role of Hannah Mae Dollar. Granted, the new role was small—barely a bit part—but in Hannah's dawning acceptance it was a part in which she played rather well; so well, in fact, it felt as though it was written specifically for her. And Hannah was glad she was playing the part well, as she had plans of playing it, one show at a time, for a long, long time.

Hannah sat at the front of the classroom waiting for yet another group of fresh, defiant and bewildered faces to fill the desks. Soon the bell rang to begin the thunderous movement of so much testosterone and estrogen descending from the corridor.

Ricky Desault, senior class and first string varsity, took a seat in the front row of Ms. Dollar's U.S. History class. He had commandeered the same seat as a junior in Hannah's Vermont History class. Ricky always sat up front.

Initially, his obvious attentions were cause enough to tweak the young teacher's self-consciousness, but on closer inspection Hannah wondered if his awkward stares did not interest her on some level. She wondered if the strapping young man's approval might have verified for her that she was still attractive, something Hannah had not felt for some time; however, regarding young Ricky's eyeful insinuations, Hannah found those laughable and ludicrous. *Imagine,* thought she, *a student carrying on so over a teacher. Whoever heard of such a thing?*

She took an early opportunity to inform the young man of his inappropriateness. "It can only develop into a serious conflict of interests when students entertain feelings for instructors, Richard," (Hannah was the only teacher who called him 'Richard') "except as they regard the shared class material." Kindly, and even complimentary, still the history teacher was firm, and of course empathetic. Ricky seemed to get the message, but while the tête-á-tête served well to increase the student's respect for the instructor, it did little to dispel the crush, for he continued sitting with dreaming eyes at the front of the class. Their talk, for Hannah, was a pleasant reminder.

Once the students were settled, the teacher began, "There are three rules regarding this class and all my classes: Be here, be on time, and do the work. If you're running late, don't bother running."

Maddie and Chelsea remained close on the other side of the river, with mom back at the hospital and the daughter enrolled in school. Maddie knew of several guys whom Hannah *just had to meet*, and Chelsea, seeming desperate for another uncle, suggested that Hannah come to her school and meet her teacher; "He doesn't got no wife," was the keystone of her pitch. The suggestion, of course, made Hannah cringe, not so much at the prospect of another man, but rather regarding the grammar used by the young cupid in trying to secure the match. Hannah first corrected the child, then suggested that she re-quiver the arrow, as auntie wasn't quite ready—yet. Chelsea couldn't understand why Auntie wasn't ready (—yet), nor did she comprehend the *arrow* reference. Chelsea was, however, accepting, and she let the matter rest … for now.

Hannah had only to travel to the other side of the high school building, but still she was late for the meeting and missed most of the opening readings. The heightened punctuality which had plagued her in the theater world had given way to her occasionally being late for appointments, meetings, and the like; her former motto, *I'd rather be an hour early than a minute late*, no longer applied. She didn't sweat small stuff, having found that the world still whirled around whether or not Hannah Mae Dollar was on board for the whirling. It even seemed to whirl a little better when she didn't have her nose so pressed into it.

The chairperson showed relief when she finally entered the auditorium. Walking down the long aisle of the room, Hannah paused briefly near the seat where Lincoln Dollar had sat during her first stage performance those eight years before, on the night when she had looked for him from the stage and was upset to have found him gone. That night, though, she was upset for but a moment before satisfied; satisfied, that though her teacher was prone to rushed exits— *skedaddling,* she called it—he would never be far from her; Hannah was satisfied that night that he would always be near, and to her perpetual delight Lincoln Dollar forever was. It was with knowing this that she went into the auditorium and was once again able to return to that stage. However, Hannah no longer needed to be *big*; she needed only be her own right-sized self.

With barely thirty in attendance, it was the smallest group for which she had ever performed. Most were consolidated in the first three rows, with a scattering of skeptical newcomers further out in the room, out in the cheap seats. They would come hither in time. Those who stuck it out sooner or later worked their way to the front.

Hannah made eye contact with each person in the room, something she never did during her many other stage performances. With the connection thus made, she began, "Thanks for having me here tonight, and an extra special thanks to Jim for asking me to speak. He said it's probably important for me to do this, and I'm thinking he's right."

She paused a moment to confront an unruly flash of stagefright. At her seasoned command, the fright turned back upon itself, and turned into a glorious burst of performance energy—the same as it always did, only now it was of different, well-grounded and spiritual proportions.

She took a long deep breath, had a drink from her water bottle, then swallowed hard. "Forgive me. I'm a little nervous." She collected her thoughts, reminding herself of the present format, her present stage direction. "Let me see; what it was like, what happened, and what it's like now."

The script was creative-nonfiction—her story, Hannah playing Hannah—but before she had chance to begin, a friendly voice called out to her from the third row center, offering the nervous, young high school teacher a gentle reminder. "Who are you?"

"Oh, right—sorry. I'm still kinda new at this." After another long breath, she introduced herself, "My name is Hannah." She smiled, with eyes straight, bright and determined. "I'm an alcoholic."

So far, so good, she thought, then settled herself down to continue, "It's been rough these past few years, and I've been tired—so tired, even my soul was tired."

Some faces in the first few rows were nodding with understanding and encouragement. They were the faces of her mother and father, the faces of her husband and her best friend—and of all her friends, past and present, and of all the friends to come—and all of the faces were smiling back at her.

"Now my soul is waking up. But for the love and help of all of you, my soul is finally waking up."

the end

ACKNOWLEDGEMENTS

Regarding this particular act in the drama, many thanks are owed Don Rowe for casting me (against a student's will) in '*Streetcar*' those many years ago. There was really never any going back. Thanks also to Dr. Rob Williams for help with river navigation, to Brad for guidance in matters spiritual, and to Cheryl Burghdurf, Jim Ellefson and Joanne Farrell for the kindness, patience and understanding needed in bringing a diffident butcher out from behind the glass. As always, thanks to O'Eric Deso for the ongoing technical and moral support.

To Brenda, Rick, Katie, Oscar, Mike, Nancy, Jim C., Fartin' Mary, Mark, Paul and Dad: I love you and miss you all.

And to Tammy Morissette, the best cousin and the best friend a guy could hope for; the beacon — *the* instigator/prompter — without whom these pages would not exist: While I might go on for a hundred thousand words about actresses and their adventures, when it comes to nailing down my admiration for you I remain a fumbling fool of a fawn in the high beams. Thank you, so so much.

Lastly, thanks to Libby, Moriah and Caroline for making the world a prettier place.

Part of the proceeds from Playing Hannah *helps to fund women's educational initiatives at home and abroad. Thank you for your continued support.*